Changeling Press, LLC

ChangelingPress.com

Thunder/Savior Duet
A Dixie Reapers Bad Boys Romance
Harley Wylde

Thunder/Savior Duet
A Dixie Reapers Bad Boys Romance
Harley Wylde

All rights reserved.
Copyright ©2023 Harley Wylde

ISBN: 978-1-60521-863-2

Publisher:
Changeling Press LLC
315 N. Centre St.
Martinsburg, WV 25404
ChangelingPress.com

Printed in the U.S.A.

Editor: Crystal Esau
Cover Artist: Bryan Keller

The individual stories in this anthology have been previously released in E-Book format.

Table of Contents

Thunder (Dixie Reapers MC 15)
A Dixie Reapers Bad Boys Romance
Harley Wylde

Amity -- I knew people could be cruel. I never thought the entire school and town would turn against me. And why? Because I trusted the wrong person. I thought Evan loved me. How could I have been so wrong? He used me. Humiliated me. Then my parents threw me out. I'd hit rock bottom when Thunder found me. He didn't just get me off the bridge that night. He saved me in every way that counted. He's my rock. My hero. My everything. I only hope one day he'll come to love me as much as I love him.

Thunder -- My club is my life. My family. And I'll do anything for them. But I've kept a secret. Something from my past. Before I became a Dixie Reaper.
When Portia asks for help, I can't deny her. So I go out into the storm. I didn't realize the impact it would have on me. Seeing Amity on the bridge, ready to jump, brought it all back. Now I'll save her because I have no other choice. I failed in the past. I won't this time. One look in her eyes, and I know she's meant to be mine. I will lay her demons to rest. Get revenge for her and our baby. Every man who's touched her, hurt her, will answer to me. And I'm sending them all straight to hell.

Prologue

Amity

Mr. Parsons droned on about *Hamlet*, while most of the class ignored him. English Lit happened to be my favorite class, so I took notes and listened to his lecture. He was mid-sentence when half the phones in the classroom went off. Then a few more.

"Oh, my God! Is that... No!"

Someone laughed.

"What a slut!"

More laughter. My phone went off, and I opened the message. I felt the blood drain from my face as I saw the video clip. It felt like someone had sucked all the air from the room, and everything started to spin. I stared, willing the video to disappear, but it didn't.

"Class! Pay attention or you'll all get detention." Mr. Parsons banged his fist on his desk.

How could he have done this to me? I glanced at those closest to me and they stared, either outright leering or casting me looks of disgust. The video kept playing on a loop. Evan fucking me from behind. My breasts bounced with every thrust, and he had a handful of my hair, calling me filthy names. I'd thought he cared about me! I'd given my virginity to him, thinking we'd be together the rest of the year and into college.

I grabbed my stuff and ran from the room.

If my parents saw that video, my life would be over. They'd never understand. It wouldn't matter that he'd said he loved me. They wouldn't care that he'd been my first and only.

I didn't make it far before I slammed into someone. I looked up to offer an apology, but it died on my lips. Evan sneered at me.

"Why? Why did you do it?" I asked. "You asked me to be your girlfriend. I thought you liked me."

"Why the hell would I want someone like you? Don't you get it, Amity? It was a joke. The entire thing. I just wanted to see if you'd spread your legs."

I felt sick to my stomach and pressed a hand to my mouth so I wouldn't throw up all over his feet. I'd given him my trust. My heart and my body too. And it had all been a game to him? Shoving past Evan, I ran from the building, not bothering to sign out at the office.

I made it down the steps and halfway across the parking lot when the campus officer gripped my arm tight. "Where are you going?" he demanded.

I couldn't face him, or anyone else. I cried harder, no longer able to hold in my pain. As I sobbed, his hold on me loosened.

"Miss Whitman?"

I nodded. "Please. I need to go."

"What's going on?" he asked. "It's not like you to try and ditch school."

I dropped my things, including my phone. He bent to pick them up and froze when he saw the screen. His gaze lifted to mine, and I saw both understanding and sorrow in his eyes. "Do you know who took this?" he asked.

"It was only me and Evan there," I said, my voice nearly a whisper.

"You need to come with me to the office. I'm going to call your parents…" He hadn't finished his sentence before I was shaking my head. If he called them, I could only imagine the awful things they'd say. He sighed. "Miss Whitman, I don't have a choice. Did this video go to anyone else?"

"I think the entire senior class received it."

He cursed and took my arm again, leading me back into the building. We went into the front office, and he didn't stop until we were in the principal's office. He explained the situation as I sat, wondering what would happen to me now.

By the time my parents arrived, I felt numb. My mother's jaw was set in a hard line and my father… he wouldn't even look at me. My mother watched the video and gasped. My cheeks burned with embarrassment, wishing they hadn't asked her to see it. I barely listened to them. I heard something about a police report, the FBI, and Evan's name.

"We're not pressing charges," my mother said. "Amity has made her bed and now she can lie in it."

The principal, Mr. Henry, sputtered a moment. "Mrs. Whitman, I don't think you understand. This isn't a case of whether you want to press charges. Your daughter is only seventeen, which makes her a minor. The boy in the video is eighteen. When he recorded your daughter, then sent the video to the senior class, he distributed child pornography."

I blinked and stared at Mr. Henry. "What? Am I in trouble too? I didn't know he was recording us!"

The campus officer kneeled by my chair. "Miss Whitman, I've already made notes of what happened, but the officers coming to arrest your boyfriend may wish to speak with you. Just be honest with them. They may ask you to testify in court if this goes to trial."

Trial. Court. That meant the entire town would know. People would stare and whisper everywhere I went. I wouldn't feel safe. They'd call me names, look at me differently. Panic welled inside me, and I tried to shove it down. If I lost it right now, my parents wouldn't be sympathetic. If anything, it would only infuriate them more. When we got home, I could only imagine what they'd say and do.

"We'll discuss this at home," my mother said. "Can

we go now?"

"Not yet," Mr. Henry said. "As Officer Charles stated, the police may need to speak with your daughter when they arrive."

My mother huffed. "This is disrupting our day. We had a schedule and now it's been tossed out the window. I hope you're happy with yourself, Amity."

Officer Charles narrowed his gaze at my mother before focusing on me again. "It's not your fault, Miss Whitman. The boy took advantage of you, recorded you without your knowledge. Be brave a little while longer."

I nodded and tried to block out the sound of my parents' voices.

By tomorrow, no one would be laughing at me. They'd hate me instead. I'd be known as the girl who sent Evan Miller to prison. I might be an unknown at our school, but he wasn't. It wouldn't matter that he was at fault. No one would care. As far as the students were concerned, Evan was a god who could do no wrong.

I wasn't sure how I'd survive the rest of senior year, but I'd need to figure it out. Otherwise, they'd eat me alive.

* * *

Two Months Later

My throat felt tight and my eyes burned as I held back my tears. I felt stupid. Why had I ever believed someone like Evan would like me? It had all been lies. And why? Because he wanted to win a stupid bet. I'd fallen for it. All of it.

When the video had gone out to the senior class, I hadn't understood why. It wasn't until the officers arrested him that I found out he'd been trying to win a bet. A group of boys had a list of girls, each worth a certain number of points. I apparently rated the highest because I'd been a virgin.

I felt awful. He'd used me. Treated me like a whore, all to win some money? I should have never gone out with him. When he'd asked, I'd known it was too good to be true. I could still hear the names they'd shouted as I'd walked by. *Whore. Slut.*

Not once had a boy tempted me to do more than kiss. Until Evan. Now I'd be paying the price until graduation. It didn't matter if I only had one month left of school. My classmates had done their best to make sure my life had been pure hell since Evan had been arrested.

One of the bitchier girls in the senior class stepped in front of me, smirking as she placed her hand on her hip. "Did you really think Evan wanted a pathetic loser like you? Why don't you do the world a favor and go kill yourself?"

I ground my teeth together so I wouldn't lose it in front of Nicole. I tried to go past her, but she sidestepped, blocking my way again. I wanted to ask why she felt the need to torment me. Evan had already embarrassed me in front of the entire school. No, not just the school. The whole town knew what happened to me. What more did she want? But a part of me worried I wouldn't like her answer.

"Leave her alone, Nicole," said a girl from somewhere behind me.

I glanced over my shoulder and saw Portia. We hadn't spoken much, even though we'd attended the same high school for four years. I knew her dad was part of the biker group on the outskirts of town. The Dixie Reapers MC. People sometimes whispered about her, but never to her face. I didn't know why she'd come to my defense, but I was grateful.

"Butt out, bitch," Nicole said.

"Really? You want to call *me* a bitch? Have you looked in the mirror, Nicole? Or were you too afraid all the ugliness inside you would make it crack?" Portia came to stand next to me. "You're a bully. An ugly, egotistical whore."

I held back my gasp. I couldn't remember anyone ever speaking to Nicole like that. At least, not when I'd been around. The way her face turned red, then nearly purple, didn't bode well.

"Do you know why you belittle everyone, Nicole?" Portia asked. "Because deep down you know you're nothing. Less than nothing. You've spread your legs and hit your knees for nearly every boy in the senior and junior classes. No one takes you seriously. And one day, that clear skin and those blue eyes aren't going to be so pretty. What then, Nicole?"

"You'll pay for that," Nicole said, glaring at Portia.

"Go ahead." Portia smirked. "You know who my daddy is. Do your worst. All I have to do is head home, tell him everything, and your life will be over. My Uncle Wire can wipe out your entire family without having to leave his damn chair. So I dare you, Nicole. Come at me. See what happens."

I swallowed the knot of fear in my throat. How the hell was Portia so brave? I'd heard the rumors and had seen her out around town with her family. Her dad looked a lot older than her mom, but he'd always had a smile for his family. He'd seemed nice, and like he actually cared about them. It was more than I could say for my parents.

"Fine. Take the little slut with you," Nicole said, flipping her hair over her shoulder. "But you won't be around to protect her all the time, Portia. Sooner or later, she'll get what's coming to her. And so will you."

Portia grinned. "Looking forward to it. I especially can't wait to see what my family does to yours afterward."

Nicole paled a bit, then stuck her nose in the air and walked off. Portia took my arm and led me outside. On the steps, I stopped and wondered where I should go. Not home. As bad as my day had been, I couldn't handle my parents right now. Neither of them liked me. I knew a lot of kids felt their parents disliked them, or even hated them, but in my case, I knew mine truly did.

"You going to be okay?" Portia asked.

I shrugged, not wanting to lie. A noncommittal answer was the best I could do. "Why did you help me?"

"Because I hate bullies." Portia smiled. "My dad and his club have taken out a lot of bad people over the years. If Nicole stays on her current path, she might be one of them someday."

I wasn't certain how to take her words. Did she mean her dad had *killed* people? Or had he helped send them to prison? I started to ask, and decided I didn't want to know.

The roar of a motorcycle snagged my attention. A guy pulled into the school lot and stopped at the curb near the stairs. Portia smiled, and I noticed her cheeks flushed a little. The man wore one of those leather vests like her dad, and it said Dixie Reapers MC on the back. The way he smirked at her only had Portia blushing harder. Did he know she liked him? It was clear for me to see, but I'd heard men could be a bit dense at times.

Portia waved to him, then flashed a smile my way. "Looks like my ride is here. You sure you're all right?"

"Go, before he decides to leave without you," I said.

"No way Merlin would leave me here. My dad would pound him into the ground. Then again, if he had any idea how much I liked riding on the back of Merlin's bike, he might lock me away forever. So let's keep it between us?"

I stared at her. "Um, Portia, when will I ever talk to your dad?"

She snorted. "Good point. Be safe heading home."

I watched her race down the stairs and get on the back of the bike. The way she put her arms around him made me feel envious. Not because of the man himself. It had more to do with the fact she liked a guy who would never hurt her the way Evan had done to me.

I gripped the strap of my backpack and decided to walk for a bit. I went down the stairs and walked across the school lot. A few boys let out whistles and made lewd comments, but I ignored them. Something told me I'd be facing more than that in the days to come. I didn't think for one moment my torture would end anytime soon. No, they'd drag it out as long as they could. Or until they found someone else to torment. Portia might have saved me today, but what about tomorrow?

My stomach churned as I thought about the remaining month in the school year. I had a bad feeling about what was to come.

Chapter One

Thunder
Three Months Later

I leaned against the porch post in front of my house and watched the storm. Lightning streaked the sky as the rain poured down. I'd always loved weather like this, which was only a small part of how I'd gotten my name. Torch had once commented that when I lost my temper, it was like the thunder booming. Needless to say, when it came time for me to patch in, they'd given me the name Thunder. Couldn't complain. It could have been worse.

Normally, I'd be at the clubhouse on a Friday night. As much as I liked to party with my brothers, some of the club sluts were getting a little too clingy. Veronica, in particular, couldn't seem to take a hint. I let her suck me off *once*, and now the bitch thought she meant something to me.

A shadow moved through the dark, and I had a feeling Merlin was making his way over. He lived two houses down, and lately, he'd been hiding from the President's daughter. Portia had her eye on Merlin, and the poor bastard didn't know how to let her down gently. He'd found her infatuation cute at first. Now that the girl had been chasing him for months, he did his best to hide every chance he had. Although, why the fucker was lurking in the shadows in the middle of a damn storm, I didn't understand. Surely Portia wasn't out in this mess.

"Would you get your ass on the porch and stop creeping along like a serial killer?" I called out.

The figure darted closer, and I realized the shadow was far too small to be Merlin. What the fuck? Portia came onto the porch, rain dropping off her, and panting for breath. "What the hell are you doing here?"

I demanded. "Does your daddy know you're running around?"

"I need help." She stared up at me with wide eyes. "Well, not me. It's someone I know. She's in trouble, Thunder. I tried to find Merlin, but he didn't answer his phone or the door. I don't know what else do to."

"Talk to your parents?" I suggested.

She shook her head. "You don't understand. Amity needs *help*. I'm grounded and Daddy took my keys. I got a voicemail from Amity that's freaking me out. I tried calling back and she's not answering. I need to find her!"

She pulled out her phone and pulled up the message. She put it on speaker and hit play. The first thing I heard was someone crying as if their heart had broken into a million pieces. She sobbed and tried to catch her breath a few times before finally speaking.

"Portia, I'm sorry. I know I promised, but I can't do this anymore. Thank you for being my friend for the past three months. None of this is your fault. I just can't... can't --" The message cut off, and I stared at Portia.

"Who the fuck is Amity and why does it sound like she's about to kill herself?" My heart pounded against my ribs. I'd never tell Portia, or anyone else, but hearing about that woman just now took me back to a dark place. One I'd never told a soul about.

"How do you *not* know?" Portia asked. "Her name has been all over town. Remember the guy at school who recorded himself having sex with his seventeen-year-old girlfriend?"

"The asshole who sent a sex video to the entire senior class?" I asked. "Are you telling me that girl is the one in the video?" Shit. I'd seen her picture in the paper, and I'd heard people talking. I'd eavesdropped on a few conversations, but I hadn't realized she and Portia were friends. Hell, if the Pres knew, he'd have been busting some heads around town. From what I heard, the punk who sent the video and screwed the girl over would be spending the next ten years in prison for child pornography. He'd put in a request to be tried as a youth. The judge had declined. And fuck if that hadn't made me smile.

It didn't matter if he'd willingly broken the law. He'd known taking that video, then sharing it, was beyond wrong. Some assholes thought the rules didn't apply to them. I might not walk the straight and narrow, but I'd never do something like that. Hurting women and kids went against everything I believed in. Same for abusing animals.

She nodded. "Amity didn't know he was playing a cruel joke on her. And she sure the hell didn't know he'd recorded them. People whisper when she walks through town, or outright call her a whore or a tramp. Her parents…"

"What about them?" I asked, pushing away from the porch post. I knew there were some shit parents in the world, but surely hers hadn't turned their backs on her. If I'd ever had a daughter, I'd have treated her like a princess. Hell, I was still young. Plenty of time to find my one and only and start a family.

"They're awful, Thunder. You should have heard some of the things they've said to her. They blame her for all of it, and only care how she's made them look to their friends. She turned eighteen last week, and they threw her out." Portia hugged her arms around her waist. "She didn't have anywhere to go. They didn't give a shit."

Sounded like her parents needed their asses kicked. But the longer we stood here talking, the worse our chances of finding Amity before she hurt herself.

"Where would she go, Portia?" I asked.

"She's been living on the streets. I have no idea where she is, Thunder. But she's alone, and she's hit rock-bottom. I think she really means to end it all." Portia sniffled and I could tell she'd be crying any moment. "I should have asked my dad to help her. I don't know why I didn't."

I cursed and pulled my keys from my pocket. "I'll find her. Go home, Portia. If your parents start looking for you, this is the last place you need to be. Since you didn't go to them first, I doubt you want them on my doorstep when I get back with Amity."

She placed her hand on her lips. I saw the sheen of tears in her eyes and knew the waterworks would start any moment now. "*If* you find her in time. That message is an hour old. What if it's too late?"

I didn't even want to contemplate not making it. I ran down the steps and around the side of the house to the carport. Didn't matter that I'd barely be able to see my hand in front of my face. I couldn't let Amity end her life. Her situation wasn't anything like the other girl I'd known, but it didn't stop me from comparing the two. As I flew down the streets, searching for the beautiful young woman, I couldn't help but go back to that awful day...

* * *

Thunder
Senior Year, High School

I'd skipped school again. No one cared, least of all my mother. Well, maybe one person. Ashley. We spent most of our free time together. Even after she hooked up with her last boyfriend, we'd been inseparable. Then he'd broken her heart and left her pregnant. I'd knocked out a few of his teeth, but it didn't matter. The thought of being a mother terrified Ashley.

I walked down the street, heading for our secret place. It wasn't much. A large flat rock near the river. We'd hang out there for hours. Sometimes we talked. Other times, we sat quietly, lost in our own thoughts. But on days like this one, when I'd stayed home, we would meet up there after school.

The rock came into view, and I smiled when I saw Ashley already there and waiting. She'd stretched out on the rock and seemed to be sleeping. As I drew closer, the smile slipped from my face.

"Ashley?"

I froze for a moment, then rushed to her side. Dropping to my knees, I reached for her, my hand shaking. I hadn't noticed from farther away, but she was far too still. Blood soaked the rock and the ground beside it. A knife lay on the ground, and Ashley was no longer breathing.

"No." I shook my head. "Not like this. Why? Why did you do it?" I buried my face in my hands and tried to pull myself together. I needed to tell someone.

I couldn't hold back my tears as I thought about the baby growing inside her. If that jackass she'd been dating hadn't knocked her up, then dumped her, would she have done something like this?

There'd been options. We'd discussed them countless times. I reached for her, my fingers brushing her cold ones. "I'm sorry. So fucking sorry."

* * *

I shook off the past as I approached the bridge over the river. My heart kicked in my chest when I saw the small figure standing in the rain. As I drew closer, she didn't even turn to face me. I shut off the bike and stood, pausing as I tried to figure out what the hell I should do. We didn't know each other. Would it freak her out if I approached?

"Amity?" I called out.

She tensed and looked ready to jump at any moment.

"Portia sent me."

Now *that* got her attention. She turned her face my way, and fuck if she didn't look beautiful. Soaked by the rain, eyes puffy from crying, and she still outshone every woman I'd ever known.

"Honey, this isn't the way to handle this," I said. "I know things are fucked up. Portia told me about your parents, and I know about that little shit from school. Can you come away from there so we can talk? Maybe I can help."

She turned to face me, and I nearly hit my fucking knees. It was Ashley all over again. It seemed that fucker had done more than humiliate her. He'd left her pregnant. The small bump wouldn't have been noticeable if the rain hadn't plastered her clothes to her. As thin as she seemed everywhere else, I knew she had to have a baby in her belly.

"No one can help me," she said, her lower lip trembling.

"You're wrong. You aren't alone, Amity. I know it feels that way. Things probably seem bleak. Your friends turned away. Your parents threw you out. Everyone knows what happened. Seems like the world is ending, doesn't it?"

She started sobbing. Her arms going around her waist, she looked down at the little bump where her baby was, then placed a hand there. She shook her head before holding my gaze again. "I can't take care of this baby. I have nowhere to live. No way to eat proper food. How can I bring a child into this ugly world?"

I swallowed the knot in my throat and moved closer to her. Holding out my hand, I waited, hoping she'd take it. For a moment, I thought she'd refused. Then she slid her fingers along mine, and I gripped her hand, pulling her closer.

"You aren't alone anymore," I said.

"Why do you care?" she asked. "You don't know me."

I patted my cut. "I'm a Dixie Reaper, which means Portia is like family to me. She considers you her friend. If that girl claims you, then you'll have the support of the club."

"Is that why you're here?" she asked, her lower lip trembling.

I swallowed hard and cupped her cheek. "Partly. But I also have my own reasons. Let me take you home. We can get you dried off, fed, and then we'll talk."

She looked at my motorcycle, and I cursed myself for being an idiot. I should have brought one of the club trucks, except someone might have asked questions I didn't want to answer. I didn't like the idea of her riding on the back while pregnant, especially in the current weather.

"Just hold on tight, okay? I'll go slow and we'll get back to my place in one piece. I won't let anything happen to you, Amity."

If only I'd made the same promise to Ashley. Would she have still taken her life? Her baby hadn't been mine. I'd never thought of her that way. Didn't mean I couldn't have offered to help. Is that what Amity needed?

I led her to the bike and helped her onto the back, then I climbed on and started the engine. Once her hands were secure around my waist, I turned the bike and headed back to the compound. I didn't go faster than thirty miles per hour, not wanting to chance Amity falling off. Thankfully, there weren't many drivers out in the storm.

When we approached the compound gates, the Prospect threw them open, and I rode through. I bypassed the clubhouse and went straight home. In all the years I'd been here, not once had I brought a woman with me. I had a feeling word would spread soon enough. With some luck, my nosy-ass brothers wouldn't drop by. I needed to figure out what to do with Amity before everyone decided to offer their assistance.

I stopped under the carport and helped her off the bike. Her legs wobbled a little. I shut off the engine and led her around to the porch and inside. She shivered and looked around my small house.

"I don't keep women's clothing here, but you can have one of my shirts. Should be long enough to fit you like a dress," I said. "Do you just want to change, or would you like a shower first?"

She clasped her hands in front of her and worried at her lower lip. "I don't want to be any trouble."

I moved closer and tucked her hair behind her ear. "Honey, you're far from trouble. I wouldn't have gone out looking for you if I hadn't wanted to help. You're safe, Amity."

Tears welled in her eyes and tried to hold back her sobs. They broke free, and she crumpled against me. I wrapped her in my arms and did my best to comfort her. Her long hair lay in a tangled mess down her back, and I stroked my hand over the locks. I didn't know what she needed from me, but I swore whatever it was, she'd have it.

I'd failed Ashley.

This time I'd get it right.

* * *

Amity

After everything Evan put me through, I should have just jumped when I saw the biker stop on the bridge. But then I'd remembered the way Portia talked about Merlin, and how she'd looked at him. She'd lived with those men all her life and out of the two of us, she'd certainly fared better. So I'd decided to trust him.

I couldn't remember the last time someone had held me while I cried. For that matter, I wasn't sure anyone *ever* had. My parents were awful people. To the community, they were trustworthy, gracious, and generous. Only because it's the persona they showed everyone. Behind closed doors had been a different story.

Reluctantly, I drew back from the man holding me. I wiped the tears from my cheeks and sucked in a shaky breath.

"I'm sorry," I said.

"No reason to be," he murmured. "Come on. I'll get you a towel, something to wear, and let you take a warm shower. Any food allergies or preferences?"

I bit back a laugh. "I've been eating only when Portia sneaks me something, or if someone else in town takes pity on me. Anything you have is more than fine."

"I'll make something hot."

"Don't you need to shower, too?" I asked, eying his wet clothing.

"I'll be fine." He took my hand and led me past the living room. A short hall only had four doors. The man pushed open the first door on the left and flipped on the light. The bathroom was relatively small, but clean. "Let me get that shirt for you. Wait right here."

I nodded and eyed the space. Opening the cabinet under the sink, I pulled out a towel. I noticed a pack of disposable razors, travel-size toothpaste and deodorant, and new toothbrushes down there as well. I grabbed what I'd need to feel truly clean. I didn't think he'd protest. If he said anything when he came back, I'd just return the items to the cabinet.

I jolted when I saw him behind me in the mirror.

"Didn't mean to scare you," he said. "By the way, they call me Thunder."

It wasn't funny. And yet it was. I started to giggle and then broke out into full on laughter. I held my sides when they started to ache, and I eventually got control of myself again.

"Um, can't say that I've had that reaction before," he said, his lips quirking into a smile.

"It's just... You said they call you Thunder, and you went out in a storm to rescue me from jumping off a bridge. It struck me as funny. Thunder was out in a thunderstorm." I snickered again and slapped my hand over my mouth.

He reached out and pried my hand loose. "Don't. You never have to hide your laughter from me, or your anger. Just be yourself, Amity."

"Thank you." I sobered at his words. No one had ever been so kind to me before. Portia had been nice, and I'd appreciated her help, but I'd always felt like she only did it because she felt sorry for me. Thunder had mentioned having his own reasons for helping me. I wondered what they were.

"Take as long of a shower as you want. Use anything you need and meet me in the kitchen when you're finished. I'll rinse off quickly and change before I start our food."

"I don't know why you're helping me, but… it's more than anyone's done for me before. You have no idea what this means to me."

He smiled sadly. "I think I have an idea."

I pressed a hand to my baby bump. "No one knows I'm pregnant. Well, nearly no one. My parents found out. It's why they threw me out of the house. And Portia knows."

"What are you saying, Amity?" he asked.

"It's not that I don't appreciate what you're doing for me, but I shouldn't stay here long. People will talk. They already call me a whore around town. I don't want anything to blow back on you. Not when you're being so nice to me."

He reached out and cupped my cheek. He'd done that before, and a weird sensation hit me. It felt like something fluttered around inside my stomach, and I wanted so badly to lean into his touch. For some reason, when he'd held me earlier, it had felt like everything would be okay.

"No one will dare say such a thing to you in my presence. If they do, I'll make sure they regret it." He leaned in and kissed my forehead.

I swallowed hard and nodded. After he left, I shut the door and pressed my hand over my racing heart. It felt like it might beat right out of my chest, and I didn't understand it. I'd thought I loved Evan, that he meant something to me. It's why I'd given myself to him. But now… I hadn't felt like this with him. What did it mean? Why did I feel like this when Thunder touched me?

"Maybe I'm what they say," I whispered to myself. What sort of woman had this kind of reaction to a strange man she'd just met? I'd only been with Evan, but had I given in to him too easily? And now with the way Thunder made me feel…

I stripped out of my clothes and took a shower. I shaved, washed my hair twice, and didn't get out until the water started to cool. No matter how much I tried not to think about it, I kept wondering if what other people saw was the real me. I felt raw inside, like someone had hollowed me out with a dull knife.

Thunder might have pulled me from the bridge tonight, but what about tomorrow? The pain seemed never ending, and I wasn't sure I wouldn't try to take my life again. What if he wasn't there next time? As much as I wanted to curl up in his arms, let him hold the world at bay, I knew that wasn't realistic. The longer I remained here, the more likely the town would turn on him. I couldn't let him suffer when he'd only been trying to help.

I dried off and pulled his shirt over my head. It fell to my knees and covered everything important. I couldn't bring myself to put on the dirty panties I'd removed, and I didn't have any others. My hair had already started soaking into the shirt, but at least I wasn't as wet I'd been before. I hadn't noticed a hairdryer when I'd been snooping, so I toweled it dry, then finger-combed it.

A tantalizing smell drew me to the kitchen, and my jaw dropped. Thunder had placed two plates on the table, nearly overflowing with spaghetti, as well as a basket of rolls, and two glasses of ice water.

"You didn't have to do all this," I said.

"Of course, I did. But before you get too excited, I used ground turkey in the sauce. I thought it might be healthier for you. Have a seat and I'll get the butter for the rolls." He paused. "Um, full disclosure. I opened the bathroom door so I could check your clothing sizes. I have someone picking up a few things for you. Nothing fancy, but you need more than what you had on tonight."

I wasn't sure how I felt about him going into the bathroom while I'd showered, but since he hadn't tried anything, I couldn't raise too much of a fuss. I pulled out a chair and sat down, staring at the food. My mouth watered, and I tried to remember the last hot meal I'd had. Portia had been great, bringing me sandwiches when she could. But something like this? It had been a while. I watched Thunder as he reached into the fridge to get the butter, and I wondered why Portia had picked him out of all the guys here. The way she talked about Merlin, I knew she adored that guy. If she'd have sent anyone after me, I'd have thought she'd pick him.

She didn't worry I'd try to steal Merlin from her, did she? As my only friend, I'd never do something like that. I worried at my bottom lip until I tasted the tang of blood. I licked it and hoped it wasn't noticeably bleeding.

Thunder placed the small tub of butter on the table, along with a knife, then sat across from me.

"Amity, you didn't have to wait on me. Go ahead and eat. I know you have to be starving."

My cheeks warmed. He wasn't wrong. I picked up my fork and took a bite, sighing in bliss as the flavors burst on my tongue. It was good. *Really* good. Thunder picked up a roll, buttered it, then placed it on the edge of my plate. I gave him a grateful smile. It was nice, having someone take care of me. For the first time in a while, I didn't feel like I had to worry about every little thing.

"I don't have beds in the spare rooms," Thunder

said. "You can sleep in my room tonight and I'll take the couch."

"What?" I blinked. "The couch?"

He nodded. "Won't be the first time I've slept in the living room. I've fallen asleep watching TV many times."

"I don't feel right kicking you out of your bedroom. The couch will be the softest place I've slept since my parents threw me out. I don't mind sleeping there."

"Amity, you're pregnant, and a guest in my home. Take the bed."

I started to argue, then realized it was pointless. The stubborn set of his jaw told me I wouldn't win this argument. Didn't make me feel any better. I finished my food, then stood to take my plate to the sink. Thunder arched an eyebrow at me, and I sighed, putting the dishes back down.

"I'm not allowed to clean either?" I asked.

He shook his head, then pointed to the hall. I folded my arms and stared at him. Was he sending me to bed like a wayward child?

"Amity, when's the last time you slept all night? When you didn't have to worry about whether it was safe to close your eyes and rest?" he asked.

"A while," I admitted.

"I'll clean this up. Get some sleep, honey. We'll talk tomorrow and figure something out. I'm not going to let you live on the street. I only wish Portia had said something sooner. I don't know why that girl waited until things were so dire."

"It's not her fault," I said. "She's been nice to me. Before this mess with Evan, we hadn't really spoken much."

"The point is that she knew you were in trouble. Not once has this club ever turned their backs on a woman in need." He paused. "You are a woman, right? Not a girl? I mean, Portia said you're eighteen, but she wasn't wrong, was she? You're legal?"

"I'm eighteen, if that's what you're asking."

"Thank fuck," he muttered.

"Wasn't it a little late to worry about that?"

"Yes and no," he said, rubbing a hand over his face. "In the morning, I'll make us breakfast, and then we can discuss your future. I'll help in whatever way I can. Make sure you and your baby have a chance."

"Thunder, you don't owe us anything."

"Maybe not, but it's my way of righting a wrong. It's not something I want to talk about, but I'll say this much... when I was in high school, my best friend killed herself. I've often wondered if I could have stopped her. Did I miss the signs? What if I'd shown up just a little sooner?"

I moved closer and reached out to place my hand on his shoulder. "It wasn't your fault. Do you think she'd want you to blame yourself?"

"No. Ashley would have kicked my ass."

"There was no one to blame for what happened earlier, either. It wouldn't have been Evan's fault, or the town's. It wasn't Portia's fault. I'm the one who decided to stand on that bridge. It was my decision to jump."

He stood so fast the chair felt over. I jolted but held my ground. If he'd wanted to hurt me, he wouldn't have brought me to his house. Right? The fury on his face made me doubt my decision not to run.

"They bullied you. Evan used you. He humiliated you, then everyone you knew turned against you. This entire fucking town has looked down on you, ridiculed you. It wasn't your *choice* to jump off the fucking bridge, Amity. Everyone drove you to it."

Tears misted my eyes. "Thunder, I…"

He reached out and gripped the back of my neck. The next thing I knew, he'd pressed his lips to mine, and it felt like the world had fallen away. I sucked in a breath, and his tongue slipped into my mouth. A whimper escaped me as I reached up and gripped the sides of his shirt. Clinging to him, I let him devour me, and not once did I even think about stopping him.

"Fucking hell. What are you doing to me?" he murmured before kissing me again. My toes curled, and I pressed closer to him. Thunder's hand slid down from my neck to my waist. "Austin. My name is Austin. When it's just us, you don't have to call me Thunder."

"Austin," I whispered. "What's happening?"

"Do you trust me, Amity?"

I didn't even hesitate. "Yes."

"You shouldn't. I didn't realize how tempting you'd be. I refuse to hurt you the way Evan did."

"I don't understand."

He pressed his forehead to mine. "I want you, Amity. I shouldn't, but I do. Tell me to sleep on the couch. Tell me to keep my distance, that you don't like me touching or kissing you."

"I…" I shut my mouth. I couldn't say it. "That kiss was the most wonderful thing I've ever experienced."

He closed his eyes. "You aren't making this easy, Amity. I'm trying to be a good guy, to do the right thing."

I took a step away from him, then another. He let me go, and I turned and walked out of the kitchen. He might say he wanted me, but clearly he didn't *want* to feel that way. I'd make it easy on him. I went to the bedroom and shut the door. After I crawled into bed, I closed my eyes and tried to sleep. Tried, and failed.

Touching my lips, I wondered if he would ever kiss me again.

Don't be silly, Amity. You just rejected him. Walked away. It had been the hardest thing I'd ever done. What the hell was wrong with me? I didn't know Thunder. Had never met him before. I didn't know why I reacted to him the way I did, or why he made me feel so… so… "You're stupid, Amity," I muttered.

I'd heard the rumors about the bikers. They could have any woman they wanted. What if Thunder only kissed me because I was convenient? Would the same thing have happened with any woman under his roof tonight? I wasn't special. Had *never* been special… to anyone. I needed to remember that.

It might be the only thing that saved me.

Chapter Two

Thunder

You're a fucking idiot!

I'd gone out searching for Amity, wanting to save her. Instead, I brought her home, kissed the hell out of her, then implied I wanted to fuck her. No wonder she'd walked out. Hell, it surprised me she hadn't run right out the front door. I wouldn't have blamed her.

My phone buzzed in my pocket, and I checked the screen. *Merlin.*

"Where the hell have you been?" I asked. "Portia was searching for you."

"I know. That's exactly why no one knows where I am."

What the fuck? "That's a dick thing to say. She's the Pres' daughter."

"Right. Do you think Torch would like any of us dating his baby girl? Because I sure the fuck don't think so. It was cute the way she followed me around and asked me to pick her up from school. Now I can't shake her."

"You're an asshole, Merlin. She needed help tonight, went looking for you, and had to settle for me."

I heard the rustle of sheets and a soft voice in the background. Figured as much. The asshole had picked up a woman somewhere and most likely gone back to her place. I hoped like hell Portia gave him a wide berth. The fucker wasn't good enough for her.

"What kind of help?" he asked.

"Remember the big ordeal about a guy at Portia's school filming himself having sex with another student?"

"What of it? Jerk's in jail, from what I hear. Portia went off about him, saying he'd used that poor girl.

Something about a bet. What does that have to do with anything?"

"Her name is Amity, and she tried to kill herself tonight. Portia went to your house, hoping you'd find Amity and save her."

"Holy shit," Merlin muttered. "You said *tried*. Does that mean you were able to stop her? Or someone did?"

"I found her. She's asleep in my room right now. And before you make any smartass remarks, I'll be on the couch tonight."

"She can't stay with you indefinitely. What are you going to do?" Merlin asked.

Instead of answering, I hung up on the fucker. Let him wonder. For that matter, I hadn't figured it out myself. Well, that wasn't entirely true. I knew what I *wanted* to do. Didn't make it the right thing. I'd failed Ashley, and I felt like I was already doing the same with Amity. Once the rest of the club heard about her, and knew she was staying at my place, I'd have one of two choices. Either hand her over to one of the old ladies and let them take it from there or claim Amity as mine.

I didn't know her. She sure the fuck didn't know me.

So why did I want to go with option two?

At least when Venom had claimed Ridley, they weren't complete strangers to one another. From what I'd heard, he hadn't seen her since she'd been a child, even though she'd had a crush on him most of her life. Then there was the Pres and his old lady... he'd had to claim Isabella in order to keep Ridley safe. Bull had rescued Darian. Preacher had knocked up Saint's sister. Tex had gone to retrieve his daughter and ended up bringing Kalani home.

Shit. We all had fucking hero complexes.

And we also knew when we'd met the woman we wanted to keep. At first, I'd thought the draw to take care of Amity was more about my past failure with Ashley. But it was more than that. Yeah, I'd cared about Ashley, but not in a romantic sense. One look in Amity's eyes on that bridge, and I'd known then and there she was mine. Just didn't know how to convince her. I'd handled things badly tonight. She'd been through so much, and I'd mauled her. I never should have kissed her. I'd promised to protect her, and now she probably thought I was like every man she'd known who expected something in return for my help.

My phone rang again. *Wire.*

"I feel special. Everyone's calling me tonight."

"Hello to you too, Thunder. You always answer your phone that way?" Wire asked.

"Just tonight. What's up, Wire?"

"Want to tell me who the woman is?" he asked.

"Well, that didn't take long. Figured I'd have until morning before someone blabbed or got nosy."

"I have this place under surveillance. The fact you never take anyone to your house made this seem a bit odd to me. So who the hell is she? And why was Portia at your home right before you ran out of there like your ass was on fire? If trouble is coming to the gates, I need to know."

Jesus. Old age hadn't mellowed Wire at all. Not that I'd ever call him old to his face. He was a scary bastard when it came to all things electronic. Wouldn't take him long to make it look like I'd never existed. Nope. Wasn't about to piss him off.

"Her name is Amity," I said.

Wire whistled. "Amity Whitman? Why did Portia ask you to go get her? And why the fuck did you make it seem so urgent?"

"She left Portia a message. Sounded like she was about to kill herself." I cleared my throat. "Wire, I stopped her from jumping off the bridge and into the river during a thunderstorm. This town has fucked with her head, ruined her life, and she felt like she didn't have any options."

"Why is she at your place?" he asked.

"I promised her I'd take care of her," I said. "Let her shower. Gave her something dry to put on. Then I fed her. She's been living on the street since her parents threw her out, and…"

"And what?"

"She's pregnant. Has the cutest little baby bump." I smiled, then quickly sobered. "She needs help, Wire."

"That video is still floating around out there. Someone sent it to one of the Prospects the other day. I'll do some digging and see if I can wipe it out."

"Thanks, Wire."

"You really want to help her?" he asked.

"Of course. I wouldn't have given her my bed otherwise."

"You'd do anything to keep her safe? Make sure the town stops terrorizing her? Give her baby a chance to have a happy life?" Wire asked.

"Why do I feel like I'm walking into a trap?" I heard laughter in the background. "You have me on speaker, don't you?"

"Hi, Thunder," Lavender called out. "You wanted a family, right?"

Oh, hell. They wouldn't. Would they? If Lavender and Wire did what they usually do… how the fuck was I going to explain that to Amity?

"Guys, you didn't just hack the county and state records, did you?" I asked.

"Oh, fuck," Lavender whispered, but not soft enough. I heard her clearly. "Um. Thunder. How protective do you feel when it comes to Amity?"

"There's some stuff you need to see," Wire said. "I'm coming over."

"No, *we're* coming over," Lavender corrected.

"You're just going to leave our kids here alone?" Wire asked.

"Of course not! I'm going to ask Darian to come sit with them."

I wasn't sure I wanted to know why both hackers felt the need to come over. Whatever they'd found, it couldn't be good. I got up and went down the hall, needing to check on Amity. I tested the knob on the bedroom door, and it turned easily. I swung the door open and saw her huddled in the middle of the bed. The way her shoulders shook, I could tell she was crying.

"Amity? Everything all right?"

She sucked in a breath but didn't respond. Moving farther into the room, I eased down onto the side of the bed and reached out to run my fingers through her hair. She stilled, but I heard the sniffles and knew I'd been right about the tears.

"Honey, what's wrong? If it's about the kiss earlier, I'm sorry if it upset you. I offered you a safe place, then took advantage."

"Why did you kiss me?" she asked.

"That's not an easy thing to explain, especially if you don't know much about my club or how things work around here."

She turned to face me, and her puffy eyes made me feel like an utter asshole. I'd done this to her. If I'd kept my hands and lips to myself, she wouldn't have been in here crying. The way she'd left the kitchen earlier, I knew then I'd gone too far. Now, with Wire and Lavender doing whatever the fuck they wanted, things were probably going to get worse.

"Am I convenient?" she asked.

"What?" I stared at her, thinking I must have misheard. She couldn't be serious, could she? "Why would you think that?"

She worried at her lower lip and didn't respond. I wasn't sure if something I'd said or done had made her ask, or if it had more to do with her past. I knew that Evan kid had fucked her over in a big way. Then the town decided to whittle down whatever confidence she might have still had. It couldn't have been easy. The months since that video went to the senior class had to have been hell on earth.

"Amity, I kissed you because… I wanted to. But it's more complicated than that. You'd have to know more about my club and the couples here. The men with the Dixie Reapers don't settle for just anyone. I truly believe everyone here is paired with their soulmate. My brothers took one look at their women and just knew."

"I don't understand," she said.

"That's what happened on that bridge tonight, Amity. One look was all it took. I knew right then, in the middle of a storm, that you were mine."

Her eyes went wide. "Yours?"

"It's not something we have to figure out tonight. I have some friends stopping by any minute. Wire and Lavender said they needed to discuss something with me. I wanted to check on you before they got here."

"Do I need to stay in here?" She seemed to curl up and make herself even smaller. What the hell had everyone done to her? If I could round up the town, and her parents, I'd kick all their asses.

"Do you want to meet them?" I asked.

"You'd be okay with that?"

"Of course. I told you, Amity. I want you to be mine. Only if that's what you want to. We're strangers, so take all the time you need. I'm not throwing you out. There are no conditions on you staying here with me, so don't feel pressured to give into me."

I heard the knock at the front door and stood. Holding out my hand to Amity, I waited for her to take it. By the time we got to the living room, Wire and Lavender had let themselves in. I'd have to remember to lock the door in the future. They each had laptops with them, but it was the way Lavender looked at Amity that had my stomach knotting. They'd found something about her, and whatever it was, it made Lavender hurt for Amity.

"Hello, Amity," Wire said. "I wish we were meeting under better circumstances."

"This is Wire and his wife Lavender."

"Do you have any hot tea?" Lavender asked. "She may need some if she's going to listen to this conversation."

Tea? Did I look like the fucking Queen of England? Of course, I didn't have any fucking tea.

"Just coffee," I said.

"I don't like tea," Amity said. "I don't need any. I only drink it iced and sweet."

"Amity, may we ask you a few questions about what happened?" Wire asked. "We were trying to permanently erase that video and ended up finding something else. But I'm not sure how much you remember from that day. The last thing we want to do is cause you more harm."

She glanced at me, and I reached out to cup her cheek. Whatever she had to say, I wouldn't think any less of her.

"Do you feel comfortable talking about that day?" I asked. "If not, that's okay."

"I don't know what's a memory and what's a nightmare. The lines blur a bit," she said.

"Amity, you don't have to do this," I said, taking her hand.

"I think I do," she murmured.

"You'll want to make that coffee," Wire said. "You and I are going to need it. And once all this is handled, you'll want something a hell of a lot stronger."

That didn't sound good. Now I dreaded hearing Amity's story, as well as whatever Wire had found. I knew about the video, and the fallout that happened afterward. How much worse was it?

"The kitchen table might be easier for the two of you, but I want to make sure Amity is comfortable. Do the two of you care if we do this in the living room?" I asked.

"Whatever is best for her," Lavender said. "Wire and I will manage."

They both sat and placed their computers in their laps. I led Amity over to the couch and helped her sit before I went to brew a pot of coffee. I took a cup to Wire but decided not to make one for myself. Not yet. I wanted my hands free in case Amity needed me. Whatever she had to say, I had a feeling it would be difficult for her.

"So, what can you tell us about the day Evan took the video?" Wire asked.

If I'd known what he'd already found, or the way that one question would affect Amity, I'd have never let them into the house.

* * *

Amity

They wanted me to relive the day of the video? I clenched my hands in my lap and stared at the floor. Had they watched it? These people said the video was still out there. I'd thought only the senior class received it. I knew the police had watched it, and the judge. Did the entire town watch? The name calling, the whispers… I'd thought it was because of the news reports based on Evan's trial. Was I wrong?

My stomach twisted and turned, and I struggled not to throw up. I'd already felt violated by what Evan had done, and now to find out more people had seen it than I'd originally thought? It was too much!

Thunder put his arm around me and pulled me closer. The heat of his body and his woodsy scent soothed me a little. I couldn't help but lean into him. He'd been so nice to me. Even though he'd kissed me, he'd apologized. I'd wanted that kiss every bit as much as he had, but the sweet man had worried he'd overstepped and hurt me in some way. Why couldn't I have met someone like him instead of dating Evan?

"Amity, do you remember anything?" Thunder asked. "If it's too painful to talk about, we'll understand. Wire and Lavender just need to know what you remember. They don't want to risk telling you something you don't already know."

My gaze jerked to his. What the hell did that mean? "Did… did something else happen?"

Oh, God! It had, hadn't it? Why else would he have phrased it that way? I knew Evan hadn't shared the entire video, or at least, more had happened that day. I only remembered things up to a point. I'd agreed to have sex with him. Thought he loved me, and I loved him. But at the end, the overall feel of what we'd been doing changed. I remembered his hand around my throat. Then everything went hazy. More like flashes of a nightmare that haunted me, yet I couldn't quite put the pieces together.

Thunder growled and glared at Wire and Lavender. "That's it. You're not making her talk about that day, and I don't want her to hear whatever the fuck it is you have to say. They have traumatized her enough as it is. Evan. Her family. Her friends. This entire fucking town. We aren't adding to it!"

"And *that* is why I did what I did," Lavender said.

"Um, I'm sorry, but what exactly did you do?" I asked.

"Tell me you didn't," Thunder said. "After all she's been through, you'd take that choice away from her?"

"She's already had more taken from her than I think she realizes, and certainly more than you know," Wire said. "Lavender was doing her best to ensure Amity would have a safe place, someone who cared, and a new family to stand beside her."

"What's going on?" I asked Thunder.

"Wire and Lavender have certain skills with a computer. They're hackers, or as Lavender says, Wire is a cracker. I'm not sure I understand the difference. The point is that they're notorious for getting into government records and marrying people. If anyone goes poking around, they'll find a marriage license on file with the vital records department."

My mouth went dry. "Are you... are you saying they *married* us?"

"Yeah, honey. That's what I'm saying." Thunder sighed. "I never would have done that without your consent. Hell, I'd have asked you the proper way, with an engagement ring, and a real wedding. They didn't just take your choice away, but they stole that from you too."

"Amity, if you don't want to hear what happened that day, you might want to leave the room," Wire said. "But I think Thunder needs to understand why we interfered."

"Because you're meddlers?" Thunder asked.

I swallowed the knot in my throat. The expression on Lavender's face was nothing but sympathetic. Wire, on the other hand, looked resigned. If they were trying to help, then I needed to tell them everything I remembered. Maybe they could fill in the blanks for me. I'd often wondered if not knowing was worse than remembering it all.

"It all started with Evan asking me out." I took a breath and told them how he'd tricked me into dating him. Made me feel special, only to discover later it all had been a cruel joke. I talked about how I felt when the kids at school got that video.

"And the day of the video?" Wire asked.

"Evan had been pressuring me to have sex. That was the day he made me dinner at his parents' lake house. He'd been so sweet and attentive all day and told me he loved me. I fell for it, like an idiot." I twisted my fingers in my lap, clenching them together until they turned stark white. "He'd opened a bottle of his mother's favorite wine and we'd had two glasses each. I never drank before so it hit me pretty hard. I remember things getting…"

"The two of you had sex," Lavender filled in.

I nodded, thankful she hadn't made me go into details. But I knew I needed to tell the rest of what I remembered. "You've seen the video. What you didn't see was what happened after that clip ends."

Thunder squeezed me tighter. "Amity, you don't have to do this."

"But I do. The trial only focused on what happened

up to the video and it being shared with the class. They never asked about when the video ends. I was too scared to say anything, and I'd already been embarrassed. I'd just wanted the entire thing to be over. So I kept quiet."

"Thunder, I need you to hold it together." Wire held his gaze. "No matter what she says, and what we fill in from there, I need to know you aren't going to lose it."

"I make no promises," he muttered. "If Evan weren't already in prison, I'd fuck up that little shit."

My heart warmed at his words. Maybe it shouldn't have made me want to smile, hearing him threaten violence, but not once during all this had anyone truly cared what happened to me. The officer at school had been kind, but he'd been more focused on the law being broken. My parents had only worried about their fake reputation around town.

"When the video ends, Evan yanks my hair, says a lot of dirty things, then he choked me. I remember struggling and blacking out. After that is when things get hazy. I feel like more happened, and I know I hurt so much when I woke up again. He'd leered at me, told me what a good little whore I'd been, then he'd taken me back home." I was almost too scared to ask my next question. "Do you know what happened to me while I wasn't conscious?"

"Thunder, put Amity in your lap and hold on to her. It's for both your sakes," Wire said.

I didn't give Thunder a chance to comply. I crawled into his lap and wrapped my arms around his neck. I clung like a damn vine, terrified that whatever was said next might be what broke me beyond repair.

"Evan used a condom, didn't he?" Wire asked.

I nodded.

"And yet you're pregnant," he said. "I don't think that baby belongs to Evan. He did upload the entire footage of what happened to you. On the dark web. People paid to watch it. The little prick has made about a million dollars off it, not to mention what he charged while it was being made."

Charged? I didn't understand. "Like one of those live streaming porn shows?"

Lavender got up and brought her laptop over. She set it on the coffee table and turned it to face us, then came to kneel by Thunder's feet. She clicked a few keys and then hesitated when a video pulled up. "There're hours of footage. We didn't watch all of it. We saw it from where the leaked video left off up to a certain point, then we skipped to the end."

Hours? I whimpered and held Thunder even tighter. What the hell had Evan done to me? Why couldn't I remember anything?

"You're scaring her," Thunder accused.

"It's why I asked if she wanted to leave the room," Wire said. "This is going to be ugly."

"How ugly?" Thunder asked.

"Like Rin and Kalani level," Lavender said, her voice soft and low. "I'd spare you both this pain, but I think it's better to know. For one, I'm certain that baby doesn't belong to Evan. We'd have to watch everything to try and figure out who it belongs to, and we will if that's what you want."

She started the video and a loud keening sound escaped me. I shook as I cried. Thunder growled, and I felt a tremor run through him. The sounds of the video were the worst. No. Knowing that Evan had used me like that, kept me drugged so men could pay to fuck me however they wanted, then acted like nothing had happened… that was the worst.

"I researched Evan a little more," Wire said. "He can't get off unless a woman is unconscious. In fact, he pays good money to use whores who let him do whatever the hell he wants. But he also knows a lot of men and teen boys just like him. It looks like he called them, offered up Amity, and cashed in on her innocence."

"He was my first," I whispered.

The video kept playing, and I cried harder. The sounds filled my ears, burrowed into my brain, and I knew they'd haunt me for the rest of my life. He'd let them violate me. Use me. The only thing he'd insisted on were condoms. He told them it would be harder to trace anything to them if they didn't leave semen behind, or give me any diseases.

"We think one of the condoms broke. But we'd have to watch everything to see if we could figure out who it was," Lavender said. "If you even want to know."

"Why?" I looked up at Thunder. "Why did he do that to me? I was so stupid. So trusting."

He cupped my cheek and kissed me softly. "No, honey. You thought he loved you, wanted to believe him. You couldn't have known what sort of monster lurked beneath the surface."

"Those men will pay," Wire said. "They wanted you because you were underage. They're pedophiles. Except the ones who were younger. If there's one thing this club can't stand, it's men and women who hurt those who are weaker than them. I've never had to take down a kid for being a rapist, but I'll do it."

"He'll fucking smile while he does his best to make that kid's life a living hell," Lavender said. "We won't let anyone get away with what they've done to you, Amity. I married you and Thunder for a reason. I could tell he felt protective of you. More than that, as his wife, you'll also have the Dixie Reapers standing beside you through all this."

"When I thought the baby belonged to Evan, I'd known he'd been a lying, manipulative asshole. Knowing my baby has a rapist for a father?" I shook my head. "I don't know what to do with that."

Thunder tipped my chin, so I had to hold his gaze. "No, your baby doesn't have a rapist for a father. Because as far as anyone is concerned, that baby is mine."

"Thunder, you can't do that," Wire said. "She was seventeen when she conceived. Do you want to go to jail for statutory rape? Because even I can't sweep that one under the rug."

"I won't let you get in trouble just because you want to protect me," I said. "But I'd much rather you be the baby's father than anyone else. You've been so kind. Heroic. You've been nicer to me than anyone ever has in my entire life. This baby would be lucky to have you as a father."

I could see the conflict in his eyes. The town might talk about the Dixie Reapers, call them killers behind their backs, but all those people were wrong. Thunder would only hurt someone who deserved it. Like Evan and those other men.

"I'm claiming Amity and the baby," Thunder said, his voice rougher than usual. Deeper. "Doesn't matter if I'm the sperm donor or not. From today onward, this baby is mine. I will educate anyone who says different."

"Is that code for you're going to hit them?" I asked.

His lips twitched into a slight smile. "Yeah, honey. I'll stomp their asses into a mud hole if they say one bad word about you or try to say this baby isn't mine.

You okay being married to a Neanderthal biker like me?"

"I'm all right being married to the kind, sweet, gentle man I know you are," I corrected.

He kissed me. His lips lingered a moment on mine, and my heart sped up. If we were married now, would we share the bed? Would he want to do… other… things? The idea both excited and scared me. It had hurt before. What if it hurt again? What if I could never enjoy sex?

"Whatever you're thinking, stop it," he said. Looking over at Wire, his expression shifted from sweet man to *I want to bathe the world in blood.* "Find every motherfucker on that video. A quick death is too forgiving. I want them to suffer. Financially. Mentally. Emotionally. Assuming any of them actually *have* emotions. Wreck their entire lives and leave them as nothing more than a shell. Then I want my time with them."

"Understood," Wire said, standing. Lavender closed her laptop and picked it up. They headed for the door, but Wire paused. "I'm going to call Torch and Venom. I'll let them know what's going on. No one is going to ask either of you to go through a vote. I can guarantee it, especially when I tell Torch your new wife is friends with his daughter."

"Thank you," I said, facing them. "I thought I was going crazy. Having weird nightmares that made no sense. Now I know it was flashes of what those men did to me. I wasn't out of it entirely. Whatever drugs Evan gave me kept me compliant and loopy. But they didn't erase everything."

"We're going to look into your parents, too," Lavender said. "From what we could tell, you were gone for more than twenty-four hours. The fact your parents never brought that up in court, or called the police when you didn't return home, raises a red flag. Whatever their part in all this, they won't come out of it unscathed."

"I don't have parents," I said. "I had a mother and father who gave birth to me, then only treated me decently in public. Their image is everything to them. I'm not even sure why they had me."

"We'll make it right. Or as much as we can," Lavender promised. "And if you want to speak with someone, the club knows a counselor. Tex's daughter saw him for a while, and Kalani has spoken to him a few times as well over the years. You aren't alone, Amity."

After they left, Thunder held me. He ran his hand over my hair. Not once did he say anything. The *thump* of his heart soothed me.

I didn't know what would happen next.

But one thing I knew for certain… those sounds, the little bit I'd seen of the video, would keep me up for many nights. I hoped Thunder knew what he was getting himself into.

Chapter Three

Thunder

I wanted to track down every motherfucker who'd touched Amity. They needed to pay. I knew Wire and Lavender didn't want to watch that nasty shit, but I was grateful they were willing to find out who'd hurt my woman. No, my wife. After they'd left, Amity held it together for a little while, until she'd completely fallen apart. She'd cried so hard she'd made herself throw up.

My phone buzzed with an incoming text. *Church. Now.*

I smoothed Amity's hair from her face, hating to wake her. Instead, I wrote a quick note to let her know I had to go to the clubhouse and would return shortly. With some luck, she would sleep until I returned.

I put on my cut and my boots, then left the house, making sure I locked it on my way out. It wasn't that I didn't trust my brothers and their old ladies. But I couldn't ignore the amount of trouble that seemed to find us every time one of us settled down with someone. I didn't delude myself into thinking I'd be any different.

By the time I got to Church, everyone else had arrived before me. Wire got up and placed a cold beer in front of me, and I knew then we'd convened to discuss Amity. Whatever he'd discovered since leaving my house, it had to be really fucking bad.

Torch stood and cleared his throat. "Before we discuss the main issue for tonight, there's something I need to tell everyone. I can admit I'm not getting any younger, and I'm more than ready to enjoy what's left of my life. So that being said, I'm going to step down as President."

I couldn't say his words shocked me. The low

murmur around the table told me my brothers felt the same. We'd known it was coming sooner or later. The fact our VP wasn't much younger worried me. Would Venom step up as President? If he did, how long before he decided to retire too?

Tank, Flicker, and Venom stood as well. Oh, fuck. This didn't look good. Not even a little. What the hell was going on?

"In fact, we're all stepping down," Venom said. "None of us are getting any younger. It's time to let the next generation take over. And we don't mean that literally. Since none of our sons have patched in, we'll be passing the responsibility of President, VP, Treasurer, and Enforcer on to those of you who are a bit younger. Or rather, Tank's position will also be transitioning to Sergeant-at-Arms. His patch never said that, so we ordered one."

I lifted my hand, feeling like I was back in high school. "How is this going to work?"

"We each have someone in mind for our positions," Tank said. "But we're going to let the club vote to see if you feel the same way we do."

"We're going to be active in the club. We'll have your backs when shit goes sideways. Hell, put us to work when you need us. But for the most part, we're going to be more like silent partners in a business firm. We want time with our families," Flicker said.

"This club hasn't had a Road Captain or Secretary in a long while," Torch said. "And we have recommendations for those two positions as well."

Flicker cleared his throat. "So, I'm going to go first. For club Treasurer, I'm recommending Grimm. Put your hands up for a vote for Yes. Leave your hand down if your vote is a No."

Every hand around the table went up, except

Grimm. He narrowed his gaze at Flicker. "Why the hell are you stepping down?"

"Because I'm sixty-four years old and I want to spend time with Pepper, Reed, and MaryJane. My priorities have shifted," Flicker said. "Do you accept the position, or not?"

Grimm sighed. "I'll take it."

Flicker tore the *Treasurer* patch from his cut and walked around to hand it to Grimm. "Your seat at the table is over there now."

Grimm and Flicker swapped spots. My throat grew tight with emotion, and I knew I'd feel wrecked by the time Church was over. I'd never expected this. I'd known things would change at some point. I just hadn't anticipated all the officers stepping down at once. I didn't think any of us had.

Tank scanned the table. "I already spoke with my successor, so he knows what's coming. I'd like Tempest to become the Sergeant-at-Arms for this club. Hand up if you vote yes. Leave your hand down for no."

Every hand went up once again. I didn't think any of us had the balls to go against the old officers. If they'd chosen a specific person for their position, I sure the fuck wasn't going to tell them I disagreed. I knew they wouldn't pick lightly and had put a lot of thought into it.

Tank handed Tempest a patch and swapped seats with him.

"Torch and I spoke with the two men we'd like to take our positions. And while Torch and Saint are extremely close, neither of us felt Saint was quite ready for that position. So, I've asked him to be the club's new VP."

Before Venom even finished his little speech, every

hand went up. Same as before, the patch was handed off and the new VP took Venom's old spot at the table.

"Before I announce your new President, I'm going to let you vote on your new Road Captain and Secretary. All the officers discussed those positions. We didn't make our decision hastily. For Road Captain, we'd like to offer the position to Viking."

Another unanimous vote. Since we hadn't had a Road Captain before, Viking remained in his regular seat.

"For Secretary, we'd like Royal to step into the position. And before you vote, you may have noticed none of the brothers we chose are older than their early forties. We were trying to choose men who could remain in their positions for a decade or more, so the club wouldn't be in turmoil. It doesn't mean we didn't feel the older brothers, like Preacher, Bull, or Sarge would be a good fit. We were just trying to choose brothers who wouldn't feel the need to step down within a few years."

Everyone voted for Royal to become the club Secretary.

Torch ran a hand over his beard. "I struggled with the decision to step down as President. I've bled for this club. Damn near died for it multiple times. But like Venom, I'm not getting any younger. In fact, I'm older than him and Flicker. The man I've selected as your next President is older than the other new officers, but he certainly doesn't have one foot in the grave."

"The suspense is killing us," Bull said. "Just spit it out, Torch."

Torch flipped him off, but I noticed Bull was smiling.

"I'd like for Savior to take over as President," Torch said.

Once again, every hand went up. Watching Savior accept the patch and take Torch's spot at the head of the table made my chest ache. Torch had been the President when I was nothing more than a Prospect. Hell, that was true for most of us. Seeing him step down was bittersweet. I knew he was ready to retire and enjoy his life, but damn would I miss seeing him sitting in his regular spot at the table during Church.

Savior remained standing and surveyed the room.

"I don't have a big speech planned, or anything like that. But Church was called for more than a change in officers. There's a rather serious matter that needs our attention." Savior's gaze swung to me. "Thunder, why don't you tell everyone about your wife, then we'll let Wire take over."

"Most of you probably heard about the girl at Portia's school. The senior whose boyfriend filmed them having sex, then sent the video out to the entire senior class. The prick is in jail for child pornography since she was seventeen when it happened.

"Her name is Amity, and she's my wife. But the story is worse than we imagined. That little shit didn't just have sex with her. He filmed the entire thing, choked her until she passed out. Drugged her. Then he charged men to rape her. And the sick little shit recorded every second."

"Holy shit," Tempest muttered.

"Amity is pregnant. I saved her before she could jump off the bridge into the river. Portia came to me, asking for help. She'd received a voicemail that terrified her. She worried Amity would end her life, and she'd been right. It's exactly what Amity planned to do. Until I stopped her."

"And the wife part?" Merlin asked.

"Lavender married them," Wire said. "Amity

wasn't aware of what happened once she passed out. She said she'd had flashes of memory that hadn't made sense. Now she knows why. We didn't show her everything, and I'm really fucking glad we didn't. She's pregnant, and since Evan and the men who paid to use Amity all wore condoms, we weren't sure who the father was. Lavender thought one of the condoms broke."

"Are you telling me that's not what happened?" I asked.

"Before I say anything else, I need a promise from you. No matter how enraged you become, you will remain in that seat. You won't storm out of here and rip the fucker to pieces. We'll make sure he pays, but we have to be smart about it. And Amity will need to know, but I'm worried about what it will do to her." Wire bit his lip. "The baby will need to be checked for possible birth defects."

"What the fuck, Wire?" I started to stand, but Tempest moved so fast I didn't see him coming. He placed his hands on my shoulders and pinned me to my seat.

"Whatever it is, tell us and do it fast," Tempest said.

"We thought we'd watched the entire video. We were wrong. Before Evan took Amity home, there was one more visitor. Her father."

Oh, fuck no. Anything but that. Bile rose in my throat, and I fought against Tempest. I knocked him to his ass and rushed to the trashcan, barely making it before I threw up. I didn't stop retching until I couldn't do more than dry heave.

"Are you saying her own father raped her?" Saint asked, looking pale and every bit as sick as I felt. "How the fuck can someone do that to their kid?"

"He raped her. On film. And he didn't use protection. The baby Amity is carrying belongs to her father, which means there will be an increased risk of blindness, deafness, limb deformities, cleft palate, and quite a few other issues." Wire held my gaze. "I'm so fucking sorry, Thunder. I didn't want to tell you but knew everyone needed to hear it. We can't let that man stay free."

My poor, sweet Amity. She'd suffered so much before she'd even realized the full extent of what Evan did to her. Now this? I wasn't sure she'd survive the news. I'd have to keep a close watch. Make sure someone stayed with her whenever I wasn't home. The fact she'd wanted to end her life already meant she was in a fragile state.

"I already called Dr. Myron and Dr. Sykes," Wire said. "They're on their way here. Go home, Thunder. Talk to Amity. And please let those men help in any way they can. She's going to need all the support she can get."

My legs felt shaky as I left Church. I got on my bike and went home. After I pulled into the carport, I let it idle as I stared at the side of the house. How did I tell her what I'd learned? It would destroy her. I finally turned off the bike and went inside. Amity sat on the couch with the TV going. She smiled when she saw me, but it slipped from her face after she got a good look at me.

"What's wrong?" she asked.

"Honey, we need to talk, but I… I don't know how to…" Shit. I was about two seconds from crying like a little bitch.

"They finished the video, didn't they?" she asked softly. I nodded. "And whatever they saw, it's worse than what we found out before?"

"Yeah, honey. It's a lot worse." I cleared my throat. "I'm going to brush my teeth and rinse off in the shower. If there's a knock at the door, it's just two friends stopping by. Dr. Myron and Dr. Sykes want to speak with you."

She stood abruptly. "Are you having me committed somewhere?"

"What?" My brow furrowed. "Amity, why the hell would you ask me that?"

"I've heard of Dr. Sykes before. I know what he does for a living."

I went to her and pulled her into a hug. "No. I'm not sending you anywhere. The counselor that was mentioned earlier? It's Dr. Sykes. He's only come to talk to you and listen if you want to discuss everything you're feeling right now."

"I don't want to be alone," she mumbled against my chest.

"Then come sit on the bed while I clean up." Honestly, I hadn't gotten dirty, even though I'd puked until I couldn't anymore. After hearing what Amity's father did to her, I *felt* like someone dragged me through manure. Twice.

She sat on the edge of the bed while I pulled out a pair of sweatpants and a tee. I went into the bathroom and left the door partially open in case she needed me. Then I scrubbed my teeth twice and took the hottest shower. By the time I'd finished and dressed, I didn't feel any more prepared for the discussion we needed to have. If I could think of a way to prolong it indefinitely, I would.

"I didn't hear anyone at the door," she said.

"They may not have arrived yet. Do you want to wait until they're here in case you need medical attention?" I asked.

"You're scaring me, Austin."

I cupped her cheek and kissed her forehead. "I'm not trying to, honey. I'm just worried how you'll handle the news. But there's something I want to say first. I know we just met. We're strangers. Even if we're married, it's not the same as you meeting someone, dating a while, falling in love, and doing all this the traditional way."

"The traditional way, as you put it, didn't work out so great for me," she said.

"Maybe not. My point is that despite all that, I care about you a great deal, Amity. I didn't lie when I said I took one look into your eyes and knew you were meant to be mine. I felt it here," I said, placing my hand over my chest. "What I learned today doesn't change that. You're still mine, and so is the baby growing inside you. Understand?"

She hesitantly nodded. "Just tell me, Austin. Not knowing is even worse."

I laced our fingers together so she couldn't run when she heard the news. Then I told her what Wire discovered. She paled and her eyes went so wide I thought they might pop out of her head.

"It wasn't a dream," she murmured. "I thought something was horribly wrong with me, for so long, and all this time…"

"Amity, what are you saying?" I asked.

"My father. I kept having this recurring dream, or I assumed it was a dream. He'd come into my room, pull down his pants, and masturbate while he watched me. Another time, it was different. I got up to get a drink of water and his office door hadn't closed all the way. I saw him inside with a girl on her knees. Younger than me. He had his cock in her mouth." She audibly swallowed. "Does this mean I didn't dream those things? He really did all that?"

"Do you know who that girl was?" I asked.

She shook her head. "I hadn't seen her before. And I never saw her after."

I got my phone and shot off a message to Wire, letting him know what Amity had told me. When I sat beside her again, she leaned into me.

"Is it wrong I almost feel relieved?" she asked.

"What?" Surely I hadn't heard her right.

"I thought there was something wrong with me. That I was disgusting and sexualizing my father all these years. I felt wrong, and like a monster."

"Amity, you heard the part where the baby is his, didn't you?" I asked slowly.

"I did." She looked up at me. "I think I'm... numb. I don't feel sorrow. No anger. No pain right now. I'm just... here. If that makes any sense."

Yeah, it did. She hadn't fully processed everything. Once she did, I had a feeling she'd be a complete wreck. Whatever it took, I'd see she got the help she needed, and I'd be there for her every step of the way. I hadn't lied when I said I cared about her. Hell, if I believed in love at first sight, I'd even say I loved her.

But that was ridiculous.

Wasn't it?

* * *

Amity

I kept waiting for the crushing weight to hit me. The urge to end it all. I stared at the table while Thunder made breakfast. I'd met with Dr. Myron and Dr. Sykes last night. They'd seemed nice, and incredibly understanding. I'd overheard Dr. Sykes tell Thunder to keep an eye on me. My new husband had held me while I slept. It was probably the safest I'd ever felt at night. At least I understood why now. I'd never known why I had trouble sleeping.

Thunder kissed the top of my head when he set a plate in front of me. *Scrambled eggs. Biscuits. Grits.* I added salt and pepper to my eggs and swirled my fork through the butter and grits, then stared at the biscuits. "Do we have apple butter?" I asked.

"No, but I'll get some," he said, taking a seat across from me.

I kept staring at the biscuits. "I can't eat them without it."

He paused, fork mid-air. "Okay. Would you prefer toast?"

I shook my head. "No. I want apple butter."

Thunder set his fork down and watched me. I could feel the weight of his gaze as I stayed focused on the biscuits. It felt like a monster was clawing its way up my insides, trying to get out. Hysterical laughter bubbled up and I tried to hold it back.

"I need it," I said, my voice coming out a little shrill.

Thunder stood and came around the table. Without a word, he picked me up and carried me to the bedroom. I beat on his shoulder, screaming at him.

"Where's the apple butter? Why don't we have any?"

A burning sensation flooded my chest, and it felt like my brain was buzzing, like a thousand volts of electricity was flowing through it. I screamed and thrashed in his arms until a sob escaped me. Then another. Tears streaked my cheeks, and my throat ached as I lashed out at the sweetest man I'd ever met.

I knew it wasn't rational. I needed to stop. But I couldn't.

I'd held back for so long. Bottled it up. Shoved it

down deep. Convinced myself I'd been having strange dreams. Nightmares. That something was incredibly wrong with me.

"Let it out," he murmured. "I'm right here, Amity. I won't go anywhere. You hit me if you need to. Scream. Cry. Whatever it takes. Purge all that negative emotion."

"Why? Why did he do it?" I asked, my voice sounding every bit as broken as I felt. "I don't understand. What did I do wrong? Was I a bad daughter? Did he hate me that much?"

"Amity, none of this is your fault. Your dad is a sick, twisted man. His perversions have nothing to do with you. He's rotten from the inside out, and I'm going to expose all the skeletons in his closet. Whatever it takes, I'll make sure you and our baby are safe."

I pressed a hand to my mouth. "The baby. What if there's something wrong with it?"

"Dr. Myron will check on the baby when you go in for a visit. He said there are some tests he can do to check for certain things. Blindness and deafness we wouldn't know about it until after the baby is born." He kissed my temple. "One day at a time, honey. That's all we can do right now."

"Do you…" I stopped and licked my lips. The question was so close to coming out, but the thought of how he might answer terrified me.

"Do I what?" he asked.

"Knowing everything about me, about what happened, does it disgust you? I know we're married, but if you don't want to ever touch me… like that… I'd understand."

He took a breath and his hold on me tightened. "Amity, I will give you all the time in the world to heal, and to be ready for us to take that step together.

But don't mistake my patience for a lack of interest. Does what happened disgust me? Yes. Do *you* disgust me? Fuck no! You're beautiful. Sweet. And most importantly, you're mine."

"I'm sorry. I shouldn't have asked."

"Of course, you should have! If you have a question, I want you to feel comfortable to talk to me about it. Doesn't matter what it's about. Your past. My past. Our future. Whatever it is, don't ever hide things from me or hold back. Understood?"

I nodded. "Will you tell me about your past?"

"Anything in particular you'd like to know?" he asked.

"I guess the usual. Your parents. Siblings. Ex-girlfriends."

"My parents weren't bad people. They didn't abuse me. Didn't starve me, or anything like that. They just didn't understand me. Then Dad took off, and it was just me and Mom. She did her best, but because she had to work two jobs, she was absent a lot. She wanted me to get a college degree, work in an office, have a wife and kids. All the things that didn't appeal to me back then. Some of it still doesn't." He leaned back against the headboard. "I left home once I turned eighteen. I reached out shortly after I became a Prospect for the Dixie Reapers about seven years later, and mom basically called me garbage for wanting to be part of the club. I walked away and never looked back."

I didn't know why they didn't see how amazing he was. If it weren't for Thunder, I'd be dead right now. He'd pulled me off the bridge, brought me here, and given me a chance at a better life. Not just me, but my baby too. How could anyone think of him as anything other than heroic? So what if he was part of the Dixie

Reapers? I knew from the rumors around town people didn't necessarily like them, but I'd also heard about the good things they'd done. Toy drives. Donating clothes to the homeless.

"As for siblings, I didn't have any. I'm not sure my parents even wanted me, much less planned to have more children. They were older. Expected things to do be done a certain way. Even when I was little, they weren't the sort to get down on the floor and play with me."

"My parents didn't do much with me either, unless we were out in public. They always portrayed themselves to be the perfect parents," I said. "Appearances are everything to them."

"You said Evan was your first. Did you mean for everything? Or did you date anyone before him?" Thunder asked.

"No one before Evan," I said. "Maybe if I had, I wouldn't have been so naïve. He said he loved me, and I believed him without question. Who does that?"

"A lot of people," Thunder said.

"What about you? Any ex-girlfriends?" Oh, God. I'd never asked if he'd been seeing someone before he brought me here! "What about... did I..."

"If you're trying to ask if I had a current girlfriend when I went out looking for you, the answer is no. I haven't dated anyone in a long time. Since before I came to the Dixie Reapers. I won't lie and say I've lived like a monk because I haven't. I've been with the various girls who go to the clubhouse for a good time. And I've gotten tested regularly."

I'd heard people talk about their parties. I guessed that's what he meant. Wait. Tested. What if someone had given me something?

"Dr. Myron took blood when he came here. Is he

testing me to make sure none of those men gave me anything?" I asked.

Thunder nodded. "It's one of the things he wanted to check. We didn't bring it up at the time because we had hit you with a lot of information at once, and none of it was good."

"I know Dr. Sykes means well, but I'm not ready to talk to him yet. Do I have to?"

"No. Do I think it would help? Sure. But I'm not going to force you to go to therapy. When you're ready, if you're ever ready, let me know and I'll set it up. Until then, I'll be here for you."

"I'm sorry for yelling and trying to hit you." My cheeks burned. "I don't know what came over me. I mean, sure, I like apple butter, but it wasn't a big deal that we don't have any."

Thunder smiled faintly. "Amity, it wasn't about the apple butter. You know how a kettle whistles when the water inside is boiling? That was you this morning. You reached your boiling point, but instead of a shrill whistle, you lashed out. And that's okay. I understood what was happening."

"But it's not okay," I mumbled.

"Honey, you yelling or hitting me isn't going to run me off. I can take it. Do I want that to happen when you're with other people? No. And that's why I think counseling would help. Dr. Sykes could help you learn the signs to watch for, and before you reach the point of erupting, you could use whatever skills he teaches you to get control over yourself and cope with what's going on."

"How do you know so much about it?" I asked.

"My best friend in high school killed herself. I spent a lot of time blaming myself for not being there. If I'd arrived a little sooner, if I'd told someone what was going on with her, maybe I could have saved her. Deep down, I know it's not my fault. Logic plays very little into the way we feel during and after a traumatic event. I saw a counselor, and it helped a little. I won't say I'm cured. I never will be. But talking about it helped at the time." He sighed. "My brothers don't know about it. I never told anyone about Ashley or what happened to her. It's a secret I've kept for a long time."

"What's going to happen to me? To my parents?" I asked.

"Well, you and I are going to do our best to live a long and happy life together. We'll love this baby, maybe have some more if you're willing, and make a lot of memories together. As for your parents, I'd rather not tell you." He shifted and held me closer. "I have plans for Todd and Helen Whitman. Best if you don't know the details."

"Did you know they don't have many pictures of us?" I asked. "Aren't family pictures a normal thing? We have one over the mantle. I think I'm about two or three in the picture. There's another when I'm a little older. After that, they didn't take any of the three of us."

"Considering what your father did to you, it seems a little odd. Unless he was overcompensating. Perhaps he didn't want pictures, fearing people would realize he had a darkness inside him. We may never know."

I looked up at him. "Could Wire and Lavender find out? They uncovered all that other stuff. What if there's more? And if he could hurt me like that, and that girl I saw in his office, what if there are others?"

Thunder nodded. "You're right. I'll ask them to check and see what they can find. I doubt you and the other girl were his only victims. There may be girls who need help. But I swear I'm taking that man down before he can hurt anyone else. I'll do whatever it takes."

"Thank you, Austin."

He kissed my temple. "You ready to try eating again? I'll make a fresh batch of eggs. The rest I think we can warm in the microwave, but those eggs won't be too pleasant."

"I promise not to have another fit," I said.

"Amity, you throw as many fits as you want right now. If it helps get all that pain out? Then go for it. You're not going to send me running."

I didn't know how I'd ended up finding such an amazing guy, but I was thankful. Thunder was more than I could have ever hoped for. He was patient. Kind. And so sweet to me.

I only hoped I was worthy of being called his.

Chapter Four

Thunder

I didn't know what the club discussed after I'd left Church. No one had given me an update, and I hadn't heard from Wire or Lavender. I didn't think I even needed to ask them to check into Todd and Helen Whitman more than they already had. More than likely, they'd been digging as deep as they could, looking for anything we could use to either put them behind bars indefinitely, or wipe them from the planet. I would be fine with either, but I really didn't want Amity going through a court hearing and having to discuss what her father had done to her.

I still couldn't believe the sick bastard had raped his own daughter. Sure, I knew monsters were out in the world. I'd helped take down some before. But this was an entirely new level of fucked up I couldn't even wrap my brain around. It wouldn't be the first time some asshole had taken advantage of their own child. I doubted it would be the last. I'd just never expected to deal it with it personally.

For Amity, I'd gladly walk through fire. Someone needed to stand by her side. Her friends and family hadn't. They'd only hurt her in unimaginable ways. I hated every one of those motherfuckers.

Speaking of her friends… I glared at Portia when I opened the front door and found her on my porch. "What the hell do you want?"

She narrowed her eyes at me and huffed. "Fine greeting. So now that my daddy isn't the President, I'm going to be treated like garbage?"

"No. This has nothing to do with your dad. It has to do with Amity. You knew she was living on the street. Knew she was starving. Did you tell anyone here what was going on so we could help her? Nope." I folded my arms. "So pardon me if I'm a little pissed you treated my wife like shit. Would a friend do that?"

She deflated and sighed softly. "I'm sorry for how I handled things. You're right. I should have told my mom or dad, or even Wire and Lavender. I didn't and because she felt like she didn't have anyone in her corner, she nearly jumped off a bridge."

"Why are you here, Portia?" I asked.

"I came to visit with her. She's been stuck in this house since you brought her home. It's been a few days now. Don't you think she needs to meet some people? You're great, Thunder, but she's going to need more than you."

I felt a small hand on my back and glanced over my shoulder. Amity had walked up behind me without me even noticing. I reached back and took her hand, threading our fingers together, and pulled her to my side. If she wanted to speak with Portia, I wouldn't stop her. Didn't mean I wouldn't be angry with Portia for a while. Something told me her dad had chewed her out for her part in all this. I knew Torch wouldn't take it well when he found out his daughter had kept Amity's problems from him. The Pres, or rather ex-Pres, might have blood on his hands, but when it came to women and kids, he'd do anything to keep them safe.

"I'm not sure I'm ready to meet anyone," Amity said. "I'm still trying to process the things I've learned in the last few days."

"Lavender isn't the only old lady here. If it makes a difference, when my mom and dad found out about you, I got into a lot of trouble. They were furious I hadn't brought you up sooner." Portia shifted on her feet, like she contemplated running. "Um. I'm really sorry, Amity. My dad said I behaved immaturely, and you could have died because I didn't let anyone know you needed help."

I put my arm around Amity's shoulders. "You did, Portia. Amity may forgive you, if not today then later, but it's going to take a while for me to get there. I could have lost her before I'd even had a chance to meet her."

Portia nodded. "I get it. Merlin isn't happy with me either. In fact, no one is. Even Wire and Lavender are pissed at me."

"Why did you keep my situation to yourself?" Amity asked.

"I think on some level, I didn't want to feel like I was competing for attention. If I'd brought you here, I knew everyone would rally around you. It was selfish of me. I guess I still have a lot of growing up to do." Portia sighed. "I hope you'll still consider me a friend, Amity. I won't say that I'll never screw up again, because I'm only human, but I'll do better to think of others and try to be a little less focused on myself all the time. Sticking up for you at school didn't cost me anything. Neither did bringing you food now and then after your parents threw you out. The club didn't know I did those things so it didn't put a spotlight on you."

"Hadrian and Ivy are watching you," I said. "You're their example of how to act. Not only here at the compound, but out in the world too."

She nodded. "I know. Dad made sure they heard how badly I'd screwed up and turned it into a lesson for all of us."

"Are there others close to our age here?" Amity asked.

"Oh, yeah. Lots of girls either slightly older or a little younger." Portia smiled hesitantly. "Would you want to meet some of them? I could ask them to come here if you're more comfortable."

I watched Amity's face and knew the offer tempted her. I kissed her temple. "Do you know Harlow, Westlyn, and Kasen? They went to your school."

"They graduated last year, didn't they?" Amity asked.

"Yeah. They're all super smart and skipped a grade," Portia said. "I only got ahead because I took classes in summer school the last two years. Otherwise, I'd have been a junior this past year."

"Portia is still seventeen," I said. "Which means she needs to stop chasing Merlin anyway. Right, Portia?"

She sighed and nodded. "Right. Dad gave me hell about that too."

"If you think the triplets would like to come over, I wouldn't mind getting to know them better. I know who they are, but we never really talked in school," Amity said. "Will you stay too, Portia?"

"Of course." Portia smiled.

"I'll order some pizza for the five of you," I said. "I'm not leaving the house, but I'll try to stay out of the way."

Amity leaned into me. "Thank you. I know you have a lot to do, and I'm probably holding you back. It means a lot to me, knowing you're here if I need you."

"Amity, you're my wife. It makes you the most important person in my life," I said. I cupped her cheek and kissed her forehead. "I'll go order the pizzas, then I'll watch TV in the bedroom."

"Thank you, Thunder."

I narrowed my gaze at Portia. "And you… make sure those three hellions treat her right. If any of you makes her cry, I don't give a fuck who your daddy is, or theirs. I will lose my shit."

"Understood," Portia said.

Amity took my hand again. "You don't have to

stay. Is there someone you'd like to visit? Or maybe have a drink with your friends?"

"You saying you want me to give you some space?" I asked.

She chewed on her bottom lip, looking uncertain. "No. Not exactly. I like having you here, but…"

"She's worried she'll smother you," Portia said. "I've heard my sisters talking about their men. Farrah thinks she's too clingy sometimes and that Demon will get tired of her. Same for Mariah and Savage."

"Portia, go talk to the girls and come back in about thirty minutes," I said, then I shut the door.

Amity gaped at me. "You shut it in her face."

"Yep. Now I think you and I need to have a conversation before Tank's three girls get here." I led her down the hall to the bedroom and sat on the bed, tugging her down onto my lap. "I know all this is new to you. Not just our relationship but being a part of the Dixie Reapers. As my wife, you not only have me as your family, but everyone else here too."

"Do I get one of those leather vest things like I've seen the other women wearing?" she asked.

I bit my lip so I wouldn't laugh. "It's called a cut. And yes, you'll get one. Yours will say *Property of Thunder* on it."

"I'm not sure what my role will be," she said. "Are there things people will expect of me?"

"Right now, the only thing anyone wants is for you to settle in and have time to heal. You've been hit with a lot, honey. It's also why I'm not pushing you for anything. Even though we kissed, I felt like a bastard afterward. I don't want to ask for more than you're willing to give. You set the pace."

"But once we're past all this? Then what?" she asked.

"You'll have to ask the other old ladies. I'm not really sure what they do. I know when we have family events at the clubhouse, they help get the place set up and prepare the food. Some of them help with charity events, like the toy drive we've done for several years." Her cheeks turned pink, and I realized that wasn't what she'd meant. "Um. You mean between us?"

She nodded and tucked her face against me. I ran my hand down her hair, thinking there were times she was too damn cute. I smiled and held her close. Never thought I'd have someone as sweet as her in my life.

"I like you, Amity. A lot. But I'm also not a monster. Even though we're married, and around here, that means forever, I won't touch you until you want me to. And if that never happens, then…" I sighed. "I want to offer you fidelity. I don't want to run around with other women or use the girls at the clubhouse. Being faithful is a big deal for this club. Not just to each other, but to our women as well."

I stopped and thought about how I wanted to phrase things. The last thing I wanted was to hurt Amity. So how could I be honest without doing that? I had no doubt when Torch was still President, if I'd even thought of hooking up with anyone else, I'd have paid a hefty price. With Savior, I didn't know what to expect.

"If you don't ever want me to touch you, then… I'll still stay by your side. You'll have my support. But I'm not going to lie to you. There may come a time that I'm tempted by the girls at the clubhouse. I've gone months without sex before. I could handle longer. A lifetime without it… I'm not sure I'm capable of that. I'd rather be honest with you than pretend I'm some saintly guy who will do no wrong."

I felt her tremble and cursed myself for being an

asshole. What I wanted was for my wife to eventually want to be with me. How could I possibly want anyone else when I had someone like her in my arms? But if the trauma she'd suffered was too much, if she could never get to a point where she'd want me in that way, then I didn't know for certain how I'd react. I wanted to be faithful to her. I also didn't want to lie and promise something, then not be able to follow through.

"I don't want anyone but you," I said. "You will always be my first choice, but I refuse to pressure you into doing something that scares you or causes you pain. Do you understand?"

"I don't want to be broken," she whispered. "I liked it when you kissed me. Could we do that again?"

I groaned and shut my eyes. She was killing me. Could I kiss her again? Hell, yes! I only hoped I could pull back and not take things too far. But first, I needed to tell her something. I had a feeling I was about to kill the mood entirely.

"Dr. Myron left a voicemail earlier today. He expedited some of your labs. You don't have any STDs, in case you wondered. As for the baby, he said our little one could be born perfectly healthy and have issues later. There's a fifty percent chance for things like deformities, developmental delays, and even early death. Some babies don't live past their toddler years when the parents are so closely related." I hugged her to me. "There's something else he wanted you to consider. You have a very narrow window left if you decide you want an abortion. In our state, you can get up to twenty-two weeks into your pregnancy. I'm not saying that's what I think you should do. I only want you to know all your options."

She pressed a hand to her belly. "Fifty percent is a high number, isn't it?"

"It is, but that means there's also a percentage who are born healthy and live regular lives. I'm not sure who knows that your father is the one who got you pregnant. If the people in town found out, that baby would have a hard life. I'd bust the heads of anyone making fun of him or her, or bullying them, but neither of us can be there all the time."

As much as it hurt my heart to even consider an abortion, part of me wondered if it wouldn't be better. For the child. For Amity. Not only because of the stigma they'd both face, but if that baby did die early, I knew it would destroy the both of us. Because I had no doubt she and I would love that baby with all our hearts, regardless of who the sperm donor had been.

But the choice was Amity's, and I'd stand by her no matter what. If she wanted to go through with the pregnancy, then that's what we'd do. We'd set up a nursery, buy lots of cute baby things, and prepare like any other parents would.

"How narrow of a window?" she asked.

"Dr. Myron said you're nearly to the twenty-one-week mark. Which means you probably have about ten days before they can't do the procedure."

She looked up at me, and I saw the fear in her eyes. I wanted to gut every motherfucker who'd hurt her. Starting with her father and that little shit, Evan.

* * *

Amity

"Will you be angry if I want to keep it?" I asked.

"Of course not." Thunder tipped my chin up and pressed his lips to mine in a short, soft kiss. "I already told you. That baby is mine, just like you are. You want to keep it? Then that's what we'll do. Whatever challenges we face, we'll tackle them head on."

He was the sweetest guy. Always saying and doing the right things. It had hurt, hearing him say he might be with someone else at some point, if I couldn't be a real wife to him. At the same time, I appreciated his honesty. He could have lied or kept his doubts to himself. What if it had driven a wedge between us? I'd rather know now than be blindsided later.

And now this. Leaving the decision to me, whether or not we kept the baby. Sure, it was my body. I thought about how he'd claimed my child without any hesitation. He'd been so passionate about it. I didn't doubt for a second he'd love the baby when it was born. Treat it like his own flesh-and-blood child.

But could I?

All this time, thinking the baby belonged to Evan, I'd told myself I loved the baby. Wanted it. The child was at no fault as to how it had been conceived. Then I'd learned the horrible truth, and it's the only thing I'd thought about since then.

Yes, Evan had hurt me. Done something awful. It hadn't been anything that detracted from how I felt about my baby. Knowing my father had gotten me pregnant was entirely different. He'd never acted like a kind and loving parent. Neither of my parents had.

"What if… what if I don't want the constant reminder of what happened to me?" I asked, trying to hold back my tears. I felt awful even asking such a thing. Did it make me a monster? A killer? Or would be the better option, not only for me, but for the baby too? "What if I say I want the abortion?"

"Then I'll call Dr. Myron and have him set it up. And no, I won't be angry. All I want is for you to be happy and healthy. If you don't think you can handle having this baby, then you tell me when you're ready, and we'll try to have another one."

"Can you call him now? I have some questions," I said. I might be considering it, but I needed to know more. I didn't want to make this decision blindly. I hated that we didn't have much time.

"All right." Thunder pulled out his phone and dialed Dr. Myron's clinic.

"This is Dr. Myron," the man said when he answered.

"It's Thunder. I spoke with Amity and she has some questions for you."

"Is this about the abortion?" he asked.

"Yes. She's here and you're on speaker."

"Amity, what concerns do you have?" Dr. Myron asked.

"If I do this, will I be able to have children later?" I asked.

"Hmm. Well, I can't answer that with any certainty. Will the procedure itself mean you'd be unable to? Not necessarily. There's a small risk involved, but most women can get pregnant again within two weeks." He cleared his throat. "There's a chance of infection afterward, so I'd recommend no sex for at least two weeks."

"Does it make me a bad person to even consider this?" I asked.

"No, Amity. You've been through something horrific. Asking you to carry a child full-term that's not only the product of rape but incest is… I don't want to say monstrous, but… It doesn't just have a physical impact on you. There are psychological ramifications a lot of people don't consider. Some women decide to not only give birth, but they raise those children and love them. Others feel as if they're reliving that trauma every time they look at their pregnant stomachs, or their children if they decide to give birth. No one can tell you which option is the right one for you, Amity. That's entirely your decision."

"Thank you, Dr. Myron." I took a breath and looked at Thunder again. I couldn't read his expression, but he leaned down to kiss me, then gave me a little nod. I guessed that meant the decision was mine to make and he'd stand by my side no matter what. "Can we call you back later or tomorrow with our decision?"

"Of course! Take your time. I know you're nearing the point where you can't have an abortion, if that's what you decide, but it doesn't mean you have to make the decision immediately. Think it over tonight, or even for another few days. Talk about it with Thunder, and then let me know what you decide."

"Thank you, Dr. Myron."

"If you decide to go this route, there will be instructions for both before and after the procedure. I'll make sure Thunder has them. If you'd like them now, in case it affects your decision, I'll text them when this call ends. Make an informed decision, but also look inside yourself for the answer. Only you know what you can handle, Amity."

The call ended and within less than a minute, Thunder's phone chimed with an incoming text. We read through them together. The entire time, Thunder didn't say one way or another how he felt about it. All he'd told me was that he'd support my decision. What did *he* want?

"You've pointed out we're married," I said. "More than once you've said this baby is yours. Doesn't that mean we should make the decision together?"

"Amity, I'm not the one who went through the trauma that resulted in the baby. Nor will I be the one to give birth to it. I don't feel like I have a right to tell you what to do."

"And I love that about you." I took his hand, lacing our fingers together. "You're not telling me what to do, Austin. I'm *asking* for your opinion. You said there's a fifty percent chance the baby could be normal."

He nodded. "I did. And the other fifty percent means the baby could die within a few years, even if they appear to be fine at first. I'm worried what that will do to you. To both of us, honestly."

"Dr. Myron said we didn't have to decide right this minute. I'm going to have some pizza with Portia, Harlow, Kasen, and Westlyn. When they leave, you and I can watch a movie or do something fun together. We can just let the idea sort of… marinate. Is that okay?"

"Yeah." He kissed me again. "Sounds perfect. And I meant what I said before, Amity. Whatever you want to do, I'm with you one hundred percent. If you want to go through with the pregnancy, and we lose our child later, then we'll grieve together. All right?"

"I don't know what I ever did to deserve someone like you, but I'm so glad Portia sent you out into that storm to find me. You're amazing, Austin. Don't ever let someone make you feel otherwise."

I stood and walked out of the room while I still could. If I'd remained in his arms another moment, I'd have never met with the girls. While I loved spending time with Thunder, Portia had been right. I did need to meet more people. If this was my home now, my family, then I needed to venture out of this house. I couldn't hide forever, and it felt like that's what I'd been doing.

I'd felt weak for so long. Ever since Evan sent the video out to the senior class, and dealing with bullies the rest of my senior year, my parents throwing me out, the town turning against me… It had worn me down until I felt like there was only one way to escape the pain. Since meeting Thunder, I'd realized there were still kind people in the world.

For him, I'd learn to be as fierce as the other ladies at the Dixie Reapers. I'd seen them around town before. The officers had often gone out to eat at the diner with their families. I hadn't known back then they were called officers, though. I'd watched Torch with Portia, her siblings, and their mom. Venom had gone out with his woman and kids. And I'd envied Kasen, Westlyn, and Harlow for having such an amazing dad. Their father was larger than life, and a bit scary, but the way he smiled at them had always left me wanting to be part of something like that.

Despite having such strong men in their corner, I'd seen them stand up to people on multiple occasions. Ridley, Farrah and Mariah's mom, didn't seem to be scared of anything. She'd gone toe to toe with people on many occasions, usually to stand up for someone. Isabella, Portia's mother, always appeared quiet. Until someone hurt those she loved. Someone from school once made the mistake of picking on Portia when her mother was within hearing range. It hadn't ended well.

No one had stood up for me until Thunder. Well, Portia did that one time at school. It wasn't the same as what Thunder had done for me. She stood up to a bully for a brief moment. Thunder had turned his life upside down for me. Still, I didn't want him to fight all my battles for me. Sooner or later, I wanted to be able to stand up to people on my own. And knowing he had my back would give me the strength I needed to pull it off. I hoped.

The doorbell rang, and I answered it, smiling when I saw the girls waiting on the porch.

Kasen peered over my shoulder. "Are you sure it's okay for us to be here?"

"Why wouldn't it be?" I asked.

"You and Thunder are still in the honeymoon phase," Westlyn said. "The guys here tend to be feral when it comes to their women."

I called out for Thunder and he came, nearly at a run. He stopped, drawing himself up short, when he saw we had company. "I thought something had happened."

"See," Westlyn said.

"They're worried it's not okay for them to come inside," I said.

Thunder placed a hand on my shoulder. "This isn't just my house. It's Amity's too. If she invites you over, then you're welcome to come in."

Harlow snorted. "Right. Unless we hurt her feelings. Then you'll boot us from the house so fast our heads will spin."

Thunder grinned, but it wasn't the friendly sort. He reminded me of a shark in that moment. "Exactly."

"Did you order the pizza yet?" I asked.

"Um. No." He rubbed the back of his neck. "I didn't know what to get."

"Cheese," Kasen said. "Please."

"I'll eat anything." Harlow stepped into the house. "Except olives."

"Pepperoni," Portia said.

"What about you, Westlyn?" I asked.

"I think they covered the basics." She entered the house, with Kasen and Portia following in her wake. They made themselves comfortable in the living room. Thunder put his hand on my waist and kissed the top of my head before going back to the bedroom. It seemed he really did intend to hide in there and watch

TV while the girls were visiting.

"For what it's worth, I think what Evan did to you was despicable," Westlyn said. "I didn't realize things were bad for you at home too, though. I'm sorry."

"I guess everyone knows?" I asked, feeling the blood drain from my face.

"I told them how you and Thunder met. That's what they meant," Portia said. "As for the rest, I overheard part of a conversation between my dad and mom. I won't say anything. It's your story to tell, if you decide you want anyone to know."

"And it's fine if you don't want to tell us," Harlow said. "We haven't earned your trust yet. One day we will. After all, we're family now, right?"

Family. I smiled, liking the sound of that.

"Are any of you dating someone?" I asked. "We didn't really have the same social circles at school."

Westlyn laughed so hard tears streaked her cheeks. "Are you kidding? My dad would kill anyone who tried to date us. None of us have been on a date. Ever. Or been kissed."

"It sucks," Kasen said. "But we understand."

"Just means we need to find someone he'll accept. Like another Dixie Reaper, or someone from a club we consider family."

I swallowed hard. All this talk of family and dating. I knew they weren't blood related, but it made me feel a little ill, comparing it to my situation.

"Not all of us see the guys here as brothers or uncles," Kasen said. "But some do. Foster chased after Preacher's daughter, Leigha. It was bad. She finally put him in his place, and he realized how much he'd fucked up. Leigha saw him as a sibling, though, and I feel the same about him and Owen, so I get it."

"They're like brothers to you, but someone else

isn't?" I asked. "You said you didn't see everyone here as a brother or uncle."

Her cheeks flushed. "They'll never look at me like that, so it doesn't matter. Kind of like Merlin and Portia. She chased after him, but he only sees her as a cute kid."

Portia sighed. "Yes, and someone pointed out to me I was on the same path as Meredith. None of us want to be like her! Everyone thought she was super sweet. Then she went all psycho when Doolittle didn't want her the same way she liked him."

"Meredith?" I asked. "I don't who how that is."

Kasen waved a hand. "She's with another club. Or she was. Grizzly, with the Devil's Fury, adopted her years ago. Once he found out what she'd done, he sent her packing. Not forever. Just to clear her head, maybe admit she was wrong, and figure out who she is."

These girls sounded more mature than others our age. I knew I'd grown up fast since I made the mistake of trusting Evan. How had they grown so wise? Even Portia had admitted she had some growing up to do. But these three? They were different.

The pizza arrived, and someone with a patch that said *Prospect* brought it to the kitchen. Thunder came out of hiding long enough to make a plate, grab a drink, and give me a kiss. Then he disappeared into our room again. Our room.

I didn't think I was ready yet for being his wife in all ways, but I did want to sleep with him at night. Would he think I was leading him on if I did that? He'd held me the last few nights. Did he want to do that every night? Had I asked him for something he wasn't ready to give? I hated feeling so uncertain.

Westlyn sighed, and I glanced at her. "What?"

"He's so into you. I want that one day."

"You really think so?" I asked, staring at the closed bedroom door before going back into the living room.

"Oh, yeah. He has it bad," Portia said. "The way he answered the door earlier? All protective and stuff? You're it for him, Amity. You're so lucky!"

She was right about me being lucky. But it wasn't just because of Thunder. It was also because of her and the rest of the Dixie Reapers. They'd given me the one thing I'd never truly had. Family.

"I hope you each find the guy you're meant to be with. Everyone deserves a man like Thunder in their lives." I smiled. "Thanks for coming over. I didn't realize how much I needed this."

"I'm going to talk to Mom about setting up something at the clubhouse," Portia said. "We need to properly welcome you. Unless a party would be too overwhelming?"

"No. I think I'd like that. Besides, like you said, I can't hide in this house forever. The sooner I get to know everyone, the better."

"Then we'll get out of your hair," Kasen said. "Besides, I think someone wants you to himself again."

I looked over my shoulder and saw Thunder leaning against the doorframe. He winked and I couldn't help but smile at him.

The girls threw away their trash and headed out, leaving me alone with my husband. I knew we still needed to talk, but for now, I just wanted to spend time with him. If all this had taught me anything, it was that we couldn't always count on there being a tomorrow. So I wanted to tackle each day like it would be our last.

"Just so you know, I'm the lucky one." He came closer and knelt at my feet. "I heard what they said. The day I met you was the best day of my life. I thought I was getting a second chance, to get it right this time. I'd lost Ashley and I refused to lose you too. But I got so much more. I'm glad Lavender worked her mojo and married us, because it means I get to spend the rest of my life with you."

And that was the very second I fell in love with my husband. How could I not? I only hoped he'd come to love me one day too.

Chapter Five
Thunder

We were almost out of time for Amity to make a decision about the baby. I'd often caught her rubbing her stomach the past few days and murmuring to the baby. I didn't know if she was apologizing for thinking about an abortion, or if she was reassuring the child, they'd have a happy life. If she decided to have the baby, I'd do everything I could to keep them safe, and make sure they knew they were wanted.

My phone rang, and I answered without looking at the screen.

"Hello."

"Thunder? Amity hasn't called Dr. Myron yet, has she?" Lavender asked, sounding almost frantic.

"Why? What's going on?"

"Todd Whitman isn't her father! She needs to know."

I stood and put a hand over my racing heart. What the hell did she mean Todd Whitman wasn't Amity's father? How the fuck had she found that out? Not that it mattered. If he wasn't her biological father, then it meant the baby could be born perfectly healthy. I knew it would change things.

"Lavender, I'm getting Amity and we're coming to your house. You need to tell her that shit in person. Then you'll need to explain how you know, and who her real father is."

"Hurry. I'll leave the door unlocked."

The line went dead. I shoved the phone back into my pocket and searched for Amity. I knew she hadn't gone far. After I checked the various rooms in the house, I went to the back door. I saw her sitting on the bottom step, staring at… nothing.

Slowly, I opened the door and stepped out.

"Amity, everything okay?"

"It would be a nice place for a little boy or girl to play, wouldn't it?" she asked.

I looked at the yard, not seeing anything special. I didn't even have a fence up, but I'd change that once our child was able to come out and play.

"Lavender needs to tell you something before you make a decision. Come on. I think you'll consider it good news." At least, the part I knew about would be considered good. Since I didn't know who the hell her father really was, that part could be worse.

"All right." She stood and smoothed her dress. I'd ordered a few maternity outfits for her in town and had a Prospect pick them up. She looked cute in the little sundresses, and she'd said they were comfortable. Even if she'd decided not to carry the baby to term, I'd wanted her to have something nice to wear. She'd come into my home with nothing more than the clothes she'd been wearing the night I'd found her on the bridge.

Now, with Lavender's news, it seemed she might need a bigger wardrobe. Excitement buzzed in my veins. As much as I'd wanted what was best for Amity and the baby, I couldn't lie and say it hadn't hurt when I'd thought she might choose to have an abortion. Maybe knowing the man who'd raped her hadn't been her father would sway her decision. Regardless, whatever she chose, I'd support her.

I stopped out front and hesitated. I didn't like the idea of her being on the back of my bike while she was pregnant, and certainly not while she had on a dress. We'd had so much going on, I hadn't had time to consider another mode of transportation. Did she even know how to drive?

"Do you have your license?" I asked.

"Yes, but I didn't get a chance to drive much. My parents wouldn't get me a car, and I seldom got to use either of theirs. Why?"

"We're going to need something other than my motorcycle. I just wasn't sure if you knew how to drive, or if I needed to teach you."

She smiled and leaned into me. "That's so sweet. I'd have probably learned better with you than the dragon they had in charge at school."

"I'm going to borrow a club truck until we can get something else." Before I could pull my phone from my pocket, Lavender pulled up out front. She waved excitedly with a big grin on her face. "Or we can ride with Lavender right now."

She rolled down her window. "I realized you only had your motorcycle and decided to pick the two of you up. Wire's working on a vehicle for you."

"Um." I scratched at my beard. "Why is he doing that?"

"He spoke with the Police Chief. They have some decent cars at the impound lot. In exchange for Wire's assistance with a case they have, he's going to give one of the cars to us. Since we don't need it, Wire is going to let you and Amity have it. I don't think it will be anything fancy, but you know the chief won't give us something that's not reliable."

"Your club works with the police department?" Amity asked.

"Not exactly." Lavender waved for us to get in. I held open the back door and helped Amity onto the seat before I slid in next to her. I put my arm around her shoulders and held her against my side as Lavender turned the SUV around. "His daughter is with another club. Since we consider that club part of our family, the chief looks the other way when he can.

He's gotten to know Tank, Torch, and Venom over the years, and knows they walk in the gray area."

She pulled up at her house and we got out, then followed her inside. Wire sat on the couch with his feet propped on the coffee table, and his laptop perched on his thighs. He'd been tapping away until he saw us.

"You'll have a car tomorrow," he said. "It's a Honda Accord that's a few years old. I already pulled the VIN on it. No accidents showing, the maintenance records don't seem to be missing anything, and it's still under warranty for another two years."

"Sounds perfect," I said. "Are you sure you want to give it to us? I could buy it from you."

Wire glared and I shut up. Right. I led Amity farther into the living room and sat down, pulling her onto my lap. Lavender sat beside Wire. I could tell she was excited to share her news with Amity.

"We know you've been facing some difficult decisions," Lavender said. "So, I kept digging into your parents. And I may have meddled a little."

"Meddled?" I asked. "What does that mean, exactly?"

"We sent someone into the Whitman house to pull DNA from both Todd and Helen. Then we asked Dr. Myron if he still had any blood left from the tests he'd run on Amity. He just so happened to have one vial he hadn't used yet. He took a small enough amount to compare the DNA to her parents." Wire shut the laptop and put his arm around Lavender. "The results show that Helen is your mother, but Todd isn't your father."

I felt Amity tense and I kissed her shoulder, hoping to calm her down. After a moment, she melted into me, and I hoped that meant she wasn't about to panic. This was good news, right?

"Any idea who her father is?" I asked.

"We ran her DNA through a few programs we have," Wire said. "There was no guarantee we'd get a hit. In this case, we lucked out because her grandfather spent time in prison."

Someone knocked on the door and I tensed, wondering what the hell was going on. Wire and Lavender shared a look before they yelled out for the person to enter. When Hammer strolled into the room, it felt like all the air had been sucked out. Were they trying to say Hammer was Amity's grandfather? I knew he'd been in prison for drug trafficking, back before the club cleaned up a bit.

"What's going on?" I asked.

Hammer looked over his shoulder and motioned to someone. A guy entered the house, looking uncomfortable as fuck. He wore grease-stained clothes, and a baseball cap that said *Camelot Towing*.

"I'd like everyone to meet my son. I've tried to keep him away from the club, so I never told anyone about him. Sam, this is Wire, Lavender, and Thunder." Hammer cleared his throat. "And the woman sitting on Thunder's lap is the reason we're here. You said you remembered a Helen Whitman."

Sam's face flushed. "Not my proudest moment, but yeah. What does that witch have to do with any of this?"

"She's my mother," Amity said.

I released Amity when she struggled to stand, and she approached Sam and Hammer, looking from one to the other. And I knew the moment Sam realized who she was. His eyes widened and he paled. Poor bastard staggered back a step. Hammer looked like he wanted to hug her.

"Sam, did Hammer explain anything to you?" Wire

asked.

"No. Just said he needed me to meet someone. But…" He held Amity's gaze. "How old are you?"

"Eighteen," she said softly. "Are you… my father?"

Sam muttered a *fucking bitch*, then reached out to run his fingers through Amity's hair. "I never knew about you. Found your mom stranded on the side of the road one night. Knew she was married, but when she came onto me, I didn't exactly fight her off. One thing led to another and…"

"Since Sam is my son, that makes me your grandfather," Hammer said. "Done some things I'm not so proud of, so I'll understand if you don't want to claim me as family."

Amity threw her arms around Hammer, then Sam. I saw her shoulders shaking and knew my sweet girl was crying. I didn't blame her. She'd not only discovered her baby hadn't been the product of incest, but learned she had a grandfather and dad who knew nothing about her.

"The connection between you and Hammer had me asking a few questions," Wire said. "That's when he came clean about having a son. For the record, Sam, I don't think anyone here will stop you from entering the compound to visit your daughter. She's going to need your support."

"Why?" Sam skimmed his gaze over her, stopping at her belly. "How far along are you?"

"About five months," she said.

"Amity Whitman," he mumbled. "Why does that… Holy shit! You're the one in the video that caused that huge stir around town. If that little punk weren't behind bars, I'd pound his ass into the ground."

Hammer patted his shoulder. "Easy, Papa Bear. There's a lot more to the story. Not sure if you want to hear it or not, but there was a reason they were searching for dirt on the Whitmans. Finding a genetic match to me was just a bonus."

So Wire and Lavender spent the next half hour filling in Sam. He couldn't stop hugging Amity, or apologizing to her. None of it had been his fault. He'd not even realized he had a daughter. No, the blame lay solely with the Whitmans, and all the other fuckers who'd laid a hand on Amity that day. Wire had managed to put a few faces and names together, and he'd already started his brand of justice. Those people would be tortured financially, then outed to the public for their atrocities, and finally put into jail.

"While they're in prison, I'll make sure they get special treatment," Hammer said. "Since they're all too high profile for us to just bury the motherfuckers."

"I didn't hear that," Sam said. "But I can't disagree either. I want all of them to suffer. Mostly, I want Helen and Todd Whitman taken down more than a few pegs. I want them in the lowest level of hell for what they've done."

"And I want to know why," Hammer said.

"I have a feeling we'll get more of the story soon. Until then, you and Sam should take some time to get to know Amity. I'm sure she's thankful to have relatives who aren't as despicable as Todd and Helen Whitman." Wire stood and so did Lavender. "We'll keep working, making people's lives a living hell, and doing whatever we can to make everyone pay for what they've done. I want more dirt on Todd and Helen before we make a move on them."

"Would the two of you like to come to dinner?" Amity asked.

"Only if we can take you out somewhere." Sam smiled. "It's not every day I learn I have a beautiful daughter, and a grandbaby on the way."

"Shit." Hammer growled. "This means I'm about to be a great-grandpa. I'm only in my fifties for fuck's sake!"

"Then I guess you shouldn't have had me when you were seventeen." Sam arched an eyebrow. "At least you did right by Mom. Mostly."

"I'm sure Amity would love to hear more of your story," I said. "I just need to get a club truck if we're leaving the compound."

"No need." Sam pulled out his keys. "I have an SUV. We can all fit. I'll bring the three of you back after dinner."

"How's your mom?" Hammer asked.

"Still uses your name as a curse word whenever I piss her off."

"I thought you said he did right by your mother?" Amity asked, her brow furrowed.

"Oh, he did. Gave her money when he wasn't locked up. She's just angry that he never married her, or made her his old lady. She was ready to dive into life here with the Dixie Reapers. Instead, he knocked her up and sent her on her way."

Hammer folded his arms over his chest. "She deserved better. This club was different back then. And you both turned out fine. She married that boring as fuck paper pusher, gave you a good life, and even had another kid. Not sure what she's griping about."

Sam shrugged. "Guess you'll have to ask her that next time you see her. Now that you both have a granddaughter and a great-grandchild on the way, I guess you better figure out how to be in one another's company for more than fifteen minutes. Or you'll both miss out."

I had a feeling holidays just became more difficult,

but the way Amity smiled so brightly, I knew I'd put up with anything. Didn't matter if Hammer and his ex sniped at each other, or if her father spoiled her and our kid. If they made her happy, then it was all worth it.

But I sure the fuck hoped there weren't any more relatives we'd find out about later. Finding out I was now related by marriage to Hammer was more than enough. Sam seemed like a nice guy. I only hoped we'd get along.

Going from being alone to having a wife and baby on the way, and now this? I was in over my head.

* * *

Amity

Thunder seemed on edge. At first, I'd been worried it was something I'd said or done. Then I'd noticed the way he kept glancing at my dad and grandfather. I'd been leery of going out to eat, worried about people whispering when I entered the restaurant. When we'd walked into the diner, the low murmur of voices came to a halt. I noticed everyone staring and would have turned around and left if Thunder hadn't laced our fingers together.

"Figures a whore like her would end up with a bunch of filthy bikers," someone said. Not low enough the men with me didn't hear them. I felt Thunder tense, and my grandfather's head turned in their direction.

Hammer and my dad both walked over to the woman who'd made the comment. Thunder led me past them to an empty table at the back near the wall. My grandfather leaned into the woman's space, and my dad glared down at her.

"That girl you're calling a whore was abused by

her so-called parents. Those pillars of the community you have on a pedestal? They're no better than anyone else," Hammer said.

"Her mom wasn't anything memorable, but my daughter?" Sam nodded his head toward me. "She's fucking amazing."

I heard a few gasps around the diner and people glanced my way. Yeah, my dad had just dropped a bomb on them. The pristine Helen Whitman had an affair with someone. Not just anyone. A blue-collar guy. She'd die of embarrassment right now if she knew what he'd just divulged. It wouldn't take long before it spread through town.

"That little shit, Evan, used her. Sent out a video of an underage girl. And I know what happened during the rest of his little show." Hammer stood and scanned the diner. "If I find out any of you were in that video, I'm coming for you. Already spent twelve years in prison. I've got no problem going back if it means my granddaughter has justice."

Tears blurred my vision, and I stood. Thunder didn't stop me as I approached my grandfather and dad. I hugged them both, feeling more loved in that moment than I had in my entire life.

"Grandpa, you shouldn't have said that. But thank you."

He hugged me tighter before letting me go. "Let's get something to eat."

We went over to the table Thunder claimed for us, and I sat beside my husband again. He kissed me, just a short, quick one. It still made me feel warm inside. I couldn't stop smiling as I looked at the men sitting with me.

"Remind me to thank Wire and Lavender," Thunder said. "Pretty sure I'm not topping this present. Ever."

I giggled, but had to agree. Finding out Todd Whitman wasn't my biological father was beyond amazing. And now I had a grandfather too? Despite everything that I'd been through, I felt happier than I'd ever been before.

I sobered a moment and stared at Hammer. "I called you Grandpa, but we're out in public and you're wearing your cut. Should I have called you Hammer?"

He shook his head. "No, little one. You call me whatever you want. I liked hearing you call me Grandpa."

I looked at Sam. "Can I call you dad?"

"I'd be honored." He winked. "Only wish I'd known about you sooner. Or picked a better mother for you. Helen Whitman has a lot to answer for."

"If you weren't already married to Thunder, I'd ask Wire to have your last name changed," Hammer said. "If I could wipe out any connection between you and those monsters, I would."

I pressed a hand to my belly and leaned into Thunder. "I didn't just gain a grandfather and father today. Finding out I wasn't related to Todd Whitman changed so much more."

Thunder put his arm around me and hugged me to his side. "Guess we better get to work on that nursery."

A darkness entered the eyes of both my grandfather and my dad. I had a feeling both were going to make Todd Whitman suffer. It didn't matter that Wire was going to do his best to take everyone down in a somewhat legal way. Something told me Todd Whitman was going to have a miserable life -- however long they left him breathing. I should have been upset by the knowledge, but I wasn't. If anyone deserved to die, it was him and the others who'd hurt me. How many other girls had they raped over the years?

I reached over and placed my hand on Thunder's thigh before leaning in to whisper to him. "Can Lavender see if those men hurt anyone else? Maybe we can help them?"

"You want to help previous victims?" he asked, keeping his voice low so the other people in the diner wouldn't hear.

I nodded. "Is that okay?"

"Count me in," my dad said. "I know I'm not part of your club, but if the monsters who hurt my little girl have done the same to other girls or women, then I'll help however I can."

Hammer leaned back in his seat. "You know, just a thought, but with Torch, Venom, Tank, and Flicker all sitting on their asses now, we're going to be a bit shorthanded. Think it's time to bring in more Prospects. We're down to two at the moment."

Dad folded his arms over his chest and shifted in his seat. "Is there an age limit on being one?"

Hammer slowly turned to face my dad. "What?"

"Look, my dad is part of the Dixie Reapers. My daughter is married to one. I know you wanted to keep me away from that lifestyle, but I'm in it anyway. If you think I'm going to keep my distance now that I have both of you there, you're mistaken. So how do I go about being a Prospect?"

"Think it's time to give Owen and Foster their shot?" Thunder asked. "I know Foster fucked up with Leigha, and he has some growing up to do, but can you think of a better way to help him?"

"I'll message Savior. Sounds like we need to have Church again," Hammer said. He pulled out his phone and shot off a text to whoever Savior was, then pocketed it again.

"Now, what do we have to do to get service in this place?" my dad asked.

Thunder stood, and bellowed in a voice that made me wince, "Is it your habit of ignoring pregnant customers?"

A young waitress scurried over, her face flushed. "I'm so sorry!"

"Weren't you working the tables on the other side?" I asked.

She nodded and glanced at a woman behind the counter. One who happened to be glaring at me. It seemed our waitress didn't want anything to do with our table and had planned to ignore us indefinitely.

"Why don't you start with a pitcher of water, four glasses, and some menus?" my dad suggested in a soft tone. "We'll be ready to give you our order shortly."

She gave him a grateful smile and rushed off to do as he said. "Poor girl. No one wanted to wait on us, and I think she took pity on us. I have a feeling it won't go over well with the other staff."

My dad narrowed his gaze, then scanned the room. "Guess I'll have to make her a better offer. The shop could use someone to answer the phones and set up appointments. Boss is always griping about needing help. I'll send her his way and give him a heads-up."

The more I got to know Sam and Hammer, the more thankful I was that Todd Whitman wasn't related to me by blood. I might be stuck with Helen as a mother, but these two made up for her shortcomings. Sort of.

The waitress brought our cups, a pitcher of ice water, and some menus. She also gave us silverware and straws. "My name is Mindy. I'll give you a few minutes and come back to check on you. Just call out if you need me before then."

She raced off and my dad shook his head. "That girl has too much energy."

By the time we'd placed our orders, and our food arrived, my stomach was rumbling loudly. Thunder gave me grief over it, but I liked his teasing. It made me feel… normal? That was as good a word as any. My dad made sure Mindy knew about a possible job with the garage where he worked, and I noticed he and my grandfather left her a hefty tip. They'd insisted on covering the check.

"Not every day I find out I'm a dad," he said.

"Or that I have a granddaughter." Hammer smiled. He pulled his phone from his pocket, his eyebrows lifted. "Savior said with everything going on as long as I vouch for my son, then Sam can prospect. He just needs to go to the clubhouse for a cut. He's going to reach out to Rocky and Bull and have them tell their sons the good news."

"Do you have a motorcycle?" Thunder asked.

"I'm Hammer's only kid. What do you think?" My dad smirked. "Vintage Harley-Davidson. I'll probably get something less flashy for everyday riding, though. Been eyeing the new Fat Bob 114."

"When we get back to the compound, I want to introduce you to some people," Hammer said. "You and Amity both. I realize she's married to Thunder, but I want everyone to know how proud I am of my granddaughter."

I felt my cheeks warm. I wasn't used to so much attention, not the positive sort, anyway. I hoped he and my dad didn't go overboard. I could tell it was making Thunder a little uncomfortable. It had just been the two of us, with a baby on the way, and now he'd gained in-laws. For someone who'd been alone all this time, I wondered if he wasn't feeling a bit overwhelmed. I wouldn't blame him.

"Portia and the triplets mentioned something about a party," I said. "What if we made it for me and Dad both? Then everyone could meet us at the same time. I don't know when they were going to have it, though. Maybe it wouldn't be soon enough if he's going to join the club."

"Amity is right," my dad said. "I'll meet a few people today and should probably speak with your President and other officers, but there's no rush. Neither of us are going anywhere. I should probably stop by the Harley-Davidson shop and check on that new bike."

"Want me to go with you?" Hammer asked.

I could tell he wanted to spend more time with my dad, and I hoped it meant the two of them would grow closer. If he'd kept my dad a secret all these years, they couldn't have had much bonding time. Then again, my grandfather had been in prison. That couldn't haven't helped their relationship.

I found it odd. My grandfather got locked up, but he was so nice. Then there was Todd Whitman. The town adored him. Thought he walked on water. But behind closed doors, he showed a different side. I wondered what all these people would think if they knew the bikers they sneered at were heroes, while the upstanding citizens had a darkness inside them that would make most people sick.

It just proved you couldn't judge someone based on their appearance.

If only I'd learned that lesson before dating Evan. But if I had, would I have ever met Thunder?

"I'm going to set up an appointment with Dr. Myron," Thunder said. "And I'll let him know we're keeping the baby. We are, aren't we?"

I cupped his cheek and kissed him. "Yes. Honestly, part of me wanted to keep it even when I thought there was a chance it wouldn't be born healthy, or wouldn't live long. It was a decision I wasn't sure I could make, and now I don't have to."

"You make a baby registry wherever you shop," Dad said. "I want to buy some stuff for my grandbaby, but I want to make sure it will be things you need or want."

"Guess that means we're going shopping," Thunder said. "We'll need the club truck, though. Wire is working on a car for Amity, but we don't have it yet. All I've got is my bike."

"Use my truck today," Dad said. "We can drop Hammer off at the clubhouse, then you can leave me at the Harley-Davidson store. Just give me a call when you're done, and I'll come get it."

"What's Wire getting her?" Hammer asked, his brow furrowed. "And why is he doing it? Shouldn't that be left to one of us?"

"He said the police chief asked for his help, and in exchange, he's getting one of the cars at the impound lot. It's a Honda Accord that's still under warranty," I said. "I've always heard those were good cars for a family. And the warranty means we won't have to worry about repairs for the first two years."

"Fine. If you don't like it, you just let us know. We'll get you something better," Hammer said, and I thought I heard him mutter something about *damn foreign cars*.

I bit my lip so I wouldn't smile. The Whitmans would only drive German cars. The more expensive the better. It seemed my grandfather preferred vehicles made here in America. Nothing wrong with either one, but after living with the Whitmans and seeing the sort of people they were, I didn't want anything that would remind me of them in the future.

"The Honda will be a good car," Dad said. "They're reliable, and they hold their value. So if you decide you want something different, or bigger like an SUV, then you should get a decent trade-in value for it. Just depends on what shape it's in and how many miles are on it."

I shrugged. "I don't really know a lot about cars, other than what I overheard the kids at school saying. I have my license, but I was never given a car of my own. I haven't driven very much. Probably better to start with something smaller than anything huge like an SUV or truck."

Hammer made a soft growling sound. "When you're no longer pregnant, I'm teaching you to ride a motorcycle. Something light since you're so tiny."

"She's not like Pepper," Thunder said. "I like the fact my wife is soft and sweet. Let's not turn her into a terror like some of the Dixie Reaper ladies."

My dad chuckled and I noticed the gleam in his eye. "I think you're outvoted. If my dad doesn't teach her, I will. And you better believe I'm going to make sure she knows how to change a tire, the oil in her car, and any other basic car maintenance. You may be there for her, but what happens if you're not? I'm not going to leave her stranded somewhere because she's clueless about those things."

Thunder held up a hand. "Fine. Teach her anything you want, as long as she's okay with it."

I kissed Thunder's cheek. "Don't worry. I don't plan on changing much, but I do want to be stronger. I didn't like the weak person I'd become. I want to feel worthy of standing by your side."

His gaze softened. "Amity, you're more than worthy. I'm the one who doesn't deserve an angel like you."

"On that sappy note, it's time to go." Hammer stood, his chair skidding across the floor. My dad winked at me as he followed my grandfather out of the diner.

"Well, now you know what it's like to have a real family," Thunder said. "Hope you're ready because I have a feeling this will be one hell of a ride."

He was right, it would be... and I couldn't wait!

Chapter Six

Thunder

I'd been married over a week, and while my wife slept in my arms every night, nothing else had happened. Every morning, I woke before her, and eased out of bed before she realized I was sporting wood. I'd take a shower and handle the issue myself, then make breakfast for us. I couldn't complain. Did I miss sex? Of course. But I also wasn't a complete bastard. I'd told Amity she could take all the time she needed, and I meant it.

If I suffered from blue balls because of it, that was for me to know. I didn't want her to feel pressured. Although, I had to wonder if Portia hadn't been right about me spending too much time with Amity. Hammer and Sam both stopped by to visit, and Portia dropped in every other day. Even Tank's daughters had been to visit once since meeting Amity. Through it all, I remained somewhere in the house.

The only times I'd left had been to take Amity somewhere, or to go out on club business. Savior had tried his best not to hand me too many things right now. He knew Amity and I needed some time to bond. Maybe I was trying too hard? Smothering her? I wanted to keep her safe, and make sure she knew she could rely on me, but had I taken things too far?

Someone knocked at the door and I went to answer, glancing at Amity, who sat on the sofa reading a book. She didn't even budge. It was nice knowing she felt safe in our home.

I opened the door and found Merlin, grinning at me like an idiot. "Are you on something?"

"Nope," he said. "But I'm here to kidnap you."

"What the hell are you talking about?"

"You're coming to the clubhouse with me. You

haven't had a beer with your brothers since you brought Amity home. Unless you want the club to revoke your man-card, I suggest you get your ass on your bike and get over there to mingle a little."

I glowered at him. "No one is taking my man-card, as you put it. There's nothing wrong with spending time with my wife."

"No, there isn't. You need to spend time with your brothers too, though, and you aren't."

"It's okay if you want to go," Amity said. "You don't have to babysit me. I promise I won't fall apart while you're gone."

Great. Either she felt bad because of what Merlin said, or she needed a break from me. I'd tried to give her space when her family or friends were over. Had that been the wrong move? I knew my brothers tended to act like cavemen with their women, and there was a part of me that wanted to do the same with Amity. Did she expect that behavior from me?

I stared at her, trying to decipher her expression. She stared up at me with guileless eyes, not giving me a damn clue as to what she actually wanted.

"Merlin, give me a minute," I said, then shut the door in his face. I heard a muffled *asshole* from him.

Amity looked from the door to me, her brow wrinkled and her nose slightly scrunched. It was cute as fucking hell. "Do you want to go with him?"

"I can have a beer with my brothers anytime. Doesn't have to be tonight, unless you want me to go. Do I need to give you some space?"

Her eyes widened slightly, and she licked her lips. "N-no. It's just… You mentioned before, about the women at the clubhouse. I thought you might want to, um… I mean, we aren't…"

I growled softly. "Did you just tell me to go fuck

another woman?"

She pressed her lips together. Slowly, she shook her head, then stopped. After a moment, she shrugged and looked away.

"Is that what you want?" I asked. "You want me to be with someone else?"

"You haven't tried to touch me," she said. "Not since that first kiss. You've been so gentle with me. When you do kiss me, it's short and quick. I know I'm not very pretty, and --"

I put my hand over her mouth to stop her before she said something to piss me off even more. "First, you're right. You're not pretty. You're fucking gorgeous, and you're *mine*. Second, I told you multiple times I was letting you set the pace. Clearly, I was wrong to do that. So I'm just going to make things abundantly clear."

I grabbed her hand and placed it over my dick, which was hard. But I was *always* hard in her presence. She whimpered and her eyes darkened. Not in fear. No, if I wasn't mistaken, there was a hint of desire in her gaze.

"I get out of bed every morning before you wake up, so you won't see how hard I am for you. I get in the shower, yank one out, then make breakfast for us. The only woman I want is the one I'm married to."

She reached up and tugged my hand away from her mouth. "When you said I could set the pace, I didn't know you meant you'd completely put the brakes on. I liked the kiss we shared. I love it when you touch me. Do you think I'm scared of you?"

"I think you're still healing," I said, cupping her cheek.

"Maybe it's not something I have to do alone," she said. "If we try to do more than kiss, and I panic or have a flashback, would you stop?"

"Of course!"

"Then I think I'd like to try."

Holy shit. Did she mean it? I opened the door, and without looking at Merlin, told him to fuck off. Once I'd shut it again, I locked it.

"We're going to make this memorable, all right? Your first time was a nightmare for you. If we're going to try and erase those memories, give you something good to hold onto, then I want to do it right."

"I'm not sure what you mean," she said.

"I'm going to make us a nice dinner. After we eat, you're going to soak in the tub while I get things set up."

"I don't need all that." Amity placed her hand over mine. "I just need you, Austin. Even though it's been incredible getting to know my real dad and my grandfather, the best part of coming here is that I got to meet you. I know Lavender married us without asking, but I'm glad she did."

"I'm glad too." I smiled. "Now, you can finish your book, or you can keep me company in the kitchen. Either way, I'm determined to make tonight special."

"I like your spaghetti. Can we have that?"

I nodded. "We can. I'll even make garlic bread."

She followed me to the kitchen, and while I cooked, she sat at the table. I set out plates, glasses, and silverware when I wasn't checking the noodles, sauce, or bread. By the time I plated our food, I could hear her stomach rumbling. She'd been so tiny when I'd brought her home that first night. With regular meals, she'd already started to fill out more. The gaunt look had faded, and she no longer had circles under her eyes.

"Was he telling the truth?" she asked as she twirled

the pasta around her fork. "Have you been staying here because of me and neglecting your club?"

"I'm not *neglecting* anyone, honey. I used to hang out with Merlin and a few others. We'd drink and blow off steam. For the record, I hadn't touched a woman in a while before I brought you home. One of the club girls started getting clingy, so I took a step back."

She took a bite, but I could see the thoughts circling her mind. "I'm not interested in her. Or anyone else. You hear me? You're the only woman for me."

"But before... you weren't sure you could be faithful."

I knew that was going to come back to bite me in the ass. "I said if we were never intimate that I didn't know whether or not I'd stray at some point. It would be something that would haunt me the rest of my life. This club is different from a lot of others out there. When we find a woman, that's it. She's ours and we don't want anyone else."

"So those women won't even tempt you a little?" she asked.

I reached across the table to take her hand. "No. I'm sorry I even mentioned it before. I was trying to be honest with you, but I should have kept my mouth shut. Even then, I knew I didn't want those women."

"Then why did you say all that before?" she asked.

"I didn't want you to feel pressured. I thought if you knew I wouldn't touch anyone but you, it might make you feel like we had to have sex. I didn't want you thinking it wasn't a choice. I'll never take anything you don't offer freely, Amity. Even now, if you change your mind, then we'll cuddle and just hang out."

She gave me a slight smile and I felt my tension ease. I'd never intended for her to hear those words and feel worse about herself. I'd been trying to help the situation and instead I fucked it to hell and back. I was starting to understand why I'd remained single all this time. A woman like Amity was special. The once-in-a-lifetime kind. If Merlin hadn't been hiding from Portia that night, I may have never met her.

"I hate everything you've been through, but I'm beyond grateful that you're here with me," I said. "I know if you hadn't been on that bridge, if you hadn't called Portia, we likely wouldn't have met."

"I'd have jumped," she said. "If you'd been a minute later, I'd have already gone into the water. Even when you rode up onto the bridge, I nearly leapt anyway. Something held me back."

"Fate." I smiled. "I think you were meant to be mine."

She nodded. "I think so too. Coming here has changed my life in so many ways. I don't want to be broken. I want to have a normal, happy life."

"You think I can give that to you?"

"You're the only one who can." She said it with such certainty. I knew I couldn't fail her.

We finished our meal, and I went to start a bath for her. I shut off the lights and set out a few candles on the bathroom counter. After I set a towel out, I went back to the kitchen to clean up. As much as I wanted to help Amity into the bath, I'd give her this time to herself. I had no idea what was going through her mind right now. This was going to be a huge step for us. I'd be lying if I said I wasn't nervous as fuck. Sure, I'd been with quite a few women over the years. None had been important.

Amity might not be a virgin, but I'd treat her as such. As far as I was concerned, this would be her first time. I'd try to make it the perfect night for her.

I finished cleaning the kitchen and went back to the bedroom. I'd pulled the bathroom door mostly shut earlier, wanting to hear her if she needed help, yet giving her privacy. I tried really fucking hard not to peek through the crack in the door as I prepared the bedroom. I took the sheets and blankets off the bed and put on fresh ones. Since I'd put the candles in the bathroom with Amity, I didn't really have any to set the mood in here.

I looked around, trying to figure out what I could do. Then I remembered the kids asking all of us to put out jack-o-lanterns last Halloween. I'd bought the flameless candles after the wind kept blowing out the tea lights. There weren't many left, but I set out two on each bedside table, and the remaining three along the dresser. I'd started with nearly twenty, but I'd used most with the pumpkins.

"Austin?"

"Everything okay?"

I heard the sloshing of water in the tub. "I can't get out. Every time I try, my feet slide out from under me."

Shit. I hadn't thought to scrub the bathtub after her last bath, and I'd added oils to the water for her. Feeling like an idiot, I went into the bathroom and made sure I kept my gaze on her face and nowhere else. She lifted a hand, and I helped her stand, putting my other hand at her waist to support her. The slick feel of her skin against my palm had me swallowing hard. Fuck but she felt incredible.

Once she'd stepped out of the tub, I handed her the towel and backed away.

"Since you're going to see me naked in the bedroom anyway, could you help me dry off?" She held the towel out to me, and I noticed her hand trembled. I took it, then gently dried her.

My cock got hard as steel, and I couldn't hold back another moment. Leaning forward, I licked her nipple. Amity gasped and went still, but she didn't tell me to stop. I lifted my gaze, and watched her face as I did it again. Her cheeks flushed and she parted her lips.

"Austin." She said my name reverently.

I sucked the hard bud into my mouth and scraped my teeth over it. She cried out and her knees buckled. I caught her, lifting her into my arms, then carried her into the bedroom and set her down on the bed. I made quick work of stripping out of my clothes. The way she looked at me, with heat and longing, made me feel like a fucking king. The others from my past had only wanted a quick ride, or bragging rights for having been with a Dixie Reaper. Amity was different.

"Remember what I said. At any time, if you need me to stop, just tell me."

She nodded then reached for me. I joined her on the bed, pulling her against me. Pressing my lips to hers, I started the kiss soft and slow, then deepened it when she gave a little whimper. Her nails bit into my shoulders.

I trailed kisses across her jaw and down her chest. I lavished attention on her breasts and eased my hand between her thighs. She wasn't soaked, but I thanked the gods she wasn't dry either. I toyed with her clit, and it wasn't long before she sucked in a breath and let out a loud keening sound.

Working my finger into her tight pussy, I groaned when I realized I'd already made her come. She'd gone from slightly wet to being drenched. My cock jerked and I could feel pre-cum smearing on the sheets. I'd have to wash the bedding again, but I didn't give a fuck right then.

"Come for me again," I murmured, playing with

her body some more. "Let me hear those sweet sounds you make when you feel good."

"Austin, I --" I kissed her, cutting off her words. I just wanted her to feel. She came twice more, her body trembling. As badly as I wanted her, I knew it was time to give her a chance to back out. We'd already done more than I'd thought would be possible this early in our relationship.

My sweet angel had given me a gift. One I'd cherish the rest of my life.

* * *

Amity

I stared at the ceiling, feeling as if I'd fallen into a whirling vortex. I'd always loved to read romances, and I'd sighed when the hero and heroine got together, but not in my wildest dreams did I think the way Austin made me feel could be a real thing. Until this moment, I'd thought it was only fiction.

He kissed me again and I ran my hand down his back. Despite giving me more pleasure than I'd ever felt in my entire life, not once had he tried to take things further. It had been all about me, and I adored him for it. He made me feel special. Important.

"You're so beautiful," he murmured, nuzzling my neck.

"We aren't… stopping… are we?" I hated how uncertain I felt suddenly. What he'd done had been beyond amazing. The fact he'd not kept going left me wondering if he worried he'd done too much, or if he didn't want me as much as he'd claimed. Doubts filled me, and I felt a flash of anger. Evan and the others had done this to me. Even now, their actions haunted me, and drove my reactions when I was with Thunder.

"That's up to you," he said. "I told you I wouldn't

take what you didn't offer. We've already gone further than I thought we would. Don't get me wrong. I'm incredibly grateful you trusted me this much. I'm in awe of you, Amity. But I also don't want to push for more if you aren't ready."

He ran a hand over my baby bump. A soft smile curved his lips as he stared at the little mound. Telling him I wanted to keep the baby hadn't only been a relief for me, but I thought it had been one for him too. I wasn't the only one who'd fallen in love with the life growing inside me.

"I'm ready," I said. "I want to have a real marriage with you, Austin. I don't want the past to hold me back from the happiness we can have together. If I do, then Evan and the others win. I won't let them break me."

He cupped my cheek and pressed his forehead to mine. "You're not broken, honey. You're so damn strong. You held out on your own for so long. Do you know how incredible you are? The entire fucking town tried to tear you down, but you're still here."

"Only because you saved me," I said.

"You didn't have to leave a message for Portia. I think it was a final cry for help. You didn't really want to die. You just wanted someone to give a damn." He brushed his nose against mine. "I see you, Amity. I care. So fucking much."

"I ruined the mood, didn't I?" I asked.

"No. I'm glad you feel like you can talk to me about this stuff. As for the mood, I'll just have to warm you back up." He winked and worked his way down my body. When his shoulders spread my thighs wide, my cheeks warmed. He wasn't about to do *that*, was he?

He parted the lips of my pussy and the first lick of his tongue had me squealing and trying to clamp my legs shut. He chuckled and flicked my clit. I didn't know what to do. My heart raced, and I gripped the sheets in my hands. As embarrassed as I felt over him looking at me down there -- tasting me -- it also felt really good.

Thunder eased a finger inside me as he nibbled, sucked, and licked at my clit. It felt like I was heating from the inside out, and soon he had me coming again. Once didn't seem to be enough for him. My orgasm didn't even have a chance to wane before he sent another crashing through me. I screamed out his name, my body tensing, and I felt my release gush from me.

Thunder settled himself over me, his tender gaze locking with mine. He didn't look away. Didn't close his eyes. He laced our fingers together with one hand as he slowly sank into me. It stretched and burned, but he didn't rush. My sweet husband took his time, and by the time he'd filled me completely, I ached for him to move.

"Do something," I begged. "Please. I need... need..."

"I've got you," he murmured. Thunder pulled his hips back, then drove into me. I cried out, gripping his bicep with my free hand. My nails bit into him as he thrust again and again. The bed rocked under us as he sent me to dizzying heights. It felt like the world was spinning as I came one last time. The moment I clamped down on his cock, he let out a low growl before driving into me with quick, deep strokes. I felt the heat of his release and wished this had been my very first time.

"You okay?" he asked.

"More than." I gave him a tired smile. "I didn't know that was even possible. To come so many times? I mean, it's happened in books I've read. I just didn't think it was a real thing."

He grinned. "Good to know. Challenge accepted."

My eyes widened. "What? What challenge?"

"You came six times. I'll try for eight after you've had time to rest."

"Eight?" The question came out as more of a squeak.

"Hmm. Not enough? We could go for ten? An even dozen?"

"You're joking. Aren't you?" I asked.

"Nope." He kissed me. "I'm going to give you so much pleasure you won't be able to walk tomorrow."

I lay quietly, absorbing his words. Thunder rolled to his side and pulled me against his chest. I cuddled against him and wondered what I'd gotten myself into. Now that I'd given the man the green light, it seemed like he planned to kill me with orgasms. I mean, it wasn't the worst way to go, but I hoped he'd been teasing me. I already felt wrung out, and like I could sleep for a week.

I'd been so scared of being intimate with him. Mostly, I'd worried I'd panic and have a flashback or something. Or worse, a repressed memory from my time with Evan coming back with a vengeance and ruining everything. Thunder had been so kind to me. I knew he wouldn't hold anything like that against me, but I'd feel awful if we had to stop because I fell apart.

Was he right? Was I stronger than I realized?

I didn't know what had come over me. I'd heard Merlin ask him to go to the clubhouse, and I'd remembered what Thunder said about the women there. Something in me had fractured. The thought of him being with someone else was the worst pain I'd ever felt. Even finding out what Evan had done to me hadn't hurt this bad. Or maybe it was just a different sort of pain. I was glad we'd talked and he hadn't left.

At the same time, I knew Merlin was right. Thunder couldn't stay home with me all the time. He had a life outside this house. A family other than me and our baby. It wasn't fair for me to hold on so tightly to him.

"Austin, you know I trust you, right?" I asked.

"What brought that up?" He raised himself up on an elbow and looked down at me.

"Merlin wanted you to go have a drink with him. I don't want to keep you from doing something like that because of the women you'll see there. If you say you don't want them, then I believe you. I was only worried because…" How did I tell him the thought of never being healed enough to satisfy him that way had filled me with fear? He might have been patient, but eventually he'd have gotten tired of having a wife who didn't want sex. Right?

"You didn't have sex with me tonight so I wouldn't be tempted at the clubhouse, did you?" His brow furrowed. "It wasn't necessary, Amity. I told you I would wait and I meant it."

"But you said you might want to be with them sometime…" I swallowed hard. "It wasn't just that, though. I care about you, Austin, and I wanted a real marriage. I won't lie. The thought of having sex terrified me. I worried I'd freak out and ruin everything between us. I think I needed to prove to myself that I could handle it."

"How are you doing? Not physically. You already told me that part. Emotionally? Mentally? Any regrets? Worries?" He ran a hand down my arm. "Do you need anything from me right now?"

I leaned up to kiss him. How the hell had I lucked out with such a great guy? He was like my perfect storybook hero. I hadn't thought men like him really existed.

"I'm good. Honest."

"I'm going to go start the shower. When it's warm, I'll come get you. We'll rinse off, you can put on your pajamas, and we'll…"

I was shaking my head before he'd even finished. "The shower part is fine. I'm not going to ask you to stay here right now, Austin. You need to go have a drink with your friends. Show them you're not on a tight leash and stuck at home. Go have some fun. I think it's something we both need anyway. You need to see I'll still be here, happy and healthy, when you get back. And I need to show the both of us I can handle being on my own, even if it's just for an hour or two."

"Fine. I don't like it, but I'll go. For *one* drink."

I nodded. "All right. One drink. I'll be here when you get back."

He leaned in, his nose nearly touching mine. "If I'm not back in an hour, Merlin kidnapped me. If you can get to the clubhouse safely, come rescue me. Or ask Hammer to come extract me."

I bit my lips so I wouldn't laugh. "Extract you? Is this a covert mission that's going to go wrong?"

"Could be. Never know." He winked and rolled out of bed. I heard the shower going a moment later and couldn't help but smile. I felt… good. Really good. Happy. Normal. I hadn't thought I'd ever experience either of those ever again.

I stared at the open bathroom door, the smile slipping from my face. "I love you, Austin," I murmured low enough I knew he couldn't hear me. It was too soon for those words, but I felt them. God help me if he never felt the same, but I couldn't shut it off. Now that I'd opened myself up to him completely, there was no turning back.

Chapter Seven

Thunder

The smoke hit me in the face when I stepped through the clubhouse doors. After avoiding this place for a little over a week, the stench made me wrinkle my nose. It wasn't just the cigarettes. Nope. The place reeked of sex and desperation. My brothers were all too happy to take the women up on their offers, but now that I had Amity at home, I could see the look in these women's eyes. Hunger. Not the sexual kind either. Greed might be a better word. They might be spreading their legs or dropping to their knees, but it wasn't just to have a good time. They wanted more.

Tessie gave me a wink as she sauntered by, putting some extra swing in her hips. Before Amity, I might have taken the bait. Didn't hurt she'd ditched everything but her thong. Not that I was looking. My brothers, however, were nearly salivating over her and the others.

Merlin came over, a big grin on his face. "It's about time!"

"Not staying long," I said. "And I'll need another shower when I get home."

He bounced his eyebrows up and down. "Don't let the officers hear you say that. You know how this club feels about stepping out on your woman. Can't deny there's some tempting women in here, though. Wouldn't blame you at all if you…"

He didn't get to finish his sentence before my fist met his face. Merlin worked his jaw and back and forth, glaring at me. My fist shook from the strength it took to hold back from nailing the bastard again.

"What the fuck is wrong with you?" I asked. "I meant because of the damn cigarette smoke. I'm not cheating on my wife, asshole."

I heard a gasp and spotted Sonja. Her lips parted and her eyes went wide. "You're married?"

"Yeah, I am. So hands off." Something told me she'd be a problem.

"You seriously hit me?" Merlin demanded. "What the hell is wrong with you?"

"You implied I was going to cheat on Amity, then sounded excited about it. Show my wife some respect. Even if I *had* fucked up and gotten sucked off by one of the girls, it wouldn't have been something to celebrate. I'd have felt like shit afterward."

Merlin shook his head. "She's fucked with your head."

"No, she hasn't. Are you telling me if you found the woman you wanted to keep, made her your old lady, that you'd come here and hook up with the club whores?" I asked. "How long before one of the officers, or another brother, handed your ass to you when they found out?"

He backed up a step. "Whatever."

"Portia wasn't too clingy, was she?" I asked. "You actually liked her. But you don't think you can be faithful to one woman, do you, Merlin?"

He dropped his gaze to the floor and shrugged a shoulder. "Won't know until I try it, but Torch's daughter? Yeah. That's like being baptized by fire. No way I'm touching any of the daughters around here. If I fucked up, every brother in this club would have my balls."

He wasn't wrong, but I thought he was a chickenshit just the same. If he liked Portia, and she clearly had a thing for him, then he should pursue her. Maybe it would settle her ass down. Amity had forgiven her. I hadn't. Not yet. Someday, perhaps.

I saw Tank, Wire, and Sarge at a table in the corner

and made my way over. They were the only men in here who had a woman at home. Seemed safer to have a beer with them than the single brothers. I hoped it would also keep the club whores away from me. If any of them screwed up what I had going with Amity, I'd kick their asses out of here. I didn't think any of the officers would disagree.

"Mind if I join you?" I asked, pulling out a chair.

"Be my guest." Wire smiled. "Here for some male bonding?"

"Something like that. Merlin stopped by earlier. Made a big stink about me not coming to the clubhouse for a beer since I brought Amity to my house. She told me to come mingle."

Wire snorted. "That poor girl has no idea what this place is like. If she did, she'd have tied you to the bed."

"And yet you're here."

"Yes, but my wife is just as good with a computer as I am. Anyone here pisses her off, and their lives will be ruined before morning." Wire took a swallow of his beer. "Have to admit it gets me rather hot thinking about it."

"I like the fact my woman isn't bloodthirsty," Tank said. "She's all soft and sweet."

"Same with Amity," I said. "I can't wait for everyone to meet her. I know Portia was going to see about setting up a family party at the clubhouse. Any word on that?"

"She roped my woman into helping," Sarge said. "Think they were going to make it a surprise but be prepared to come to the clubhouse for lunch tomorrow. Once things wrap up tonight, the Prospects will be scrubbing every surface in here. Doubt they'll be sleeping much."

I looked over at the bar and saw Owen filling drink

orders. I held up my hand, and he gave me a chin lift. I knew he'd be over when he had a second.

"Think Owen, Foster, and Sam are going to work out as Prospects?" I asked.

"Well, with Sam being Hammer's kid, and your father-in-law, as long as he doesn't fuck up, I think it's safe to say he'll patch in. Same goes for Owen. He's a good kid. Always follows the rules. Foster…" Tank shook his head. "I'm still not convinced he has what it takes. Not after that mess with Leigha."

"Yeah, I worried about that too. I don't think he meant to be so pushy with her. Guess we'll find out sooner or later. Now Bull isn't just his daddy. He's a patched member who has a say in whether he makes it as a Dixie Reaper. I hope it makes him toe the line a bit more." Owen dropped off my favorite bottle of beer and was gone before I could even say thanks. I popped the top and took a swallow before scanning the room. "How did I ever think this was fun?"

"You really like her, don't you?" Wire asked.

I nodded. "Yeah. I think I'm falling for her."

Tank smirked. "Nope. Not falling. *Fallen.*"

"Huh?" My brow furrowed. "What's that supposed to mean?"

"Why haven't you been here lately?" he asked.

"Well, I didn't like the idea of leaving Amity by herself. Before that, I was getting tired of the clingy club whores. You know damn well they all want a brother to claim them. It wasn't going to be me."

"Something wrong with claiming one of us?" Tessie asked from behind me.

I looked over my shoulder at her. "I wouldn't want to claim a woman who'd been with nearly every brother here."

"So you're only into virgins?" she demanded,

hands on her hips.

"No. What I don't want is a woman who's been intimate with men I consider family. How awkward would it be for their old ladies? Being with any of you is fine for blowing off steam. None of you are my idea of forever, though," I said.

"If you wanted someone here to claim you, then you shouldn't have become a club whore," Tank said. "I don't know a single brother who wouldn't be thinking the same thing Thunder just said. As for me, my wife was a virgin our first time together. I fucking love the fact she's never been with a man other than me."

Tessie pressed her lips together. I saw her give the room a quick scan, but her gaze lingered for a moment on Savior. "None of you will? Not for any reason?"

"If you're thinking of getting knocked up on purpose to trap someone, I wouldn't," Wire said. "I don't think it would end favorably for you. I know if it had happened to me, I'd have claimed the child, but I sure the fuck wouldn't have claimed the whore who gave birth to them."

She flinched a little and her face paled. I wondered what the hell she was up to. Had that been her plan? To trap Savior? I hoped she didn't follow through with it. Now that he was the President, I didn't think he'd handle it nearly as well as he would have before. Not to mention he had an adopted daughter now.

Tessie didn't say another word, but I noticed she found her clothes, pulled them on, and rushed out of the clubhouse. I looked back at Tank and Wire and saw the calculating look in their eyes. Tank might have stepped down as the Sergeant at Arms, but that wasn't a switch you could turn off. He'd be keeping an eye on her.

"Think I'm going to go home and look into the women here a bit more," Wire said. "Call me if you need anything."

He stood and walked out, and I had a feeling the club whores were in for a rude awakening. If Wire dug up anything on them, there would be hell to pay. At least, if it was something that could harm the club, or if they were after a brother in a malicious way. I wouldn't want to be in their shoes if that happened.

"Think I've been here long enough?" I asked.

"Um." Tank smirked. "Since Hammer just walked in and seems to be looking for you, I'd say so. Think your woman called her grandpa and asked him to bring you home?"

I angled my chair, and sure enough, Hammer stood inside the door. I waved at him, and he started pushing his way through the crowded room.

"What the fuck did you say to piss off Merlin?" Hammer asked when he was within hearing range.

"Merlin? He misunderstood something I said. Thought we'd cleared the air already." My nape prickled. "Why? What's going on?"

"Sam may put him in the ground if you don't hurry," Hammer said. "Told my boy not to do anything stupid, but Merlin is at your house."

"Shit." I stood so fast my chair fell over, and I was rushing to the doors. I heard Tank right behind me. He called out to Savior and Tempest before we made it outside. I got on my bike and went straight home, not even slowing for the curves in the road. When I reached the house, I saw Sam on the porch, arms crossed, and snarling at Merlin.

"What the fuck is going on?" I asked.

Merlin swayed and I wondered how drunk he was. Or worse, was he high? He'd seemed fine at the clubhouse. An asshole, but fine.

"I stopped by to see my daughter before heading home. Found this one scaring the shit out of her," Sam said.

"Merlin, why are you here?" I asked. "What did you do to Amity?"

"Amity," he muttered. "Stuck up fucking bitch. She's no better than the girls at the clubhouse. Spreads her legs like the others."

I fisted my hands and stomped closer, so fucking close to losing it. "What did you just say?"

"Your wife is a whore, isn't she? Got fucked three ways to Sunday by a bunch of men, including the one who raised her." Merlin sneered. "Your precious Amity is nothing but a dirty slut."

A red haze settled over my vision, and I took a swing. I couldn't stop at just one. No. I beat the hell out of Merlin. I felt hands grabbing me, pulling me back, and I struggled to reach him again. Panting for breath, I finally stilled.

"Stand him up," Tempest said. He released me and moved closer to Merlin.

I'd done a number on him. One eye already swelled shut, and his jaw had started to turn purple in places. I'd split his lip, and his nose bled.

"Why?" I asked. "Why the hell would you say those things? You know what happened to her. Everyone in Church heard the story."

"Did he just scare her?" Tempest asked, focusing on Sam. "Or did he hurt her?"

"He'd grabbed her arm and dragged her out onto the porch. Saw him shake her a few times. I sent her inside." Sam looked at the house. "She was crying so hard she could barely catch her breath."

"Check on her," Tempest said. "Let me know how

bad it is. Then we can decide what to do with Merlin."

Savior came up beside me. "I'll come with you."

I went into the house and heard Amity sobbing from the back of the house. I followed the sound and found her curled up on our bed. Savior stopped in the hall, giving us some space.

Easing down on the side of the bed, I ran my fingers through her hair. "I'm here now."

She threw herself into my arms and I held her close, trying to soothe her. I caught Savior's gaze over her head. The man looked torn between his heart breaking for my wife and wanting to beat the shit out of Merlin. If I'd known how badly he'd scared her, I might have done more damage to him.

"Honey, I need to see if he left any marks on you. And the club President is here. I think he'd like to meet you." She sniffled and buried her face in my shirt. I kissed the top of her head. "Come on. You'll smell like smoke."

She finally pulled back, and I checked her arms, letting loose a low growl when I saw the finger-shaped bruises on her arms. Savior came closer and kneeled beside the bed.

"Amity, this is Savior. He's the President of the Dixie Reapers now that Torch stepped down. Can you tell us what happened?" I laced our fingers together. Tears still streaked her cheeks, and she drew in a shaky breath. I hated that he'd scared her so badly. It made me want to pound on him some more.

"I heard a knock on the door. Everyone says I'm safe here, so I opened it." She curled against my chest. "Merlin was on the other side. He started yelling at me, calling me names. I tried to shut the door, but he grabbed me and dragged me onto the porch."

"He pulled you from your home?" Savior asked.

She nodded. "I don't understand what I did wrong."

"Nothing." Savior stood. "I'll go find out what's going on with Merlin. He and Thunder are close. It doesn't make sense that he'd attack you like this."

"I think he's on something," I said. "He was swaying. I just saw him at the clubhouse not even a half hour ago and he seemed fine. His usual asshole self, but he wasn't drunk or high."

"We'll get to the bottom of it," Savior said. "Stay with Amity."

I shook my head. "Not happening, Pres. Sorry. I need to be there and hear what he has to say. If someone put him up to it, or if he's pissed because I'm spending so much time with my wife, I need to know."

"Amity, your dad is outside. Would you like him to stay with you until Thunder returns?" Savior asked.

She nodded and held onto me. I hugged her and kissed the top of her head again before standing. I eased her down onto the bed and waited for Sam to come inside. He stood in the bedroom doorway, refusing to enter. The tortured look in his eyes told me enough. He felt like he'd failed her again. Hell, I did too. It never crossed my mind that Merlin would do something like this.

"I'll be back soon. If anything happens, call me."

I followed Savior from the house, and we went to interrogate Merlin. Since he was a brother, and trustworthy up until now, we went to Savior's office at the clubhouse. Tempest shoved Merlin down onto a chair and stood in the doorway, blocking his escape.

"You take anything?" Savior asked.

Merlin shook his head. "Just beer."

Tempest yelled out for Owen. The Prospect showed in the hallway a moment later. "Ask Wire to check the feed at the clubhouse. See if anyone dosed Merlin with something. Tell him it's urgent."

Owen took off at a run. I tried to hold back. Something had to be wrong with Merlin. He'd never acted like this before. Even earlier, the way he'd seemed thrilled with the idea of me cheating on Amity hadn't been like him. I didn't know what was going on, but I hoped we figured it out soon. Savior was right. Merlin and I had always been close. Best friends, even before we became brothers.

"Why did you attack my wife?" I asked, trying to keep my voice even.

"Little whore is ruining everything."

I pressed my lips together so I wouldn't yell at him. Or worse. I wanted to throw another punch, or ten.

"What did she ruin?" Tempest asked.

"He's supposed to fall for Sonja. She had it all planned out." Merlin started to slide sideways, and Tempest moved quickly to hold him upright. "Now it's ruined."

"Why do you want me to be with Sonja?" I asked. "She's just a club whore. Easy pussy. You knew I wasn't interested in her, or anyone else. Until Amity, I had no plans to settle down."

"It's the only way." His words started to slur. "Can't get him if I don't play along."

Savior's gaze sharpened. "Get who?"

A knock sounded in the hallway, and I glanced over as Wire stepped inside. "You need to see this."

He set up his laptop and showed Savior whatever was on the screen. The President's eyebrows shot up.

"Are you shitting me?" Savior asked. "That fucking cunt! Find her and bring her here."

"What's going on, Pres?" Tempest asked.

"Merlin, why didn't you tell anyone you had a

kid?" Savior asked.

He gave a humorless laugh. "Not just me. Bitch has yours too."

Savior stood and leaned forward, bracing his hands on the desk. "What did you just say?"

Merlin's eyes started to droop, and I knew he was about to pass out. I reached over and smacked him on the cheek, jolting him. He blinked and looked around. "Where am I?"

"In the President's office," I said. "What did you mean they have your kid and Savior's? Who does? What kids?"

"Candy had Savior's baby. It's why she left," Merlin muttered. "Anya had mine. They didn't say anything. Just left. But Sonja knew. She took them. Those bitches gave them up. Now she's using them."

"Using them how?" Savior asked.

"To get Thunder."

Shit. The look on Savior's face didn't bode well for any of those women. I couldn't believe Merlin had known about this and didn't say anything. Was that why he'd been acting strange since Amity came here? How long had Sonja had the children? Was she hurting them?

Why the fuck hadn't he said something? We would have helped him. Didn't he know that we had his back?

Wire cleared his throat. "You have another daughter, Savior. She's two. Merlin has a son who is three. From what I was able to trace, it looks like Anya didn't want a kid with a Prospect. Candy knew you'd take the kid and leave her high and dry, so she ran. At least, that's what I'm getting from this, but it's a bit unclear. They essentially sold the kids to Sonja."

"I want that bitch here now," Savior said. "And

find the others."

"Why did they run?" I asked. "So what if Savior had wanted his kid? If she was going to hand the little girl over anyway, what did it matter?"

Wire shrugged. "No idea. Maybe they were scared? There's not a lot in the emails and texts between the women and Sonja. It's possible motherhood was just too much for them. Or maybe she threatened to out them. They've moved on in other towns. No longer club whores."

"We'll see that it's done," Tempest said. "What do we do with Merlin?"

"Take him to his house, but have someone watch him. If they dosed him with something, he may need medical care. Once he's sober again, we can find out why he didn't tell us. I have a feeling we won't like the answer," Savior said. "Either way, he's a brother and his kid is caught up in this mess, too."

"If no one else needs me, I'm going home to my wife. I know you and Merlin have more of a right to take care of Sonja, but she sent him after Amity. I want my pound of flesh. I don't care if she's a woman or not. She crossed a fucking line."

Savior nodded. "You can have a go at her, once we have all the answers we need, and our kids. Stay vigilant. Who knows who else she roped into this scheme?"

Why the fuck couldn't anything ever be easy? Not only did we still need to take care of the men who'd hurt Amity, but now we had a club whore running wild. I was starting to understand why the officers had stepped down. I wasn't anywhere near their age, and I was already starting to feel too old for this shit.

Chapter Eight

Amity

My dad made coffee for him and a glass of sweet tea for me. We sat at the kitchen table, waiting for Thunder to return. I hadn't seen my grandfather either. I knew he'd run to the clubhouse to get my husband, but had he stayed there? Why hadn't he come back?

"The club will handle it," my dad said. "Whatever is going on, they'll take care of it and make sure you're safe."

"How can you sound so certain? I thought being inside the compound meant I'd be protected. Then Merlin shows up, starts calling me names, bruises me and drags me from my house." I twisted my glass in circles on the table. "If Merlin came for me, who else will? And what did he plan to do to me if you hadn't shown up to stop him?"

My dad's features tightened, and I knew he hadn't liked the reminder. Thunder's club brothers were supposed to be on our side. If they weren't, was there a chance enemies had surrounded me? If Merlin didn't want me here, how many others didn't? Portia and the other three girls had been nice. But they were the offspring of the members. I didn't think they had a say in anything that happened here.

I knew it was possible the things I'd been through made me a bit paranoid. Just because Merlin hated me didn't mean everyone else did. Some part of me recognized that. It didn't stop me from being afraid, though. I wasn't just protecting myself. I had the baby to consider as well.

"I think that's what they're trying to figure out. Mostly, they'll want to know why he did it."

The front door opened and shut. I tensed until I saw my grandfather. He sighed and came over to kiss the top of my head, then poured himself a cup of coffee and sat next to my dad.

"She's worried someone else will try to hurt her," Dad said.

"If they do, I have a feeling Thunder will rip them to pieces. Merlin is his best friend, and he beat the hell out of him." Hammer leaned back in his chair. "I don't think there's anything he wouldn't do to keep you safe, Amity. That boy cares about you a great deal. In the time I've known him, not once has he been so tender and sweet with a woman. Only you get that side of him."

"I love him, but I'm worried he'll never feel the same about me," I confessed.

"Pretty sure he already does," Dad said with a smile. "I could tell just by watching the two of you."

He couldn't be right, could he? Thunder couldn't love me. Not this soon. Sure, I'd fallen for him, but look at how much he'd changed my life. Not just physical things like this house or food to eat. He'd helped give me back my pride and self-worth. Because of him, I felt like I could hold my head up. Most of the time. I still struggled.

"I feel a little out of my depth," I admitted. "I don't know anything about being in a motorcycle club. I know Portia, and I got better acquainted with Kasen, Westlyn, and Harlow. But I don't feel like I'm really a part of things here."

"That's because you've been hiding in the house," Hammer said. "And technically, your husband is in the club. You're his property."

If the word *property* was supposed to make me feel inferior or insulted, he was wrong. I didn't care what term Thunder used, as long as I was his.

"I know. I need to make more of an effort. Portia

mentioned a party so I could meet everyone, but I haven't heard more about it."

Hammer nodded. "They wanted to surprise you. The old ladies set it up for tomorrow, but with all the shit going on tonight, I have no idea if they'll still have it or not. The question is whether you're going to stay here, waiting patiently for Thunder to come home, or are you going to go get some answers?"

I gaped at him. "What? But he told me…"

Hammer smirked. "He told you to wait here, and like a good little wife, you're doing as you're told. Admirable. Not exactly the way some of the women around here handle things, but there are quieter ones. Like Tank's woman, or Wraith's. They're not as in your face about matters around here, unlike Venom's woman. Then again, her daddy is a Dixie Reaper, too."

I narrowed my eyes at him. "And I'm married to one and the granddaughter of one. My daddy is prospecting. That's what it's called, right? Are you saying I need to put on my big girl panties and go ask what's going on?"

"I think your grandpa is trying to earn you a spanking. Thunder said to stay here. If you leave, he may not go easy on you. Especially if Merlin is dangerous." My dad sighed. "But you do whatever you feel is right. Either wait or go after him. I'll tag along if you decide to leave. Can't leave my daughter unprotected."

I wasn't sure what I should do. As my dad said, Thunder told me to wait here. But I didn't want anyone to see me as weak. They probably already thought I was, since I'd hidden myself away. I wanted to know why Merlin had hurt me, why he'd said all those things. Thunder had told me, as his wife, I'd have the support of the club. It didn't seem to be the case. If I needed to be more cautious, I'd like to know. What if I opened the door again, and someone else tried to hurt me? My dad might not be around next time to save me. What then?

"I need to know why he did it," I said.

My dad and grandfather both stood. I followed them outside, then stopped to stare at their motorcycles. Wire hadn't gotten the car for me yet, which meant I didn't have a way to get to the clubhouse unless I rode with one of them. If Hammer thought Thunder would be angry I showed up at the clubhouse, it would be worse if he found out I rode a motorcycle while I was pregnant.

"How far is it?" I asked, not remembering how long it had taken by car.

"You're not walking," Dad said.

"Wait here. I'll ride over to the clubhouse and get one of the trucks," Hammer said.

"Just ride behind me," Dad said. "I'll creep along so it won't be dangerous."

Hammer shook his head. "Your husband is going to be pissed, but go ahead."

Dad got on his motorcycle, and I climbed on behind him, holding on tight. True to his word, he went at such a slow pace, it felt like we were barely moving. My grandfather rode ahead. By the time we got to the clubhouse, Thunder stood on the front steps, arms crossed, and a scowl on his face.

"I told you to stay home," he said.

My dad helped me off the bike, and I walked up to Thunder. Tipping my head back, I held his gaze. "I didn't feel safe anymore. If Merlin came after me, what if someone else did?"

He sighed and ran a hand over his hair. "I've wondered the same thing. I don't like the idea of you walking through the clubhouse right now. Lots of smoke, and things you don't want to see."

I wasn't sure what to make of that last part. Did he mean the women? The ones he'd said he might sleep with at some point? He was right. I didn't want to see them, to acknowledge they existed and could pose a threat to my marriage. Even though we'd been intimate now, and I'd asked to be his wife in more than name, could I be absolutely certain he'd never be tempted by them?

Stop doubting yourself, Amity. I gave myself a mental slap.

"Did he say why he did it?" I asked.

"It's club business, Amity. I can't talk to you about it. But if you want Savior to reassure you about your safety here, then come on. Just don't give me shit about what's going on behind these doors."

It sounded ominous, but I gave him a slight nod and followed him inside. I grabbed onto his cut so I wouldn't lose him in the crowd. My eyes went wide as I saw the partially and fully naked women parading around. He hadn't been wrong. Not about the fact I wouldn't want to see what happened behind the doors, nor about the smoke. It burned my nose as we went across the room and down a hall.

Thunder stopped in an open doorway, and I saw several men inside, including Merlin. I tightened my hold on Thunder, not wanting anyone to see how scared I was right then. The thought of facing Merlin terrified me.

"Pres, can I have a minute?" Thunder asked.

"What the hell is wrong now?" Savior asked.

Thunder tugged me from behind him. "She came to the clubhouse to find me. The house doesn't feel safe for her anymore. She doesn't understand why Merlin wanted to hurt her, and she's worried someone else will, too."

Savior sighed and pinched the bridge of his nose. "I now understand why Torch went prematurely gray."

"I'm tired of feeling scared," I said softly. "The town hates me. I don't have any friends, except Portia. I think Kasen, Westlyn, and Harlow might be friends, but it's too new to say. Being here was supposed to give me a layer of protection. Then Merlin dragged me out of my house and left bruises. What if someone else does the same thing? Does the club not want me here?"

Savior glared at Merlin. "Do you see what you've fucking done? That woman has been through hell, then you pull this shit. I can't begin to tell you how pissed I am, for multiple reasons."

Merlin sneered at me. Then his gaze met Thunder's, and he looked almost ashamed. I didn't understand what was happening. Thunder said it was club business. Did it not have anything to do with me? And why did that man look at me with open hatred, yet change the moment he gazed at my husband?

"He made it seem personal, but Thunder said it was club business. Did it not have anything to do with me? Was I just convenient?" I asked. "I want to understand. No, I need to. If my dad hadn't come by and stopped him, what did he plan to do to me?"

Savior leaned back in his seat. "I won't tell you all the details, but I will say this much. One of the club whores wanted Thunder. Guess she thought he'd claim her. She has a hold over Merlin, so he wanted to drive you away."

His words only confused me even more. "So it was just him? No one else wants to hurt me?"

Merlin's head drooped. "I never intended to hurt you. I just wanted you to leave."

Thunder held out my arm and showed off the bruises Merlin had left. "Well, you did hurt her, asshole. And not just physically. She doesn't feel safe in her own home because of you."

The man didn't look up. Maybe he was remorseful, but what if he was acting? Did the men in this room believe him? The President seemed pissed. Would he punish Merlin?

"I just want my son," Merlin whispered.

I gasped. What? The man had a son? What did that have to do with anything? I broke free of Thunder to move closer to Merlin. "Your son?"

"Your girl is too soft," Savior said. "She looks seconds away from forgiving him. Everything she's suffered, and still has a gentle soul. It's a fucking miracle."

They weren't entirely wrong. If I thought Merlin was truly regretful, if it had been a mistake, then I could have forgiven him. But something told me this was all an act. He knew they had caught him. Understood he'd fucked up with Thunder and the other men in this room. Because of that, he wanted them to feel sorry for him, to think he was a puppet on a string. And he may have been. It made me wonder who was the puppeteer.

The man scared me, but if he hadn't acted alone, the person calling the shots worried me even more. He said he only meant to scare me. To make me leave. I'd have never gone willingly. How far would he have gone to ensure I left Thunder? And what did his child have to do with all this?

"Am I safe?" I asked Savior. "The next time someone knocks on the door, do I need to ignore it?"

"By morning, I should have a better picture of what's going on," Savior said. "Go home with

Thunder. I'll get word to him once I know if anyone else is involved. He needs to explain a few things about the club to you. I'd recommend befriending the old ladies sooner rather than later. They'll be able to fill in more gaps in your knowledge, since they've lived this life for a while. The last woman claimed was about four years ago."

"I'll call a few of them tomorrow and see if they'll stop by," Thunder said. "I'm going to assume the party tomorrow is now off."

"Yeah. For now," Savior said.

"Let me know if I can help with anything," Thunder said. "I'm going to leave my bike here tonight. Need to get a club truck to take her home."

"Wait!" I took a breath and gripped Merlin's hair, lifted his head. Before he had a chance to school his features, I'd seen the smirk. I hoped someone else had noticed as well. "Why do you hate me?"

"You'd have to be important for me to hate you." He narrowed his gaze. "Thunder never wanted to settle down. Then you show up, all pathetic and pregnant. Even knowing all those men fucked you, he still kept you. I lost my best friend because of you."

Thunder shook his head. "No, Merlin. You lost me because of your actions. Yes, I've been spending a lot of time with Amity, hoping to ease her into this way of life, and ensure she was safe. I'll get vengeance for the wrongs those men committed, including the man who raised her. But her real father is here, a Prospect for this club, and her grandfather is one of our brothers."

Merlin's brow furrowed and I took a step back. He looked from me to Thunder then back again. "Your grandfather?"

"No one told you?" I asked.

"What the fuck? Who the hell is your grandfather?

The new Prospect, Sam, is your dad, right?"

I nodded. "My dad is Hammer's son. I thought the club had been told."

"They were," Savior said. "Or at least most were. I haven't held Church yet, so it's not been officially announced. We were going to handle that at the party tomorrow. The old officers, and the new ones, all know. The other Prospects know."

"You're patched into this club," Thunder said. "My wife is a Dixie Reaper by blood. So, out of the two of you, who do you think has more of a right to be here?"

Merlin audibly swallowed. "I didn't know."

"And that excuses your behavior?" Savior asked. "She's right to be wary of you. What exactly were your plans for Amity? If Sam hadn't stopped you, what were you going to do to her? It's clear she'd have never left Thunder. Not willingly. How far would you go, Merlin?"

His jaw tensed, and he pressed his lips together. It seemed we weren't going to find out. Not right now. Possibly not ever. I hated the look in Thunder's eyes, and the way Savior looked so betrayed. Merlin may have scared me and physically harmed me, but he'd broken the trust of men who considered him family.

Thunder took my hand and led me back through the clubhouse. I noticed the women eyeing me, and more than one looked hostile. Were these the women he'd mentioned before? The ones he'd said might tempt him to stray before we'd been intimate? I didn't know how I felt about them. The thought of them touching Thunder made me want to yank out their hair. But more than one seemed a bit run down. Haunted. I wondered if this was the only way they could feel special or wanted. For that reason, I didn't blame them for wanting a man like Thunder to claim them. He was beyond amazing.

But he was also mine, and they'd better keep their hands off. I would no longer be the downtrodden woman who wouldn't stand up for herself. Any of them so much as touched him, I'd fight for what was mine.

* * *

Thunder

I knew I should paddle her ass for disobeying and coming to the clubhouse, and yet, I couldn't bring myself to do it. Not only had she faced her fears and stood up to Merlin, but she'd asked some valid questions. Because she hadn't fallen for his act, I'd seen his true face. I didn't know what happened to the man I'd considered my best friend, my brother, but he'd changed. Or he could have always been that rotten, and I'd just missed it. We all had.

All this time, I'd thought he was hiding from Portia. What if he'd worried she'd get too close and see the real him? It gave him a reason to be absent. What had he been doing all those times?

I led Amity into our home and shut the door, twisting the lock. I didn't like the fact I felt it necessary to lock my brothers out of my house, but right now, I wasn't sure who to trust. Clearly the officers, Hammer, and Sam. Other than them? I didn't feel as confident as I did before. For Merlin to be so different from what I'd thought, I couldn't trust my instincts when it came to the others.

"Am I in trouble?" she asked, folding her arms around herself.

"Yes." I needed to stand firm with her. Didn't matter how proud I was that she'd stood up for herself. She'd disobeyed me, and it could have ended badly. If

Merlin had an accomplice somewhere in the compound, they could have gotten their hands on her. Or worse. If Merlin had broken free, he could have hurt her before any of us had a chance to react.

"My grandfather said you'd spank me." She shifted from foot to foot, refusing to meet my gaze.

With another woman, I might have done exactly that. I hoped one day I'd feel like Amity had healed enough for me to treat her as I would anyone else. Well, any other woman I'd claimed.

"I'm not going to spank you," I said. "Do you understand why I'm upset?"

"Because I didn't listen?" she asked, sounding as if she weren't certain.

"Partly. There's a reason I told you to stay here. I didn't know what to expect of Merlin. I have no idea if anyone is working with him, aside from the club whore. You had your father with you. What if Merlin had multiple brothers who felt the same as him? They would have overpowered Sam, and you'd have been gone. I have no idea what Merlin planned to do with you." I moved closer and tucked her hair behind her ear. "It would kill me to lose you, Amity. I'd tear the world apart trying to find you, but what if it was too late? You could suffer the same fate as before, or someone could kill you."

She paled and swayed a little. It made me wonder if she'd ever considered how dangerous this world truly was. Sure, she'd experienced some of the darkness firsthand, and yet, as Savior had said, she remained tender and sweet. She'd reached a low point the day she wanted to jump from the bridge. Since then, she'd blossomed. The Amity I'd brought home would have never come to the clubhouse. I loved the fact she was feeling stronger, more confident. But I also worried it would get her killed.

"You and our child are my world, Amity. I can't bear the thought of anything happening to either of you. When I tell you to do something, it's not because I'm being a high-handed asshole. I'm trying to protect you."

"I'm sorry," she said. "My dad cautioned me to stay put. But my grandfather..."

I groaned. I should have known Hammer had something to do with this. "He egged you on, didn't he? Encouraged you to leave the house."

She shrugged a shoulder. "He wasn't entirely wrong. I don't want to be some weak woman you need to watch over like a baby chick. I want to be strong. Independent. He said Venom's woman wouldn't have sat at home meekly waiting for him to return. What if your club thinks I don't have what it takes to be your woman? Will they ask me to leave?"

"How long have you been worrying about this?" I asked.

"I don't know. A while? My grandfather said I've been hiding, and he's not wrong. I haven't made an effort to go meet people. Do they think I'm a coward?"

I hugged her to me, running my hand down her hair. My beautiful, brave, sweet wife. If I lived to be one hundred, I'd probably never figure her out. It hadn't occurred to me she'd worry about something like that.

"No one thinks that of you," I assured her. "They're eager to meet you, but they've been holding back. They understand the trauma you've suffered and haven't wanted to overwhelm you. The party was their way of welcoming you, but since it's been put on hold..."

I pulled out my phone and called Ridley, putting

the call on speaker.

"Thunder? Is something wrong?" she asked the moment the call connected.

"Not exactly." I wasn't about to tell her what Merlin had done. I'd leave that to Venom. He could decide how much she learned about what happened with the club. "Amity is worried everyone thinks she's a coward for not introducing herself. You're on speaker right now. Would you mind telling her she's wrong?"

"Are you serious? Fuck that. Prepare for company." Ridley disconnected the call, and I smirked. I'd had a feeling she'd react that way. I only hoped Amity was up for the old ladies to descend on our house. Something told me Ridley wouldn't be coming alone.

"What just happened?" she asked.

"I think this is a more fitting punishment than anything I could do," I said.

"What?" She backed up a step.

"I won't be spanking you, Amity. The old ladies will be told the party is canceled tomorrow. You can't tell them why. Not one word about Merlin or what happened here or at the clubhouse. Understood?"

"Is this about the club business thing you mentioned when I showed up?" she asked.

"Yes. You know more than they possibly do. It's up to their husbands to decide what they learn. For all I know, Venom and the others don't have a clue what's going on just yet. That's for Savior to disclose, not us."

"That's my punishment? Being silent?"

"No. Your punishment is getting a full dose of Ridley and the others in your home, where you can't be rude and kick them out." I smiled. "You'll be a gracious hostess, get to know them, and after they've visited for at least an hour, then you may ask them to leave. Or I'll do it if I think they aren't going to budge."

"You make it sound like a rabid pack of hyenas are about to enter the house," she said.

"That's not far off. You'll see. I'll carry in a few chairs from the kitchen, just in case. I'm not sure how many are coming."

Amity started muttering to herself and went to sit on the couch. I knew I was throwing her to the wolves, but it was time. If she didn't want to be seen as weak, didn't want to feel that way, this was the best solution. I knew those women would welcome her with open arms. They also tended to be a little crazy and over the top. Especially Ridley. Her girls might be terrors, but they were a perfect blend of Venom and Ridley.

"It's late, but I'd imagine they'll stay long enough to need drinks and maybe some snacks. Come to the kitchen with me," I said.

She stood and followed, looking a bit dazed. I made sure we had plenty of sweet tea and soda available and put a few bottles of water in the freezer, so they'd get cold faster. We didn't have a ton of snack items in the house, but we put together a bowl of pretzels, some kettle corn, and a package of cookies.

"I wish I'd had more time. This looks pathetic," she said, eying the offerings on the coffee table.

"Honey, they aren't expecting much since they're springing this visit on you. What you've got here is plenty. Do you need to splash some water on your face? Want to change? I'd imagine they'll be here any minute."

She smoothed her hand over her clothes. "I look a mess, don't I?"

I pulled her to me and kissed her soft and slow. "No, you look beautiful, like always. I'm the luckiest bastard on the planet because I get to call you my wife."

"I want to make a good impression."

"They're going to have on their property cuts, and most likely jeans. You don't need to get dressed up," I said.

She worried at her lower lip, and I knew what she was thinking. I hadn't given her cut to her yet. Didn't mean I didn't have it. I'd been waiting for the right moment. Looked like it had arrived. I took her hand and led her into the bedroom. Reaching into the top of the closet, I pulled down a box and handed it to her.

"What's this?" she asked.

"Open it. Before you decide whether you're going to change, see what's inside."

She pulled off the top and carefully reached inside. She pulled out the cut, examining the front and back. I took it from her and eased it over her shoulders. I had to admit, I fucking loved seeing my name across her back.

"Fits perfect," I said, clearing my throat. Or rather it would once she could fasten it. I hadn't realized I'd get a little choked up when I gave her the property cut. I wondered if my other brothers had felt the same way.

"Help me change into something that will make me fit in with the others?" she asked, running her hands over the cut.

"Sure, honey. Let's see what you have." We went through her clothes, and she selected a solid-colored v-neck tee. Granted, it was in lilac, but she looked cute as hell in it, especially with the way it hugged her baby bump. She paired it with her maternity jeans, and I convinced her to go barefoot since she wasn't leaving the house. She braided her hair and washed her face.

"I want you to be proud of me," she said, turning

to face me.

"Hell, Amity. What makes you think I'm not? Do you have any idea how amazing you are? You know what I like most about your property cut?" She shook her head. "It tells the world you belong to me. Maybe you need a reminder?"

She blinked at me. I started to unfasten my belt and watched the pulse in her neck flutter. She licked her lips and backed up a step. Then another. I advanced on her as I tugged down my zipper. Seeing my name on her, knowing she was mine not only in the eyes of the law but the club too? It made me want to beat my chest like a caveman and shout to the world this woman belonged to me body and soul.

Amity let out a little squeak and turned to run, but I caught her around the waist. I spun her to face the bed and worked on her pants, shoving them down her legs.

"Austin, what are you... I mean... you said they'd be here soon, and..."

"Do you know how hot it makes me seeing my name on you like this?" I asked.

She shivered and I saw goose bumps break out across her skin. I worked her panties down, and she stepped out of both them and the pants. Once I had her naked from the waist down, I bent her over the side of the bed. She pushed her ass out, and I damn near came at how perfect she looked. Didn't escape my notice her pussy was nice and slick. Seemed my girl wanted me as much as I wanted her.

I reached between her and the bed, slipping my hand between her legs, and circled her clit. "How badly do you want me?"

"We don't have time," she said, but I heard the lack of conviction in her tone.

"We'll make time. I will *always* have time to make my beautiful wife scream my name. You want to come? Do you need this as much as I do?" I asked.

"Yes! Yes, Austin. Please."

I rubbed her clit a little harder as I lined my cock up with her pussy. I sank into her, giving her body time to adjust. My sexy woman was still tight as a fucking virgin, and while I wasn't huge, I was big enough I could hurt her if I weren't careful.

"That's it, beautiful. Let me in."

Once I'd slid in balls-deep, I pulled back and thrust forward again. On the second stroke, she came, screaming out my name. That was all it took. I knew I couldn't hold back. I gripped her hips and drove into her, fucking her like it would be our last time. I took what I wanted, angling my hips so I'd stroke that special spot inside her.

"Austin!" She gripped the bedding so tight she nearly ripped it off the mattress. Her pussy gushed around my cock, and I felt my balls draw up. I slammed into her again, and again, not stopping until I'd filled her with the last drop of cum.

I kissed her neck and rubbed my beard against her. "You're amazing, Amity. I will tell you that every day for the rest of our lives."

She opened her mouth to respond, and the doorbell sounded. I grinned as I pulled out and watched my cum slide out of her. When she started to head into the bathroom, I stopped her.

"Sorry, honey. You get to meet the old ladies with my cum soaking your panties. I want you to remember you're mine and you belong here."

I helped her back into her clothes and took her by the hand. I led her to the front of the house, then I left her at the door and went to the kitchen. I heard a squeak leave her and smiled. Yeah, I'd tossed her into shark-infested waters, but I had no doubt she'd do just fine. Those ladies wouldn't eat her alive, but they might teach her a few bad habits. Either way, by the end of the night, she'd feel more like she belonged, and she'd have some new friends.

Ridley might be a wild card at times. Hell, most of the time. I also knew she'd take Amity under her wing, make sure my woman learned the ropes, and she'd make her feel at home with the club. And I pitied anyone who tried to stand up against her.

Chapter Nine

Amity

I swallowed my fear and opened the door, wishing Thunder hadn't left me. Seven women stood outside, smiling at me. They bustled past me and into the house, leaving me no choice but to take a step back and let them enter. I shut the door and twisted the lock, which made the first one pause.

"You lock the doors?" she asked.

Another elbowed her. "Shut it, Ridley. Maybe she doesn't feel safe here yet."

So that was Ridley. She didn't look old enough to be Mariah and Farrah's mother. They'd graduated long before I did, but I knew who they were. I also knew they'd moved out of town. Only because the people around here liked to gossip like it was an Olympic sport.

"I'm Amity," I said. "Anyone want something to drink? We have sweet tea, soda, or bottled water. Not sure how cold the water is, though."

"I'm Ridley," the blonde woman said. "The one who thinks I'm being rude is Darian, my stepmother."

I felt my eyes widen, and Ridley snickered. Darian smacked her on the arm.

"You're going to give her a bad impression of us right off," Darian said. "But it's true that her dad claimed me. She's a shit too. Taught her kids to call me Grandma, even though I'm younger than her."

Oh, my. I wasn't sure what to make of these two, but it was clear they were close. I looked at the others, hoping they'd introduce themselves.

"I'm Isabella, Torch's woman." She smiled and waved to the woman standing next to her. "This is Kayla. She's with Preacher, and Saint is her twin brother."

Another woman introduced herself. "I'm Kalani. I'm with Tex."

"I'm Mara. I'm with Rocky."

The woman next to her gave her a nudge. "This one likes to hide in her house, so you may not see much of her. I'm Delphine. Zipper is the club tattoo artist, and he's mine."

Ridley snickered. "You introduce yourself that way all the time? He's yours? Or are you his?"

Delphine rolled her eyes. "We belong to each other. Just like you and Venom. As I recall, someone said you went into Church and laid claim to that man in front of everyone."

Ridley's cheeks flushed, but she got a sappy smile on her face. "Yeah, I did. Best decision I've ever made."

"To answer your question, yes, we'll take drinks, but we can get them ourselves. Just point us to the kitchen," Isabella said.

They followed me and I opened the fridge, then took out the pitcher of sweet tea. I set it on the table and got out some cups. I didn't see Thunder, even though he'd come this way. But the backdoor stood partially open. I figured he'd stepped outside when he heard us coming to the kitchen. The women who wanted soda helped themselves.

"The water is in the freezer. Thunder put it there so it would get cold faster," I said.

Only Delphine got a bottle. I noticed she put the others in the fridge. Once we had our drinks, we went back to the living room and took a seat. I still felt nervous, being with so many people I'd just met. I almost wished Portia had come with her mother, but I understood why she hadn't. While Portia was Torch's daughter, Isabella was his woman.

"So, we've heard a little about you," Ridley said.

"You don't need to go into your past or anything. Portia filled in Isabella, then she told the rest of us. We're here because you're one of us, Amity. Thunder took you as his wife and old lady. That means you're family."

Isabella reached over and put her hand over mine. "From what I hear, the one you were given by birth was pretty shitty. Until you met your real dad and Hammer. You're a Dixie Reaper by blood, Amity. Don't let anyone make you feel like you don't belong here. Understand?"

I wasn't entirely sure I did. Was she implying she knew what happened tonight? I couldn't tell by the look in her eyes, nor from the other ladies. I just nodded and decided to go with it.

"We have your back. All of us. Even the ones who aren't here," Kalani said. "Tex saved me. I'd been locked up in an asylum that didn't care about legalities. They tortured me. Raped me. Not once did he hold my past against me, and neither did these ladies."

"My mother and stepfather wanted to sell me to a man old enough to be my grandfather," Ridley said. "I ran and came to my daddy. Instead, it was Venom who found me at the gate. I grabbed hold and never let go."

"My stepmother kept trying to kill me," Delphine said. "Zipper gave me his protection."

Ridley snorted. "He gave you far more than that."

Delphine narrowed her eyes at the other woman but didn't contradict her.

"My supposed boyfriend tricked me into coming to this town with him." Darian sighed. "He tried to drug me so a party full of guys could do whatever they wanted with me. I ran. Found the Dixie Reapers by accident, and Bull took me in."

"My turn?" Mara asked, looking around. "My mother decided to marry into a bad family. My stepbrother had plans for me. I didn't agree with them. Ended up wrecking my car on a mountain, and Rocky found me. Found out he'd known my father. He decided to keep me."

Kayla smiled. "I'm afraid my story isn't quite as adventurous as theirs. I met Preacher at a club event. That same night, my brother helped me move to another town. Found out later I was pregnant."

"You're leaving part of the story out," Ridley said.

Kayla sighed. "I was nearly raped. My brother's friend saved me, and hauled my ass back here, which is when Preacher found out he'd knocked me up."

"So everyone had some sort of trauma that brought them here?" I asked. "Is that true for the others too?"

"Not sure Katya's past was necessarily traumatic, but she did deal with some shit. She's with Sarge. And Laken…" Isabella trailed off a moment. "She's Flicker's sister and hooked up with Ryker, who now goes by Dice. They had some drama between the two of them, but nothing I'd call traumatic. Not like everyone else."

"Then there's Isabella," Ridley said. "Her daddy pretty much sold her to Torch in exchange for his help with my stepfamily. It worked out, though. They're crazy about each other."

"But everyone else?" I asked.

Ridley nodded. "The rest of us have some fucked-up shit we've dealt with. So you fit right in."

"I can't decide if I should thank you, or be worried about the lot of us," I said.

Ridley threw her head back and laughed. "Be worried. Very worried. I'm sure our men are. Lord knows Venom never knows what to expect from me."

She didn't look the least bit sorry about it either. I

hoped one day I'd have her confidence. Baby steps. Tonight was a good start. And I had to admit, Thunder had been right to call Ridley. I'd needed this, even if I hadn't realized it.

With one visit, these women made me feel welcome. Like I'd always belonged.

Coming home with Thunder had been the best thing I'd ever done. It had not only given me an incredible man I'd fallen in love with, but it had given me a family. A true family. It was the greatest gift I could have ever received.

* * *

Thunder

I met Savior, Tempest, Hammer, Saint, Grim, and Royal at our secret location. Merlin sat in a chair in the center of the room, blood dripping from his mouth and nose. The whore, Sonja, sat beside him. Neither of them had fared well, and I knew they weren't leaving this room. I'd make damn sure of it, even if no one else did.

Flicker entered the room, not even looking at Merlin. "It's done. Wire located the kids. Extracting them will be a bit of fun, but I'm sure you can handle it."

"Thanks, Flicker," Savior said.

"Guess that means these two are no longer useful." Tempest grinned. "You know what that means, Thunder."

Yeah. I knew exactly what it meant. I could have revenge for what these two tried to do to my wife.

"It was all his idea," Sonja said. "I just said to get rid of the bitch. I never told him how to do it."

Didn't surprise me she'd thrown Merlin under the bus. Of course, I'd had a feeling he'd had a particular plan for Amity that had nothing to do with Sonja's orders. For whatever reason, he hated my wife.

"What exactly were you going to do with my wife?" I asked.

"Give her back to her father." He smiled, blood coating his teeth. "He said she had the tightest cunt he'd ever felt. Wanted to take another ride, especially after he heard she wasn't his kid."

I picked up the brass knuckles off the table and slid them on. I landed blow after blow against his ribs, his face, his arms. Anywhere was fair game. I stopped when my chest was heaving with every breath I took, and Merlin looked half dead.

"He'll be sitting where you are soon enough." I spat on Merlin. "You're both pieces of shit and deserve everything you get. I'm disgusted I ever called you my friend or my brother."

"You done with him?" Savior asked.

"Yeah. Have at it, Pres. As long as I have permission to bring Todd Whitman here."

"I have a feeling if I say no, you'll do it, anyway. Can't say that I blame you. Take a few brothers with you. Grab Sarge, Bats, and…"

"Me," Hammer said. "That fucker hurt my granddaughter. I want in on it."

Savior nodded. "All right. Sarge, Bats, and Hammer will go with you. Be careful, and for fuck's sake, don't get caught. Ask Wire to scope out any camera feeds in the area and make sure they suffer a sudden glitch."

"Done," I said.

Hammer followed me out, and I heard Merlin scream like a girl. I knew Savior would make him hurt a while longer before he ended the man's suffering. Or maybe he'd let him bleed out. I didn't give a shit what they did to that bitch, Sonja.

I found our other brothers in the clubhouse having a beer.

"Sarge and Bats. You're coming with us," I called out.

They stood and approached me. Both knew about Merlin and Sonja, as well as what we'd been doing to them. The club knew about the ways those two had fucked up. Every last brother wanted them dead.

My phone rang, and I pulled it from my pocket. *Wire.* "Hello."

"Hold off about thirty minutes. Maybe a little longer," Wire said.

"Why? I want that fucker's blood and I want it now."

"I'm aware. You've waited this long. Just do as I say. Please. I'm going to make this as easy as I can for you. I need a bit of time, though. Go be with your wife, and I'll send a text when everything is in place."

"What the hell, Wire?"

"You'll need the cops to be distracted, right? I'm going to offer up some of the men who hurt your wife. If you want Whitman, then I need to give Daniels something. Let him have some of the others. Evan is already behind bars. He and Whitman were the worst of the lot. You'll get your pound of flesh."

"Fine. I'll go sit with Amity until you say it's time." I hung up, and the others went back to the bar, with Hammer following. If he wasn't going with me, then it meant I had Amity all to myself. "I'll be back as soon as Wire gives us the signal."

I went out to my bike and drove straight home. I knew I had Merlin's blood on me and didn't want any of it touching Amity. Who knew what that fucker might be carrying?

When I got home, I went inside and didn't stop to say anything. I needed to wash the blood off. In the bathroom, I removed my cut and set it on the counter. I quickly stripped out of my clothes and put them in the hamper before I started the shower. Amity appeared in the doorway.

"Is everything okay?" she asked.

"Need to get cleaned up, and I'll be leaving again shortly." I stepped into the shower and shut the door. The water turned pink and ran down the drain as I scrubbed my skin. A slight breeze caught my attention, and I saw my wife joining me. "Amity, I'm covered in blood."

"Then let me help you wash," she said.

She took the shower gel and squirted a generous amount into her hands before spreading it across my shoulders and chest. Her light touch, the gentle scrape of her nails, had my cock hardening.

"You're playing with fire."

She smiled. "Maybe I like it when you burn me."

I cupped her cheek and pressed my lips to hers. "I already bent you over the bed and took you like a damn savage. Now you're tempting me to take you here in the shower. You're my queen, Amity. You deserve better than this."

She traced a pattern on my chest, and it took me a moment to realize what it was. I pressed my hand over hers. My heart thudded against my ribs.

"You love me?" I asked.

"How could I not?"

"Amity." I kissed her long and deep, my tongue stroking hers. She whimpered as I pulled her closer. "I love you too."

"So how can I deserve better than my husband making love to me? I don't care if we're in the shower, or if you bend me over the bed. Because it's you, it makes it special. You're all I need, Austin."

I kissed her again, then backed her against the wall. Lifting her thigh over my hip, I rubbed my cock against her pussy. Thankfully, the water had already rinsed the blood and soap off me. I sank into her as I pressed my lips to hers again.

"I love you, Amity. So fucking much."

"Less talk. More orgasms."

I couldn't hold back my laughter. "You're perfect. Don't ever change. I don't need a badass for a wife. I just need you exactly as you are."

I made sure I rubbed against her clit with every stroke, and it didn't take long for her to claw at my back. I used long, deep strokes, wanting to draw the moment out. I knew we didn't have a lot of time, but I'd make the most of it. I pinched her nipple between my thumb and forefinger, then rolled it. Amity moaned and tipped her head back. I felt her pussy get even hotter.

"That's it, honey. Show me how much you love this."

"So good," she murmured.

"You like that?" She hmm'd, and I did the same to the other side. "Come for me, Amity. Squeeze my cock and show me how much you want my cum."

"Oh, God! Austin…"

"You like it when I talk dirty to you?" She nodded and bit her lip. "I love filling you with cum and not letting you wash it off. Makes me hot knowing you're walking around with my scent on you. A reminder of how much I want you."

She whimpered, and she gave a cry as she came. Looked like my wife was more of a treasure than I'd already known. She liked me saying filthy things during sex, then I'd make sure I did it often.

"Hold on, honey."

She gripped me tighter as I stroked in and out of her. With her pussy clenching me tight, I came inside her. If I hadn't been waiting on a call from Wire, I'd have taken more time with her.

"Since we're in the shower, does that mean I get to wash off before I get out?" she asked.

I smirked. "If I said no?"

She gave a soft growl that sounded cute as fuck. "Seriously?"

"You can wash, Amity. I'm only teasing you." I heard my phone buzzing and knew it was the message I'd been waiting for. "I have to hurry, honey. They're waiting for me, but I'll be home as soon as I can. I want you to stay here, understand? I'm locking the door behind me. Don't let anyone in. Not even your dad."

"What about Grandpa?" she asked.

"He's going with me. Promise me, Amity. I need to know you're safe while I'm gone. All this will be over soon enough. Until then, I need to focus and not worry about you."

She nodded. "I promise. I'll make sure the doors stay locked, and I won't go anywhere. If someone comes by, I'll just yell through the door."

"If they don't go away, call Lavender."

I washed and got out, then pulled on clean clothes. Before I left, I paused to watch my wife as she finished her shower. I was doing this for her, so she'd sleep at night knowing the monsters weren't coming for her ever again.

I locked the back door, then made sure I locked the front one when I left. It was a quick ride to the clubhouse, and my brothers were waiting for me by the gate. We pulled out and went to the coordinates

Wire sent. I trusted him to have cut the feed to any cameras, or make it seem like they were malfunctioning. When we reached the Whitmans' subdivision, I realized the bastard had done better than that. The power was out for more than ten blocks in any direction. I didn't know how Wire planned to stall the company turning it back on, but I knew he'd have something up his sleeve.

"Can't say he doesn't deliver," Bats said.

"Anyone know where the wife is?" I asked.

"You taking her too?" Hammer asked. "Sam might like to have a few words with her."

"Hadn't planned on it, but I wouldn't mind. Maybe Wire can make it look like these two went on vacation and had an accident," I said.

"How exactly are we getting them out of here since we all brought our bikes?" Sarge asked.

Shit. I'd been so hell bent on making this bastard pay. I hadn't thought about how I would get him out of the house. Change of plans.

"All right. Hammer, if Sam wants in on this, call him. Get him here now." I got off my bike and killed the engine, then hid it among some bushes. The others did the same. "We aren't taking them with us. We're finishing this here."

"What?" Bats gripped the back of his neck. "Isn't this a little messy?"

"Power's out in this area. We'll make it look like a break-in. Smash some shit, take the woman's jewelry. Whatever it takes to make it look like a robbery gone wrong." I looked at my brothers. "We can do this."

"I'll let Wire know about the change of plans," Sarge said. "Better to clue him in now, in case he needs to do anything on his end."

I prowled around the mansion, looking for the best

entry point. The rest of the neighborhood couldn't see the back door on the patio. A trellis hid it from view on the sides, and giant flowering trees would obscure us from the back. I motioned for the others to follow. Sarge used his gloved hand to bust out the window. The sound seemed loud in the otherwise quiet evening.

A beam of light scanned the ground beyond the patio, and I knew it came from an upstairs window. It seemed the Whitmans knew we were here. Or they at least suspected someone was on the premises. I hoped like fuck Wire had made sure they couldn't call this in. Cops being busy didn't mean no one was around to respond to a 9-1-1 call. As for any weapons, the family didn't have guns registered to them. Didn't mean they couldn't have bought some under the table. And of course, they could always try to stab us. But people like these thought they were invincible. As awful as they were, they believed themselves to be the big bad wolf. I had news for them. I had more teeth and bit harder.

"Sam is on his way," Hammer said. "Should be here in a minute. I told him where to enter the house."

"And Wire said he's got everything covered, but to be careful," Sarge said.

"Let's do this." I opened the door and stepped inside, careful not to walk through the broken glass. I didn't want to risk leaving any clues behind.

I heard rustling upstairs and wondered what the fuck those two were doing. Never in a million years would anything have prepared me for the sight that greeted us. I wanted to throw up and rip the fucker apart at the same time. It seemed Amity had been right about him bringing young girls here. Wire hadn't been able to locate the one she'd seen before. Unless it was the same girl he had now. Only Wire or Amity would know. The rest of us had never seen her face. As for the room, I didn't see any indication she lived here. No, he'd brought her here to play. If he kept her long-term, he had to hold her elsewhere.

"You son of a bitch," Hammer muttered.

The girl was sprawled across the bed. Tied down and naked. I knew exactly what he'd been doing.

"You make me sick," I said. "I came here to avenge Amity, but it looks like she won't be the only one who sleeps better once you're dead."

"You can't touch me. Don't you know who I am?" he demanded.

"Yeah. You're the piece of shit who raped my wife, this girl, and who knows how many others. And you're the man who's going to die tonight."

Sarge kneeled beside the girl and murmured to her softly. The glazed look in her eyes told me the bastard had at least drugged her before he'd started. I hoped that meant she hadn't been in any pain.

I heard booted steps coming down the hall and shifted so I could see who was passing. Sam gave us a nod and kept hunting for Amity's mother. I hoped he didn't end her life quickly. The bitch deserved to suffer awhile.

"How do you want to handle this?" Bats asked.

"Someone needs to get this girl out of here. Take her to the clubhouse and get the doc to come take a look. No idea if she's missing, or if he bought her." Sarge helped the girl stand, but her legs wouldn't hold her.

She glanced around at us and whimpered, until she saw Hammer. I don't know what made her like the big bastard. On wobbly legs, she approached, then fell into him when she couldn't stay upright.

"Guess I'm taking her out of here," he said. He

didn't sound thrilled, and I knew he wanted a piece of Whitman.

"You're the one she trusts," I said.

He nodded. "I know. Can't understand why, but I'll get her to safety. Make him pay, Thunder. He hurt my granddaughter."

"Oh, he's going to hurt," I promised.

Sarge clapped me on the back. "I'm going to keep an eye on Sam. Let me know if you need anything."

And that left me and Bats with Whitman. The man didn't look the least bit afraid. He also hadn't closed his robe, or gotten soft. What the fuck?

"Can you only get it up for underage girls?" I asked.

A scream came from down the hall, then another. By the third, I knew we were running out of time. There was no way someone hadn't heard that.

"Motherfucking Sam!" I glared at the hallway.

"We need to do this quick," Bats said.

"Hold him." I pulled a knife and approached Whitman. Bats yanked the man's arms behind him and held tight. The way Whitman remained silent either meant the asshole was braver than I gave him credit for, or he didn't believe I'd actually hurt him. Idiot.

"You raped my wife. Then you threw her out of the house. I found her on a bridge, ready to end her life because she thought everyone in this fucking town hated her." I ran the blade of my knife over one of his ears.

"Easy, Thunder. Remember, we want this to look like a robbery. You can't torture the guy no matter how many you want to."

Shit. He was right. I didn't fucking like it, but I couldn't disagree with his assessment. "Fine."

I stabbed Whitman in the gut three times. He

snarled at me after the first one. By the third, his eyes widened and the fucker knew I wasn't playing around. I sliced his throat, ending things far too soon. The devil inside me wanted to make the fucker suffer more. His blood sprayed me and the room, which would leave a fucking void. They'd be able to tell the height and build of whoever killed him, which would narrow their suspect list. Not ideal, but hopefully the chief didn't come knocking at our door. Even if he suspected we might be involved, all we'd have to do was show him the evidence of the sort of monster Whitman truly was. Chief Daniels might uphold the law, but even he wouldn't shed a tear over the death of someone like this man.

"Let's check on Sam. It's quiet," Bats said, letting the body fall to the floor.

We found Sam and Sarge in the master bedroom. I stared at the carnage he'd left behind and decided the man had earned his spot with the club. Whenever it came time to patch him in, I had no problem voting for him. Hell, I'd have done it just because he was my father-in-law.

"Think it's time to wrap up the party. Start breaking shit, and find small items to steal, like jewelry. I'll look for Whitman's wallet and take any cash and the credit cards. Then we need to get the fuck out of here," I said.

"Let's do it." Sam reached for a vase near the door and smashed it on the floor. I pulled out the dresser drawers and dumped stuff out of them, making it look like we'd been searching for valuables. Sarge found the jewelry boxes and pocketed what he could carry.

"Give me a few pieces," I said, holding out my hand. He gave me some and I made sure to leave a trail to the backdoor and onto the patio. By the time we'd finished, I knew it wouldn't be long before the power was on and the cops showed up.

"Let's head home," Sarge said. "I'll let Wire know we're leaving."

We didn't start our bikes until we were a block away, not wanting to cause more noise than necessary. I wasn't sure what Amity would think when I came back covered in blood. Again. At least I could tell her that she would be safe after tonight. Wire had sent the police after the others. There wasn't anyone left to haunt my sweet wife.

The past would be behind us, and now we could focus on each other and the baby. It was time to lay her demons to rest.

Epilogue

Amity

I had a hard time believing it was all over. Even though Thunder came home covered in blood -- twice -- it didn't seem real. He said Merlin wasn't an issue anymore. Same for the Whitmans, and anyone else who'd hurt me. But hearing it wasn't enough. Not even when the news reported the deaths of Todd and Helen Whitman. It seemed the club made it look like a robbery.

"Did you… or my dad…" I couldn't even say the words.

"Did we kill them?" Thunder asked.

"Yeah."

"I took out Whitman with some help from Bats. Sarge and your dad handled your mom. And Hammer…" He stood and opened the door. My grandfather came in with a girl in tow. She clung to him like he was her lifeline. "He saved the girl Whitman had drugged and raped."

I covered my hand with my mouth, tears gathering in my eyes. She didn't look much younger than me, and she'd suffered like I had. It didn't seem right. Why were there monsters in the world? Men like Todd Whitman should have never been born.

"Aura, this is my granddaughter, Amity. That man hurt her too. She's the one I was telling you about," Hammer said.

I went to her and stopped before I reached out to hug her. I remembered how I'd felt when I heard what happened to me. I didn't know if she'd welcome my touch or not. She seemed to feel safe with my grandfather, and I couldn't blame her. He was pretty awesome.

"How old are you?" I asked.

"Sixteen," she said. "You?"

"I'm eighteen now. I was seventeen when he hurt me."

She nodded. "We aren't the only ones."

I didn't like hearing that. Could we find the others? Help them in some way?

"Wire is looking into it," Thunder said, putting his arm around my waist. "We'll track down as many as we can. Make sure they get the help they need. A safe home, if that's what they want."

"Do you have a family looking for you?" I asked.

"No. My junkie mother sold me to that man. He gave her enough to keep her high for weeks." Aura leaned into Hammer. "He said I can stay with him. Will that bother you?"

"No. I understand. He makes you feel safe, and that's important right now."

"I'm going to ask Wire to put through an adoption," Hammer said. "Might be weird for your aunt to be younger than you, and Sam may have a shit fit, but Aura doesn't have anyone. She needs us, Amity."

I hugged my grandpa and gave Aura a smile. "Welcome to the family."

Adoption. It made me wonder what would happen to Merlin's son. Did he really have one? I hadn't seen the child, but the club had kept it rather quiet. It seemed to be one of those things that fell under "club business."

Aura relaxed and smiled back. "I thought you'd tell me to leave."

"No. I'd never turn away someone who'd suffered the way we have. I hope the club will offer refuge to anyone else who needs a home." I looked at Thunder. "If I found my home here, there's no reason others can't."

Aura nodded at my stomach. "Any idea what you're having?"

"A baby," Thunder said with a straight face.

Aura snickered. "I figured as much. I meant, is it a boy or girl?"

"We don't know yet, but I think we'll find out soon," I said. "Would you want to help with the nursery? We haven't set it up yet."

"Are you sure?" Aura asked.

"Of course. Like I said, we're family now." I reached for her hand, and when she didn't resist, I led her to what would be the baby's room. "I want to paint the walls after we find out if it's a boy or girl. But I want to go ahead and get the furniture, and maybe some toys."

"I'd love to help."

"I still get input, right?" Thunder asked. "Seeing as how it's my child too."

"You know I wouldn't leave you out." I smiled at him. "I fully expect you to go to every appointment with me and hold my hand when I give birth. I want you there for every moment of this pregnancy, and all the firsts our baby has."

"You better." He winked.

I lowered my voice so the others wouldn't hear my question to Aura. "How are you really?"

"A basket case," she said. "But I'm trying to be strong, you know? I don't remember much of what happened. He drugged me. I know it happened. They caught him in the act. Doesn't seem real, though. Like it happened to someone else."

"The club knows a counselor who's helped some of the other women here. I haven't had the courage to see him yet. I'm sure someone would set up an appointment if you want to talk to him, though. I've heard he's really nice. And gay."

"I'll think about it," she murmured.

"I'm sorry that happened to you, but I'm glad they brought you here. I think you'll love living with the Dixie Reapers. I know I do." I bumped her shoulder. "Who knows? One day, maybe you'll be married to someone here."

She shook her head. "I don't know that I'll ever want that. For now, I just want to forget everything that happened."

"You aren't alone, Aura. Not anymore." I looked over my shoulder and saw Thunder and my grandfather in the doorway. She wasn't the only one. Something horrific happened to both of us, but we'd found a family in the end. People who accepted us. Would love us. "I hope one day you find someone who loves you the way Thunder loves me. He's everything to me. The day he found me was the worst and best day of my life. The worst because I'd given up. And the best because this kind, sweet, incredible man found me and brought me home."

Thunder came closer and pulled me in for a hug. "I love you, Amity. You and our baby."

"We love you too."

"To think I went from being single and going to prison, to coming back to my brothers, reconnecting with my son, finding out I had a granddaughter, and now I have a second chance at being a dad." Hammer smiled. "I think the gods are smiling down on our family."

"Couldn't have said it better," Thunder said. "I didn't think I ever wanted a woman in my life. Not after I'd fucked up so bad as a teenager. It never occurred to me what I needed was the *right* woman."

"All of you are too sappy," Aura said.

"No. We're happy," I said. "And one day you will be too. I guarantee it."

I didn't miss the haunted look in her eyes, or the way she twisted her fingers together. I saw the pain. The worry. I understood all her emotions and knew it would take time for her to heal. With the Dixie Reapers in her corner, and my grandfather adopting her, I knew she'd be okay.

Thunder tipped up my chin and kissed me. "The monsters have been dealt with. I won't say we won't have problems in the future. We very well may. But I promise you lots of laughter, smiles, and happy memories. With every day we're together, I'll replace the bad ones."

I cupped his cheek. "You've already been doing that. And I love you for it."

He leaned in closer, placing his lips by my ear. "After this baby, how many more do you want? Because I think we need at least one more. Maybe two."

I pulled up to look at him. "Really?"

He nodded. "Yeah. Nice big family so our kids can look out for one another. Maybe have them somewhat close together?"

"Let's see if I survive this first one." I cuddled into his side. "But I'm not saying no."

My husband hugged me tight, and it felt like everything was right in my world.

The club might be scary to some. To me, they were angels. They loved fiercely, protected those they considered family, and would help Aura heal just like they had helped me.

I hadn't just found my home here. I'd found my family, my friends, and the place where I belonged.

Savior (Dixie Reapers MC 16)
A Dixie Reapers Bad Boys Romance
Harley Wylde

Dessa -- I've always known Sonja, my foster sister, thrives on chaos. It never occurred to me she'd go so far as to buy children, then use them as leverage against a club of bikers. When armed men burst through the door, I'm terrified. Not only of them, but of losing little Junie and Judd. Those kids mean everything to me, but they're not really mine. I know I can't keep them. And when the bikers walk out with the children, I don't even try to stop them. Without Sonja and the kids, I'm alone. The darkness I've held at bay starts to close in on me, and I have to wonder... how much longer before I join my family on the other side?

Savior -- I only wanted my daughter. When I find her, I didn't count on a sweet angel keeping watch. I should walk away. But Dessa's loved my little girl as if she were her own. I feel like a monster taking Junie from Dessa. There's a sadness in her eyes. It tugs at me, makes me want to protect her. So I give in to my instincts, and I take Dessa with me. I didn't count on falling under her spell. She's wrapped me around her finger, and I'm not sure I really mind.

Prologue

Savior
Three Months Ago

"I'm going to ask you again, Sonja. Where the fuck is my kid?"

She grinned, blood covering her teeth. What was left of them. The boys had worked her over already, and I'd had my turn. I didn't know why the fuck she hadn't broken yet. I'd seen men four times her size bawl like a baby by now. The bitch was psychotic.

"I'll never tell."

I hated torturing women. Even club whores like this one. She'd overstepped. Not only did I have a daughter I'd never known about, but she'd thought to use my child as leverage to get what she wanted. I couldn't let it stand. Thunder had taken his pound of flesh. All this started because the stupid bitch wanted Thunder for herself. He'd never once looked at her as anything other than a club whore. Never would have either, even if he hadn't married Amity.

The fact Sonja had pushed Merlin to help her, and he'd then tried to drag Amity from the house, had sealed her fate. At least where Thunder was concerned. For me, she'd done that the moment she bought my kid from another woman.

Merlin might have claimed he'd done everything as a way to save his kid, but I wasn't sure I believed him. He'd shown no true remorse over the way he'd treated Amity. If anything, I thought he'd been jealous of the time Thunder had spent with his new wife, and Merlin had decided to use the children and Sonja as an excuse to get rid of her. Since the fucker was buried six feet under, we'd never know for sure.

"Anything new?" I asked, looking over at Wire.

He'd been working on this nonstop ever since we

discovered the kids. And yet, we weren't any closer to bringing them home. Clearly, Sonja had someone else helping her. We'd already checked her place here in town. Other than roaches, drugs, and empty alcohol bottles, we hadn't found anything. Even a stupid cunt like her wouldn't leave small children unattended. As often as she came here to party, it meant someone else had the kids. But who?

He shook his head. "If she's got a place where she's stashed the kids, it's under a different name."

"So look into her family. Even a bitch like her had to have come from somewhere."

The smile slipped from her face, and I knew I was onto something. I didn't know anything about Sonja. Were her parents alive? Did she have siblings or cousins who might help her hide the kids? If Wire had already checked those angles, I wasn't aware of it. I knew he'd vetted the women who came here. Dug into their backgrounds. Made sure he didn't find incriminating texts or messages from any of their electronic devices. He'd watched their social media accounts.

How had Sonja slipped past us all? The woman was short a few screws. To hear Thunder tell it, he'd worried about Veronica latching onto him. Something about her wanting more than he'd been willing to give. Yet, it had been Sonja who tried to lure him in by any means necessary. He was a good kid, and he'd treated the women well. I could understand why they'd want to keep him. Didn't mean it would ever happen. Even if he were single right now, he wouldn't have claimed a club whore.

"She should have broken by now," Tempest said.

"If I can't have what I want, you can't have what *you* want," Sonja said.

"Thunder is married, you crazy whore," Tempest said.

It didn't matter. I knew her type. She wouldn't stop until she had what she wanted, or until we put her in the ground. It was only a matter of time. She wasn't walking out of here. Bitch had to know it. Maybe that was the problem. She had nothing left to lose.

"No family that I could find," Wire said. "But Sonja was adopted. Maybe I can track her foster siblings and parents. This might take a while."

"Do it. I'll keep working on her. Maybe we can still break her," I said.

Wire gave a nod and walked out, carrying his laptop with him. I faced Sonja, ignoring the sneer on her face. I was running out of options. We'd knocked out some of her teeth. Burned her. Cut off hunks of her hair. Sliced her up. The woman had bruises from the top of her head to the tips of her toes. Yet she still refused to tell me where the kids were.

"Foster families. Tell me about them. And remember, the longer it takes Wire to find my kid, the worse things will be for you." I walked over to the table and picked up a small knife. She eyed the blade and tried to hide her fear. Didn't work. I could see right through her. We'd tied her hands and feet to the chair, which made my next step easy enough.

"You son of a bitch!" she screamed as I removed one of her fingernails. She ranted and raved as I took off another one. By the third, she couldn't hold back her tears. My stomach twisted as I looked at her bloody fingers. I hated this fucking shit.

"Where's my daughter, Sonja? Let's end this now. Do you really want to keep suffering? Because it's only going to get worse."

"I won't tell you," she said, pressing her lips

together in a tight line.

"Fine." I made shallow cuts along her arms, shoulders, and the tops of her breasts. Her blood flowed, and tears streaked her cheeks. She still wouldn't give up the location. We'd been at this for days now. I didn't know how she'd managed to hold out for so long.

I should have known she'd never tell us what we needed to know. Instead, I watched as she slowly bled out from her various wounds. No closer to finding my daughter, or Merlin's son. I wouldn't rest until those kids were home, where they belonged. Whatever it took, we'd find them. When I'd realized she wouldn't give in, I'd ended it. No point listening to her plead and cry. It wouldn't change anything, and everything she'd done, I wasn't about to let her live.

Tempest folded his arms and stared at the carnage in front of us. "What do you want me to do with her?"

"I don't care. Make her disappear. Burn her. Feed her to some pigs. Bury her. What the fuck ever you think will work best."

I cleaned off my hands and left the room. I might not know where my biological child was right now, but I did have another daughter waiting for me. One I'd adopted. Ares might be mostly grown up, but she still needed me. And so did this club. I couldn't wallow in agony, wondering if my other kid was even still alive. I'd have to hold on to the hope that I'd find her one day. Until I found evidence she was gone for good. Only then would I stop searching.

I walked in my door and Ares shut off the TV, watching me expectantly. "Any luck?"

I shook my head. "Wire is going to look into something. We think she's got them in a house under someone else's name. Maybe someone she knew in the foster system. It's all we've got right now."

"You'll find her," Ares said. "And when you do, she's going to be the luckiest little girl because you're an amazing dad. I should know."

I smiled and shook my head. "Wish I could take credit for you, but you were already incredible. I'm just along for the ride, and to make sure you get to be a teenager before you have to finish growing up. After everything you went through, you've earned it."

"When you do find her…" Ares dropped her gaze. I knew what she would say. We'd already had this discussion a few times.

"Ares, you're my daughter, even if we aren't related by blood. I'm not throwing you out. There's enough room here for you to keep your bedroom, and for your little sister to have one of her own. Besides, I'll need your help. I have no fucking clue what to do with a little girl."

She flashed me a smile. "All right. I can do the big sister thing."

I nodded. "Good. I'm going to take a shower, then I'll make dinner for us."

I knew once my other daughter came home, Ares would feel like she didn't belong. I'd have to make sure she knew I still loved her. I may not have been her sperm donor, but that girl had my heart. She was tough as nails, and I knew she'd take the world by storm when the time came.

Chapter One

Dessa

I didn't know where my sister had found the children, but little Junie and Judd were the sweetest kids. They weren't hers. No matter what she implied, I knew she'd never been pregnant. Not to mention, she didn't have a maternal bone in her body. Of course, I'd seen plenty of parents who didn't have what it took to take care of children. Which was why I'd ended up in foster care, along with Sonja.

It bothered me, not knowing where the children came from. Did they have parents searching for them? Had Sonja stolen them to try and give them a better life? I had too many questions, and she never offered any answers. Not that I'd seen her lately. She usually stopped by every other week with some cash and would buy groceries. Until the day she'd walked out and not returned. Had she grown bored with the kids? It wouldn't have surprised me.

I rolled my chair forward and scooped Junie onto my lap. She giggled and clapped her hands, always enjoying a ride. To her, it was a game. For me… Well, it was a reminder of the life I'd never get to have. Jeremy had made it clear no one would want a woman like me for a wife. The accident hadn't been my fault. He'd walked away, and I hadn't. Thanks to the drunk driver, and nerve damage, I'd never walk again.

I could have wallowed in self-pity, or let depression drag me down. It had been close for a while. Once Jeremy dumped me, I'd spiraled. I'd barely been existing when Sonja found me. She'd asked for my help, even though she hadn't explained what she needed. I'd agreed, as long as it wasn't illegal. She'd smirked and said I'd be fine. Then she'd vanished again, only to show up about five months ago with two kids in tow.

The first two months after the accident had been rough. Adjusting to life in a wheelchair hadn't been easy. Hell, most days I still struggled. I wondered if I always would.

"How's my sweet girl today?" I asked, kissing her cheek.

I glanced at the kitchen and knew I'd have to order supplies soon. The money Sonja had left was long gone. She should have returned months ago. Part of me worried she'd forgotten about us. Or worse, she'd gotten into trouble. Being unable to drive made life a little difficult at times. Even if I'd had a car, I wasn't sure how I'd manage. I hadn't had insurance when the accident happened. If the drunk driver hadn't covered my medical expenses, I'd have never gotten my wheelchair. The damn things cost entirely too much.

Thankfully, there were apps for nearly everything these days. I could have groceries delivered, as long as I had money. Maybe someday I could afford a car and figure out how to drive without the use of my legs. It just wouldn't happen anytime soon.

Chasing the little ones didn't give me much time for work, and my job barely covered our expenses. If Sonja didn't return soon, we'd be in trouble. I had enough for some groceries, as long as I bought cheap things like macaroni or spaghetti. I knew the kids needed healthier options, but it was better to feed them than to make them starve.

Judd held his arms up, and I lifted him onto my lap as well. They both curled against me, and I knew they were ready for a nap. Wheeling us into the living room, I picked up their favorite book off the coffee table. We'd read *Goodnight Moon* so many times, I had it memorized. And yet, the kids wanted to listen to it every day. Sometimes more than once.

We were on page four when someone pounded on the door. I clutched the children to me and stared, too scared to open it. It rattled on the hinges, and I knew it had to be a man on the other side. I'd never met a woman with that much force behind their fist. Didn't mean there weren't any. I'd just never known any.

"Who's there?" I called out.

"You have to the count of three to open this damn door or I'm breaking it down," a deep voice said from the other side.

My heart leaped into my throat, and I started backing my chair toward the hall. I knew if they really wanted in, there wasn't any way I could stop them. The way he beat on the door made me fear not only for my life, but the lives of the children. When he made it into the house, we'd be helpless.

I whispered to the kids, hoping they'd listen. "I need you both to go hide. Don't come out unless I call you. Understand?"

Junie blinked at me and didn't say anything. Judd stared and refused to move. I whimpered, not wanting anything bad to happen to them. Stuck in my chair, I knew I wouldn't be able to fight off whoever was trying to break in.

"Lady, you let me in or I swear to Christ it won't be pretty when I get my hands on you."

I backed up even more. The door nearly exploded off the hinges as a group of large men came barreling into the house. I screamed, and the children started crying. I held them tight, hoping to soothe them, but I was just as terrified. What did these men want?

"Please, we don't have anything valuable. Take whatever you want. Just don't hurt us," I begged. More men came into the house, and the breath in my lungs froze when I recognized one of them. "Johnny?"

He blinked, and his eyebrows lifted. "Dessa?"

"What's going on?" Some of my tension eased. It had been a long time since I'd last seen him, but unless he'd drastically changed, I knew he wouldn't hurt us. Hopefully, that meant the other men wouldn't either.

"I go by Saint now," he said, coming farther into the house. "I think the better question is why are *you* here and with those two kids?"

"You seem surprised to see her. No one mentioned who was keeping the kids?" one of the others asked. "Maybe we should be asking how the two of you know each other?"

The man's words set me on edge. Something bad was going on. Clearly, the door being knocked off the hinges had been a big clue, but they'd come here for the children, and Johnny was with them. *Sonja, what were you thinking?*

"Oh, God." I looked down at the sweet babies in my arms. "What did she do? I knew they weren't hers. I knew it, but I…"

One of them walked over and hunkered down in front of my chair. His gaze latched onto Junie and a softness entered his eyes. The more I studied the man, the more I began to see similarities between him and Junie. Was this her father? Had I unknowingly kept the two apart? What about Judd?

All this time, Sonja had lied to me. In my gut, I'd known it. Still, I'd hoped the children hadn't been taken from their parents. I couldn't think of anything worse than having a loving family and being ripped away from them. How could she have done that? And even worse, she'd made me be a part of it. I'd kept these sweet babies from their daddy.

"How do you know Saint?" the man asked, not

even bothering to look at me.

"My ex-fiancé is a friend of his," I said.

I saw Saint wince and look away. I hadn't spoken to Jeremy in a long time. For all I knew, Saint hadn't kept in touch with him. I certainly hadn't kept up with Saint. But then, he and Jeremy had been close. I'd only tagged along because I'd been engaged to Jeremy.

"You're Sonja's foster sister," the man said, finally lifting his gaze to mine. I stared, dumbstruck by how handsome he was, and couldn't manage to do more than nod. He didn't say anything, and I realized he wanted a verbal answer.

"Y-yes," I said.

"You expect me to believe you had no idea these kids weren't hers?" he asked.

"I didn't think it was likely, but she denied they didn't belong to her. She set us up in this rental, then she'd disappear for a while. Sonja only came back to check on us and leave some money. Then she'd disappear again."

My stomach knotted. The fact they were here, and Sonja wasn't, made me think she'd never return. Had they hurt her? And why had she tried to keep the children from their dad? I didn't understand any of it. When we'd been in foster care together, we'd often talked about our families, and how much we wished we had a dad or mom who'd wanted us. So why did she take Junie and Judd from people who clearly cared about them?

"You didn't find it strange she didn't come back for several months?" the man asked.

"It worried me, but it wasn't like I could leave and go look for her."

His gaze dropped to my legs, and I felt my cheeks burn. I'd gotten used to the stares and questions since the accident. Except he didn't ask why I was in the wheelchair.

"You know you can't keep the kids," Saint said. "They're coming with us. The little girl belongs to our President. He's the one kneeling in front of you. The boy belongs to a brother who is no longer with us, but someone will take him in. They aren't yours, Dessa."

Little Junie whimpered, and Judd leaned into me. I heard a soft *Momma* before he buried his face against me. I knew their President heard it too, from his sharp inhale and the way his gaze jerked to mine.

"I didn't tell them to call me that," I assured him.

"Someone get their things," the man said, then stood. He reached down and plucked Junie from my lap, cradling her against his broad chest. She stiffened a moment, and I worried she'd pitch a fit. But after a moment, she laid her head on his chest and closed her eyes.

"I'll go to their room and pack their clothes," I said, my throat feeling tight and raw. My eyes burned, and I knew I was close to crying. Someone came to take Judd from me, and I turned my chair and wheeled it down the hall to their bedroom.

As I shoved their things into a duffle bag, I let the tears fall.

Sonja was gone now. With Junie and Judd leaving with the men, I'd be alone. Trapped. What would happen when I couldn't pay the rent? Even if I got an eviction notice, it wasn't like I could leave on my own. I didn't have transportation, other than the wheelchair.

I swiped the tears off my cheeks as I finished packing the children's clothes. Then I started on the few books they had, and their toys. I set the bags into the hall, then wheeled myself farther into the house and into my room. It was cowardly to hide, but I couldn't stand the thought of telling those sweet babies goodbye. I already felt like someone had ripped out my heart.

"Dessa, want me to call Jeremy?" Saint asked from the doorway.

I gave a humorless laugh. Right. As if Jeremy would give a crap about me. He hadn't in a long time, and I didn't think he'd start now. "There's no one to call. Just go. Take the kids and..."

I bit my lip so hard I tasted blood. I heard him walk away, and I let myself break. I cried so hard my throat ached and my nose ran. It wasn't that I hadn't been alone before. I had. But when Sonja brought those small children to me, I'd felt hope for the first time in so long. Now those men were taking them away, and I'd never see them again. Any chance I had at having a family had just been yanked out from under me.

Someone spun my chair around and I screamed, gripping the armrests. My eyes went wide as I stared up at the scariest man I'd ever met. His jaw tightened and his nose flared as he stared me down.

"You can cut the shit. You might have the others fooled, but you couldn't have been stupid enough to not realize those kids didn't belong here. You didn't care, though, did you? They made you feel important. You come after them, and I'll make you regret it."

I shook so hard, I worried I'd vibrate out of my chair. My bladder felt like it might release at any moment, and I hoped it wouldn't. The man terrified me, but I didn't want him to know it.

"I'm stuck in this chair. Even if I weren't, I'd never try to take them from their father," I said.

He gripped my chin so hard it hurt. "Sonja was a fucking bitch. For your sake, I hope you're different. If you aren't, I'm happy to bury you right beside her."

I whimpered and tried to wheel my chair away from him, but I couldn't. He snarled and got in my face. *Oh, God!* He'd killed her! Did Saint know? Had he been part of it? I'd felt safer when he came into the house. Now I wondered if he was every bit as monstrous as this man.

"Tempest," someone shouted.

"Coming." He released me and walked off, pausing in the doorway. "I meant what I said. Don't come looking for those kids. Stay the fuck away from them. Because if you don't, I'll make you sorry you were ever born."

Too late. Someone already beat you to it. I already regretted it every day. Ever since Jeremy walked out on me, ended our engagement, and said he couldn't be with a broken woman, I'd struggled to keep living. Before I'd met him, my life had been miserable. No one had ever given me a second look. Until the day Jeremy asked me on a date, I'd never had a boyfriend. He'd been my first date. My first kiss.

Sonja was gone. The children too.

Would anyone miss me if I disappeared? If that man did come back, and he buried me next to Sonja, how long before anyone realized I was gone? Would they ever? The landlord wouldn't care. He'd just think I skipped out on rent. I couldn't think of a single friend, and I didn't have family anymore.

I was alone. Again.

And this time, I wasn't sure I'd make it back into the light. I felt the darkness pulling at me, trying to drag me under.

I stared at the floor long after the men left. My appetite had fled, and I couldn't bring myself to go watch TV. I hadn't even checked the door since they'd broken in.

None of it mattered.

I looked at the bed and wheeled myself over to it. I locked my chair into place, then started the process of dragging myself onto the mattress. Nothing was quick or easy anymore. Something as simple as rolling over in bed now took several minutes. Curling around my pillow, I fought the monsters inside my head. The voices whispered to me, no matter how hard I tried to ignore them. *You're worthless. Stupid. No one wants you. You should give up.*

I'd heard them all before. Would this be the time they won? Or could I claw my way back again?

Did I even want to?

Chapter Two

Savior

Something felt off. For one, both kids had been screaming since we walked out of the house. Judd kept asking for his mom, which I assumed meant Dessa. And second... I wanted to hate that woman. She'd kept my daughter from me, but she claimed she hadn't known. As fucked up as Sonja had been, it was possible she'd lied to her foster sister. What if Dessa was just as much a victim in all this as I'd been?

Tempest had laid into Dessa. Any other time, I'd have pulled him back. I'd heard it all and had decided not to intervene. I'd noticed the way Saint shifted uncomfortably, which meant he knew something the rest of us didn't. He'd known who she was and seemed surprised to find her there. Where had they met? What was she to him?

We pulled off the highway to fill up the tank, and I wanted to grab some snacks for the kids. The more upset they became, the more I wished we'd thought about bringing an old lady with us. Any of them would have known what to do in this situation. Saint had kids, and so did a few others. I'd jumped into fatherhood with a teenager, so I didn't know shit about small children.

While someone pumped gas, I got out to stretch my legs and go into the convenience store. I grabbed two bottles of white milk and perused the snacks for something that seemed appropriate for toddlers. Wraith had tagged along for the trip and rolled his eyes at me when he realized my dilemma.

"Here," he said, pulling down two packages of animal crackers.

I grabbed a soda for myself, then went to pay. While I waited, I wondered if we'd done the right thing. Sure, the kids belonged to the club. But Dessa had seemed devastated over the loss of the children. She lived too far from the compound for us to offer visitation. Assuming she was truly innocent in all this.

I'd heard Tempest laying into her and knew I should have stopped him. I didn't know what crawled up his ass, but I'd have to figure it out sooner or later. I couldn't have him going off half-cocked again. I knew he took his new role as Sergeant-at-Arms seriously. However, threatening a woman was going too far, especially when she claimed to be innocent.

The children adored her. That much was clear. I still didn't know where I'd put Judd when we got home. I'd already fixed a room at my house for Junie. Since Merlin was no longer breathing, and I had no fucking idea where Judd's whore of a mother had gotten to, it left me with a problem. No one had come forward and asked to take him in. As the President, maybe I should do it. He and Junie had lived together for at least three or four months, maybe longer. After separating them both from Dessa, how much trauma would they suffer if they had to live apart from one another?

I stepped outside and motioned to Saint, who remained on his bike not too far away. He walked over, and I noticed he scanned the lot along the way. It was a habit most of us had, always aware of our surroundings. As a kid, he'd had to grow up too fast. Since joining the Dixie Reapers, he'd been through a lot of shit, and I trusted him. Not only to have my back, but to be truthful.

"What is it, Pres?" Saint asked.

"The woman. Dessa. How do you know her?"

He rubbed the back of his neck. "We weren't close or anything. Remember my friend who helped Kayla?"

I nodded. I didn't remember much, but I did recall some guy not only saving Kayla from a rogue Prospect, but he'd also brought her home. Which was when Preacher found out he'd knocked her up, and he'd decided to claim her. Seemed like forever ago. Now their twins were all grown up and living their own lives. Shit. Made me feel old.

"Jeremy came back here once he'd handed over Kayla. He's never dated anyone seriously. Until Dessa. One day, I came up to visit and found out they were engaged. She knows me as Johnny because that's what Jeremy still calls me. I let it slide since we've known each other so long. I hung out with them a few times. She seemed sweet." He cleared his throat. "A drunk driver hit them one night. It totaled Jeremy's car, but he walked away with only bumps and bruises. Dessa's legs were pinned under the dashboard. She has nerve damage, which means she has some feeling in her legs, but she can't walk."

"What aren't you telling me?" I asked.

"Jeremy couldn't handle it. Still can't. Every time he sees her, he feels guilty. Even though it wasn't his fault, he blames himself. A few days after the accident, he broke their engagement. Walked away and never looked back. That was about ten months ago, I think. I lost touch with her. We hadn't really been friends. Only acquaintances through Jeremy. I didn't realize she knew Sonja."

Saint looked away, and I saw the worry in his eyes. He may not have been friends with Dessa, but he clearly didn't like leaving her alone. I'd heard him offer to call Jeremy. She'd refused. If she couldn't walk, and there wasn't a car parked in the driveway, how did she get the things she needed? Did she work? Had Sonja been providing for her and the kids? Even if Sonja stopped by now and then, how did she manage the rest of the time? I knew Sonja wasn't rolling in cash. I'd seen the beater she drove, and noticed her clothes and shoes were far from new. Not that I'd ever gone there. Not once had I touched her intimately.

My stomach knotted at the thought of leaving her without a way to take care of herself. I knew being in a wheelchair didn't make her useless. But if it had really only been ten months, I had a feeling she was still adjusting to the hand life had dealt her. How many things had she had to relearn?

I gave myself a mental slap. None of my concern. I had my daughter, and Merlin's son. That's all that mattered.

"Pres," Wraith said, stepping up beside me. "Think Tempest is trying to get your attention. Something seems to be wrong with the kids."

I glanced over and saw him looking a little green as he waved at me. I wondered what the hell could go wrong this early on the trip and strode over to the truck to see what was going on. The moment I opened the back door, the smell hit me.

"What the hell?" I covered my nose with my shirtsleeve.

"Merlin's kid cried and screamed so much he puked everywhere."

"I guess that's a no to the milk, then," I said. "Someone go back inside and see if they have a roll of paper towels. If not that, then maybe some shop rags. And plastic bags."

"I want Momma." Judd whimpered. A tear slid down his cheek. "Where's Momma?"

Shit. I felt like an asshole. "That woman wasn't your mother, Judd."

He started crying harder, then the retching began

again. At this rate, the kid couldn't have anything left in his stomach. I'd only thought to get the kids and take them home. It never occurred to me they'd bond with whoever had been taking care of them. Of course, I hadn't expected someone like Dessa either. When we'd burst into the house, she'd asked us not to hurt them. Not once had she offered up the kids in order to save herself. She'd held them as if she wanted to protect them.

"We're not going back for that bitch, are we?" Tempest asked. "She kept the kids from us."

"She didn't know," Saint said. "I believe her. The Dessa I knew would have never done something like that. Not willingly. Sonja used her the same as she used Merlin and the kids' mothers."

"You think because she's a fucking cripple that she couldn't have been in on it?" Tempest asked.

I fisted my hand and ground my teeth together. I didn't know where all the animosity was coming from. Tempest had a short fuse, hence his name, but this was fucking ridiculous.

"Don't call her that," Saint said. "You have no idea what she's been through. Her fiancé walked out on her because of that chair. Now her foster sister is gone, and we took these kids from her. We left her with nothing."

Fuck. Fuck, fuck, fuck. Saint was right. "I'm going back," I said.

"Fine. But we need to get the kids back to the compound and settled. You want to go back for that woman afterward that's on you." Tempest walked off, and I knew I'd need to have a few words with him later. Something was wrong. In all the years I'd known him, not once had he acted like this, especially when it came to a woman. Club whores didn't count. They tended to be manipulative and calculating. Dessa hadn't seemed to be like that.

He wasn't wrong about taking the kids home. I'd leave them with Ares, then head back for Dessa. They didn't need to be in the truck longer than necessary, but if I didn't talk to them first, the next hour would be miserable.

Someone handed me a sack. I peered inside and saw baby wipes, a small roll of trash bags, and paper towels. I handed off the snacks to Saint, then got to work cleaning the back seat. Sure, I was the President and could make someone else clean it up, but the kids were mine. *Fuck.* It looked like I'd not only gained a second daughter, but now I had a son too. With some luck, he wouldn't inherit his parents' traits. "I'm going to go back to get Dessa, all right?" I looked from one to the other.

"Momma?" Judd asked.

I nodded. "Yes. I'm going to go back for your mother, but not until after I get the two of you home. I didn't plan for two of you, so we'll figure out rooms for everyone tomorrow. For tonight, the two of you can share Junie's room."

"Who's Ares?" Judd asked.

Had I mentioned her? I couldn't remember. Maybe he'd overhead me talking to one of my brothers. "My daughter. She's in high school, and she'll help you get settled into your new home."

"Sister?" Judd asked.

I nodded. "Yes, Ares is your sister. Big sister."

Junie hadn't said a word since we'd left the house. I worried about her. For a two-year-old, she seemed far too quiet. I didn't know if she'd talked more with Dessa, or if she was always like this. *My kid.* She was a stranger to me, but I wanted to get to know her.

I finished cleaning up Judd and the back seat, then

threw the trash away. I also tossed the milk, not wanting to take a chance on making the kid sick again. By the time we got home, the drinks would have been too warm. After the way Judd threw up all over the car and himself, I wasn't about to give it to him now. "Let's get back on the road. The sooner I get you home, the faster I can go back for Dessa. All right?"

Judd nodded and seemed to settle down. He didn't act the way the three-year- olds at the compound did. I wondered what he'd experienced in his short life. The fact his mother sold him to Sonja gave me a few ideas. From now on, these two would get to be kids. They'd play, make friends, and when they were old enough, they'd go to school.

I got back in the truck, and we hit the road again. By the time we got to the compound, both kids were asleep, and I wasn't looking forward to another four hours on the road. Two to get back to Dessa, and another two home again. But I'd told Judd I'd go back for her, and I'd keep my word to him.

Ares came out when we pulled in. She didn't rush over but let us go to her. I didn't know if that was because she worried she'd be replaced, or it was concern for the kids. I'd already told her she had a home with me forever. Finding out I had a daughter hadn't changed anything. Well, not as it pertained to her anyway. "Ares, come meet your brother and sister."

Her eyebrows went up. "Brother?"

I nodded. "Judd and Junie."

She came down the steps and approached the truck, curiosity blazing in her eyes. She peeked into the back seat, and I saw a soft smile curve her lips as she stared at the kids. She reached in and unbuckled Junie, bringing her into her arms. Saint stood on the other side of the truck and got Judd out. I led the way into the house and wondered about sleeping arrangements. I didn't think both kids would fit in one bed. Or maybe they'd shared at the other house. I hadn't gone into their room.

I carried their bags into Junie's room and set them down, then flicked on the light. Not having thought about Judd living here, there wasn't much he'd probably enjoy playing with. I'd have to fix that tomorrow. I wanted him to feel at home here.

"Tomorrow we'll work on a room for you," I told him.

He shook his head. "With Junie."

"You want to stay with Junie? In here?" I asked. He nodded. "Well, all right. We'll get a second bed and change the curtains. Butterflies were fine when it was just Junie staying in here, but I think we'll get some plain ones since you'll be sharing the space. Tomorrow, we can figure out what the two of you need. For now, are you hungry?"

"Yes," Judd said.

"I'll feed them." Ares headed for the kitchen, and I followed.

"You okay?" I leaned a hip against the kitchen counter. She pulled out ingredients from the cabinet and fridge, refusing to look at me. "Ares, this doesn't change anything."

"Do you want me to stay because you think of me as your daughter? Or is it because you need a babysitter?" she asked.

"The first one. As for the second, there was a woman taking care of the kids. Judd screamed and cried half the way here. Made himself sick. He calls her Momma, even though she's no relation to him."

She faced me. "I call you Dad, but we don't share

DNA. What's the difference?"

She had me there. "It was wrong to leave her. I'm going back, so I do need you to babysit the kids right now. Dessa is…"

I didn't know what else to say. Should I warn Ares Dessa was in a wheelchair? Shit. At least the house was one story, but if I expected her to come sit with the children sometimes, I'd need to have a ramp installed. Would her chair fit through my doorways? For that matter, where the fuck would she stay once I brought her home tonight?

I wished I had more time to plan, but something told me waiting until tomorrow would be a bad idea. I'd told Judd I'd bring Dessa home tonight, and I needed to follow through. I pulled out my phone and called one of the Prospects. As long as Sam didn't fuck up, he was pretty much guaranteed a spot with the club. His dad was a patched member, and his daughter was Thunder's old lady. I still had to put him through the paces, though. I couldn't just hand him a cut because of those two things.

He answered on the fourth ring.

"You need something, Pres?" he asked.

"You any good with woodworking?"

"Um. Like making furniture or installing a deck? Because there's a big difference."

"I need a ramp installed. Preferably now."

"Ramp for what?" he asked. "Not trying to be nosy, but there's different types of ramps. To make sure it's functional, I need to know what you'll use it for."

"Wheelchair access to the house," I said, holding Ares's gaze. Her eyes widened and her lips parted. Yeah, I'd shocked her with that one.

"Might take me two or three hours, but I'll get it

done. I'll come take some measurements now, then head to the hardware store."

"Can you do some research and see if the doorways in my house are wide enough for a wheelchair to get through? If not, we'll need to handle that soon too."

"I'm on it, Pres. Anyone going to be home to let me in?"

"Ares is here, and so are the children. Judd and Junie."

"I'll get it done." Sam ended the call, and I knew Ares would have some questions for me.

"The woman you're going to get is in a wheelchair?" she asked. "Guess that means you weren't romantically interested in her."

For some reason, her words pissed me off. Of course, I *hadn't* thought of Dessa like that, but only because I'd been so angry at the time. Now that I thought about her, I realized she'd been rather pretty. Not runway model gorgeous. Then again, I'd never gone for those types. Dessa's strawberry blonde hair and pale green eyes had been pleasing. I hadn't been able to see much of her body. She'd seemed petite. "Judd calls her Momma. She's been taking care of the kids, and they don't seem to be starving. As for not being interested because she's in a wheelchair, I'm not even sure where to start with how wrong that statement is. Why the fuck would you say something like that, Ares?"

"So, you plan to fuck her?"

I pinched the bridge of my nose and prayed for patience. "One, I'm your dad and that's not the sort of conversation we'll ever be having. My love life is out of bounds. Two, when I bring Dessa home, I expect you to be nice to her. Her fiancé left her when an accident put her in that chair. If I find out you've been a bitch to her, there will be consequences."

She nodded. "All right."

I pushed away from the counter and went to hug her. "Ares, no one is kicking you out of your home. Not the kids, not Dessa, and sure as hell not me. You're my daughter, and that's not changing. We went over this before, but I'll tell you as many times as I need to before it sinks in."

"Thanks, Dad."

"Feed the kids, maybe give them a bath, and let them watch a cartoon. They fell asleep on the way here, so I'd imagine they'll be in bed before too long."

"Be careful," she said.

"Always am." I kissed her cheek, checked on the kids once more, then went back to the truck. I wasn't looking forward to the two-hour drive and wanted to get on the road as soon as possible.

At the gate, I rolled down the window to speak with the Prospect, Rocky's son. "Owen, Ares is watching the kids. I'm going back, so I'll be gone for several hours. If anything needs to be addressed, take it up with Saint."

I pulled through the gates and headed back to Dessa's house. There was one stop I wanted to make along the way. I needed to visit Jeremy and find out what happened between him and Dessa. If he still had feelings for her, I'd rather know before I hauled her all the way home. I messaged Saint and asked for the address, then let the truck eat up the miles.

By the time I pulled back into Dessa's town, it was late and I was ready for some coffee. Instead, I found myself outside a little bungalow not too far from where Dessa lived. I wondered if they realized they lived so close to one another. Had it been intentional?

I got out and knocked on the door. The man who answered reeked of sex and alcohol. No shirt. No shoes. Pants unzipped. It seemed I'd interrupted.

"You're with Saint's club. He in trouble?" the man asked.

"Jeremy, right?"

He nodded. "Yeah. If you're not here about Saint, what do you need?"

"I wanted to ask you about Dessa."

He shut down. That one name wiped all expression from his face. "Why are you asking about her?"

"Saint asked her earlier if she'd like for him to call you. She had upsetting news."

His jaw tightened, and he looked away. "Dessa is better off without me."

"Because you're a chickenshit bastard?"

"She didn't want to go anywhere that night. I made her. Told her if she loved me, she'd go. I walked away from that accident, and she didn't. She'll never walk again. It's best if Dessa and I avoid each other."

"You saved Kayla once. I know Preacher and Saint were both grateful. But when your fiancé is injured, you turn tail and run?"

"Jeremy! Come back to bed," a woman called out from somewhere inside.

I shook my head. I may not know Dessa, or Jeremy, but clearly she was better off without him. He'd dumped her and started over, while she remained in a house by herself. It made me feel even worse for what I'd done today.

"Your whore is calling." I noticed he didn't correct me as I turned and walked away. Before I got in the truck, I turned to face him again. "Don't come looking for Dessa. You may have thrown her out like trash, but the Dixie Reapers will make sure she has everything she needs. Unlike you, my club knows what it means to be a real man."

He stepped back into the house and shut the door as I backed down the driveway. When I reached Dessa's house, all the lights were off. I noticed the door hadn't been repaired. Hell, it still stood partially open. I didn't like the thought of someone being able to go inside and hurt her. We'd left her vulnerable. What the fuck was wrong with us? Sure, we'd focused on the kids, but still…

I stepped over the threshold and looked around. Everything seemed to be just as we'd left it. "Dessa! Are you here?"

Not a single sound came from anywhere in the house. I made my way down the hall and into her bedroom. Inky blackness made it difficult to see. I flicked on the light and nearly hit the ground. No. Fuck no.

"Dessa!" I rushed to the bed, shoving her chair out of the way. An empty pill bottle lay next to her. I checked the label. It looked like she'd filled it a week ago. *Oxycodone.* "Dessa, please open your eyes."

I felt for a pulse and found one. She moaned and her lashes fluttered for a moment. When her eyes opened, I breathed a sigh of relief.

"How many did you take?" I asked.

Her brow furrowed. "What?"

I lifted the pill bottle and her eyes went wide. "One."

I felt my temper rising. There was no fucking way she'd taken only one when the bottle was empty. How stupid did she think I was? "You had thirty and only got these a week ago. Where are the rest if you didn't take them?"

"It wasn't empty," she whispered. She paled, and I

felt like an asshole. If she hadn't taken the last one, then it meant someone had been in here with her.

"What other pills do you have? Where do you keep them?"

"Bathroom."

I went back into the hall and found the bathroom. I opened the cabinet over the sink, all the drawers, and checked the closet. Nothing. Not a single pill bottle. It made me check the rest of the house, doing a better job than I had when I'd arrived. I realized the TV was gone. I didn't know how I'd missed that when I'd arrived. Not knowing what else she'd had in the house, I couldn't say for sure if anything else had been taken.

"Dessa, someone robbed you while you were asleep," I said as I entered the bedroom again. She'd sat up on the side of the bed and stared at her chair where I'd shoved it across the room. I wheeled it over to her, and before she could protest, I lifted her into my arms. I'd intended to put her down in the chair until I'd felt her slight weight and gentle curves pressed against me.

When was the last time she'd eaten? Had she spent all her money on the children and barely been surviving herself? Tempest had been awful to her, and we'd not repaired the door we'd broken. We'd left her vulnerable, and at the mercy of anyone who wanted to hurt her. They'd stolen from her, but what if a murderer or rapist had come in here instead? It made me sick, and I hated myself at that moment.

"You can put me down," she said.

"No." I sat on the edge of the bed and held her on my lap. "I fucked up, Dessa. I focused on the kids and hardly gave you a second glance. When we left, we didn't fix the door. Someone could have hurt you."

She licked her lips. "They could have, but they

didn't."

"How do you know? What if they did, and you slept through it? Those pills…"

"You don't understand. No one here wants me. They know who I am. Nobody wants a broken woman."

I closed my eyes and fought not to scream out my rage. At myself. The world.

"Can you put me down?" Dessa asked.

"You're coming with me. Is there a bag I can use for your stuff?"

She gaped. "What do you mean, I'm going with you?"

"I promised Judd I'd bring his mom home," I said softly. "That's you, in case you were wondering. He cried so much he threw up on the way to the compound. I'm not returning without you."

"So you finally believe me when I say I didn't know what Sonja was doing?" she asked.

"I think I believed you all along but couldn't admit it to myself. I never should have left you here, Dessa. I'm sorry."

She sagged against me, and I had a feeling we weren't going home tonight. The dark circles under her eyes bothered me. When had she last had a good night's sleep? Her stomach rumbled, and I wondered when she'd last eaten.

I carried her to the truck and buckled her in. Then I went back for her chair. After I stashed it in the bed of the truck, I made short work of packing her things. Whether I liked it or not, we'd be staying in town overnight. I called Ares to let her know, then found the nearest motel that seemed to be in a safe area. I had no idea how Dessa would react when she woke. In the morning, we'd have a conversation about her expectations, and I'd make her a few promises. One thing was for certain... we needed to talk and make sure we were on the same page.

And I'd make sure the club knew Dessa was family. My children considered her their mother, and I didn't want to do anything to upset them. They'd been through enough already.

I got us settled in the motel room, brought in Dessa's chair and some of her clothes, then called Wire.

"Pres, it's getting late," Wire said in a hushed tone.

"Right, and your kids are asleep. Sorry. I'm bringing Dessa home with me in the morning. We're staying overnight at a motel. Poor thing passed out from exhaustion, and possibly fear. Someone went into her house after we left. Took her medication, the TV, and who knows what else."

"The woman who had the kids? That's who you're bringing home? Why?"

It seemed no one had filled him in yet. "Judd calls her Momma. I promised the children I'd bring her back with me."

"Momma?" He seemed more alert. "Is she going to stay at your place?"

"I guess so. Haven't really thought too much about it yet. I did ask Sam to install a ramp on my house and to check the size of the doorways. I know she'll want to be near the children, and they'll want to have her around."

I heard clicking and knew he'd pulled out his laptop. Then I heard a whistle. "Damn, Pres. She's pretty."

"Yeah, she is. What are you doing?" Unease pricked at me. When Wire said something like that and had his computer out, it usually meant trouble.

"Checking into her more thoroughly. I'd have done

it sooner if I'd realized you were bringing her here. I'll have a full workup done by morning."

"Thanks, Wire. Spread the word, will you? I don't want anyone making her feel unwelcome."

"You got it."

The line went dead, and I hoped like hell he wasn't going to do anything more than research Dessa. Ever since he'd claimed Lavender, he had a bad habit of marrying people. Most asked for it. Some hadn't.

I should have told him not to even think about it.

And yet... I watched Dessa sleep and realized it wouldn't be the most awful thing ever. She didn't have anyone to watch out for her, and the children loved her already. Didn't mean we had to have a real marriage, but my name would offer her some protection.

I'd talk to her about it and see how she felt. No sense rushing into anything. We'd done plenty of that already and look how it had turned out.

I smoothed her hair back from her face. "Goodnight, sweetheart. Sorry I was such an asshole before."

She murmured something but didn't wake up. Something told me it was going to be a long night.

Chapter Three

Dessa

Sunlight streamed into the room, and I closed my eyes tighter. It felt like hammers were pounding inside my skull, and my body ached. As I stretched, I felt a body lying next to me. My eyes flew open, and I jolted upright, looking around the room. I didn't recognize the space, but as the fog of sleep fully lifted, I realized I knew the man in bed beside me. He'd taken off his boots and the leather vest they'd all been wearing yesterday. Otherwise, he remained clothed.

I saw my chair and scooted down toward the foot of the bed so I could reach it. Tugging it closer, I set the brakes and lifted myself off the bed and onto the seat. After I placed my feet on the footrests, I released the brakes and wheeled myself to the bathroom, only to stop outside the door. Crap.

"Dessa?" The man rubbed at his face and sat up. "Everything all right?"

"Um." I looked at the bathroom again, then my chair. "I can't get through the door, and I need to pee."

He yawned and stood, then came over to me. He pulled my chair back, then reached down and lifted me into his arms. As he stepped into the bathroom, he paused and looked at me. "Not entirely sure how to do this and protect your modesty."

I sighed. "When I woke up and realized I wouldn't walk again, my dignity took a big hit. I've had more people help me bathe and pee in the last ten months than have probably helped the rest of my entire life. It's fine. Just… hold me steady?"

He nodded and stared at the wall over my head as he lowered my feet to the floor. I winced at the pain, but managed to shove my pants and panties down, then tapped his arm. He lowered me onto the toilet, still refusing to look anywhere other than the wall while I did my business. By the time I had my pants back up and the toilet flushed, I was back to hating my life. A grown woman shouldn't need help to pee in the morning. I hated my wheelchair. Hated the fact my legs would never work again. Hated… just about everything.

He carried me to the sink, and I washed my hands, then he took me back to the bed, easing me down on the mattress. I reclined against the headboard and studied him. When he'd arrived yesterday, I'd noticed how handsome he was. Didn't mean it hadn't felt like he'd gutted me when he left with the kids. So why had he returned? He'd mentioned something about Judd asking for his mom. Had the big, tough biker really come back for me, all because a three-year-old wanted him to?

"My name is Savior and I'm the President of the Dixie Reapers," he said, sitting at the foot of the bed facing me. "I'm afraid none of us made a good impression yesterday. Sonja used the children as leverage. She convinced one of our brothers to help her, and it nearly cost Thunder his wife. All because Sonja wanted Thunder for herself."

"I'm lost," I admitted.

He spent the next twenty minutes telling me what Sonja had done to their club, and about a man called Merlin. It all seemed a bit crazy. Then again, Sonja had always been a wild card. It didn't surprise me she'd used the children to try and get what she wanted, or that she'd lied to me about it.

"Why am I here?" I asked. "And where is here?"

"When Judd kept asking for you, and made himself sick, I promised to come back for you. Except when I arrived, the door stood partially open, and I found you lying next to an empty pill bottle. I'd worried you'd taken them all."

Bits and pieces of last night came back to me. "Someone broke in."

He nodded. "Although, the police probably wouldn't consider it a break-in since the door was open. That's our fault, and I'm so fucking sorry. If anything bad happened to you, I'd have never forgiven myself. That's not who I am. I'm not the asshole who leaves a woman defenseless."

"And we're where exactly?"

"Still in your town, but at one of the motels. You passed out in my arms before I could get you to the truck. I thought it would be better to stay overnight and head back this morning. I'm taking you with me."

"Because Judd asked you to?" I needed clarification. What did this man expect from me? I knew it couldn't be sex. No one had looked my way twice, not in a romantic way, since I'd ended up in the wheelchair. For some reason, busted legs made me less pretty. Or so it seemed.

"It started out that way." He cleared his throat. "I don't know what your situation is, and I'm not trying to pry. I get the feeling you would have struggled without Sonja's help. Honestly, I have no idea what to do with two toddlers. Maybe we can help each other."

"So you need a babysitter."

"I have a teenage daughter. While she's already let me know how she feels about babysitting the kids, I know she'd help if I asked her to. Those are her siblings now, whether she likes it or not. She'll adjust."

"So… not a babysitter?" My brow furrowed. I couldn't remember the last time I'd felt this confused.

"The children need a mother. All three of them."

Right. They needed a mom. And Judd already

called me Momma. "You aren't married?"

He shook his head. "Ares is my adopted daughter. Some people hurt her in truly awful ways. Another club rescued her, and I happened to be there helping where I could. I brought her home with me, and Wire, our club hacker, worked his magic. If anyone were to go digging, it would look like I went through the same process as everyone else who adopts a kid."

Had he ever been married? Been in a committed relationship? We were strangers. Knew nothing about each other. Now he had three kids and wanted me to be their mother. He hadn't asked me to marry him. Hadn't actually said anything about where I'd be living when we reached his hometown. Would I have a place of my own and we'd co-parent? Would I live with him but have my own room?

"We should probably come up with a plan before heading home," he said.

"Do you impulsively take people home with you all the time?"

He smiled a little. "No. Taking Ares home worked out all right. I didn't plan for Judd to remain with me, until I realized he and Junie had been together for a while. Seemed cruel to separate them, especially since neither of his birth parents can take care of him. We'll need to get a few things for him today, and for Junie. I want the place to feel like their home."

I looked down at my hands, locking my fingers together in my lap. "They haven't really had one of those, I don't think. I don't know where they lived before Sonja brought them to me, but the rental wasn't anything spectacular. I tried to make it comfortable for them."

He moved closer and placed his hand over mine. "You did a great job, Dessa. They clearly love you and trust you to take care of them."

"The children were the only ones who made me feel like I wasn't useless," I admitted softly, refusing to hold his gaze. "When Jeremy left, I didn't have anyone. The pain was constant, both physically and emotionally. Sonja only came around when she needed something, even though she tried to make it sound like she was doing me a favor. Then she brought Judd and Junie to me. I had a purpose. Little people who needed me. Loved me. I knew it was the closest I'd ever get to having children."

"Just because Jeremy is a fucking idiot doesn't mean no one would ever want you, Dessa. Do you not realize how pretty you are?"

"It's not that. Well, not *only* that." I lifted my shirt to right below my breasts. I ran my finger over the pink, puffy scar. "A piece of the windshield broke off and went into my abdomen. It damaged my uterus. The doctor said my chance of getting pregnant and carrying a baby to term were slim. So even if I did have a guy who wanted to marry me, I may not be able to give him children. Who wants a woman stuck in a wheelchair who can't do something as simple as getting pregnant? Even the stray cats can do that much."

"Hey." His harsh tone had my head jerking up. He moved even closer and reached out, fisting my hair in his hand. I had no choice but to look at him. "You listen to me. Being able to have babies doesn't make you a woman. The fact you're in a wheelchair doesn't detract from you as a person."

I stared at him, not sure what to say. No one had ever said such a thing to me before. Were there really men out there who wouldn't care if I couldn't give them babies? Or who wouldn't see me as less because I couldn't walk? At one time, I'd thought decent people existed. Then the accident happened, and all I'd seen since then was the ugliness in the world. No matter how hard I'd tried to stay positive, life kept smacking me down. Jeremy. Sonja. Even the people who stared and whispered when I wheeled past them.

His eyes darkened and his gaze dropped to my lips. Before I could process what he was doing, he leaned closer and pressed his mouth to mine. I sucked in a breath, shock holding me immobile. After a moment, I kissed him back. It was the first time a man had touched me intimately since the accident.

His lips brushed mine, then I felt his tongue slide across my bottom lip. I opened, letting him in, and it felt like the earth fell away. I'd been with Jeremy for a year, and not once had he made me feel this way. My heart began to race, and I trembled. When Savior pulled back, it felt like I couldn't catch my breath.

"What... what was that?" I asked, reaching up to touch my lips. They tingled, and when I licked them, I could taste him.

His lips kicked up on one corner. "If you don't know, I must not have done it right. Should I try again?"

I knew I should say no. This was insanity. And yet... I nodded. Savior kissed me again. Longer. Deeper. I reached up and placed my hands on his shirt, clinging to him. I didn't know why he'd kissed me. He'd called me pretty. Was it possible the sexy man was actually attracted to me?

He pulled back and rubbed his thumb across my bottom lip. "I think we have a few things to talk about."

My brain was buzzing, and he wanted to *talk*? I wasn't sure anything I said would make sense right now. How could he want to have a conversation at a time like this?

"I asked someone to install a ramp at my house." He released my hair only to caress my cheek. "They're also checking the doorways to make sure your chair will fit through them."

"My wheelchair is the standard size, so the doors wouldn't be an issue. Unless you had narrow ones. I'm assuming they're regular doorways?"

"Far as I know."

"You really asked someone to install a ramp before you came back for me?" I worried at my bottom lip. "Or did you do that this morning while I was sleeping?"

"Last night. I got the kids settled, gave Ares some instructions, then I called one of the Prospects. He said he'd get it done within a few hours. I wanted to make sure you could come and go without needing someone to help you. I don't want you to feel like a prisoner at the house."

Tears misted my eyes. Why couldn't I have met someone like him before now? If it weren't for Sonja bringing those kids to me, I'd have never met this incredible man. Sure, he'd scared me yesterday, and taken the children away. But he'd also come back for me. Protected me. Kissed me like I'd never been kissed before.

"When you said the kids needed a mother... you meant for me to live with you?"

"Yeah, I did." He ran his finger down the bridge of my nose. "And now I'd like to ask you something else. It's going to sound crazy but hear me out."

"Crazy seems to be the theme these days," I said.

He smirked. "Fair enough. Since it seems we have some chemistry, would you consider not only coming back with me to be a mom for the kids, but would you marry me?"

My jaw dropped and I stared. He'd lost his mind! I couldn't think of another explanation. Men didn't propose to strangers. Especially ones who looked like him. I had no doubt he could have any woman he wanted. Why did he need to marry me?

"You said you have a teenage daughter. What does she think of this?" I asked.

"I didn't ask her."

The way his jaw tightened told me enough. "She's not happy about the kids being there, is she? And she probably doesn't want me intruding in her territory either."

"She's a kid. She doesn't get a say in who lives in our house. I do."

Right. Clearly, he didn't know how teenage girls worked. And he said she'd been through something traumatic. That made things even worse. He was her safe haven, and now he'd opened up the house to three more people. I could only imagine the emotions rolling through her right now. She'd have to share her dad. Her home. Everything. The poor girl was probably freaking out, and possibly even lashing out because of it.

"Savior, I'm thinking you got your name because you like rushing in to save those who can't help themselves." He didn't disagree, so I figured I was right. "You should take me back to the rental house."

"Are you fucking kidding me?" he demanded. "The door is smashed in. Someone took all your pills and your TV. You want to go back?"

"You have three children who need you. While my presence might be good for Judd and Junie, your other daughter isn't going to see it that way. Taking me home with you, and telling her you want to marry me, is going to upset her more."

"She's being… difficult," he said. "I have a feeling it will be an uphill battle with her once we get home. She's a teenager, but she's never acted out before."

I shook my head. "No, Savior. She's not. I don't know what she's suffered, but clearly you were her hero. Still are. However long you've been together, she's had her dad to herself. Now you want her to share you with others, and your home. It's bad enough those people are other kids. But adding a wife to the mix? One who's in a wheelchair at that, is not a smart idea."

"I'm not taking you back. You're going to get in the truck, and we're going home." He leaned in until our noses nearly touched. "And don't think of arguing. If you don't want to wheel yourself out there, fine. I have no problem putting you where I want you."

My eyes went wide, and I gasped. "Did you just threaten to haul me wherever you please because I can't use my legs to run away?"

He winced. "Maybe."

"If you try to force me into your truck, I'm going to call the police and tell them I'm being kidnapped."

"You wouldn't." He narrowed his eyes.

"Try me." I wasn't about to make a young girl feel like she'd been replaced in her dad's life. He might not understand right now, but he would. Eventually. I hoped. I was doing this for all of them. Not one person would be better with me in their lives. The kids would adjust, and after a while, they might even forget me. He'd find someone to love and be grateful I'd refused to marry him.

"You brought this on yourself. Just remember that." He pulled out his phone and called someone. His gaze locked with mine. "Wire, I need you to do something for me. A certain woman is being too stubborn for her own good. Since she won't agree to marry me the traditional way, I need you to handle it."

"No! Are you kidding me right now?" I tried to grab the phone, but he pulled back out of reach.

"She didn't say she didn't want to marry me. Only that she thought it was a bad idea. Something about Ares." He narrowed his eyes, and I had a feeling if I reached for the phone again, I'd regret it. "Make it happen. That's an order, as your President."

He ended the call, and I stared at him. I didn't know what the hell to say. Had he really just told someone to marry us? Sure, he'd said the guy had something to make it look like Ares was his legally adopted daughter. But a marriage? He couldn't really do something like that, could he?

"Congratulations. You're going to be Dessa Black within the hour."

"I can't believe you just did that. Do the wants and needs of other people not even register in your brain?"

He softened and leaned in, kissing my forehead. "Honey, I *am* thinking of other people. Whether Ares will admit it or not, she needs a mom. Judd and Junie need you, and after that kiss we shared, I think you might be what's been missing from my life too. Can you honestly say your life won't be better with us in it? You won't have to struggle to pay the bills. You'll have three kids, and a faithful husband."

"Will you? Be faithful?"

"Every Dixie Reaper who's ever claimed a woman has remained true to her. And if I ever catch one stepping out with another woman, or fucking a club whore, when they have a wife or old lady at home, I will personally beat their asses. Fidelity is a big deal in my club."

"What's a club whore?" I asked.

"Sonja."

"Wh-what?"

He nodded. "She was a club whore. Spread her legs for any brother who crooked a finger at her. Got it in her head she wanted to be Thunder's old lady, except he never saw her that way. They serve a purpose for the single men. But no, I won't be touching any of them. Haven't in fact. Not in a long-ass time. When I brought Ares home, I focused on her. Last thing she needed was her new dad staying at the clubhouse to fuck random women."

"You really want to marry me?" I asked.

"I do. I wouldn't have asked otherwise. I'm no prize, Dessa. I'm set in my ways. Stubborn. And I'm damn near fifty years old, which probably makes me entirely too old to even think of kissing you much less the things I'd like to do."

My cheeks warmed. *Oh my.* Now I wondered exactly what he wanted to do to me. I'd never been intimate with Jeremy, and only shared kisses before the accident. It had been so long ago.

"How old do you think I am?" I asked.

He shrugged and scanned my face. "Maybe late teens, early twenties. People are going to think I have four kids when we go out."

I bit my lip so I wouldn't laugh. "Savior…"

He placed a finger over my lips. "Gabriel. Or Gabe. When it's just us, you can call me either name. When the club is present or the other old ladies, then it's Savior. And before you ask, no, they aren't physically old. It's just a title."

"Gabriel, I'm older than you think. I'm twenty-six."

He rolled his eyes. "Honey, that's only a few years

older than early twenties. I'm still old enough to be your dad."

"Do you care?"

"No. I want you. Maybe I shouldn't, but I won't lie. When I carried you out of your house last night, I got semi-hard. Made me feel like an asshole."

"And now?" I asked.

He reached over and took my hand, then pressed it down on the front of his jeans. The breath in my lungs stalled as I explored the hard length of him. My cheeks warmed as I realized he really did want me.

"I'm going to ask Wire's woman to check on the kids and see if Ares needs help. I think you and me need another night away."

"For what?" I asked.

"Honeymoon. Just not here. Somewhere nicer. Come on, sweetheart. Let's hit the road and figure out our next stop. Then we're going to get much better acquainted."

It felt like my heart my beat right out of my chest it was thumping so hard. But I had to admit the thought of a honeymoon with Savior excited me.

I'd called him crazy for telling that man to marry us.

Now I had to wonder if the insanity was contagious, because I was ready to ride the train to crazy town right next to him.

Chapter Four

Savior

We'd been on the road for a little while. Dessa's head rested against the window, and she slept. I kept glancing her way. I'd never met someone like her before. It wasn't the wheelchair, although that definitely made her different from the women I'd been with. The way she'd protected the kids, shielding them when we'd entered the house, said a lot about her as a person.

I felt like shit for letting Tempest tear into her. Should have stopped him then and there. I don't know why I hadn't. Still didn't know what caused his reaction. No one else had lit into her. If anything, I think finding her in a wheelchair had surprised the fuck out of all of us. Except Saint. The fact it was Dessa had been what shocked him.

I found myself watching Dessa again. The longer I looked, the more unsettled I felt. At first, I'd thought she was the girl-next-door sort of pretty. Every time I studied her face, I noticed something new. The light dusting of freckles across her nose and cheeks. A small strand of hair that curled while the rest of her hair remained straight. The delicate arch of her eyebrows.

I'd watched my brothers fall fast and hard, one after another. Two decades had passed since I'd become a Prospect for the Dixie Reapers. Not once had I found a woman who made me want to settle down. I hadn't lived like a monk. Not until I adopted Ares. Even with all those women, I'd had fun, but nothing more. Did it make me crazy for wanting to keep Dessa? Probably.

We were strangers. I didn't know anything about her, and all she knew about me was that I'd been an asshole to her. I might have gone back for her because

Judd wanted his mom. Wanting to marry her had nothing to do with the kids, even if I'd used it as an excuse. The moment I'd picked her up at the house, felt her slight weight in my arms, I'd been a goner. I'd known then I wouldn't walk away from her.

I'd gone through a drive-thru to pick up breakfast after we left the motel and hit the open highway. A little research had gifted me the perfect location for our honeymoon. It would take us a half hour out of the way, but I didn't care. Lavender assured me the kids were fine, and she'd even stayed over and slept on the couch so Ares wouldn't feel responsible for the little ones. I owed her a new pair of Converse when I got home. She'd gone above and beyond, like always.

Once Sam had finished the ramp, he'd noticed Judd didn't have his own bed. From what I'd heard, he'd gone to the store and gotten a racecar toddler bed and new mattress, as well as bedding for the little guy. I'd wanted to take him shopping for something. It felt like I should have done it, as his new dad. At the same time, I knew I needed this time with Dessa.

The children were struggling enough already. We needed to present a united front with them, be able to set them at ease. I couldn't think of a better way to do that than to have some quality time with Dessa before we went home.

The hotel sat back in a wooded area. The lot seemed small considering the structure rose three stories. Of course, a small town like this one probably didn't see much in the way of tourists. I had a feeling no one came here unless it was intentional. It wasn't the sort of place you ran across by accident. If I hadn't been looking for a nice hotel, I'd have never known it was here.

I reached over and ran my hand down her arm.

Her lashes fluttered and she gave me a sleepy look.

"I'll be back in a minute. Honk the horn if you need me."

I went into the lobby and rang the bell at the counter. An older woman, who looked like she'd seen the other side of ninety, slowly made her way over. She gave me a smile, and her eyes looked huge behind her thick glasses. Tight curls covered her head, the white strands still thick.

"Do you need some help?" she asked.

"Yes, ma'am. I'd like a room if you have one available."

"Passing through?" she asked.

"Actually, it's my honeymoon. The wife and I get one night away from the kids, and I thought we'd spend it here. Seems like a nice, quiet place." And I seriously needed to get this right. I hadn't given her a choice when it came to marrying me. I'd taken the children from her. The thought of being intimate with her scared the shit out of me. I couldn't treat her like a club whore. Not to mention, I didn't know enough about her condition to understand how I needed to handle her.

The woman clasped her hands in front of her. "Oh, how romantic! I have something even better! Instead of the standard honeymoon suite, like some hotels, we have honeymoon cabins. Would you like one of those?"

"Well, ma'am, that sounds pretty nice. But I have to ask. Are they wheelchair accessible?"

Her lips formed an O, and she nodded. "We do have one. Your bride is in a wheelchair? Poor little thing."

"I'll take the cabin." And I hoped Dessa didn't run into the woman. Something told me she wouldn't appreciate the woman's sympathy. I knew the wheelchair was still relatively new to her, and someone feeling sorry for her would likely make her feel worse about herself.

She pushed a book toward me, and I filled it out. I couldn't remember the last time I'd had to do such a thing. Everywhere seemed to use computers these days. Then she handed me an actual key and not one of those card things.

"How much? And do you take credit cards?" Since the place seemed a little archaic, I should have asked before now.

"One twenty for the night. Breakfast is included, and we take all major credit cards."

I pulled out my wallet and handed her my bank card. She pulled out an old credit card slip with a carbon paper copy, and an old credit card machine. After she slid it over the card, my number imprinted on the paper, she handed it back.

"We'll keep this on file until you check out," she said. "We'll total the charges and have you sign it, then."

I smiled and put my card away. "Thank you, ma'am."

When I got back to the truck, Dessa had fallen asleep again with her head resting against the window. She'd slept the entire night, but it had been an emotional twenty-four hours for her. If she kept dozing off, I'd need to have a doctor take a look at her. What if they'd missed something after her accident? Then again, for all I knew, the sleeping was normal for her.

I saw the cabins, then parked in front of the one that matched the number on our key. I carried some of Dessa's things inside, as well as her chair, before I woke her.

"Sorry," she murmured.

"It's okay, honey. You're wiped out. Let's get you inside and I'll check out our food options for lunch and dinner. The lady in the lobby said they would include breakfast with our cabin."

I lifted her into my arms and carried her inside, easing her down into her chair. While she checked the place out, I took her bathroom items into the adjoining room and noticed the handicap rail by the toilet, and the fact the tub had a bench seat inside and a door that opened on the side. I'd seen commercials with something similar years ago.

"You don't have any clean clothes, do you?" she asked as I went back into the main area. A large bed took up one wall. There was also a kitchenette, loveseat, and bistro table with two chairs. The wall opposite the loveseat had a TV mounted, and I found the remote on a table by the door.

"I stopped on the way into town. I didn't want to wake you since it was a quick in and out. I just grabbed an extra shirt and some clean underwear. Also snagged a toothbrush." I folded my arms and studied the room. "If you need anything, I can run back out in a bit."

"I have everything I need." She rubbed at her arm. "Um, do you think you could help me take a bath?"

"The bathroom is set up with handrails and a special tub, but I'll help if you need me to. As long as you're comfortable with that…"

"Gabriel, we came here for a honeymoon. I'm assuming that means you'll see me naked today, eventually."

She made a good point. I knew I needed to ask what limitations she might have when it came to sex, but I couldn't seem to find the right words. The last thing I wanted was to make her feel like she was lacking in some way. At the same time, I didn't want to accidentally hurt her either.

"Come on. Let's see if we can figure out this strange bathtub."

She wheeled along behind me. I noticed the tub had a detachable showerhead. I figured out how to open the door and let Dessa take a look.

"It might still be easier for you to lift me into it."

I folded my arms over my chest. "Really? Can you honestly not do it, or do you just want my hands on you?"

I should have felt like an asshole for teasing her. But when her cheeks flushed a bright pink, I had to hold back a smile. Too fucking cute. Making her blush might become my new favorite thing to do.

"It might be the last one. I've taken baths at home by myself plenty of times. It wasn't easy, but I managed." She cleared her throat and looked away. "No one's given me a second look since the accident. And before... Jeremy didn't seem very interested in sex."

I nearly winced. From what I'd noticed when I stopped by Jeremy's house, he didn't seem to have an issue with sex. It made me wonder about his relationship with Dessa. Something seemed off, but I'd have to dig into it later.

I eyed the standing shower and noticed it had a small bench inside. The cube wasn't overly large. Then again, Dessa was the size of a pixie.

"I can help you into the tub, or if you want, we can take a shower together. I'll leave the decision to you."

She licked her lips and looked from the tub to the shower and back again. I was trying to be nice and let her decide. But I had to wonder, would I be treating her this way if she weren't in that chair? If she didn't have a disability, would I have flat out told her to get her ass in the shower?

I needed to stop treating her like she was different. Being in a wheelchair didn't mean she didn't want the same things other women did. Jeremy had treated her like trash. Thrown her away as if she'd meant nothing. When I'd told her she was marrying me, she hadn't put up much of a fight. Maybe that's what she needed now… for me to tell her she was taking a shower.

I reached in and started the water, then yanked my shirt over my head. Her jaw dropped and her eyes went wide. I smirked as I toed off my boots, then reached for my belt. Her mouth snapped shut. I finished undressing.

"Need help?" I asked.

She mutely nodded and lifted her arms. It took a bit of work to get her undressed since she couldn't stand on her own. Once I'd removed the last of her clothing, I picked her up and set her on the bench inside the shower. There were multiple showerheads, and one sprayed across her abdomen and legs.

I shut the shower door and wet my hair before kneeling at her feet. There were travel-size sealed bottles on a ledge. I picked up one that said *shower gel*. Pouring some into my hand, I reached for Dessa's arm and started to lather her skin.

"I'm capable of washing myself," she said.

"I'm aware." I kept washing her, taking my time. My hands spanned her waist, and I worked my way up. When I soaped her breasts, her nipples hardened against my palms. She sucked in a breath and went incredibly still.

I watched her face as my hands explored her body. Despite her slight stature, she had curves in all the right places. Her breasts weren't overly large. And yet,

I thought they were rather perfect. I traced the scar on her abdomen and leaned forward, pressing a kiss to the raised flesh.

I felt her fingers comb through my hair and looked up at her. A soft smile curved her lips. The way she studied me -- it was as if I were a puzzle she couldn't figure out. I knew how she felt because it was how I saw her. Something shiny and new that I needed to explore. I wanted to learn everything about her.

"Before things go any further, I need to know if you have limitations I should be aware of, or if certain things might cause you pain." I laced my fingers with hers. "The last thing I want to do is hurt you."

"My legs are in constant pain. I can't stand. This is all new for me too. If you do something that hurts, I can let you know. We'll have to figure it out as we go."

I nodded. "All right. I think sex in the bed will be the easiest on you, but that doesn't mean I can't make you feel good now."

Her brow furrowed, as if I'd confused her with my words. Had that idiot, Jeremy, never bothered to make sure she enjoyed herself with him? It made me want to go back and kick his ass.

I rubbed my thumb across her nipple before lightly pinching it. She gasped and her eyes dilated with pleasure. I rolled the hard bud between my fingers and gave it a slight tug. Her hips bucked, and Dessa gripped the edge of the bench.

"Feel good?" I asked.

"Yes," she murmured.

I leaned forward and took her nipple into my mouth, sucking on it, as I worked my hand between her thighs and rubbed her clit. It only took a few swipes before she was coming, screaming out my name, her body trembling from the force of her release.

I'd never met anyone so responsive before, and it made me eager to get her into bed.

But first… I leaned in, pushing her thighs wider apart. I lapped at her pussy, licking up her release and flicking my tongue against her clit. She squealed and tensed. I gripped her hips, holding her still, as I fucked her with my tongue. She tasted so damn good, and I loved the sweet sounds she made. I especially liked it when she screamed my name.

I made her come twice more before I kissed my way up her body and sucked on her nipples again. I couldn't wait to play with her more, preferably in a bed. I was so fucking hard, I wasn't sure I'd be able to last right now. I needed her. It had been far too long since I'd had sex and she had me burning hotter than I ever had before.

Our first time would be over entirely too quick, but I'd make it up to her. All night long, if I could get hard multiple times. I didn't remember the last time I'd been able to do that. It had been a while. But with Dessa, I had a feeling it would be possible.

"I'm going to wash off, then we're moving this elsewhere."

I felt her gaze on me as I scrubbed my skin and shampooed my hair. And I had to admit, I liked the attention. In the past year or so, I hadn't given a shit if women checked me out. I'd had other things on my mind, and the easy pussy at the clubhouse had started to get old. Then I'd adopted Ares, and she'd been my main focus. Being a dad to her had been more important than getting laid.

Now I had a sweet, sexy wife. The fact she liked the way I looked was a bonus. And I damn sure liked looking at *her*.

I shut off the water, dried us off, and carried her to

the bed. My hands shook slightly, but I hoped she didn't notice. The thought of hurting her, or worse, not making her come again, had me nervous as fuck. I hoped I didn't screw this shit up. It almost felt like my first time.

I stretched out alongside her and lightly ran my fingers over her body. I noticed she tried more than once to cover her legs. On the fourth attempt, I tossed the covers off the foot of the bed.

"Don't hide from me." I narrowed my eyes at her. "You're beautiful, Dessa. Do you think your legs bother me? They don't. I hate that they cause you pain. If you think I find them ugly, then you're wrong."

She reached up and placed her hand on my cheek. "Make love to me, Gabriel. I don't want to wait. You don't need to give me pretty words or draw things out. Just make me yours."

I smiled and pressed my lips to hers. "With pleasure."

I eased her legs apart, keeping an eye on her face to make sure I didn't see signs of pain. Settling between her thighs, I rubbed my cock up and down her wet pussy. Every time the head bumped her clit, her pulse fluttered.

Slowly, I eased inside her. She placed her hands on my shoulders, and I felt the bite of her nails in my skin. My jaw clenched as I forced my way inside her. I'd never felt anyone so tight.

"Jesus, Dessa. You're squeezing my cock." I pulled my hips back, then pushed forward again. It took several minutes before I managed to get all the way inside her. The tension eased from her body, and I reached between us to rub her clit. I needed her to loosen up, and the best way would be to give her an orgasm.

"Focus on me, honey," I said. "Eyes on mine."

She nodded and held my gaze. I worked her clit with quick, short strokes. I felt her pussy get hotter and wetter. Her hold on me lessened until she clenched so tight I damn near saw stars. She cried out my name as she came, and I couldn't hold back another moment.

All thoughts of taking things slow and being tender flew out the window. I pounded my sweet wife into the mattress, taking what I wanted. She felt too incredible, and I didn't last as long as I'd have liked. My balls drew up, and then I was coming, filling her up with hot, sticky cum.

"That was wonderful," she said, a soft smile on her lips. "Better than I'd ever imagined."

Her words gave me pause. "What does that mean?"

"You were my first," she said. She trailed her fingers over my cheek. "My only."

Holy. Fucking. Shit.

My heart raced as I realized I'd just taken her virginity without even realizing. I was a damn asshole and would have to make it up to her. How the hell did I not figure out she'd been innocent? The tight fit. The way she'd tensed when I entered her. All the signs were there. I'd just been too stupid to recognize them.

"Give me about thirty minutes and we're doing this again. If I'd known you were a virgin, I'd have done things a little different. You deserved better than a quick fuck."

"If it gets much better, I might pass out from pleasure."

I grinned. "Challenge accepted, sweetheart."

Chapter Five

Dessa

He thought the sex had been lacking? At least, that's how it seemed from what he'd said. Granted, I didn't have anything to compare it to, but I'd come so many times already, I wasn't sure I could have another orgasm. I didn't know how to feel. I wasn't a virgin anymore. That part honestly excited me.

But Savior said he was my husband now. When I'd dreamed of my wedding night, it had always been Jeremy I'd pictured. Even after he'd dumped me and moved on. Savior was the exact opposite of my ex-fiancé, but that wasn't a bad thing. The man might be a stranger, but he was growing on me. He could be sweet and tender. Thoughtful. And I couldn't wait to have sex with him again. My toes curled at the mere thought of it.

I winced as I shifted my legs. I still had a full range of movement, but the way I'd healed, thanks to the nerve damage, my legs wouldn't hold my weight without causing me excruciating pain. Even moving like I had just now made me want to scream.

"Can I ask you something personal?" Savior asked, propping his head on his hand so he could watch me.

"Sure." He'd already had his mouth in places no one else ever had. Compared to that, a question wasn't a big deal.

"How is it you were engaged, but you were still a virgin? How the hell did that idiot keep his hands off you?"

My cheeks burned. I should have known he'd wonder about that. When Jeremy proposed, I'd been thrilled. Up to that point, we'd only held hands and kissed. I'd thought things would change once I had his ring on my finger. It hadn't. If anything, he'd become more distant.

Savior reached over with his other hand and traced the bridge of my nose with his finger. The way he looked at me made me feel special. How could a man I'd just met treat me so much better than someone I'd known for years before I agreed to marry them? None of it made sense.

"Jeremy and I dated for a while. I wouldn't call it a passionate relationship. We kissed and held hands. He'd take me on dinner dates or out to a movie. But he owns his own business, so he was always busy."

"Too busy to spend time with you?" he asked.

I shrugged. "Yeah. I didn't think much of it. I'd never really had someone pay attention to me before Jeremy. I guess I felt honored he wanted to date me, much less marry me. Sure, he spent a lot of time at his garage working on cars, but I saw it as him building a future for us."

"You didn't find it strange he never tried to have sex with you? Or did you just hold him off until after the wedding?"

I swallowed hard and looked away. Did he know he was bringing up all my insecurities? Jeremy had said he loved me. Asked me to be his wife. Then the accident happened, and he ran from me. Broke our engagement and my heart. If I were being truthful, I'd admit he'd been distant from the beginning. "I'm not beautiful. Men haven't flocked to me, even before the accident. When Jeremy asked me out, I figured I wouldn't see him again after our first date. Like all the others before him. Except, he called for a second date. Then a third and a fourth."

"And you settled for him?" Savior asked.

"I guess so. I thought I was in love. Clearly, it was one-sided. If he'd ever loved me, he wouldn't have left after I got stuck in the wheelchair. Would he?"

Savior shook his head. "No, honey. A man doesn't run out on the woman he loves just because she can't walk anymore. He's a chickenshit and an asshole. He might have thrown you away, but I can promise I never will."

"Why did you marry me?" I asked. "You didn't have to. I would have gone with you and helped with the kids."

"I thought about you a lot before I got to your house. Even if Judd hadn't begged for me to go back for you, I think I would have, anyway. Maybe not quite as fast, which would have been bad. I can never apologize enough for leaving you vulnerable the way we did. And I'll have a talk with Tempest. He was too harsh with you and should have made sure you were safe before we left." He sighed. "We all should have. We shouldn't have left without making sure you could shut and lock the door. It wasn't safe."

"We can't change the past, Gabriel. There's no point dwelling on it." I reached up and trailed my fingers over his close-cropped beard. "That still doesn't tell me why you wanted me for your wife. We're strangers. What if we end up hating each other? What if you get tired of having someone stuck in a wheelchair for the rest of her life? What if…"

He placed a finger over my lips to silence me. I flicked my tongue out, and he growled softly, his eyes getting darker. His cock hardened and brushed against my thigh. It thrilled me. I'd never had a man react to me the way he did.

"I won't get tired of you, Dessa. Not today, tomorrow, or fifteen years from now. How do I know? Because you're a sweet, beautiful angel. More importantly, you're mine." He leaned in closer, our noses nearly touching. "If you wanted a way out, you should have never given me your virginity. Knowing I'm the only man who's been inside you changes things. Anyone touches you, kisses you, or even thinks of fucking you, and I will end them. I don't share."

His words should have scared me. Instead, he was only turning me on more. There might be women who wouldn't like his caveman tendencies, but I found him to be refreshing. Then again, I'd been told more than once I had a submissive personality. Even Sonja had taken charge whenever she was at the house, and I'd fallen in line. Mostly. When it came to the kids, I'd always fought for what was best for them. Or as much as I could.

"Your daughter is going to hate me, isn't she?" I asked.

"Ares has had a rough life. I adopted her after saving her. She was a part of a human trafficking ring, one that preferred children and teens. She needed a home, so I gave her one. It's been the two of us for about a year now." He ran his fingers through my hair. "She won't hate you, but she may be resistant at first."

"I'll be patient with her," I promised.

"Are you hungry? I could go grab some dinner for us. Or do you feel like going out?"

"I hate asking you to go out and bring something back. But if I go, then you have to deal with my wheelchair."

"Whatever you want to do is fine with me, Dessa. Want to go? I'll put your chair in the truck. Want to stay here? I'll bring back whatever you want. It's our honeymoon. Tonight is special."

I moved closer to him. "Why do you do that?"
"What?"
"Make it seem like it's no big deal that I can't walk.

You didn't go easy on me earlier. At least, I don't think you did. I'd thought you'd treat me like I was made of glass. Most people act like all of me broke when my legs did. They speak to me differently, treat me like I'm no longer the same woman I was before."

"You aren't your wheelchair, Dessa. Did it stop you from being a mother to Judd and Junie?"

I shook my head.

"Did it stop you from having multiple orgasms tonight?" he asked with a wicked smile.

"No." My cheeks burned again.

"Does it mean you don't feel or think the way you did before? Are you less of a woman because you can't walk?"

I stiffened. "No."

"Right. The only thing it means is you need help getting around. It's no different from being nearsighted and needing glasses."

"Well, maybe it's a *little* different."

He shook his head. "No. Your wheelchair is a medical device, like eyeglasses. Necessary in order to make your life easier. Would you die without the chair?"

"Well... I don't guess I would. Unless I needed to escape from something dangerous and couldn't."

"Right. If you didn't have it, then someone would help you get around. It's there to help you, Dessa. Nothing more. It doesn't define who you are, and it doesn't make me see you differently. If it changed how Jeremy felt about you, then he wasn't much of a man and you're better off without him."

Tears burned my eyes. No one had been so nice to me, not even before the accident. I might not have agreed with everything Sonja did, and taking those children had been wrong, but it brought Savior to me.

If she hadn't screwed up, and dragged me into her mess, I'd have lived the rest of my life alone.

"Anything is fine," I said. "But I think I'll stay here."

He leaned in and kissed me. "All right. Any food allergies? Anything you absolutely hate to eat?"

"I'm allergic to shellfish, so I tend to avoid all seafood."

"Okay. I'm going to rinse off and get dressed. I'll write my number down in case you need me while I'm gone."

"I'll be fine, Gabriel. I did manage to survive before I met you. I'm sure I can handle being in this cabin alone until you bring dinner back."

He winked and got out of bed. And yes, I admit it. I watched him walk away. I'd never paid much attention to a man's ass before. Until Savior. The man was a work of art from behind and in front. And for some reason, he was mine.

You're in so much trouble, Dessa. That man is way out of your league.

I only hoped he never figured that out.

* * *

Savior

I'm not sure what I expected when we got home. The Prospects hadn't only installed a ramp, they'd also made the porch larger. Dessa would be able to easily maneuver her chair up the ramp and have plenty of room to get the door open. There was another small ramp that would allow her to roll through the door and into the house.

I hopped into the bed of the truck and removed the tarp and tie downs from her chair. I'd picked them up before we'd headed home, wanting to make sure the chair stayed secured. Easing it over the side, my muscles strained. Why did it seem heavier than before?

Once I had it on the ground, I got down and opened the passenger door. Dessa had already removed her seat belt, so I reached in and lifted her into my arms. She smiled as she leaned into me, but I saw the strain on her face. As eager as she was to see Judd and Junie again, I knew meeting Ares had her nervous. Hell, I wasn't too sure how my daughter would react. Too many changes in too short a time.

Once Dessa was in her chair, and had unlocked the wheels, I hurried ahead to open the door. She wheeled herself up the ramp and into the house, stopping not too far inside.

I went in and shut the door behind me, checking the place out. Lavender sat on the couch with Junie and Judd on either side of her. A cartoon played on the TV. What I didn't see was Ares, even though her car was out front. Which told me she was likely hiding in her bedroom.

"Thanks for watching them," I said.

Lavender stood and hurried over. She held her hand out to Dessa. "I'm Lavender. Wire and I don't live too far from here."

"Dessa." She cleared her throat. "I'm his wife."

Lavender's smile broadened. "I know. My husband is the one who made it happen. We're so happy to have you here."

The two kids got off the couch and rushed toward Dessa. Once they were close enough, she reached down and lifted them onto her lap, one at a time. They both cuddled against her, and the look of pure bliss on all three faces told me I'd made the right decision.

"Where's Ares?" I asked.

Lavender shoved her hands into her back pockets

and rocked back on her heels. "Um. Well…"

I narrowed my eyes at her. "Spill it."

"She's with Dawson." Lavender winced. "I figured you'd prefer her hanging out at Venom's house with his son rather than chasing after one of the older boys."

"I'd rather she not hang out with any of them," I mumbled. Of course, with her past, I doubted she was doing anything more than playing a video game or watching a movie. She hadn't shown a romantic interest in anyone. Usually, if a boy got too close, she snarled at them like a rabid badger. The exceptions were the boys at the compound. I'd promised they would help keep her safe, and she took me at my word.

"Momma staying?" Judd asked.

Dessa nodded. "Yes. I'm here to stay. Want to show me the house?"

He smiled and scrambled out of her lap. She followed in the chair, with Junie still in her lap. I went along with them, wanting to see what changes had been made. Lavender tagged along, murmuring things as we went.

"They said the doorways were thirty-six inches, so they didn't need to widen them. The guys were thorough. They looked up the type of chair she had to make sure Dessa could get around easily. They added handrails to the master bathroom, and they gutted your kitchen. It's not finished yet."

I stopped. "They did what?"

She nodded. "They said the counters were too high. Something about needing a space under the kitchen sink and making the shelves on the bottom cabinets where they'll pull out."

"Damn. They put some thought into it."

"They did."

I peeked into the kids' room and saw the bed Sam purchased for Judd. It looked like someone had added a few toys too. I saw a handful of cars, some large building blocks, and other items a boy might prefer. They'd also bought Junie a few dolls and a play kitchen with dishes and plastic food.

"Everyone went overboard. I was only gone a day and a half."

"Did you really think no one would spoil your kids? You're the President now, Savior. Sam did a lot of the work, but Thunder stopped by to help with a few things, and so did Grimm and Viking."

The front door opened and slammed shut. "Did you bring her home with you?"

I winced at how loud Ares was and turned to face her as she stormed down the hallway. I heard Dessa in the master bedroom, talking to the kids. Better to get this out of the way, before my daughter tried to run Dessa out of town.

"I did. There's something we need to discuss."

Ares sighed and leaned against the wall. "I already know. I heard Lavender talking to Wire. You married that woman."

I nodded. "Yeah, I did. She's the only mother Judd and Junie remember, and if you let her, she'll be a mom to you too. I know you're nearly an adult, Ares, but she's a really sweet woman who's been dealt a shitty hand. I'd like for you to give her a chance."

"Fine. Guess I better meet her."

I went into the master bedroom. I blinked as I stared at the bed. It seemed… shorter. Then again, if they'd ripped out my kitchen to lower the counters, they'd probably made changes in here too. I noticed the room seemed more open as well.

"Dessa, I'd like you to meet Ares." I reached

behind me and tugged my daughter forward. "She recently turned sixteen and has her own transportation. Her bedroom is the one next to the kids' room."

Ares took a hesitant step forward, then another. "Um. Hi."

Dessa gave her a warm smile. "Hello, Ares. I'm so happy to meet you. Your dad didn't tell me a lot, but I can tell he's really proud of you."

"He's been an amazing dad."

"I know things are changing. You have two new siblings, and now I'm here." Dessa pressed her lips together for a moment. "I'm not trying to push you out of the house. This is your home, and Savior will always be your dad. I hope you know that. But I'd like to be your friend, if you'll let me."

I saw Ares's jaw tighten. Dessa might have been trying to ease her way into Ares's life, but she'd just screwed up. I placed a hand on my daughter's shoulder.

"Calm down, Ares. She wasn't trying to hurt your feelings."

Dessa's jaw dropped. "Oh, no. What did I say? I didn't mean to upset her."

"When you said you'd be her friend, she assumed it meant you didn't want to claim her as your daughter," I said.

Dessa wheeled a little closer and reached out to Ares. "I'm so sorry! I didn't mean it that way at all. I'd love to be your mom, but I didn't want you to feel like I was pushing my way into your life. I'll be here if you need me. I also don't want to smother you with attention if that's not what you want or need."

"Whatever," Ares mumbled. She broke free of me and rushed off. I heard the door slam again as she left the house.

"I fucked up," Dessa mumbled.

"She'll come around," Lavender said. "Kid has had it rough. Once she calms down, and gets used to you being in the house, she'll realize you aren't a monster and won't steal Savior from her."

"Might take her some time." I glanced down the hall and wondered if there was anything I could do to smooth things over. "She can be stubborn, but it's largely due to what she's been through. She's not as tough as she tries to appear."

"I'll be here if she wants to talk. At the same time, I won't force her to spend time with me." Dessa looked up at me and I saw the sheen of tears in her eyes. "What if she never likes me?"

I kneeled down next to her. "Honey, it's impossible to hate you. She'll come around. Promise. Until then, we'll get this house remodeled, so it's easy for you to get around and access everything. You can meet the other wives and old ladies, even the kids. Just take things one day at a time."

"Everyone's eager to meet you," Lavender said.

"I have to admit I'm nervous," Dessa said.

"Your husband is the President of this club, which means he's in charge. He's rather new to the position, and clearly hasn't had a woman before now. If you want to find out more about being the old lady of the club President, you should talk to Isabella. She's married to Torch, and he was our President before he stepped down." Lavender smiled. "You aren't in this alone, Dessa."

"Have Junie and Judd had a chance to meet the other kids around their age?" I asked.

Lavender shook her head. "It's a nice day, though. Not too hot. Want me to take them over to the playground? I can text Delphine, Pepper, and Katya on the way there. I'm sure at least one, if not all three, will bring their kids over."

"Thanks. I'd like to get Dessa settled into the house and talk to Sam about how long it will take on the kitchen remodel. If you could keep them busy for about an hour, I'll try to have things wrapped up by then." I ran my fingers through Dessa's hair. "I'll bring your things in, and you can put them away."

"I might have already cleared some drawer space for her," Lavender said. "Wire fussed at me for snooping, but I hung your jeans and T-shirts in the closet. I wasn't sure if she'd be able to reach anything hanging up and thought the drawers might be easier."

"Thank you," Dessa said. "That was sweet of you."

"Come on, kids. Ready to make some new friends?" Lavender asked, holding her hands out.

Both Junie and Judd went to her, but only after hugging Dessa. Once we were alone, I brought Dessa's things inside. While she put them away, I called Sam.

"Hey, Pres. You home now?" he asked when the call connected.

"Yeah. About the kitchen…"

"Thunder, my dad, and several others have offered to help. We're going to custom build your cabinets. And while we're at it, we're putting in new appliances. That was Amity's idea. We also need to talk about the hall bathroom."

"What about it?" I asked. "And how long before the kitchen is functional?"

"Give us a week on the kitchen, unless anything comes up. Barring any issues, or bullshit that comes knocking at the gate, six or seven days should be plenty of time. For the bathroom in the hall, there's not really anything we can do. It's too small to make it wheelchair accessible."

Once the kids were older, that wouldn't be an issue. It was their bathroom. Until then, Dessa would have to bathe the kids in our bathroom. Or Ares would have to help.

"We'll figure it out," I said. "Anything else I need to know?"

"No, I think we'll have the house fully functional for her within a week. Maybe two weeks. I wasn't sure about adding anything to the bedroom. I don't know how she manages to get in and out of bed, or into the tub, for that matter. I Googled some stuff to find the most common alterations and used what I could."

"I appreciate it," I said.

"The rails on the toilet screwed in. We added rails for the tub. I have plans for a handicap accessible shower but wanted to run that one by you first. I'd basically have to rip out what's in there. If you want to see the plans I found, I'll bring them by tomorrow. I'd also like to rip out your bathroom cabinets and sink. But if I do that, you'll need to set up some storage, some other way for your towels and shit."

"Yeah. I'd love to see the plans and do whatever is necessary to make this house a safe place for Dessa. I don't want her to struggle when I'm not around. She should be able to bathe herself, use the sink, make meals... I don't want her to have trouble with those things because the house isn't set up correctly."

We talked about the changes around the house for another minute or two, then I ended the call and went to check on Dessa. She hadn't owned a lot of things, so it hadn't taken her long to put her clothes away. I knew I'd need to check her sizes and surprise her with some new clothes and shoes.

I also wanted to make a few calls and look at

another motorcycle. The one I had was great for everyday use. But I wanted to take Dessa for rides too. Since she couldn't use her legs, I'd need to get a sidecar. I wasn't about to risk her riding on the back of my bike.

Which made me wonder how she'd get around town on her own. She hadn't had a car at the rental house where she'd been living with the kids. Did she know how to drive? Would she be able to? I honestly had no idea what her limitations were. Looked like I needed to ask some questions and do some research.

For that matter, I needed to make sure she could move around the compound without having to wheel herself everywhere. Until we got it all figured out, she'd be stuck at home, or at least close to the house.

I'd have to introduce her to everyone and make sure she had their numbers. Worst-case scenario, someone could take her to the store or wherever else she needed to go. It wasn't ideal, and wouldn't be a good long-term solution, but we could only tackle things one at a time. House first. Transportation later.

I braced my hands on the arms of her chair and leaned in, kissing her softly. "Welcome home, Dessa. It's not perfect, and needs some work, but I promise you'll have everything you need or want."

She reached up to cup my cheek. "I already do. All I need is you and the kids."

I snorted. "You need more than that, and we both know it. But the house will come together. Until then, you just let me know how I can help."

"You're the sweetest man," she said before pressing her lips to mine again.

"No. I'm not." I smiled. "But for you, I'll try to be. At least, in this house. Out there, I have to be the tough, no-nonsense President of the club. I may say or do things you don't like."

She audibly swallowed and nodded. "Right. Like Sonja."

My stomach clenched. "Yeah. I'm sorry, honey. I know you considered her family, but she tried to get rid of Thunder's wife because she wanted him for herself. She blackmailed a brother into helping her and used those kids as leverage. Sonja wasn't a nice person. She'd have done whatever it took to get what she wanted."

"I know she had problems. I wish I'd known about the children. Even if I couldn't drive them here myself, I'd have found a way to bring them home to you."

"Dessa, the one thing I can swear to you is that I will always protect you and our family. I'll die for all of you. For this club. There will be times I can't tell you what I'm doing or where I'm going. Club business is exactly that. But I will be faithful to you, provide for you and the kids, and will do whatever I can to make you happy."

"That's more than I've ever had before." She stared at me with sad eyes. "In just the short time we've been together, you've treated me better than Jeremy ever did. I'll be a good wife to you, Gabriel, and the best mom to our kids. But I'll have bad days. Depression might try to drag me down, and I'll struggle. Just promise you'll be patient with me."

"Always." I pressed my forehead to hers. "You start sinking into the darkness and I'll drag you back into the light. We're a team, Dessa. Whatever life throws at us, we'll handle it together. You're my wife, and you're stronger than you realize. I hope one day you can see how amazing you are."

The doubtful expression on her face nearly killed me. Whatever it took, I'd prove to her that she wasn't useless, or whatever thoughts ran through her head. She was amazing. Kind. Beautiful. Competent. And I'd make sure I told her frequently. Maybe one day she'd finally believe me.

Chapter Six

Dessa

My head felt like someone had beaten on my skull with a hammer. I pressed a hand to my forehead and winced. The lights hurt. Every little sound hurt. Lying in the dark hadn't worked. I didn't get migraines often, but they did hit a few times a month. I'd had them long before the accident.

Savior hadn't been home since early this morning, and as much as I loved Judd and Junie, they were making the pain a million times worse. Ares hadn't stuck around after her dad left. She'd glared at me as she stomped out of the house and slammed the door behind her. I'd known it wouldn't be easy to win her over, but I'd hoped she would at least give me the chance. Instead, she ran every time Savior wasn't home, and gave me attitude when no one else was around. I'd been here a week and didn't seem to be gaining any ground with her.

Junie squealed again, and I felt the bile rising in my throat. I quickly wheeled toward the bedroom. I didn't even clear the door before I threw up on myself. Not once. Not twice. No, I had to be an overachiever and do it three times. I sobbed as tears and snot streaked my face and lifted a shaky hand to swipe at my mouth.

"Dessa, are you okay?" one of the guys called out.

They'd been working on the kitchen the last few hours, which also hadn't helped my head any. Viking entered the room, and I hunched my shoulders, wishing I could disappear. I was their President's wife, and I couldn't have felt less worthy.

"Dessa?" He called my name softly as he came and hunkered down beside my chair. "Why didn't you let one of us know you were sick?"

"I'm an adult. I should be able to take care of

myself."

"If we'd finished the renovations already, I'm sure you would have been fine. We'll have the kitchen done by tomorrow night, assuming there aren't any other delays. Then we can rip out the shower and put in a new one."

A throat cleared behind us. "Savior said we're done after the kitchen. He's not making more renovations right now."

I swallowed hard. I'd only been here a week, and I was already a burden to him. Why had I agreed to this? I should have refused to come with him. Fought him off when he said I was going to be his wife. Instead, I'd thought it sounded so wonderful to be part of a family, to have a man like him pay attention to me.

Stupid. You're an idiot, Dessa.

"Call Savior," Viking said to the other man.

"No!" I winced when the sound of my own voice sent pain shooting through my hair. "Just… close the door and watch the kids while I clean up. Please."

They left, and I heard the door click shut. I took out a clean bra and panties, as well as a knit dress. I stared at the stack on top of the dresser and wondered how I'd get the clothes into the bathroom without having to set them in my lap. A quick look around the room didn't give me any ideas. I eyed the distance from the bed to the dresser and tossed the clothes over. They landed on the edge of the mattress, but it was good enough.

Heading into the bathroom, I removed my shirt and bra. I opened the cabinet under the sink and took out a rag. As much as I would have loved a bath or shower, I wasn't going to ask the men to watch the children that long. I wet the rag with warm water and added a little soap, then wiped down my torso. The next part would be difficult, but I could do it. Sweat coated my skin by the time I'd removed my leggings and panties.

I rinsed the rag and added more soap, then cleaned myself again. Put on a little more deodorant, and then wheeled myself into the bedroom. I shifted the clothes where they'd be easy to grab once I made it onto the bed. Steeling myself, I transferred from my chair to the bed. It wasn't as easy for me as it was for some people. At least I didn't struggle quite as much as I had at first. As the months passed, it took a little less time to get from my chair to the bed, toilet, or tub.

After more struggling, I got my panties and bra on, then slipped my dress over my head. I lay back on the bed, feeling exhausted. Every movement made my head pound more, and I worried I'd throw up again. Maybe I needed to get some large bowls or small trash cans and scatter them around the house today. I didn't know why I hadn't considered it sooner. Except for the part where my brain hurt, so thinking caused me more pain.

"Dessa, are you all right?" Viking called through the door.

"I need a few more minutes to get back in my chair, then I can watch the kids again." I squeezed my eyes shut. "I'm sorry."

"Are you dressed?" he asked after a moment.

"Yes."

I heard the door open, then the heavy tread of his steps. The bed dipped, and I cracked my eyes open slightly to look at him. The concern on his face nearly made me cry. Then again, after being on day two of this migraine from hell, almost everything made me want to cry.

"Asking for help doesn't make you weak," he said

softly. "We can all see you're trying. You've been dropped into this new world with a teenage girl who seems intent on making your life hell, and a house that isn't properly equipped for your wheelchair. I know your rental had its issues, but you'd improvised, and it looked like the landlord had added rails in the bathroom. But this is your home. You shouldn't have to struggle to do everyday things."

"I'm tired, Viking. So very tired." I felt a tear slip from my eye and slide down into my hair. "You're right. The house doesn't make things easier. Ares disliking me doesn't help. And to add to it all…"

"What? Are you sick?"

"Migraine," I murmured. "It won't go away."

"And we're sawing and hammering, which is probably making it worse. Not to mention the kids squealing while they play." He paused. "Does Savior know?"

"No. It wasn't this bad until today. Usually, the first day I can fake it and function enough no one notices. I'll be fine. Just give me some time to get back into my chair and I'll come watch them again."

"You know, as a patched member of this club, it's my job to have the President's back. Since you're his wife, that means it's also my responsibility to watch over you and his kids. I know you need the kitchen finished so you can function without assistance. But I think, for today, the kitchen can wait. I'm going to take the kids to the play area for an hour. You lie here and rest."

"I probably shouldn't," I said. "If I throw up again…"

"I'll make sure you have something within reach. We can prop your pillows up so you aren't lying flat on your back. Whatever you need, just tell us."

"Thank you."

Viking reached out and tugged me against his chest, then reached behind me and adjusted the pillows. He eased me back and made sure I was comfortable before he went into the bathroom and grabbed the small trash can. He placed it on the bedside table within reach.

"Rest for a while. The kids will be safe. Do you need me to bring your phone in here?"

I hesitated only a moment. "Yes, please. I left it on the coffee table."

"I'll be right back."

He walked out and I stared at the ceiling. I hated when they were so nice to me. Everyone had been understanding. Well, except Ares, who seemed to dislike me the moment I arrived. But the kinder everyone was toward me, the worse I felt when I failed at something. Savior needed a strong woman by his side. He seemed to think that was me, but I was starting to doubt I'd ever be what he truly needed.

Viking set my phone down and left. I heard him talking to the kids, and a short time later, the front door shut.

The vision in my right eye had blurred to the point attempting to see out of it made my head hurt more. Sadly, I was losing my vision *because* of the migraine. It was a vicious cycle. I couldn't exactly lie in the dark with my eyes closed for days on end until the pain finally went away. Past experience told me if a migraine lasted more than a day, I could have it for as long as seven to ten days.

The doctors hadn't found anything to cause them. I'd gone through multiple types of tests, tried every migraine medication out there, and nothing worked. The doctor said some people had hereditary migraines, and since I didn't know much about my birth family, it was likely I'd gotten it from one of them, but I'd never know for certain.

I shut my eyes and tried not to think of all the things I wasn't able to accomplish right now. I wanted to wow my husband and prove to him he could rely on me. Instead, I seemed to be doing the opposite. I hoped no one said anything to him. The fact he hadn't rushed home gave me hope that Viking and the others had remained quiet about my migraine. Savior knew my head was hurting yesterday, but I hadn't admitted how bad it was.

I winced, thinking of Jeremy's reaction whenever I got a bad one that lasted for days. More than once, he'd told me to suck it up because I had stuff to do and couldn't lie around all day. Since he'd never had anything worse than a tension headache, he couldn't understand what it felt like. Not only the intense pain, but the nausea and vomiting, loss of vision, and eventually the pain would creep its way down from my head into my ears, down my neck, and settle into my shoulders so that everything from the shoulders up hurt like hell.

Something told me Savior wouldn't react like that, but at the same time, I didn't know for certain. What if he didn't understand how this felt? It wasn't something you could really explain to people. Sure, you could describe how it felt. They could witness you throw up, or stumble into walls. Not that I did that since I couldn't walk anymore, but I had before ending up in the wheelchair. Until they experienced a migraine, they had no idea what it felt like.

I opened my eyes and groaned. I could see out of my left eye, mostly, but the vision in my right had gone out entirely. If I shut my left eye, all I saw was an inky blackness with my right eye open. I knew it would pass once the migraine did. However, that didn't help me now. The fact the left side was starting to blur meant I could be blind in both eyes within another day or two if the migraine didn't pass.

The front door slammed, and I flinched at the stab of pain shooting through my brain. Ares made her appearance in the doorway, arms folded, and a scowl on her face.

"I saw Viking at the playground with the kids. You can't even be bothered to take care of them now?" The louder she spoke, the worse the pain got. She ranted another minute or two before the bile started rising in my throat again. I made a grab for the small trash can and barely got it in my lap before I threw up. I hugged the plastic bin and wanted to cry, but I refused to show that much weakness in front of her.

"Ares, I know you don't like me and don't want me here, but… shut up."

She inched a little closer. "What's wrong?"

"Migraine, and now I can't see out of my right eye. Viking took the kids to play after I threw up all over myself. So please, just… can we not fight right now?"

I didn't have the strength or energy to deal with her. I knew I wasn't much older than she was, so I never expected her to see me as her mother. But I would have liked to be her friend. Sadly, she didn't seem to want that.

"You can't see?" she asked, her voice dropping low. I squinted at her from my somewhat good eye and saw the look of horror on her face.

"My vision will come back when the migraine goes away. I just need some quiet, and to close my eyes for a while."

She walked up to the side of the bed and took the

trash can from me. I heard her walk off, then the water running. When she returned, she set the trash can on the table again where I could reach it.

"You didn't have to do that," I murmured.

"Yes, I did. I've been a bitch to you, and I'm sorry. It's got nothing to do with you personally."

I smiled faintly. "I know, Ares. The kids and I showed up and stole all the time you had with your dad. I get it. I told him from the beginning you wouldn't want me here. He argued and said you'd adjust, that you needed a mom as much as Judd and Junie do. It didn't occur to him you might not want one, especially since I'm only ten years older than you."

"You told him that?" she asked.

"I did. Then he made a phone call, got this stubborn look on his face, and told me we were married." I sighed. "I'd have fought him harder if I'd known how much you'd hate me being here. I'm sorry if you think I've ruined your life."

I heard a sniffle and looked up at her. A tear slid down her cheek and her lip trembled. I held up my hand to her, and she placed hers in mine, then sat on the edge of the bed. Before I knew it, she'd thrown herself down and sobbed against me. I wrapped my arms around her and smoothed a hand over her hair.

"It's not the end of the world, Ares. This is still your home. Savior is still your dad. The only difference is you have two little siblings, and someone who would like to be your friend, if you'll let me. I'm not asking you to call me Mom or even think of me as one."

"I'm sorry," she said. "I've been so horrible to you, and all you've done is try to be nice to me. I don't know why I've been such a bitch. I guess I thought he wouldn't want me here anymore once you and the kids came. He'd have the family he always wanted. Why would he need me?"

"Because you're his daughter, Ares. It doesn't matter that you don't share the same DNA. I'm not related to Judd or Junie, but I love them with all my heart. I'd love you too, if you'd let me."

She sat up and wiped the tears off her cheeks. "Can we start over?"

"I'd like that. But can we start over later? Right now, I really need to close my eyes and have some peace and quiet. I'm not trying to be mean or chase you off. I'd just like to be able to see, stop throwing up, and not want to smash my head into the wall in the hopes of knocking myself out."

"I'll be in my room, but I'll leave the door open. If you need anything, just call out my name. I'll help however I can."

"Thank you, Ares."

She smiled and hurried out of the room. With a sigh, I shut my eyes again. Maybe being here wasn't a mistake after all. If Ares was willing to give me another chance, then I must not be doing too bad a job at being Savior's wife.

Only time would tell.

Chapter Seven
Savior

I pinched the bridge of my nose and wondered if I'd be able to get through all the paperwork after I downed a few beers. Narrowing my gaze at the two empty bottles on my desk, I amended my thought to a few *more* beers. How the fuck had Torch dealt with all this shit while raising a family?

A knock sounded at the door, and I tipped my head back. If I ignored them, would they go away? They knocked again, and I realized I'd have to let them in.

"Enter," I called out.

"Hey, Pres." Sam came in and shut the door behind him. "Just wanted to give you an update."

"Shouldn't you be finishing up the kitchen?"

"We were working on it, but…" He looked away for a moment. "Dessa is sick. Threw up all over herself. Says she suffers from migraines. The noise wasn't helping her any, so we stopped for the day. But I mentioned not remodeling the shower, and it looked like I'd gutted her."

"We haven't had a chance to talk about future plans. She doesn't know I'm having a new house built with wider doorways and everything she could ever need or want to make her life easier. I'll talk to her about it soon."

I stared at the desk. She had migraines? It was the first I'd heard of it, which drove home the fact we knew very little about one another. In a perfect world, we'd have had time to date and learn all the little details. But something always fucked things up. If it wasn't one thing going wrong, it was another. The club seemed to always need me, or I had a mountain of paperwork to go through, bills to approve for payment, schedules to create. Torch had warned it was a lot of work. It hadn't seemed so bad when I only had Ares. Now that I had a wife and two small children, things were different.

Of course, when I'd agreed to accept the position, it never crossed my mind my family would expand so quickly, or so soon. I'd have never thought I had a child out there somewhere. Junie had been a surprise. Then finding out a club whore had bought her… We'd faced worse. Probably would again in the future. None of it had allowed for much time to bond with my new family. I felt like shit when I realized how badly I'd been neglecting them.

"Something else you should know. Saw Ares heading back home when I came here. I heard she's been giving your wife hell. She doesn't do it in front of you. When you're not home, Ares is a bit mouthy with Dessa. Or she flat-out ignores her. I've caught her twice, glaring daggers at Dessa, then storming off when Dessa is mid-sentence. Not sure what's up, but she's being a little shit."

Fuck. Just what I needed. I looked at the mess on my desk and knew it would have to wait. No fucking way I could let my daughter make Dessa even sicker. Wait. If the noise from the construction had bothered her, then…

"Where are Junie and Judd?"

Sam smiled. "Viking took them to the playground. Said he'd give her an hour to rest, but I have a feeling he'll keep them longer. She was in bad shape, Savior."

"I'll go check on her. Make sure Ares is behaving, and see if there's anything I can do to ease her pain."

"I know I'm just a Prospect, and it's none of my business, but I think there's more going on with her than a migraine. She seems to be hard on herself. We all realize she can't walk, and it's more difficult for her to do everyday things. However, I get the feeling she believes this club expects her to take charge or something."

"Did she say something?" I asked.

"No. It's only a feeling I have after watching her off and on the last week. When she thinks no one is watching, a sad look crosses her face. If you don't mind me asking, how long has she been in that chair?"

"I think she said about ten months."

Sam nodded. "Then she's still figuring things out, and now you've dumped her into an entirely foreign situation. Being part of the club is different from anything she's probably experienced before. Want me to have Amity visit with her? She's the newest addition and is still settling in."

"I'd appreciate it. Since I've had everyone working on the house, I haven't had a chance to get a ramp added to the clubhouse. But I don't want to cover the steps. Think we could take off the rail at the end of the porch and add a ramp that snakes down to the parking lot? She'll need easy access for family events, or if there's an emergency, and she needs to get to me."

"Since I can't work on the kitchen today, want me to get started? I can take some measurements and figure out what supplies we'll need," Sam said.

"That would be great. Now, if you'll excuse me, I think I need to check on my wife."

It felt like everyone was pulling me in twenty different directions. I either needed to become one of those old Stretch Armstrong toys, or I'd be ripped apart before I'd been President for a year. I locked up the office and headed out to my bike, waving to my brothers as I passed them. Thankfully, it was too fucking early in the day for the club whores. Most already knew to avoid me, since I hadn't touched them in the last year, but some of the newer ones still tried to get my attention. It would never happen.

On the way to the house, I saw Viking with the kids. I stopped and waved. Neither kid noticed me, and I didn't want to risk them asking to go back home, so I got back on the road without speaking to them. Viking had given me a chin lift, so I knew he'd seen me. By the time I reached the house, I'd tensed up, not knowing what the hell to expect.

The fact the house remained quiet scared the shit out of me. Ever since I'd brought Dessa home, it hadn't been this quiet except in the middle of the night when everyone was asleep. If Ares was awake, she was banging things around, stomping through the house, or giving Dessa a hard time. I'd tried to let the two of them figure it out, but I felt like an asshole for not saying or doing anything. Dessa insisted she needed to figure things out with Ares on her own, and I was trying to honor her request.

I crept down the hall when I didn't see anyone in the kitchen or living room. Ares's door stood open, and I peeked inside. She was stretched out on her bed with a magazine and glanced up when she felt me watching her.

"Dad, everything okay?" she whispered.

"What's going on?" I asked.

"Dessa has a migraine. She's been throwing up, and she said she can't see out of one eye. I'm worried about her."

I smiled a little. "Good to hear the two of you aren't fighting today."

She winced and sat up. "I'm sorry. I didn't give her a chance, and it was wrong of me. I was scared. You had two new kids, a wife... I felt like you didn't need me anymore. I know you said nothing would change. I guess…"

"You've been through hell, Ares. I don't blame you for worrying you'd lose your home. I knew things wouldn't be easy when I brought Dessa home, but she's a sweet woman. I think you'll like her if you give yourself a chance to know her better."

"I will. I promise."

I nodded. "I'm going to go check on her."

I made my way to the bedroom and quietly entered the room. She seemed to be sleeping. Until I studied her closer. Her brow furrowed, and I could see the pain etched into her features. It worried me that Ares said Dessa had lost the vision in one of her eyes. Was that a normal thing for her? I'd never had a migraine, so I didn't know much about them. Had she ever been to the doctor for it?

"You're staring," she murmured.

I eased my cut off my shoulders and sat it on the dresser before toeing off my boots. I walked around to the other side and slid into bed next to her. Drawing her against my chest, I held her close.

"You get these often?" I whispered.

"Several times a month. I was overdue," she said. "And before you ask, no, there's nothing I can take for them. A neurologist is too expensive. I've been to one before. They ran all sorts of tests and couldn't find a cause for them. Tried various medications. None worked. I could have kept going, but I didn't see the point. So I just suffer through them. I've tried all the tricks. Room temperature sports drinks, an ice pack, a heat pack, taking a hot or cold shower, soaking my hands and feet in cold or hot water. None of it helps even a little bit."

"You have to tell me when you get one of these. I'll

get someone to help with the kids on those days. If Junie and Judd are here, screaming and playing, you'll never get rid of your migraine."

"I'm already too much trouble," she said.

And there it was. Seemed that Sam had been right. She felt like a burden or something, and I needed to set her straight.

"Sam said he mentioned the shower renovation being canceled. I haven't had a chance to talk to you about it yet. I got to thinking. Even though there's no guarantee you'll ever get pregnant, Junie and Judd will eventually want their own rooms. Ares might move out at some point, but she'll start a family of her own, and we'll need a bedroom for any grandkids to spend the night."

She snorted. "I'm twenty-six. Please stop trying to make me both a mother and a grandmother all at once. You're going to make my brain hurt more."

I kissed the top of her head. "Just thinking ahead, sweetheart. No sense putting a ton of money into this place, especially since there's nothing I can do to fix the hall bathroom. So I thought it would be better to start from scratch. I'm going to have a custom-built house added farther back in the compound."

"Sounds pricey," she said.

"It will be, but it's also worth it. I want you to have easy access to every room in the house. And I'd like a bit more space than we have now."

"We can talk about it later," she said, snuggling in.

"Want me to stay here for a little while?"

She nodded. "I like it when you hold me. Only if you don't have something important to do."

"Honey, nothing means more to me than my family, which includes you. So no, I don't have to go do anything else right now. I'll lie here and hold you while you rest."

"There's only one thing I've never tried that I've heard might work. Maybe not right now while the pain is so awful, though."

"What's that?" I asked, ready to give her whatever she needed.

"Orgasms."

I bit my lip so I wouldn't laugh. "Really? Well, when the pain has lessened enough you feel up to having sex, you let me know. I'll give you a few orgasms and you can see if it helps or makes it worse. Then we'll know for next time."

"Gabriel?"

"What is it, Dessa?" I asked softly.

"Thank you. I know I've said it before, but you're amazing and so kind. I'm glad you came back for me that night."

I was too. If I hadn't, I could only imagine what might have happened to her. Whoever had entered the house and stolen her pills could have done so much worse while they were there. It scared the shit out of me, thinking about how vulnerable we'd left her. I still needed to have a conversation with Tempest, but I hadn't had a chance yet. I'd find him later. After I knew Dessa would be all right.

She said she'd been to a neurologist before. I had to wonder if maybe a different doctor might have better luck. It wouldn't hurt to get a second opinion, would it? The thought of her being like this every month gutted me. How the hell had she functioned before now? She'd had the kids all to herself for the most part. Had she just suffered through it and taken care of them, even when she was in so much pain she was throwing up?

It made me hate Sonja even more. If she weren't

already dead, I'd probably kill her all over again. She'd not only stolen the children from the club, but she'd treated Dessa horribly.

Once I knew she slept soundly, I slipped out from under her and left the bedroom. I didn't bother putting my cut or boots back on because I wasn't going to leave the house while she was like this. But it didn't mean I couldn't handle a few club matters over the phone. Starting with my Sergeant-at-Arms. I shot off a quick text while I set up the Keurig in the living room. It was the best I could do until the kitchen had been put back together.

My house. Now. And be fucking quiet.

A light knock sounded at the door about ten minutes later, and I opened it, letting Tempest inside. I motioned for him to have a seat.

"Dessa has a migraine, so keep it down," I said.

He grunted as he sat. "Did you need something?"

"Yeah. I need to know what's crawled up your ass. The way you treated her when we went to get the kids isn't like you. Not to mention, you didn't make sure someone repaired her door. When I went back to get her, it was still busted open. Someone had been in there while she slept, Tempest. They'd stolen her medication, but they could have raped her. Killed her. And we'd have been responsible."

He winced and looked away. "Sorry, Pres. Guess my mind was elsewhere."

"So… talk to me about it. Why did you tear into Dessa that way?"

"I had a kid. Long time ago. I was only sixteen. My girlfriend was fifteen. They shipped her off to some family in another state, and she wrote a letter telling me the baby had died."

I leaned back in my seat. "What does that have to

do with Dessa?"

"Reminded me of it, I guess. Found out the baby hadn't died. Not then, anyway. They put *father unknown* on the birth certificate and adopted to it a husband and wife who claimed they couldn't have kids. Except they didn't go through legal channels. It was an under the table deal, and my baby died when she was only three years old."

"Dessa didn't hurt the kids, Tempest. If anyone needed that anger from you, it was Sonja. My wife was just as much a victim of that bitch as the kids were."

He nodded. "I know, and I'm sorry. It's also… the wheelchair."

"What about it? You have a problem with her because she can't walk? It's not her fault," I said.

"My girlfriend… she'd been in one too. Had a bad fall when she was only a toddler. Broke her back. I know it sounds fucked-up, having sex with a girl who couldn't walk or feel anything below the waist. She begged me. Said she wanted to feel normal, and I gave in. I was too stupid to think about protection."

"I'm sorry you went through that, but Dessa isn't your lying ex-girlfriend. She's my wife. You need to treat her with respect, and you owe her a fucking apology. Since she's the sweetest woman I've ever met, I have no doubt she'll forgive you. It's going to take me a little while, though. Hell, I can't even forgive myself for what we did."

"Understood," he said, standing up. "I know I've been avoiding her since you brought her home. I'll make an effort to say I'm sorry and get acquainted with her. Okay to leave now?"

"Yeah. Get out of here. I'm staying home the rest of the day. Dessa's vision is going out, and she's been throwing up because of her migraine." I paused. "See if anyone knows of a good neurologist in the area. I'd like her to get a second opinion. The doctor she saw said there wasn't anything else they could try. I'm not convinced it's a lost cause. There has to be something they can do for her."

"I'll text you if I find anything."

After he left, I sipped my coffee and wondered about the woman sleeping down the hall. What else did she need from me? I wanted her to feel welcome here. To realize she wasn't alone anymore. And yet, she still kept me at a distance. Why the fuck hadn't she called me when she'd realized she had a migraine? Did she think I'd call her weak? Or get angry she needed help?

No, the stubborn woman probably refused to admit she needed anyone. Ever since she'd realized what it meant to be mine, the position it put her in with the club, she'd been determined to prove she was worthy of being my wife. Foolish woman. I shook my head but couldn't stop the smile that spread across my lips. She hadn't realized it yet, but I was the one unworthy of *her.*

I'd just have to do everything I could to make her fall in love with me. Because if she was as smart as I thought, then one day she'd wake up and realize she could do so much better than me. And if that ever happened, she'd find out what kind of asshole she'd married... I'd never let her go. Hell, it didn't matter what I had to do to keep her here. I'd do it.

It had only been a week. So why did it feel like my life would be over if she left me? Waking up with her in my arms was the most wonderful feeling. We'd had sex several times since I'd brought her home. Each time was more amazing than the last.

As soon as her migraine eased or went away

entirely, I'd have her under me again. She didn't think she could have kids, but she could be wrong. I'd find out who the best doctors were in the area. No. In the entire fucking state. I'd make sure she saw them, and we'd find out together exactly what needed to be done to help her. Not only with her migraines, but I hoped they might have better news for us about having children.

Watching her with the kids, I could tell she was a natural. She'd confessed how much she'd wanted a family. Now she had one.

I only wished she realized that we needed her as much as she needed us. She would. One day. Until then, I'd do everything I could to take care of her, prove to her she hadn't made a mistake coming here. And hopefully, someday soon, she'd tell me she loved me. I had no doubt I'd be in love with her before long. I already had feelings for her. It would be incredibly difficult to *not* fall in love with her. Jeremy had been a fucking moron to let her go, but I was grateful. If he hadn't, she wouldn't be in my bed right now.

Asshole didn't deserve her anyway. I hope he rots in hell.

Chapter Eight
Dessa

It took three more days before my migraine finally subsided enough I could function. Ares had helped with the children, and so had several of the old ladies. Even though I still hadn't met anyone other than Lavender, Savior had asked someone named Ridley and another woman named Darian to help. I'd been in bed when they picked Judd and Junie up. It made me feel like the worst mother ever. Not only couldn't I take care of them, but people I'd never met had fed my children and entertained them while I rested.

I eyed the door from my wheelchair. It had taken me a while, but I'd bathed this morning and put on a pale pink sundress with a small daisy print. I'd even pulled my hair back in a clip with a few tendrils hanging on either side of my face. While I didn't care much for makeup, I'd used a tinted lip balm so I wouldn't look so pale.

I gathered my courage and opened the front door, then rolled out onto the porch. I went down the ramp and into the driveway. Since I didn't have a way to drive, I took my time wheeling toward the clubhouse. Savior had said I could stop by anytime I needed to see him. Although, my trip had more to do with what I'd overheard last night. Ares had been on the phone with one of her friends in the compound -- Aura. I hadn't met the girl yet, but they'd said something about club whores.

The term whore was simple enough to understand. Adding club to it, I figured they were women who entertained the bikers here at the Dixie Reapers. I vaguely remembered him calling Sonja one, and he'd said she'd given herself up to whoever wanted her. But I hadn't had time to really question it. Too much had happened too fast. Ares had said they were at the clubhouse, which is where Savior spent so much of his time. It wasn't that I didn't trust him. He'd said he would be faithful to me, and I didn't have a reason to doubt him. But I'd met plenty of women who went after married men, and I knew they could be relentless.

I made it down the road past six houses and I saw the clubhouse in the distance. Now would have been a good time to have a motorized chair. I'd never had to wheel myself very far, and I knew my arms would be aching by the time I got back to the house. Unless someone gave me a ride home.

"What in the hell are you doing?" a man called out from a nearby house.

I glanced his way. "Riding a pony. What's it look like?"

He snorted. "And here I thought you'd be the least amount of trouble of all the ladies. Already getting sassy and haven't even met all of them yet."

I wasn't sure how to take his words. Deciding his statement didn't require anything else from me, I kept rolling forward. I heard him curse, then the sound of his boots on the grass and finally on the pavement. My chair jolted, and I yelped, letting go of the wheels as he pushed me.

"Savior would have my ass if I didn't lend a hand." He sighed. "My name is Tank. I'm the retired Sergeant-at-Arms. You'll eventually meet my woman, Emmie, and our three hellions."

"It's nice to meet you. I'm Dessa."

"I know." I heard the humor in his voice. "It's big news around here when the club President takes a wife. Everyone's been eager to meet you but thought we should let you settle in a bit. Not to mention all the renovations in the house. You probably haven't had much time for yourself."

"Not exactly. Although, the migraine I had for five days did a fair job of clearing everyone out. Including the children."

"Heard about that," he said. "I'm glad you seem to be feeling better."

I gaped when we got to the clubhouse. Savior had put a ramp in for me. I didn't remember seeing it before, when we'd first arrived. I'd wondered how I would get inside once I got here. I felt a flutter in my stomach as I stared at it. The man was always doing sweet things like this. If he kept it up, I'd be head over heels in love with him before long.

Tank helped me into the building, and my eyes adjusted to the dim lighting and smoke-filled air. My jaw dropped as I looked around. Even though it was still daylight outside, three women were here, and didn't have a stitch of clothing on. One was on her knees with a man's cock in her mouth. My cheeks burned bright, and I quickly looked away, only to see a pretty blonde glaring at me. She folded her arms, pushing her breasts up, and I had a feeling I'd just been judged and found lacking.

Tank leaned down and whispered to me. "Don't let them get to you. Any of them gives you attitude, you put them in their place. You're Savior's wife, and if anyone has a right to be here, it's you. Don't take their shit, or they'll walk all over you. Got it?"

I nodded, appreciating the advice. Since all this was new to me, I wasn't sure how I'd react if those women spoke to me. And how exactly was I supposed to put them in their place? Did he mean verbally or physically? The first would be easy enough. The second not so much. I had a feeling they could run faster than I could roll.

I wheeled farther into the clubhouse and hoped I'd make it to Savior's office without any drama. The blonde eyed me, and I had a feeling she wouldn't keep her mouth shut. According to Tank, I couldn't ignore her. Would she attack me?

"I think you're in the wrong place," the woman said. "This isn't a school. It's a club for bikers."

My brow furrowed. "What the hell are you talking about?"

She smirked. "You look like you teach little kids, or maybe a Sunday school class. Clearly, you don't belong here."

My eyebrows rose as I stared at her. So she had a problem with how I'd dressed? Did my wardrobe need an upgrade? Should I look more badass than I currently did? Savior hadn't complained about the way I dressed.

"My husband seems to like my clothes just fine. He likes taking me out of them too."

I heard Tank cough behind me and mumble, "O*h shit*." Well, he'd said I should stand up for myself. That's what I was doing. Had he changed his mind? Because it was a little late now.

"Husband? Who would marry a cripple like you?" She sneered and took a step closer. "Was it a pity fuck, and then he felt like he was stuck with you? That has to be it. I don't see a property cut. If he hasn't given you one, then you're not his old lady."

Ouch. That actually hurt. I lifted my chin and refused to let her see her words had caused me pain. The bitch would probably enjoy it too much. And what the hell did she mean by a property cut? I remembered Lavender wearing a cut like the other men. Right. The back of hers said *Property of Wire*. Why hadn't Savior given me one? Did I not need it since I couldn't ride on his bike with him?

Wait. Could Savior have an old lady *and* a wife? What the hell was the difference? Something told me if this woman knew I'd married Savior, she'd come out swinging. She looked like the type.

"Since my husband seems to think I'm incredible and the best he's ever had, I'm going to assume he just hasn't had a chance to have a property cut made for me yet. But we can ask him. Care to join me?"

She looked around the room. "So which of these sorry assholes is yours? Because they've all been balls-deep in one or more of us today."

Eww. Did she have to be so crude? My nose wrinkled as if I'd smelled something bad. I refused to look around and figure out which men were present. I'd never be able to look at them the same way again. Did Viking sleep with these women? I hope he used disinfectant when he showered afterward. Surely a sweet guy like him didn't use these women. Not that it was any of my business.

"I'm married to Savior," I said.

Her eyes widened and her lips parted. "What?"

I nodded. "Still want to go ask him which of us is better?"

She snapped her mouth shut, and it looked like she might be grinding her teeth. The way her cheeks flushed, and she looked away, I knew she had to be too new to have ever been with him. He'd mentioned not being with a woman in about a year. I'd assumed that meant the club whores as well as a possible ex-girlfriend.

"Since you've become mute, I guess that means you don't want to go with me." I rolled past her and down the hallway. It only took a moment to find his office and I knocked on the door.

"Come in," he called out.

I pushed the door open and started to go inside, only to discover there wouldn't be enough room. I stayed in the doorway and smiled when he looked up. He stood so fast his chair slammed in the wall behind him.

"Dessa! Is everything okay?" He rushed around the desk and dropped to one knee in front of me.

"I'm fine. I can't just come say hi?" I asked.

He looked over my shoulder. "Anyone give you any trouble?"

I folded my hands in my lap. "You mean the whores?"

He hung his head and groaned. "I should have better prepared you for what you'd face here. I'm starting to feel like I'm not giving you enough of my attention. Same for the kids and the club. I'll figure out how to balance everything. I hope."

I reached out and ran my fingers through his hair. "We're fine. I can only imagine how stressful it is to be the President of a club like this. You have so many people counting on you, and the paperwork on your desk looks a bit crazy."

He nodded. "Yeah. I inherited most of this stuff. Just trying to sort through it and figure out what the most important things are so I can get those out of the way before tackling something else. It wasn't the ideal time to bring home a wife and two kids."

Right. Because we weren't planned. Although he'd at least known about Junie and Judd. I wouldn't let his words get to me. "Is there anything I can do to help?"

"Sorry, sweetheart. We consider all this stuff club business, which means it's a bunch of things you shouldn't see. I want to keep you and the kids safe. While the club is mostly legit these days, there will still be things I can't talk about with you. The club backed off from the really bad shit once the brothers started taking old ladies and starting families. Not sure we'll ever go completely legal, though."

"I met Tank. He said he has a wife and three kids."

Savior nodded. "Not sure I consider Kasen, Westlyn, and Harlow children. They're eighteen or nineteen now. Can't really keep up. Wouldn't surprise me if they settled down soon or went off to college. Depends on how much Tank loosens the leash he has on them."

"I'd love to meet more of the people here."

He smiled at me. "Would you? How about now?"

"You mean, do I want to meet them right this second?"

He nodded. "Yep. That's what I meant. I'm about to go clear out the clubhouse. No whores allowed until later tonight. Since you're here already, I can make some calls and get some of the ladies here. Is Ares watching the kids?"

"She took them to play with kids close to their age. At least, that's what she said. Since she put on some makeup and fixed her hair, I think there may be a boy involved somehow."

"Dawson is a year older than her. It's probably him. Unless she's set her sights on someone a little older. A few of the boys are between nineteen and twenty-one. Have to admit, if she's going after one of the older ones, I hope its Cowboy's son, Jackson. Kid has a good head on his shoulders, and he's usually off chasing the next rodeo. Less chance he'll get her pregnant."

"Wait. She's only sixteen. You were entirely too calm just now when you mentioned Ares getting pregnant. What the hell kind of circus did I land in?"

He sighed and stood up. "Do I want it to happen? Nope. But I'm realistic. I can't watch her twenty-four-seven, and if she wants to have sex, she will. Besides, the life she had before this one, there's no way she's letting anyone touch her unless they've won her trust first."

I backed up into the hall. "Let's go clear those women out. I'm ready to meet the rest of your club family. Or as many as I can today."

Savior shut his office door, then leaned down to kiss me. When he walked off, I followed, my lips tingling. He yelled at the women to get dressed and get the fuck out. Each of them scurried to grab their clothes and hastily pulled them on before dashing out the door. They hadn't wasted anytime following his order.

"As for the rest of you, Dessa would like to meet more of the club members, as well as the old ladies and children. I want this place cleaned up. Now." He looked over at Tank. "I see you're still here. Think your woman and girls will want to come say hi?"

Tank grinned. "Yeah. I'll go get them. I'll knock on a few doors on my way home and send more people over here."

"Appreciate it, Tank," Savior said.

As he stepped outside, two women hurried into the clubhouse. They stopped in front of Savior and gave me a quick smile.

"So, did you or your wife send those women running?" the blonde asked.

"I did. Dessa wanted to meet more people. Dessa, this is Ridley. She's Venom's old lady. The woman next to her is Isabella. She's married to Torch, who was the President before me."

Ridley sat at the nearest table, and Isabella slid a chair out of the way before claiming another. Their kindness touched me. Not many people would have thought to remove a chair for me. I rolled up to the table and wondered if I was about to make two new friends.

Savior kissed the top of my head. "I need to get more work done. The Prospects will clean up and more people will probably show up soon. Just give me a shout if you need anything."

I reached up and ran my fingers over his jaw. "I will. And thank you."

He kissed me quickly, then hurried down the hall. Ridley and Isabella were both smiling widely when I looked at them again. I felt like touching my face to see if I was drooling or something.

"You have no idea how happy we are that Savior has you now," Ridley said. "He's wanted an old lady and family for so long."

"What have I gotten myself into?" I asked.

"Trouble," Ridley said. "But usually the fun kind. There's always a bit of drama with the club whores, especially the new ones. It blows over and things get quiet for a while. Sometimes there's other stuff going on."

Isabella snorted. "Way to simplify it. What she means is trouble does come knocking, and we're sent into hiding... Oh shit. I don't think Savior thought about that."

"What?" I asked.

"There's an underground bunker for the women and kids. There's no way to get down there in your chair. Someone would have to carry you down, and I'm not sure if they'd have time to get your chair into the bunker as well. Hell, the entire place will need to be renovated."

Ridley rolled her eyes. "Since there was a giant hole

in the ceiling, and other damage, pretty sure they're doing that anyway. Making it wheelchair accessible shouldn't be an issue."

"I… No. I don't think I want to know why there's a hole in the ceiling, or what sort of trouble comes here. I'll pretend I didn't hear any of that."

Isabella nodded. "Don't blame you."

"If you want to drive Savior crazy, you can join us for our morning ogling," Ridley said. I didn't have any clue what she meant, and it must have been obvious since she explained a moment later. "The single guys tend to work out near the playground in the mornings when the weather is nice. They challenge each other. They're usually shirtless. Our men hate it when we go stare at them."

"Why would you want to?" I asked.

"Aww. She must really like Savior," Ridley said to Isabella. "Doesn't even want to look at another man. I keep telling Venom I'm not blind or dead. I can look and not touch."

"And if he looked at the naked women Savior just threw out of here?" I asked.

She narrowed her eyes. "Then I'd rip them to pieces and make him sleep on the couch."

I waited for her to realize what she'd said, but it never happened. "Um. Ridley, I know we just met, but that doesn't seem very fair. You can go check out the other men, but he can't look at the naked women running around the clubhouse?"

Isabella held up a hand. "I'm going to stop you right there. One, Venom, would never look at another woman. He adores Ridley. And two, she does it so he'll come find her. He always tosses her over his shoulder, threatens to spank her, and they go off and have sex. It's a game she plays. I just go along for moral support."

"Y'all are crazy," I said.

Ridley threw back her head and laughed. "Yes, we are. No worries, you will be too."

"Not everyone turns into a psycho after being with the club," Isabella pointed out. "Emmie is still a sweetheart. Delphine is quiet most of the time. Not all the women here are like you and Pepper. You've just rubbed off on me over the years."

"Right." Ridley rubbed her hands together. "So, let's corrupt Dessa. It should be fun."

I was starting to second-guess myself. Maybe I shouldn't have met these particular women first. Or at least, not so soon. Was I really ready to jump into this life headfirst? Looked like I was about to find out.

How bad could it be?

Chapter Nine
Savior

By the time I'd worked through one of the small mountains of crap in my office, I could tell the party was in full swing. I'd had a feeling a few old ladies would turn into a full family affair within an hour or two, and I'd been right. It wasn't that I minded. Hell, I was grateful they were so welcoming to Dessa. I knew she'd been worried since coming here, and I hoped this set her at ease.

Someone knocked on the door and I yelled out for them to enter. Ares stepped inside and shut the door behind her. I hoped like fuck nothing was wrong. The way she chewed on her lips and shifted on her feet told me this wouldn't be a quick conversation.

"Out with it," I said.

"There's something I've wanted to ask for the last few weeks, but it never seemed like a good time. I realized tonight, while everyone was out there making Dessa feel like she belonged, and you holed up in your office, there might never *be* a good time. You're always working."

"You're not wrong." I leaned back in my chair. "Eventually, things will calm down. I'll get the hang of being the club President, and I won't spend nearly as much time in the office. After we have the new house built, I'll have a place at home where I can work, so that will help too."

"So, I'm sixteen now, and I have a car. You must think I'm responsible if you let me drive."

"Uh-huh." I motioned for her to continue.

"I want to go on dates," she blurted.

I had a feeling this would happen sooner or later. I'd hoped for much, much later. "Anyone in particular you want to date?"

Something told me it was Dawson. I knew the two had been spending a lot of time together. I wasn't sure how I felt about Ares dating. The girl had been through so much, she'd matured faster than most girls her age. But I needed to know exactly where she was going with this. Just a date? Or did she hope for something more?

"About that…" She looked away and seemed to be gathering her courage. "What if the guy is older than me?"

"How much older? A year? Two years?" I asked. Dawson was a year older, but there were five boys who were now nineteen, and a few who were already in their twenties. Since Logan had moved to Tennessee to prospect for the Reckless Kings, I didn't think it was him.

"I want to date Foster," she said.

She wanted to… Oh, hell no! I was shaking my head before I'd even given her a verbal answer. "That boy is all kinds of trouble. Look at what he did to Leigha. Ran her straight to the Reckless Kings and still made a pest of himself. He's not nearly mature enough for a relationship, not to mention he's twenty-one and you're sixteen."

She folded her arms over her chest. "And you're fifty to Dessa's… twenty-six?"

"I am," I said.

"Ah-ha!" She pointed a finger at me. "See! You're twice her age."

"Yes, and we're both adults. When you're nineteen or twenty, you can love whomever you want. But you're sixteen, Ares, and still a minor. It would be illegal for you to date Foster, and the last thing we need is the police nosing around. So no, you can't date Foster. End of discussion."

She stuck her lip out in a pout. "But Dawson is my best friend. It would be weird to date him. Same for the others who are closer to my age. They're like a bunch of big brothers."

Another knock on the door had Ares growling and yanking it open. She opened her mouth, then snapped it shut as Viking entered my office. The way she stared up at him nearly made me groan. She'd just been begging to date Foster, and now she was making calf eyes at Viking. The girl's hormones were clearly running wild. I wondered if she'd talk to Dessa about this. Get a woman's perspective.

"Something wrong?" I asked Viking.

"Not exactly. I think Dessa needs to use the bathroom and is too embarrassed to say anything. The ones at the clubhouse aren't wheelchair accessible. We'll need to fix that before we have another family event."

Christ. I should have thought to check on her sooner. "I'll come help her. See if you can talk sense into Ares. She thinks Foster is boyfriend material."

Viking barked a laugh, then covered it up with a cough. "Sure. I can do that."

I walked out, leaving him to it. Pausing in the hall after I shut the door, I listened for just a moment. I had no doubt Viking wouldn't touch her. He'd always been respectful of the women and girls at the compound. The age difference alone would deter him. If Ares were legal, it might be a different story. Although, I hadn't noticed him paying particular attention to anyone.

"Foster? Why the fuck do you want that asshole?" Viking asked. "You can do better, Ares."

"He doesn't treat me like I'm a child," she said.

"He won't give you the respect you deserve, either. He's still wild and not ready to settle down. Not to mention you're not exactly legal yet."

I hoped he got further with her than I had. I found Dessa near the hallway and turned the chair so I could lift her into my arms. She squealed and grabbed hold of me.

"A little birdie said you might need to use the bathroom," I whispered in her ear.

"Yes, but I can't use the ones here."

"I'm going to help you." I went into the bathroom and kicked the door shut. Keeping my arms around Dessa, I held her upright without putting pressure on her feet. She worked her panties down her hips, and I helped her sit, then stepped back and looked away while she used the toilet. I waited until she was finished before helping her back up. I carried her to the sink and let her wash her hands before taking her back into the hall and easing her down into her chair.

I'd need to have the clubhouse bathroom renovated sometime soon, which was just another thing to add to my ever-growing list. At this point, I'd never cross everything off. It seemed to get exponentially bigger every day.

Since I'd been neglecting Dessa and the kids, I knew I needed to take a break and join the party. It looked like all the families were here, even the smallest of the kids. Junie and Judd were across the room at a table with Cole and MaryJane. Pepper stood nearby, along with Lavender, so I knew they were in good hands. And it gave Dessa a break.

I wheeled her to the nearest table and pulled out a chair. She adjusted herself so her legs were under the table, and I took the seat next to her. She gave me a tired smile, and I wondered why I hadn't noticed the circles under her eyes. Tension bracketed her mouth, and her eyes seemed darker. It was obvious my wife was stressed the hell out, and I'd been oblivious.

"I haven't been taking very good care of you," I said. "I'm sorry."

"You've had a lot going on. When you mentioned me watching the kids while you were busy with the club, I figured you weren't going to be home most of the day."

"True. But I can do better. I *will*. You and the kids are important to me, and I haven't been acting like it. Hell, Sam had to tell me you had a migraine." I reached over and took her hand. "Have you met everyone here?"

"I did. Just don't ask me to tell you who is who. I've already forgotten most of their names. Especially the kids. I didn't realize how big the club was."

"It's grown a lot over the years. Thunder married Amity not too long ago. The couple before them was over four years ago. Sarge and Katya. Lavender and Wire got together about six years before that. For a while, it seemed like we had a new couple every year. Sometimes twice a year. Then we'd go stretches where no one settled down."

"Everyone seems happy together," she said.

"They are. I won't say there are never any arguments, because there are, but I think that's true with any couple. Doesn't matter if they're fated to be together or not."

She smiled softly. "You believe in fate?"

"Of course. If I hadn't gone to help another club, I'd have never met Ares or adopted her. If Sonja hadn't wanted Thunder bad enough to buy Junie and Judd from two other club whores, I'd have never known I had a daughter out there. Or that Merlin was a piece-of-shit traitor. Not that I'll ever tell Judd that about his birth father. Sperm donor might be a better term. Not sure he'd have ever been a good dad to that boy. Too wild. Still young and stupid, and only worried about himself."

"Does that mean you think it was fate the two of us met?" she asked.

I reached out to cup her cheek. "Yes, Dessa. There's no divorce with the Dixie Reapers. Torch held fast to that rule, and I will too. Telling Wire to marry us wasn't done lightly. I knew it would be forever, and I'd have never done that if I thought for one moment you weren't someone I'd want to keep the rest of my life. I'm only sorry I didn't take you with us when we showed up to get the kids."

"I don't blame you for what happened."

"Don't have to. I blame myself enough for the both of us. I should have pulled my head out of my ass sooner." I leaned in and kissed her on the lips. It was only a quick, soft kiss, but the dreamy look in her eyes when I pulled back was enough to make me want more. I hoped like hell the kids went to bed early tonight, and Dessa felt well enough for us to have some quality time together in the bedroom.

"I like the women here," she said. "Ridley and Isabella were nice. Maybe a little crazy, but I think I can see myself being friends with them."

I chuckled. "Yeah, that's a good way to describe them. Especially when they're together. They were the first two old ladies in the club. Even though you're my wife, and I'm the new President, I have a feeling Ridley and Isabella will still try to meddle and take over from time to time. It's up to you if you want to let them."

"Let them?" She stared at me like I'd lost my mind. "I may have just met them, but I don't think anyone *lets* them do anything."

"You're not wrong." I kissed her again. "Want

anything to drink? Something to eat?"

"A drink sounds good," she said.

"I'll be right back." I got up and went to the coolers set up under one of the long folding tables. The first had wine coolers and mini bottles of wine. The second had juice and milk for the kids. I finally found the sodas and grabbed one for Dessa, and another for myself. While I'd have enjoyed a beer, I didn't want to drink if I was going to take her home in a little while. I'd have to leave my bike here and use a club truck. I glanced at Dessa. How the hell had she gotten here? Had the stubborn woman wheeled herself all the way to the clubhouse?

Even though she hadn't asked for food, I tucked the sodas under one arm and grabbed a plate, adding some chips and two sandwiches. Since I hadn't eaten in a while, I was starving, and I had a feeling Dessa hadn't eaten much either. Especially if she'd been worried about being able to get to the bathroom on her own. There were times I needed to kick my own ass. Like now. How the fuck had I not thought about the bathroom at the clubhouse?

I carried the plate and drinks back to the table and set them down before reclaiming my chair. She reached out for a chip and nibbled on it. When she went to grab another, she paused, hand hovering over the plate.

"I didn't think to ask. I'm just eating your food."

I kissed her cheek. "I got it for both of us. Eat as much as you want."

Tempest came through the doors and scanned the room. When he saw me sitting with Dessa, he headed straight for us. Looked like my woman was about to get that apology, even though I knew Tempest didn't want to do it. He'd never been one to admit when he was wrong. If I hadn't been his President, and I'd told him to apologize to my wife, he'd have given me attitude.

He plunked down in the chair next to me and stared at Dessa. She froze, eyes wide. Shit. I reached over and place my hand on her thigh and leaned in to whisper everything would be fine. I could see her pulse pounding. I should have warned her Tempest would want to speak with her sooner or later.

"I'm sorry I was an asshole and scared you when we came to get the kids," Tempest said, his jaw tight. "You didn't know what Sonja had done. It wasn't right to take it out on you."

That was his apology? Jesus. I kicked him under the table, and he scowled at me. I'd heard more sincere apologies from the Prospects, or even the teenagers living here. Hell, Farrah and Mariah, when they were younger, had done a better job at saying they were sorry. If he didn't pull his head out of his ass, I was going to beat the shit out of him to drive home my point.

"I-i-it's fine," she stammered.

"No, it fucking isn't," I said. "Outside. Now."

Tempest stood and stormed off. I got up to follow, and Dessa reached over to take my hand.

"It's really all right, Savior."

"Like fuck it is. I already talked to him. Thought he understood and would give you a true apology. Not this half-assed shit."

"What are you going to do?"

"Knock some sense into him."

I left, going outside where Tempest waited in the parking lot. It didn't escape my notice several people came outside to watch, and one of them happened to be my wife. She worried at her bottom lip, and I knew she didn't like what I was about to do. At the same time, I needed Tempest and everyone else to realize I meant business. I wasn't going to let them ignore my orders or walk all over me.

"I told you to tell Dessa you were sorry for how you treated her. You got in her face and threatened her. Then you give some bullshit apology you don't even mean?" I asked. "You think I'm going to let that slide?"

"I don't care," he said. "You're the only one who hasn't realized she's not fit to be the wife of the club President. So she wasn't in on it with Sonja. Fine. But how the fuck is she going to stand by your side in a time of crisis? How is she going to be any help to you at all?"

I fisted my hand and took a swing at him, colliding with his jaw. He worked it back and forth and glowered at me. But it seemed I hadn't sufficiently shut him up. I landed a right hook to his cheek, slammed my fist into his abdomen, then hit his chin with an uppercut that had him staggering and nearly falling to the ground.

"What crawled up your ass?" I asked. "You seemed fine after we spoke. Something had to have happened between now and then."

"One of the club whores gave her shit. If she'd gone after your wife physically, do you think Dessa would have had a chance against her? Because I don't. The girl let your woman give her a verbal smackdown, but that's it. If she's not tough enough to handle one of the dumb sluts spreading their legs for the club, how is she going to be a help to you any other way?"

I looked over my shoulder at Dessa. Her cheeks had flushed, and she wouldn't hold my gaze. His words had made a direct hit, and I had a feeling she'd be questioning her place here. Every time I thought I was gaining ground with her, making her see her value, someone knocked us back a few steps. The sight of her feeling so defeated lit a fire inside me.

I went after Tempest with everything I had, landing blow after blow until I had him on the ground. Even then, I didn't stop. It wasn't until my chest was heaving and I'd split open my knuckles that I stepped back. The fucker was pissing me off with this shit.

"What would you do if you wrecked your bike tomorrow and could never walk again? You couldn't ride your motorcycle. Had to relearn everything. Bathing. Dressing. Using the bathroom. Could no longer live in your home without some renovations. What would you do, Tempest?"

He shrugged. "Probably put a bullet in my brain because if I can't ride my bike what's the point in living?"

I pointed to Dessa. "She's been through all that. Not being able to drive. Learning how to cook, bathe, dress... All the things you do every day, she's had to learn a new way to do them. That woman is braver than you'll ever be, Tempest, and you dare say she's not tough enough to be at my side?"

Saint came down to stand next to me. He folded his arms and stared down Tempest. Then Grimm, Royal, and Viking joined us. When Tempest realized every officer stood against him, his shoulder sagged. He tipped his head back and stared up at the sky before finally getting to his feet. He didn't even bother brushing himself off or stopping the blood that ran down his chin.

"What's going to happen if a whore gets violent with her? What if someone sees her as your weakness and comes after her? How is she going to defend herself?" he asked. "If something happens to her, you're going to fall apart. The club needs you to be strong at all times. Can you do that if she's hurt or killed?"

No. It would fucking gut me. But letting her go wouldn't make it any easier. We hadn't been together long. As my brothers had often said, sometimes you just knew when you found the right woman. It had been that way for me and Dessa. I couldn't let her go. Wouldn't. She was mine, and that was the end of it. Tempest could fall in line, or I'd kick his ass again.

"I actually looked into a few things," Saint said. "There are self-defense classes for people in wheelchairs. There's no reason she can't learn to protect herself if someone tries to grab her, or attacks. As the Sergeant-at-Arms, maybe you should have looked into that instead of using her disability as an excuse to belittle her."

Tempest rocked back on his heels. "There is?"

I had to admit it hadn't crossed my mind, either. I owed Saint a beer after this. Maybe a few cases of beer. Having someone teach Dessa to protect herself would certainly set my mind at ease when I wasn't with her.

"Yes. In fact, I was going to ask Dessa when she might want to learn. There's a class in the next town that starts this week. If that's too soon, another will begin in a month." Saint glanced at me. "Hadn't had a chance to mention it to you yet."

"Thanks for looking into it." I held Tempest's gaze. "So, are you going to fall in line and support my wife, or do we need to go a few more rounds? I might be getting old, but I can keep going."

He held up his hands. "I'm done. And, Dessa, I'm sorry. Truly."

"Even if Dessa accepts, I don't," I said. "You need to earn my forgiveness. Whatever is making you act like such a dick, get it figured and move the fuck on. We aren't going to keep doing this. Understood?"

He nodded. "Got it."

I sure the fuck hoped so. I had enough shit to deal with. The last thing I needed was one of my officers acting like a damn toddler throwing a tantrum.

I left Tempest in the parking lot and went up onto the porch with Dessa. I kneeled in front of her, took her hands in mine, and waited for her to look at me.

"You're *not* unworthy of being my wife. You're stronger than anyone gives you credit for, and you amaze me every fucking day. Understood? All the bullshit Tempest spewed is utter nonsense. As Saint mentioned, you can learn to defend yourself. If that's something you want to do."

"I'd like that," she whispered.

"Then you can talk to Saint and figure out when and where. He can handle it for you. We'll discuss transportation later. I don't like the thought of you coming all the way to the clubhouse in your chair, either, so it's something we need to talk about anyway."

She nodded and I leaned in to kiss her, then stood and pushed her back into the clubhouse. I refused to let Tempest ruin the fun everyone had been having. The club needed days like this one. If we didn't take time to be one big family, relax, and enjoy each other's company, then what the fuck were we fighting for the rest of the time?

Chapter Ten

Dessa

The phone rang for the tenth time, and I hurried to answer it. The screen on the phone said *Private Number*, just like all the other times. I answered, wondering if someone would actually speak this time.

"Hello?" Heavy breathing and nothing else. "I know you're there. Look, if you have the wrong number, just stop calling."

"Do you know what he likes?" a woman asked, her voice a near whisper. "He likes to hurt people."

I knew she couldn't be talking about Savior. "Who?"

"Jeremy," she said. "He beats us. Cuts us. Wraps his hands around our throats while he rapes us."

Bile rose in my throat. No. She had to be wrong. Not my Jeremy. Sure, he'd been distant, and he'd walked out on me when I needed him most. But I couldn't have been engaged to a monster like that. Right?

"How did you get this number?" I asked.

"He knows where you are," she said. "You were a duty and nothing more. Too soft. Too sweet."

My hand started to shake, and I nearly dropped the phone. "Are you telling me that Jeremy is coming for me?"

She laughed. "No, silly. You're the untouchable one. It's not you he wants. It's the filthy whores. He's watching you, Dessa. He's watching everyone and waiting oh so patiently."

"M-my children. Is he going to…"

"No. Although, he does enjoy a virgin now and then."

"Why are you telling me this? Why have you been calling?" I asked.

"Are you scared?" she asked, her voice taking on a hard edge. "You should be. Jeremy may not want to hurt you, Dessa, but I do. What makes you so special? Why shouldn't you feel the bite of his knife? Gasp for air as he takes what he wants? It's not very fair, is it? No. No, it's not fair at all. He treated you decent. Never hurt you. And your husband now is always kissing you. What's it like, Dessa? To be so perfect? So loved?"

I swallowed hard. Perfect? Not hardly. Loved? Did Savior love me? It was too soon. Although, I knew with each passing day I fell for him a little more. Was it possible he felt the same?

"I'm not perfect, and Savior doesn't love me," I forced myself to say.

She gave a maniacal laugh that made me wince and pull the phone away from my ear until she'd stopped. "Don't worry, Dessa. Once I'm finished with you, I'll make sure your husband isn't cold at night. I'll warm his bed. Show him what a real woman can do. Ready or not, Dessa, here I come."

The line went dead, and I set the phone down. I stared at it, wondering if the woman was completely insane, or if she was a real threat. And Jeremy… had that all been a lie? Or was he really that much of a monster? They were both watching me. Why? Clearly, the woman wanted to hurt me. But Jeremy? Why did he watch me? She said he didn't want to hurt me. He hadn't wanted to marry me after the accident. So…

I rubbed my forehead, hoping to ease the ache building. I heard a creak behind me and spun my chair, my heart in my throat as that woman's words haunted me. Was this it? Was she already here?

"Sorry," Ares said. "Didn't mean to scare you. Who was that?"

"I'm not sure."

"Are you in danger? Are the rest of us?" she asked.

"She said the children were safe. I'm assuming that means you too." I swallowed hard. "She doesn't want to hurt your dad. I think she plans to take my place."

"You need to tell him."

"What? That we got some creepy phone calls today? Nothing has happened. What if it's all a bluff just to scare me?" I asked.

"And what if it isn't?" Ares asked. "At least call Lavender and Wire. Maybe they can check the phone records and figure out who called or where they called from."

"I could do that," I said. I eyed the phone, not sure I wanted to touch it again. The woman had wanted to frighten me, and she'd succeeded.

"I'll call them," Ares offered. She stepped out of the room, and I heard the low murmur of her voice. It didn't take long before the front door opened. I'd expected one of the club hackers. Instead, I got Tempest, Saint, and my husband. I glared at Ares, and she only shrugged. Traitor!

"Wire is on his way," Savior said. He came straight for me, then lifted me into his arms. When he sat in his favorite chair, he settled me on his lap.

"She wasn't supposed to call you," I said.

"Good thing she follows my orders better than yours, then." He narrowed his gaze at me. "We'll talk when everyone else leaves. I'm not happy about the fact our daughter had to tell me what was going on instead of my wife."

I sighed. "I didn't want to worry you until I knew there was something to actually be concerned about. You have enough to deal with already."

"I appreciate you wanting to lighten my load, Dessa, but protecting you is high on my list of priorities." He hugged me tight. "When Wire gets here, tell us everything."

"There's not much to say." I squirmed on his lap, wishing I could escape. My chair was too far away, and I didn't think he'd let me transfer to it anyway.

"That's one," he said, his voice a low growl.

My eyes went wide. One? One what? I opened my mouth to ask, but the look in his eyes told me I probably didn't want to know.

Saint cleared his throat. "Ares, why don't you take the kids for some ice cream? My treat. Make sure you take at least one of the brothers and a Prospect with you. Make that, two brothers. Whoever you pick, tell them it's on my orders."

He pulled out his wallet and handed her a twenty. She smiled widely and raced off. I heard Judd's excited chatter a moment before Ares raced through the living room with a kid in each arm. Tempest opened the door for her, and she practically ran for her car. I wasn't sure it was entirely smart to send them off if someone was watching the clubhouse, but the woman didn't seem interested in our kids. I didn't think they were necessarily in any danger. With two brothers and a Prospect with them, they should be safe enough. Right? Especially if they were vigilant. I hoped someone told those men what was going on before they all left the compound.

Saint looked over at Savior and smirked. "You owe me one."

"I already owe you several for looking for self-defense for Dessa. Add it to my tab," Savior said.

I felt like I was missing something. What the hell was going on? Before I could ask, Wire stepped into the house with a laptop under his arm.

"Should have known this wouldn't be easy," Wire

said as he took a seat. "I did some quick digging on the calls from today. They're pinging from towers not only here, but as far away as New York City and somewhere outside of Austin. Hard to get a lock on them."

"And Jeremy?" Savior asked.

"I'll see what I can find." Wire focused on me. "Tell me about the calls."

"The first nine were silent. I heard breathing, but no one ever spoke. If I tried to get them to talk, they'd hang up. The tenth time, a woman talked to me. Said some horrible things about Jeremy."

"Like what?" Wire asked, opening his laptop.

"She said he liked to hurt women. Cut them. Strangle them." I pressed my lips together a moment. "Rape them."

Wire's gaze flicked to Savior, and I saw him shake his head from the corner of my eye. Did that mean they were all as shocked as I was? How could a man like Jeremy walk around in the open and no one be the wiser about his true character?

"What else?" Wire asked.

"She didn't think it was fair he never touched me or hurt me. Said she would change that, then she'd take my place in Savior's bed."

His hold tightened even more, and I winced at the bite of pain. "Like fuck she will. One, I'll gut the bitch if she lays one finger on you. And two, I don't want anyone but you, Dessa."

His words were sweet. The fierce expression on his face told me he meant every word too. I didn't know how I'd gotten so lucky to end up with Savior, but when he said things like that, I fell for him even more. I might as well admit it, at least to myself. I was completely in love with him. It had only been a little over a week, and yet, I couldn't imagine my life without him.

"Tell me more about Jeremy," Wire said.

"My personal experiences, or what the woman said?"

"Both." He cracked his knuckles. "The more info I have, the better my chances of figuring out what's a lie and what's the truth."

"Um, well… When we were dating, he never did more than hold my hand or kiss me. I'd thought he was waiting for our wedding since I'd never been with anyone before. I knew he'd dated a lot of women before me. It never crossed my mind he wouldn't be faithful to me, or that he was hiding a dark side."

Wire snickered. "There's a *Star Wars* joke in there somewhere."

I blinked and didn't dare tell him I'd never watched it. I had a feeling he'd take offense. Even if the man was a biker, he was also a computer genius, according to Savior and Ares. I figured he had to be a geek, even if you couldn't tell by looking.

"The woman said he enjoyed virgins sometimes. She said…" I bit my lip and forced myself to keep going. "She said he liked to strangle women while he took what he wanted. I think that's how she phrased it."

"So I need to check for bodies that show signs of being strangled and raped. You mentioned a knife?" I nodded. "Right, I'll add cuts and stab wounds to the list."

"Do you think he's really like that?" I asked. "How could I date him? Get engaged to him, and never know?"

"Maybe he didn't want you to," Wire said.

Savior shifted under me. "When I went back for

Dessa, I stopped at Jeremy's house first. Not entirely sure I felt the need, but I did. A woman called out to him from somewhere in the house. It's possibly the same one who called Dessa today. Maybe a new girlfriend, and she's jealous for some reason?"

"Um. She said Jeremy was watching me."

"Shit," Wire muttered. "Not good. If this guy really is a murderous psycho, that's the last thing we need. Savior, when you spoke to him, did he seem like the type to come after her?"

Savior shook his head. "No. I got the feeling he was completely over her. Not sure why he'd decide to watch her now."

"She called me perfect," I said. "And said it must be nice to be so loved. Do you think he still loves me, assuming he ever did?"

"I guess it's possible. Although, if he really is a psychopath, I'm not sure he's capable of love. Not in the normal sense, at any rate. He could fixate on you for some reason."

None of that sounded good. Things had been rough already. Even though meeting all the families had helped me feel more like I belonged here, Tempest's words at the gathering had made me feel inferior. I knew if I felt more confident about myself, it wouldn't have bothered me as much. Would I ever get used to people looking down on me because I couldn't walk? I had a feeling people would treat me differently for the rest of my life.

"I'm going to call Surge and a few others," Wire said. "The more people we have looking into this, the better our chances of figuring shit out. Think we need to call in reinforcements?"

"Not yet," Savior said. "Until we know for sure this woman isn't just spouting a bunch of bullshit, we'll sit tight and just be extra vigilant. Make sure all the women, teens too, know to check in now and then if they're leaving the compound. If anyone leaves and doesn't text or call every hour on the hour, we'll go looking for them. Make sure any GPS trackers are activated too."

"Not taking any chances?" Tempest asked.

"No. Not with Dessa or anyone else. Until we know what's going on, I'm not going to put any of our families at risk."

He nodded. "Good. I'm going to stop by Wraith's place. Make sure he knows to keep an eye on Rin and Akira. After all Rin went through, she doesn't need this shit."

"None of the women do," Wire said. "Rin isn't the only one who was dealt a shitty hand."

I eyed Tempest. I didn't know him, but something seemed different when he spoke of that family. His fingers twitched slightly, and I noticed a tic in his jaw. Who was Akira? Was she old enough he might be interested? Or did he just see them as sisters or something?

"We're going to head out," Saint said. "Wire, keep us up to date on anything you find. Group text with the officers is fine. Once we have all the pieces, or most of them, I'll feel more prepared."

"I'll call Church once we have this shit somewhat sorted. But we do need to make sure everyone is cautious. Just don't... don't blow things out of proportion. Tell them there might be an issue with someone stalking the club, and we'd rather be safe than sorry." Savior sighed. "I don't want to cause panic if there's no reason."

Everyone walked out, leaving us alone. Ares hadn't returned with the children yet, which meant Savior and I were alone. The heated way he looked at me spoke volumes, and I knew we were about to take advantage of the empty house.

* * *

Savior

I owed my delectable wife a spanking, and a lot of orgasms. Lifting her into my arms, I carried her to our bedroom and kicked the door shut. I eased her down onto the bed and helped her undress. She leaned back on her elbows and watched as I stripped off my clothes, not saying a word. I caught her licking her lips as I shoved my underwear down my thighs and couldn't help but smirk.

I'd had plenty of women in my life, but when my sweet little Dessa looked at me like that, it made me feel like a fucking king. I stepped closer and ran my hands up her thighs. Her breath caught as she stared at me. I didn't know how much she could feel when I touched her like this. Whatever damage the accident had done to her body, she could still orgasm, and definitely felt it when I was inside her or played with her clit. But her legs? Other than the pain she mentioned, I didn't know if she felt my touch.

"You're so sexy and beautiful," I said.

She shook her head. "My legs are getting too thin. Not being able to walk means I lost all the muscle in them."

I reached down and stroked my cock. "Do you think if you weren't sexy, I would be this damn hard? I don't care if your legs are thin and scarred. Does it bother me you might be in pain? Of course. Do I wish you could walk so your life would be easier? Yes. But the way your legs look doesn't detract from your beauty, Dessa."

Her cheeks flushed, and she looked away, her fingers tracing a pattern on the bedding. "I sometimes have a hard time seeing myself the way you see me. I'm trying to do better. It doesn't help that no one wanted me before the accident, except Jeremy. I didn't have much self-esteem to begin with."

"Then I'll have to remember to tell you every day how much I love your body, enjoy your kisses, and crave your touch." I slid my hands under her thighs and shifted her legs until her knees bent and spread. "Already wet and ready for me. I bet I could slide right in."

"Touch me, Gabriel. Please."

I cupped her breast and rubbed my thumb across her nipple. It pebbled, and I leaned down to suck it into my mouth. While I teased the hard peak with my lips, teeth, and tongue, I reached between us to rub her clit. I'd give anything to take her from behind, but since she couldn't get on her hands and knees, I hadn't yet figured out how we'd do it.

I still owed her a spanking. I pulled back and eyed the pillows. I wondered if those would work to prop her up?

"Do you trust me?" I asked her.

"What kind of question is that? Of course, I do."

"Are you willing to try something new?"

She nodded. I reached for the four pillows at the top of the bed and stacked them. I picked Dessa up and flipped her to her stomach. She squealed a moment and threw her hands out to brace herself. Her stomach hit the pillows and her eyes went wide.

"Oh. Oh! I think… this might be easier over the side of the bed?"

I lifted her and positioned so that her torso pressed to the mattress with her legs over the side. Then I took a pillow to wedge under her hips to lift her a little higher. I ran my hand over her ass, thinking about the spanking I still owed her.

"Remember when I told you that was one?"

She glanced at me over her shoulder. "In the living room?"

I nodded. "I meant you'd earned yourself a spanking. But now I'm worried you'd feel it and it would cause you pain. Not the sexy kind, either. So I think that's going to be a no for us, at least right now. I need to make an appointment for you to see a local doctor, get your files transferred, and ask him some questions. I want to make sure I don't do anything to hurt you."

"Gabriel… no offense, but shut up and fuck me."

Damn! She kept surprising me. "If that's what you want, that's what you'll get."

I stood behind her and bent my knees. She was too high up for me to kneel, and not high enough for me to stand up straight. I gripped her hips and lined my cock up with her slit, I sank into her wet heat. Fuck, but she felt incredible! I leaned over her, my chest to her back, and braced my weight with one hand while holding her hip with the other. I used long, deep strokes, taking my time to enjoy this moment with her.

"So good," she murmured.

"You okay? Not uncomfortable or in any pain?" I asked.

"Just don't stop. Please."

"I need more hands. I want to play with your clit, but I need to keep my weight off you too."

"Not going to break, Gabriel."

I kissed her shoulder and rubbed my beard against her skin. "I know. Just savoring the moment, and not wanting to possibly injure you. We haven't tried it this way before."

"Harder," she begged.

I growled softly and gave her what she wanted. I drove into her, each thrust harder and faster than the one before. Soon, the only sounds in the bedroom were her pants and our flesh slapping together. I felt her tighten on my cock a moment before the heat of her release hit me. I couldn't hold back. I took her like I'd been possessed, treating her more like a whore than a wife.

I shouted her name as I came inside her, filling her with my cum. Worried it might have been too much for her, I pulled out quickly and rolled her onto her back. She gave me the sappiest smile I'd ever seen.

"That was amazing, and I felt like…"

"Like what?" I asked, tossing the pillow aside so I could settle her higher on the bed, so she didn't dangle off the edge. I lay down next to her, placing my hand on her belly.

"Like I was whole."

I ran my fingers over her cheek, across her lips, then push her hair from out of her eyes. I knew there was a shop in town that sold sex toys and such. I wondered if they might have something that would work better than the pillows had. And maybe something that would tease her clit while I fucked her from behind.

"Do you want to go into town with me?" I asked.

"Now?"

"Well, not right this very second. We can rest a little, take a shower, and then go. There's a shop I'd like you to see. Might find some fun things in there to try."

"All right." She pressed her lips to mine. "But I'm greedy. Can I have another orgasm before we go?"

I snorted, then laughed. "Yeah, sweetheart. I can do that."

Sliding my hand between her legs, I worked her clit as I watched her face. I loved the way her eyes darkened and her cheeks flushed. She had the most expressive face. One of these days, I'd get Ares to take the kids and leave the house all day. Then I'd make love to my wife for as long as possible. I couldn't think of anything I'd love doing more.

She came again, calling out my name as she threw her head back. I kept rubbing, wanting to give her another orgasm. Her body trembled, and one orgasm rolled into two, then three. Our mingled released dripped from her pussy and pooled on the sheets under her. I knew I'd have to change the bedding later, but I didn't care. It was the hottest thing I'd ever seen.

"Maybe one more time," I murmured, settling my body over hers. I thrust hard and deep, filling her with one stroke. Her nails bit into my shoulder as I fucked her, pounding her sweet little body into the mattress. She tossed her head from side to side, and her nipples hardened even more. When she came yet again, I pumped another load of cum into her.

She might not know if she could have kids, but I was going to try my hardest to knock her up. Sure, we had a house full of kids, and if we never had another, I'd be fine with it. And at the same time, I really wanted to see her belly swollen with my kid. A little girl or boy who was half of each of us.

"I'd love nothing more than to keep you naked in bed for days, making you come over and over again." I kissed her, my cock still buried in her warm, wet pussy. I didn't know how, but I was still fucking hard. What the hell did this woman do to me? I felt like a teenager again, able to go for hours.

"I think I'd like that too," she said, a shy smile on her lips.

"Maybe one day. We can send the kids to spend the night with someone. Two nights. And we won't leave this bed except to use the bathroom and eat."

"It sounds rather nice."

Yeah, it really did. I rolled to my side and curled my arm around her waist. This little slip of a woman had me wrapped around her finger, and I wasn't sure she even realized it. There wasn't a damn thing I wouldn't do for her.

Which meant I needed to start acting like it. No more long days at the clubhouse office, trying to sort through shit. I'd go every day if need be, but not for eight to ten hours a day. I had a family here at home, and I wasn't going to spend so much time away from them. Not anymore.

"You mean so much to me," I told her. "I hope you know that."

"I love you, Gabriel. I don't expect you to say it back, and I know it's too soon, but it's how I feel."

I leaned up on my elbow and looked down into her beautiful eyes. "I love you too, Dessa. Think I have from the moment I carried you out of that house."

She gave me a big smile and drew me down so she could kiss me. I didn't know what trouble was heading our way, if any, but I'd do whatever it took to keep her safe. Dessa was my entire world, her and the kids. No one would touch them. If they did, they'd pay the ultimate price. I'd torture the fuckers before I buried them.

I fumbled for my phone in my jeans pocket and shot off a text to Ares. *Take the kids to Sarge's house. Ask him to keep them. You should stay with Akira.*

She sent me a green-faced emoji back with a

thumbs-up, which meant she knew exactly why I wanted them gone. I smiled and tossed the phone aside. Now I had Dessa all to myself for the rest of the day and into tomorrow morning. And I knew just how I wanted to spend our time.

Chapter Eleven

Dessa

It took Wire and the others four days to dig up some dirt on Jeremy, but no one had any idea who the woman was. She'd called every day. If I didn't answer, she continued to call until I did. Every time, my stomach bubbled, and I felt like I might throw up. Whoever she was, it was apparent she wanted Jeremy to be hers, and for some reason, thought the man was in love with me.

The more I thought about it, I realized he'd never loved me. It made me question why he'd asked me to marry him. Had I only been convenient? It would explain why he walked after the accident. Savior often told me anyone who loved me wouldn't see my disability as a problem. It was just a part of who I am now.

The entire club now knew there could be a threat to the women and teen girls. Which meant no one left the compound without two or three men with them. From what I'd been told, club business was exactly that, and they left the women out of Church and any discussions about matters like this one.

Until now.

Savior called Church this morning. Typically, I'd have been left at home, or the women would gather at the clubhouse to wait. At least, that's what Ridley told me. So why was I now in Church with my chair right beside Savior's? The looks of surprise on everyone's faces when they came in and saw me made me wonder if this would come back to bite Savior on the ass.

"Why is your wife here?" Grimm asked. "I can count on one hand the number of times this club has allowed a woman in here."

So, I wasn't the first.

"She'll be here the entire time," Savior said. "We've permitted women before, on a case-by-case basis. Didn't Ridley lay claim to Venom in Church?"

She did? No one had mentioned it to me. Then again, other than the first day I'd met her, we'd only had time to visit once. She's stopped by to check on me the next morning, and we'd talked for about an hour before she went home.

"And why is that?" Rocky asked. "I guess we're just wondering if the rules are changing. Since we have a new President, you can technically request us to reconsider certain bylaws. Are we going to permit the women to sit in on Church in the future?"

"All right. I guess let's start there," Savior said. "When it's necessary, and the officers are in agreement, old ladies and wives may attend Church as long as the discussion pertains to them or their safety. Everyone in agreement?"

Every hand went up around the table.

"We were technically doing that anyway. Ridley wasn't the only one who's been in Church before. But Royal can add it to the minutes, so we'll have an official record. That brings us to why Dessa is here. We're meeting today to discuss a threat she's received, and to determine if her ex-fiancé is involved."

Wire cleared his throat. "Guess that means it's my turn. I've been working with Lavender, Surge, Wizard, and Shield. Jeremy hasn't been as careful as he thinks, so we have a decent amount of information on him. Everything but his current location. As for the woman, none of us have been able to find her. She's using a burner phone with a signal that bounces all over the country. She could be outside the gates, or several states away."

"What do you have on Jeremy?" Tempest asked.

Savior reached over to take my hand and gave it a squeeze. I wasn't sure I wanted to hear this. I'd been engaged to him. If he hadn't left me after the accident, we would have been married by now. Exactly how awful was he? And why hadn't I noticed? There had been little things Savior had shared with me before we came here today, but I knew he hadn't told me everything.

"Saint, most of this is going to be hard for you to hear. Dessa too," Wire said. "But I know the two of you were friends. And, Preacher... when you hear the sort of man who was watching over your pregnant woman, you're going to lose your shit. Just brace yourselves."

Great. That didn't sound the least bit ominous. It made me wish I could just roll right out of here and pretend none of this was happening. If I didn't worry so much about the sort of trouble I'd brought to the Dixie Reapers, I might have done exactly that. Instead, I sat and waited, wondering how badly Wire was going to destroy my world.

"Jeremy grew up here in Saint's old neighborhood. Supposedly left town for better opportunities and started his own garage. It's how he got the money and continues to earn extra cash that's part of the trouble. His twisted desires are another problem." Wire pulled out a stack of papers and slid them to the center of the table. "Savior, don't let her see those. In fact, anyone with a weak stomach should avoid looking. It's pretty fucked up."

"Are you telling me I handed my sister over to a monster?" Saint asked.

"Afraid so." Wire leaned back in his chair. "Jeremy is in pretty deep with the closest thing this area has to the mob. He helps them run drugs by hiding them in vehicles, then doing just enough modifications so people won't question if the wheel well isn't regulation, or if it rides too low in the back. Seems to be profitable. His garage isn't earning enough to remain open, considering his overhead costs. His extracurricular activities are what pays the bills and then some."

"How long?" Preacher asked.

"From what we've been able to track, since before he moved there. He made connections through some local thugs and made himself useful to the right men. Or, the wrong ones by our standards." Wire pointed to the papers. "Those have nothing to do with his business, though. Jeremy gets off on causing pain. Some bodies have been turning up. Fresh enough the medical examiner determined the women were sexually assaulted and strangled to death. They sustained other wounds, leaving multiple contusions and cuts all over their bodies. He likes to slice the soles of their feet so they can't run."

"Jesus," Savior muttered. His hold on my hand tightened even more, and I knew he was thinking about what might have happened to me if I'd married Jeremy.

"Lavender found messages between Jeremy and a man called Santi. He's not the big guy, but he's higher up the food chain than Jeremy, and seems to call at least some of the shots. He advised Jeremy to date and act as normal as possible, even get married some day and start a family. I think that's where Dessa comes in. She probably came across as biddable. The type of woman who wouldn't question him if he stayed out late, or didn't want to discuss his day." Wire held my gaze. "Can you tell us what it was like between you and Jeremy?"

"Like you said, I didn't ask questions. I was so

thankful he loved me enough to marry me, it never crossed my mind he wasn't my Prince Charming. Even before I ended up in this chair, I wasn't the type of woman to draw the attention of men. The first time Jeremy asked me out, I figured that would be it. When he called for a second date, it shocked me."

"Did he ever hurt you? Abuse you in any way?" Tempest asked.

"No. We'd hold hands when we were out in public. Shared a few kisses. I'd told him I was a virgin, so I thought he was taking things slow. Once he asked me to marry him, he said he wanted to wait until I was his wife before we had sex."

"None that seemed odd to you?" Tempest asked.

"I thought he was being a gentleman." Now that I said the words, I realized how stupid that sounded. I'd heard him cussing at work. Watched him throw tools when he got angry. When he was with me, he'd been different. But at the garage, he didn't come across as the type of man to wait until marriage for sex. "I was stupid. I should have asked more questions, paid better attention to what was going on around me."

"You fell for every lie he told you," Savior said. "I'm sure he was convincing."

"You said he's been hurting women? What did they look like before he hurt them? Did they… look similar to me?" I asked.

"No. They were all petite like you but had a range of hair and eye color. He didn't care if they were black, white, Asian, Hispanic… But a lot of them have one thing in common. They were prostitutes. Because of their type of work, the police determined the evidence of long-term abuse could have been from that and not necessarily the person who killed them."

"Any DNA left behind?" Saint asked.

"No." Wire flipped open a file folder and skimmed the page inside. "They aren't linking the crimes right now. The cuts were made by various blades. The contusions could have been from anything. No distinguishing marks to say otherwise. No DNA under their nails or elsewhere."

His glaze lifted to mine briefly and I understood he'd cleaned that up a little because of my presence. It meant the person who attacked them used a condom. Then again, if they were prostitutes, couldn't the signs of sexual assault have actually been from paying clients?

"They're sure those women were raped?" I asked.

Savior focused on me. "You think it was just from their job?"

"I don't know much about prostitution, but I would assume if men are paying to use those women, they wouldn't necessarily be gentle with them."

"She's right," Wire said. "There's no way to know for certain. The only reason I've connected these women to Jeremy is that he's known to purchase women from a particular pimp in the area. All the bodies found can be tied back to the same pimp."

"What else did you find when you dug into his texts and emails?" Savior asked.

"He sometimes buys a whore to keep for several days. He does whatever he wants to her, then sends her home. Mostly. I found three communications that indicated he'd have to pay for loss of property. While it's vague as shit, I think it means he killed those women, and the pimp wanted more money." Wire ran a hand down his beard. "I don't have anything concrete enough the police would pick him up. However, I have enough to make me believe he's the one killing these women. I have a feeling if we were to dig up the lot near his garage, we'd probably find some bodies. His earliest victims most likely."

"You don't have even a clue as to who the woman might be?" Tempest asked me.

"I didn't recognize her voice if that's what you mean. She made it sound like she wanted Jeremy to love her, and she believed he was still in love with me. Except I don't think he ever felt that way about me."

"So she knows enough about Jeremy to know who you are and where you are," Tempest said.

"There was a woman at his house the night I showed up on his doorstep," Savior said. "I thought he'd moved on from Dessa and had a girlfriend living with him or over for a visit. I'm going to stick close to Dessa the next two days. If that woman calls while I'm home, I can see if the voice sounds the same."

"Still wouldn't tell us who she is," Saint pointed out.

"No, but it would mean she's been in his house. It's possible they were dating. Or she could have been a whore he bought for a night or two. For whatever reason, she's fixated on Jeremy. Wants him to belong to her, and she sees Dessa as a threat to that ever happening," Savior said.

"If Jeremy shows his face in town, I'll know," Wire said. "I've got every camera feed in town watching and waiting for a facial match. So far, he hasn't popped up anywhere. I honestly don't think he's in town. I think this woman is delusional. She makes her own version of reality and believes it with every fiber of her being."

"But you said Jeremy wasn't in his town either, right?" I asked.

Wire nodded. "That's correct."

"What about the lake?" I asked. "He often said he liked going to the lake with some friends to hang out on their boat. Is there a way to check for him at the area lakes?"

Wire made a note in his file. "I'll do that when I get home. Thank you, Dessa. Anything else you remember about your time with Jeremy, any hints about his habits or places he likes to visit, would be a great help."

"I'll let Savior know if I think of anything else."

My husband stood and rapped his knuckles on the table. "I don't want club whores on the premises for now. I wouldn't put it past this woman to try and slip in with the pretense of attending a party, so I'm shutting all that down. Don't bring women back here unless they're family, or you have Wire and Lavender run a background check on them. Church is dismissed. For now."

Savior pushed my chair out of Church and into the main part of the clubhouse. He eyed the women in the room, in various states of undress.

"Get the fuck out. Until I say otherwise, the Dixie Reapers compound is accessible to members, Prospects, and their families only."

I heard them whine, but Savior pushed me past all of them and outside. His words haunted me. He'd mentioned the crazy person calling me could easily slip into the compound, pretending to be here for a party. What if she was already here? How much did they know about the club whores?

I'd ask about it later. Right now, I just wanted to get home to our kids.

* * *

Savior

I got Dessa into the club truck and stored her chair in the back. As I tied it down, Saint came over. I wondered if he had Dessa's property cut. I should have taken it to a vote while we were in Church, but I didn't want to do that while she was present. Since she was my wife, I wasn't giving them an option on this one. The other old ladies accepted her, and I'd married her, so she wasn't going anywhere. If anyone had a problem with it, I'd be happy to settle the matter. Preferably by knocking them on their ass.

"Did you get it?" I asked when he stood beside the truck bed.

"I did. Sofia wanted to bring it by later, along with Rin and Kayla. With the way Tempest acted, they wanted to make sure she understood the club is glad she's here."

"I appreciate that," I said. I hopped out of the bed of the truck and clapped him on the back. Saint had just been a kid when he'd first come to the Dixie Reapers. He'd started prospecting before me, but we'd often talked about his life before the club.

"Have you thought about getting your own vehicle?" Saint asked. "Or something Dessa could drive?"

"I know we need to have that discussion, but with everything going on, there hasn't been time. Once things settle down, we'll figure it out. I think I need my own truck either way, though. If she wants to drive her own vehicle, we can look into that too."

"Sofia did some research when she saw me looking up self-defense for people in wheelchairs. She asked if Dessa can transfer easily or if she struggles with it."

"It's not exactly a fast process for her, but I've seen her do it."

"There are two options for her, then. She can drive a regular car with a hand brake, if she can transfer into it and break her chair down. Or you can look at the type she'd wheel herself into."

"Can you send me the links or print the info off? I'll sit down with her soon and see what she prefers, but I want to make sure we have all the facts."

"Sofia can bring it with the property cut," Saint said.

I waved to Saint and got into the truck. On the way home, I glanced at Dessa a few times. Wire had hit her with a pretty big blow during Church. I could only imagine how she'd felt hearing that shit about Jeremy. She hadn't cried, screamed, or showed anything but a calm exterior. I was damn proud of her.

"Anything you want to talk about before we go inside and see the kids?" I asked.

"You mean about my psycho ex who seems to be a serial killer?" she asked.

"Yep."

"I feel stupid for not realizing who he really was. And pathetic. I was so eager to have attention from a guy, it never occurred to me he might be something other than what he projected when we were together."

I pulled into the driveway and put the truck in park before reaching for her. I turned her chin, so she had little choice but to look at me. "Let's get one thing straight. You are *not* pathetic. Jeremy even had Saint fooled, and they've known each other for a long-ass time. He's either good at fitting in, or someone has been coaching him on how to appear more human."

"You don't think he's human?" she asked, a slight smile on her lips. "Is he the monster under the bed? Does his true form have horns and fur?"

"If he did kill those girls and torture them, it's possible he's completely emotionless, except for when he's inflicting pain."

"I'm okay," she said. "Or as okay as I can be. I

know you'll do everything you can to keep me safe, and there's a chance Jeremy isn't even part of what's happening now. I can't change the past. Dwelling on it won't make a difference, except to add more stress to my life."

As reasonable as her explanation seemed, I had a feeling sooner or later the weight of what she'd learned would hit her like a ton of bricks. I'd be ready and give her whatever support she needed. Despite the fact she'd dated Jeremy, I had a feeling she'd lived a rather quiet life. I'd never met anyone like Dessa.

"Ready to go in and see the kids?" I asked.

"I'm always ready." She flashed me a smile. "You have no idea how happy it made me to have Judd and Junie to look after. Even though I worried about where Sonja had found them, I couldn't help but love them and feel like fate or God had given me a second chance. I'd always wanted children, then suddenly I had two little angels who needed me."

"I wish I'd handled things differently when we came to get them. It's something I'll regret the rest of my life."

She put her hand over mine. "It turned out okay. Was it scary when it happened? Of course. And it broke my heart when they left, and I thought I'd never see them again. Then you showed up, took me away from that rental house, and gave me a new life. I love you, Gabriel, and I like living here with you and the kids. Ares too."

"I'll get your chair."

"Can you just take me in for now? You can come back for the wheelchair in a minute. After everything we found out today, I need to hug all three of them. I don't want to wait."

I leaned over to kiss her. "All right. Sit tight and I'll

come around to get you."

I shut off the truck and pocketed the keys before walking around to the other side. I opened Dessa's door and lifted her into arms, then carried her into the house. Ares sat on the couch with Judd and Junie playing on the floor. I eased Dessa down beside Ares before picking up Judd and Junie to give them each a hug.

"Did the three of you behave while we were gone?" I asked, arching an eyebrow at Ares.

She stared at me, with a resting bitch face. "Nope. We threw a rave. Invited all the Prospects and any sons over the age of fifteen."

"Smart ass," I mumbled.

"The kids watched part of a cartoon, then lost interest, so I brought a few toys in here for them," Ares said. "We were fine. Believe it or not, I can keep them alive for a few hours without someone looking over my shoulder. Just because I had help when you went back for Dessa, doesn't mean I needed it."

"Yeah, well, until we catch the woman calling the house, you'll have a shadow every time you leave the compound. Get over it."

She stuck her tongue out at me, but I knew she understood why the extra protection was necessary. Even if she got a little sassy from time to time, she'd been a good kid since I'd brought her here. The idea of her dating someone didn't thrill me, though. She hadn't brought it up again, which I hoped meant she hadn't figured out who she wanted to ask out. Or was she waiting for a particular guy to notice her?

I sat on the other side of Dessa and placed Judd in her lap while I cuddled Junie. We needed more afternoons and nights like this one. I'd worked tirelessly to find the kids, and since I'd brought them home, there hadn't been much time to bond with them.

"Do all of you want to go out tonight for dinner?" I asked.

"Is it safe?" Dessa's brow furrowed. "What if she really is out there, waiting for us to leave?"

"It's possible. The bunker isn't ready for you yet, and I don't want to put you down there indefinitely. So we have a choice. We can hide out inside the compound while we wait for the woman to make a move or lose interest. Or we can go about our lives and do the best we can to keep you safe. I'll leave the choice up to you."

Ares frowned at me. "Okay, what did you do with my dad? Are you secretly an alien and body-snatched him?"

"What does that mean?" Dessa asked her.

"The Savior I know would never have given you that option. He'd have been like the others, beaten on his chest, and told you to stay put. Ask any of the old ladies. When it comes to them being in danger, their men are over the top protective. They will threaten to chain them to a bed if it means they'll be safe. So why is my dad acting so casual about all this?"

I cracked my neck. This wasn't a conversation I really wanted to have, but I guess now that Ares had brought it up, I couldn't shove that genie back in the bottle.

"Dessa has spent ten months in a wheelchair, feeling as if she's stuck. Helpless. Worthless. Before that, she didn't think a man would ever want her. She hasn't experienced life much from what I've gathered, so I don't want to lock her up and keep her from doing that now." I looked at Dessa and saw her eyes had misted with tears. "I love you, and I will do whatever I can to keep you safe without having to cage you. I want you to experience life, to feel free."

"If you wanted me to stay at the compound, I'd understand," Dessa said. "We have our entire lives to go out and do fun things together. If it's safer for me to stay here right now, then I'll do it."

"I know you will." I reached out to place my hand on her thigh. "You are the most understanding woman I've ever met. When I forgot you needed help at the clubhouse, you didn't berate me. I got bogged down with work and wasn't home much the first week you were here, and not once did you complain. Which made me realize if something did bother you, I don't think you'd tell me."

"I don't like confrontation," she said softly. "Never have."

Junie reached up and tugged on my beard. I smiled down at her and kissed her chubby cheek. This is what I'd wanted for so long. A family. Now I had one, and I hadn't taken the time to enjoy them, or start making memories.

"Ares, is your camera charged?" I asked.

"No, but I can use my phone," she said, pulling it from her pocket. She stood and went to the other side of the coffee table and snapped a picture of me and Junie, then one of Judd and Dessa. I put my arm around my wife, and Ares took one of the four of us.

"Peek outside and see if anyone is around. If they are, ask them to come inside for a moment," I said.

She went to the door, and I heard her yell for Prophet. He stepped into the house, looking like he was off to the gallows. I crooked a finger for him to come into the living room.

"Ares, give him your phone, then come over here."

She hesitated a moment, which made me wonder if there was something on there she didn't want anyone to see. I'd have to ask later. She handed it to him and then kneeled in front of me and Dessa. Prophet took a picture and started to hand the phone back. He paused when it chimed and narrowed his eyes at Ares.

"Why the fuck are you getting texts from Dylan?" Prophet demanded.

"None of your business! Give it back," Ares said, holding out her hand.

"Better yet, give it to me," I said.

Prophet brought it over and I tried to unlock the phone. When it said the passcode was wrong, I stared at Ares. She knew the rules. If I wanted to see her phone, I could. Which meant I needed to know how to unlock it. The fact she'd changed the code and not told me, was a huge flag that she was hiding something.

"Unlock it, Ares."

She took it, her cheeks burning, as she unlocked the phone. I opened the messages from Dylan and wasn't sure who I should beat first. Him or Ares. While he should have been the adult and ignored her, or even blocked her ass, she'd started it by sending him pictures of her in a bikini. She'd flirted with him shamelessly, and he'd flirted back.

I looked up at Prophet. "Bring him to me."

"On it, Pres." He bolted from the house, and Ares started to stand. I placed a hand on her shoulder and kept her in place.

"Not you. You're going to wait right there while we sort this shit out."

"Gabriel, don't be so hard on her," Dessa said. "If one of your club brothers know who this Dylan person is, then I'm assuming he's part of the Dixie Reapers in some way. Which means you trust him, right?"

"Your point?"

"Did he do anything other than flirt?" she asked.

"Maybe it was all harmless and you're getting worked up over nothing."

"He's twenty-five to her sixteen. If she were an adult, then I wouldn't have a problem with it. But she's not."

"Dad, he didn't do anything wrong," Ares said.

"It started weeks ago. Why were you asking about Foster? How many boys are you interested in, Ares? I'd think one would be enough," I said.

"I knew you'd say Dylan was too old, so I thought maybe you'd be okay with me dating Foster. Until you said no."

The door opened and Prophet literally dragged Dylan into the house, not releasing him until the man sprawled at my feet. I showed him Ares's phone and the messages they'd been sending one another. "I'll give you one chance to explain. Make it good."

"I like Ares," he said, getting up on his knees. "And I know she's too young, which is why I haven't done more than text her. I'd never break your trust and do something I shouldn't. I respect you and her."

"So what's this?" I asked, shaking the phone.

"Harmless flirting?" he asked. "I don't know if she really likes me, or if she just wanted someone to pay her attention."

Ares gasped. "Are you for real right now? You think I send that picture to just anyone? You're such an asshole!"

"Settle down," I told her. I focused on Dylan. "It seems she wants you in particular. So my question is what do you plan to do about it?"

"Nothing." He rubbed his hands up and down his denim clad thighs. "Until she's eighteen. If she still wants me then, I'll ask your permission to take her on a date."

"That's two years away," Ares said.

Dylan shrugged. "Unless I'm booted from the Dixie Reapers, I don't plan to go anywhere. I can wait."

She huffed. "Right. Wait. I'm sure you'll be celibate that entire time."

"If that's what it takes, then yes. Only if you promise to tell me the moment you no longer want me to wait for you," he said.

Jesus. These two were fucking killing me. And Prophet looked like he might murder Dylan on the spot, which made me question his motives. Not that I was going to get into that crap tonight. It could wait.

"Fine. The two of you can keep texting, as long as you keep it clean. I *will* check her messages from time to time. The moment you step a toe out of line, we're going to have a problem."

"Seriously, Pres?" Prophet asked.

I held his gaze, waiting to see if he'd break. He didn't, which made me smile. "Feel free to text her too, Prophet, since you seem so upset over the fact she's messaging Dylan. But same rules apply."

"He's nearly twice my age," Ares said.

"So? Dylan is only five years younger than Prophet. When you're an adult, age is only a number. Or haven't you learned that already by living here?"

Dessa reached out to run her fingers through Ares's hair. "Don't do anything that makes you feel uncomfortable, Ares. No one is pressuring you to do anything right now. You should be grateful your dad didn't demand you stop talking to Dylan. Most parents wouldn't be so lenient."

Her shoulders sagged. "You're right. I'm sorry, and I promise we won't do more than talk. If you want to text me, Prophet, you can."

"But you don't see me that way," he said, taking a

step back. "Fair enough. Dylan can wait for you. I won't."

He turned and walked off, and I wondered when I'd been dropped into the middle of a soap opera. Sometimes the drama at the club rivaled anything I'd find on TV. Dylan got up and cast one last glance at Ares before leaving the house as well.

"How about we order pizza and stay home?" Dessa asked.

I nodded. "I think that might be a good idea."

Something told me I needed to keep a closer eye on Ares. The girl was courting trouble by chasing older men. At least for now. Once she was eighteen, I wouldn't stop her unless I thought she was going to get hurt. Otherwise, I would trust her to make the right decision for herself. She'd grown up fast, and I had to remember she wasn't a child, even if her birth certificate said otherwise.

Chapter Twelve

Dessa

I bit into my slice of cheese pizza before cutting one into bites for Judd. The last time I'd let him eat one the regular way, he'd worn more than he'd gotten into his mouth. Little Junie was still a bit young for pizza, so she sat in Savior's lap while he fed her small bits of chicken and green beans. It was cute seeing them together. He'd spoon some food into her mouth, then take a bite of his pizza, before doing it all over again.

Ares leaned over and wiped my chin with a napkin. "Stop drooling."

My cheeks flushed. "Can't help it. Nothing sexier than watching my husband with our youngest."

Savior winked at me, then kept eating and feeding Junie. I reached over to take Ares's hand and gave it a squeeze. She'd checked her phone at least a dozen times in the last hour. From what I'd gathered, Dylan hadn't returned her last text. I didn't know if he'd changed his mind, or if he was just busy. Either way, the girl was about to go bonkers, waiting for some sort of response.

I hadn't had much of a chance to speak with her. First because she'd avoided me as much as possible. Since she'd begun to warm up to me, things had been hectic. Even though we were communicating now, I still didn't know much about her.

"Tell me about school," I said. "You're in high school, right?"

Ares nodded. "The other kids here usually carpool, so we take turns driving. Although, there's too many of us at the high school right now to only take one car, so two of us drive each day. We alternate since we all have cars."

"You're lucky. All of you. I lived in foster care

when I was in high school. The only way I'd have gotten a car would have been to work and save up for it myself. Except that any money I had went toward clothes and shoes. Our foster family used anything they received from the state to buy groceries. If you wanted clothes, it was either the donation bin at the local churches or hitting the local thrift stores."

Ares grew quiet, and I worried I'd said something to upset her. When she spoke again, I realized how little I still knew about her and Savior.

"I don't know if Dad told you how I ended up living with him. The things I went through were brutal. The family I had before that wasn't the type you see on TV, unless you're watching a crime show and the family is the villains. But I know I have it good being here with Dad and the Dixie Reapers. They've treated me well and made sure I have everything I could ever need or want."

"I'm sorry, Ares. I didn't mean to belittle what you went through before coming here. I spoke without thinking," I said. She seemed so well-adjusted, I often forgot she'd had a hard life before Savior found her.

"Well, that dampened the mood," Savior said. "How about a game night after we tuck the little ones in?"

"I wanna play," Judd said.

"I'll find some games you can play for next time," Savior said. "I only have adult games right now."

Judd pouted but didn't argue. He'd been such a sweet boy, even from the first day Sonja brought him to me. I didn't know why his mother hadn't wanted him. If I'd been lucky enough to give birth to either Judd or Junie, I'd have never let them go. Before the accident, I'd wanted a house full of children.

We finished dinner, then Savior bathed Judd while

Ares took care of Junie. We gave both kids ten minutes to splash and play before having to wash. Ares brought Junie to me first, wrapped in a towel. I dried her hair a little better before dressing her for bed, then wheeled her into their bedroom. I tucked her into her bed and pulled the pink blankets up over her. Kissing her forehead, I whispered, "I love you, Junie bug."

She reached up to hug me. I backed away after she let go and went to check on Savior and Judd. When I went into our bedroom, he already had Judd dried and in his pajamas. I reached for him, but Savior shook his head.

"Nope. I've got him. Go help Ares pick a game. We can sit at the kitchen table to play."

I watched him carry our son off to bed and felt a warmth spread through me. Savior was a kind, honorable man who loved deeply. I felt grateful to be part of his life. I'd thought guys like him only existed in fairytales until I'd met one in real life. Our first encounter hadn't gone very well, but he'd more than made it up to me since then.

I went into the kitchen and found Ares. "Your dad said we should pick a game. He's putting Judd to bed."

"We don't have a lot, but he did buy some games when I first came to live here. He'd let me invite the other kids over, or he'd sit and play with me. We have UNO, Monopoly, Cards Against Humanity, and Trouble."

"Cards Against Humanity?" I asked. "Isn't that rather…"

"Adult?" she asked. "It is, but all things considered, there's nothing in there written or implied that would shock me. I usually play it with Portia and Isadora. Although, Amity joined us last time. She's friends with Portia and is now married to Thunder."

"Would you be okay with us playing Trouble tonight?" I asked.

"Sure. That's actually Dad's favorite out of the options we have. I'll grab it. Do you want to get us some sodas? Maybe make some popcorn?"

"Sounds good, although how can you think about eating again already?"

"I'll just nibble on it, but watch… Dad will clean the bowl without even realizing he's doing it. Happens every time. The man loves his popcorn."

She left the room, and I rolled over to the fridge. I took out three cans of soda and set them in my lap to carrying them to the table. After I put them down, I grabbed the popcorn off the counter. Since the kitchen was still a mess, Ares had placed various snacks down low so I could reach them if no one was available to help.

I put a bag in the microwave and got a bowl out from a bottom cabinet while I waited. Once the ding sounded, I opened the bag and poured it into the bowl before carrying it to the table. It would have been easier to take it unopened, but I didn't want the hot, oily bag against my legs.

Someone knocked on the door and I heard Ares yell out that she'd get it. I rolled up to my spot at the table and waited. When neither Ares nor Savior returned, I started to worry.

"Do the two of you need some help?" I called out. "Ares? Savior?"

It felt like a vise squeezed my chest and I backed away from the table. Slowly, I made my way to the front door. It stood open and I didn't see anyone. Not at first. I started to turn and check down the hall when something caught my attention. A shoe. Inching closer to the door, I looked down and saw Ares sprawled on the front porch. Her back rose and fell, so I knew she was alive, but what the hell happened to her?

"Ares?" I couldn't check on her. If I got out of my chair and managed to get down on the porch, I wouldn't have a way to get back up, and I knew I wasn't any good to her if I couldn't reach a phone quickly.

I backed up and headed for the cordless phone on the kitchen counter. I grabbed it and called the only number I'd memorized. Wire's house. While it rang, I wheeled myself farther into the house, looking for Savior. I didn't see any sign of him. In a panic, I checked the children. Both slept soundly and seemed all right.

"What's going on?" I murmured to myself. Then I called out for Savior again. No answer, just like the phone ringing in my lap.

I ditched the phone and grabbed my cell from the living room. As much as I didn't want to leave Junie and Judd alone, I needed to get help for Ares. But I wasn't dumb enough to leave the house without a way to at least call 9-1-1. It would have been smart to add some numbers to Savior's brothers, or even the old ladies, but I hadn't. The only number I knew by heart was Lavender's.

I went back to the front porch and down the ramp to the driveway. None of the houses here had ramps, which meant I couldn't get to any of their doors. My palms started to sweat, and my heart pounded against my chest so hard I thought it might crack a rib.

Savior's motorcycle and the truck were still in the driveway. He couldn't have left, could he? No, with Ares down, something had to have happened. I thought about the creepy phone calls, and what I'd learned about Jeremy.

I paused. Jeremy. If I called him, would he answer? Did he even still have the same number? My hand trembled as I dialed the number to his house. The fact he answered, relieved me to some extent. It meant he wasn't behind whatever was going on. Or at least, he wasn't here to cause mischief.

"Hello," he said.

"Jeremy, it's Dessa."

"What do you want?" he asked.

I licked my lips and scanned my surroundings. "I've been getting calls from someone. She says she loves you and that I'm in her way. I've moved on, Jeremy. I live with the Dixie Reapers now, but my husband's adopted daughter was knocked out and my husband is missing. I'm worried the woman is here somewhere."

It was so quiet I thought he'd hung up and I checked the screen. It showed the call was still connected.

"Did she give a name?" he asked.

"No. But she said you'd never love her because you still loved me. I knew that wasn't right. I'm not sure you ever loved me at all. She wouldn't listen. Said she's been watching me. I'm scared, Jeremy."

He huffed, and I heard a door slam. "Look, I'm two hours away from the Dixie Reapers. Even if I came there, I'd likely be too late. Tell Saint or some other hero that you need help. And, Dessa, lose my damn number."

He ended the call, and I tried not to cry. I'd hoped he might at least know who was doing this. Or admit that he'd sent her after me. I kept rolling farther down the road, getting farther away from Ares and the children. As much as I didn't like leaving them vulnerable, it seemed the woman wanted me and not them. I'd give myself to her if it meant my family would be safe.

"Where are you?" I screamed. "Leave my family alone! You want me? Come get me!"

Nothing. In fact, it seemed almost too quiet. I turned in a circle and noticed most of the homes didn't have lights on. It wasn't late enough for everyone to be asleep. I kept going, getting closer to the clubhouse, and hoping I was heading in the right direction.

"Come on, bitch! You've harassed me every fucking day. Now you can't show your face? You're such a coward!" I screamed the words at the top of my lungs.

A door opened and one of the club brothers stepped out. I didn't recognize him, but I was still figuring out who was who.

"Dessa? What's going on?" he asked.

As he came closer, I saw the patches on his cut. *Warden.*

"Ares is on the porch. I think someone did something to her. She won't wake up, and Savior is missing. They were both in the house. We were about to play a game when someone knocked on the door."

He held up a hand. "Slow down and take a breath."

I did as he said and started over, telling him everything I knew. I even admitted to having called Jeremy, and his response.

"Savior wasn't anywhere in the house?"

"Not that I saw, and he didn't answer when I called him. Junie and Judd were still asleep. I don't know what happened to Ares. She wouldn't wake up."

He pulled out his phone and made a call. "Prophet, go to Savior's house. We have trouble and someone knocked out Ares. The little ones are still in their beds."

He switched the phone to his other ear and sighed. I couldn't hear what Prophet was saying, but it didn't seem like Warden was happy with him. The man's jaw tightened, and he looked like he might argue with him.

"Fine. Take Ares to the hospital but get someone to sit with Junie and Judd. I'm going to send out a text to see who can help find the Pres and figure out what the fuck is going on here."

He ended the call and immediately sent out a text. Doors started opening all around us as more bikers came out. If they were all home, why hadn't any of them come to check on me while I was screaming my head off? Only Warden had bothered to see what was going on.

"Is there a reason I'm the only one who came out when Dessa was screaming?" Warden asked. Good. I was glad I wasn't the only one wandering that very thing. I knew not everyone here liked me. Well, mostly Tempest had an issue with me. But they wouldn't let me get hurt on purpose, would they?

"Had the TV up loud and didn't hear anything," Grimm said.

"I was, um, otherwise occupied." Thunder's cheeks flushed a little, and I remembered Ares saying he was married to Amity. I could imagine what those two were doing while I panicked out here.

The rest of them all denied having heard me. We got excuses from music or TVs being too loud, to them just shrugging as if not hearing me wasn't a big deal. I didn't think that was possible. I'd shouted so loud my throat hurt. How could not one single man have heard me screaming my head off out here? Not that it mattered right now. Prophet would make sure Ares was all right, and see that Junie and Judd were looked after. That left the rest of us locating Savior.

"I tried to call Wire and Lavender before I left the house. No one answered," I said.

"We'll start there. Mind if one of us pushes your chair?" Warden asked.

"No, that's fine."

Grimm walked around behind me and started to push me down the road to Wire's house. When we got there, their door stood open as well. I remembered they had children and wondered where they were.

"I'll check the house to see if anyone is home," Thunder said. I noticed he had pulled a gun from somewhere before he went inside. When he returned, he shook his head. "No one's here. Not even the children."

"Anyone know if the kids are spending the night elsewhere?" Grimm asked.

"They're at my house," a man said. His hair had gone completely silver and had a harsh look to him. I saw the name *Torch* and realized he was the old club President. Isabella's husband. "My wife is watching them, along with our kids."

"Savior is missing," Grimm said.

"Not missing." Torch scanned the group of us, his gaze resting on me. "Your man is fine. Pissed as hell, though. It's why I'm here."

"Where is he?" I asked.

"Same place as Wire and Saint. They're at the clubhouse, and the bitch calling the shots is waiting for you, Dessa." Torch came closer. "It's not just one woman. We can't risk going in full force. Savior, Wire, and Saint could all die if we did that. So I have to ask a favor of you."

"Wait." Thunder folded his arms. "No offense, Torch, but why the hell are we just hearing about this? How long have they had Savior, Saint, and Wire?"

"Not long. As for why it took me so long, I'm getting old, fucker. Why the hell do you think I stepped down?" He narrowed his eyes at Thunder. "I called Grimm, but he didn't answer. For that matter, I called you too."

"Anything," I said. "I'll do anything to save him. All of them."

Torch smiled. "Good girl. I know some had their doubts about whether you were suited to be a President's wife and old lady, but I knew you had it in you."

Part of me warmed at his praise. The other half bristled over there, being more than Tempest, who didn't think I belonged with Savior. What would it take to make them accept me as an equal? Savior said my chair didn't define me. Yet, it seemed people saw it and did exactly that.

"Go in there and give them what they want," he said. "Or at least, make them think that's what's happening. You distract them, and the rest of us can get into position."

I nodded. "I can do that. But what about Lavender and Sofia? Were they hurt too?"

"Sofia is at the clubhouse in one of the rooms. When I saw her on the feed, she seemed to be unconscious. I think they're using her to control Saint. As for Lavender, I haven't seen her." Torch looked around, as if he expected her to pop up at any moment. "I don't think they have her. If she wasn't home, she may be creating havoc with her laptop somewhere. Wouldn't surprise me if she already knows what's going on and is doing what she can to help."

I knew Lavender was a badass. I wished I was more like her. If I had been, maybe I could have done something when they came to take Savior and hurt

Ares. And speaking of Ares, I saw Prophet race past us in the truck we'd had parked in the driveway. Ares seemed to be slumped against the window, which meant she hadn't woken yet. I wondered why it had taken him so long to get her out of there.

"I think they have someone watching the road. I noticed someone peeking at me as I walked past the clubhouse," Torch said.

"How do you know all this?" Thunder asked.

"You don't think I gave up complete control just yet, do you? I still have access to the camera feeds inside the clubhouse. The people inside are armed. I've only seen women and one man. How brave can you be, Dessa?"

"As much as need be," I said.

His lips twitched in a faint smile. "Good. We'll wait here. Give you time to reach the clubhouse and get inside. Stay alive. Savior is going to lose his shit when you get there. Don't let them kill him."

I nodded and took a breath to steady my nerves, then made my way to the clubhouse. I rolled up the ramp when I arrived and through the doors. My eyes took a moment to adjust to the dim lighting inside, and I saw Savior, Wire, and Saint tied to chairs in the middle of the room. They had gagged each of them. How the hell had these people gotten the drop on three men?

They had to have been at our house, since Ares was knocked out on the porch. Why take Savior and not me? Wasn't that the end goal? Or was this more about ego, and for whatever reason, they wanted me to go to them?

I scanned the room and saw the four women Torch mentioned, as well as two shadows down the hallway. They could have been male. The ex-President had said he'd seen a guy. Were there two or more, and they hadn't been caught on camera? My stomach knotted.

"I'm here. Which of you keeps calling me?" I asked.

A blonde stepped forward, hatred burning in her eyes. "That would be me."

"Who are you? What do you want?"

She snarled. "I already told you what I want, you fucking cunt! As to who I am, my name is Bridget, and I'll be the one taking your place when this is finished."

Savior thrashed in his chair and yelled against his gag. I didn't have to hear the words to know what he wanted to tell her. It didn't matter what she did to me, she'd never have him. I also knew Savior wasn't the one she really wanted. No, that honor belonged to Jeremy. Maybe I could use him as a way to create the distraction Torch asked for.

"I called Jeremy," I said. Savior went still, and Bridget came even closer. "Told him some woman kept calling and threatening me."

"And is your white knight on his way to rescue you?" she asked, smiling widely.

She was batshit crazy. I'd told her Jeremy didn't care about me, and she still insisted he'd come to save me? What the hell was wrong with her? Aside from the fact she wanted a serial killer to love her. Clearly, she had issues.

"No. He told me to lose his number and hung up on me."

The smile slipped from her face. "What?"

"I told you he didn't love me. I don't know why you think he does. If he'd loved me, would he have broken our engagement after the accident? I know Savior wouldn't have, if he'd been in Jeremy's shoes. *He* loves me. I think I was just convenient for Jeremy. Until I wasn't."

Her face flushed red, and she screamed. I didn't have to time to move out of the way. Her fist came straight for my face, and she clocked me on the cheek. It felt like my eye might explode from the impact, and I gasped at the pain shooting through that side of my face.

Come on, Torch. How much more of a distraction do you need? Save us before this woman kills me!

If I died, I was going to come back and haunt him.

Chapter Thirteen
Savior

I was going to kill her. My sweet, naïve wife was in over her head. How the fuck could she have rolled right in here and given these bitches what they wanted? When Bridget punched her, I'd wanted to rip the woman to shreds. If Dessa made it out of this alive, I was going to lose my shit once we were alone.

President for such a short time and here I was, tied to a chair, watching someone beat on my wife. It wouldn't surprise me if the club asked for my patch after this. Same for Saint, since they'd tied him up right next to me.

And how were we caught? They'd known where to hit us the hardest -- our families. When I'd seen Ares go down, I'd wanted to charge the bitch who'd dosed her with something. Fucking Bridget. She'd aimed a gun at my chest and told me to come along nicely, or every woman and child at the compound would be dead before morning. I'd seen the cold, calculating look in her eyes and realized she meant it. Whatever it took, she'd do her best to see her threat through to the end.

One of the women came closer. I recognized her as a club whore. One of the newer ones. I knew Wire had dug into each of their backgrounds. She had to have passed, so why was she joining in this fucked up shit now? Couldn't remember her name, though. She smiled and stroked my beard. I yanked my head away, not wanting her to touch me.

"You wouldn't let me take you for a ride when I came here. Not so high and mighty now, are you?" she asked. The bitch swung her leg over me and settled herself on my lap. If they hadn't tied both my hands and feet, I'd have tossed her off me. She ground against me and pushed her tits up. "Maybe I should have a little sample? We can let your wife watch. What do you say?"

I growled and stared at her with pure hatred. If she even thought of taking my cock out, when I got free, I'd bury the bitch. Hell, I might do that anyway. She wriggled some more. If she thought I'd get hard for her, she was going to be disappointed.

"What's the plan, Bridget?" Dessa asked. "I'm here. Now what? Jeremy isn't going to show up, if that's what you'd hoped for. There's an entire club of bikers inside the gates. Even if you manage to kill the four of us, you'll never get out of here alive."

I wanted to tell her to stop trying to piss them off. If she got herself killed, I'd resurrect her ass just so I could spank her. I hoped like fuck Ares was all right. And Sofia. Shit. Did Dessa not know there weren't just the four of us? I'd watched them carry Sofia down the hall. The man hadn't come back either. I had no idea what they were doing to her, and I knew Saint was holding on by a thread. If anyone hurt his woman, there would be hell to pay.

I'd complied with these crazy women, thinking I'd find a way out of this mess. Instead, my wife came into the clubhouse like she was here to meet friends. Just bold as brass entered the building, even though I had a feeling she'd known her stalker was here. She must have found Ares and come looking for me. What I wanted to know was where the fuck my brothers were? Why hadn't they busted in here to do something about these whores?

Or was that it? Did Dessa have help? Were my brothers outside just waiting for some sort of signal? I glanced at Saint, and he gave me a slight nod. Seemed we were thinking the same thing. No, the club wouldn't have let Dessa come here alone. Not without a plan.

The whore continued to rub against me like a cat in heat. Another woman stood near the bar, and a third was somewhere behind me. I could hear people in the hallway, even though I'd only seen the one man, it sounded like there were two or more people back there. Then there was Bridget, the bitch who kept threatening my woman.

The heavy tread coming from behind us told me the man was going to make his presence known. Assuming there was only one. No fucking way it was anyone from my club. They'd never walk that loud unless it was on purpose.

"Bridget, dear, this isn't what we discussed," a man said.

"But, Santi…"

He came into view and held his hand up to stop her. "Jeremy will never be yours. I said you could have the biker, if you could tame him. I will return Dessa to Jeremy, and I'll make sure he follows the rules from now on. Damaging her isn't going to make my job any easier."

"He doesn't want me," Dessa said. "You could wrap me up and stick a bow on my head, and he still wouldn't take me."

Santi slid his hands into his pockets. "Oh, he will. Jeremy always does as he's told. It's why he asked you to marry him. The moment I saw you, I knew you would be perfect. You never asked questions. Seldom spoke unless someone spoke to you first. Yes, the perfect wife for him. Then he fucked it all up."

"You're the one," Dessa murmured. "You were his contact before he moved. The one who pulls his strings."

"Hmm. It seems someone has been filling your head with stories. What else do you know, sweet little Dessa?"

No! Don't tell him! I knew if she confessed everything, the man would likely kill her. I didn't know if Dessa realized that or not. The man was baiting her. He'd clearly thought she would fall in line again, but if she confessed to all she knew, he'd know she was a threat.

"I know about the drugs, that he likes to hurt women, and about his whores," she said. Then she swung her gaze to Bridget. "Is that where he found you? Were you on a street corner and he paid for your time?"

Oh, fuck. Under other circumstances, I'd have been smiling at how feisty she was. Right now, I was too busy hoping she didn't get herself killed. I tried to loosen the ropes holding my wrists, but it wasn't any use. I was stuck watching everything unfold, and helpless to save my wife or anyone else.

Santi threw his head back and laughed. "You're positively delightful! I think I prefer this version of you, Dessa. So you know Jeremy likes to buy women for a night or three? It's part of why he never touched you. I told him he'd have to get tested first. Couldn't have our little broodmare getting sick."

"Broodmare?" she asked, her eyes going wide.

"Of course. Jeremy would need children, show the town he had the perfect family. I told him to make sure he had a daughter to use as a bargaining chip in future negotiations and a son to take over one day. Didn't matter how many tries it took before he had a son. He'd breed you until he got one."

Bile rose in my throat at the image he painted. The sad part was that Dessa would have gladly had as many children as that monster wanted, since she'd been clueless about how depraved he really was.

"I can give him children!" Bridget said.

Santi arched his eyebrows. "How do you plan to do that? It's a little difficult to have a child when you don't have reproductive organs."

Bridget paled. "What? What are you talking about?"

Santi leaned in closer, giving her a smile that sent chills down my spine. I saw Dessa back up a little and wished like hell she would get out of here. I doubted they'd let her leave. Not now, or ever. She knew too much.

"Did you think your precious Jeremy only sliced you up a bit? Oh no. Not our Jeremy. He cut you open and removed part of your insides. I don't know how you managed to survive in all honesty. If he'd known you didn't die, I bet he would have gone back to finish the job. The doctor who put you back together went a step further and made sure you'd never have children."

Dessa placed a hand over her mouth. Even after all Bridget had done to her, I knew my woman was likely feeling sorry for her. Her tender heart was part of what I loved about her.

Sofia screamed down the hall, and that was all it took. Saint gave me a wild look before he rocked forward onto his toes, then launched himself backward. The chair broke. Santi turned, and brave little Dessa rolled her chair forward at a brisk pace, running it right into the man. I tipped forward, dumping the whore on the floor, then slammed backward.

By the time Saint and I were both free, the whore I'd tossed had gotten back on her feet, and the other two were racing toward us. I swung on the whore in front of me, knocking her out cold with one blow. Saint ran for the back hall, intent on reaching his woman, and I handled the other two whores.

Wire had managed to knock his chair over, but the damn thing hadn't broken. I started to kneel and untie him when I heard a loud *crack* and turned. It felt like the world tipped sideways when I saw a small pistol in Santi's hand and blood blossoming across Dessa's abdomen.

"No!" I let out a roar and charged the man. He got off another round, and I felt the burn in my shoulder, but it didn't slow me down. I tackled him to the floor and slammed my fists into his face. Punch after punch landed until he looked like raw, bloody meat.

I felt hands grab me, and I struggled to fight them off until I heard Torch's voice.

"Easy! He's down, Savior. That man isn't getting up anytime soon."

I whirled, trying to find Dessa. I didn't see her chair, or her, anywhere. "Dessa…"

"Tempest has her. He's loading her into a truck and Grimm is calling one of his contacts at the hospital. Prophet already took Ares to get checked out." Torch waved a hand at me. "Looks like you need to go there too. Go get in the truck with her and get stitched up."

I looked around the room. Saint came out of the back hall with Sofia in his arms. Her clothes were torn, and I hoped like fuck he'd gotten to her before anything happened. She'd already lived through that kind of hell once.

"Savior." I faced Torch again. "We've got this. Get the fuck out of here. You're no good to any of us until your head is back in the game."

Even though the man wasn't my President

anymore, I still gave him a nod and followed his orders. Maybe it was instinct. Or perhaps I was only doing it because that's what I wanted most -- to be with Dessa.

"Junie and Judd?" I asked.

"They're safe, and they'll be fine for tonight."

I walked out and raced after the truck. Tempest had already pulled away from the clubhouse and approached the gates. He saw me and stopped. Since Dessa was in the front seat, I opened the back door and jumped inside. As I eyed the open gate, I wondered where the fuck the Prospect was, and how everyone had gotten into the compound.

But Torch was right. At the moment, I needed to focus on Dessa and Ares. Everything else could wait until tomorrow.

* * *

The doctor had already stitched my shoulder and released me. Ares was awake, but they were holding her overnight for observation since they didn't know what the bitches dosed her with. I sat beside Ares's bed, staring at the open doorway.

"They say no news is good news," Ares said.

"Yep. Doesn't mean I like not knowing whether your mother is okay."

She smiled a little. "I'm glad you married her. She's a great mom. I only wish I hadn't given her such a hard time at first."

I swung my gaze to her. "She loves you. You know that, right?"

Ares nodded, then yawned. It seemed the drugs were still kicking her butt. I stood and went to the door, peering into the hall. A nurse bustled by, and I called out to her. She huffed at me, giving a stern glare.

"I've already told you. I don't have any news about

your wife."

"She's still in surgery?" I asked.

"Yes. Now, please. Sit down and wait patiently."

Right. My woman could be dying, and she wanted me to be *patient*. Was she fucking crazy? My phone buzzed in my pocket, and I connected the call, needing the distraction.

"What?" I asked, instead of my usual greeting.

"Thought you'd want to know Sofia is fine. Saint has her at home, and asked Dr. Myron to come take a look. She swore nothing happened to her while she was in the back room, but I don't think Saint believes her," Grimm said.

"Do we know how they got inside? Everyone else safe?" I asked.

"We found Lavender. She was out back, hiding. Had her laptop with her and was doing her best to assess the situation and fuck with the people inside at the same time."

"I hadn't even thought about where she might be," I said. "What exactly does that mean?"

"Well… the women all have long rap sheets now. Mostly prostitution, but also possession with intent to sell, child endangerment, and assault. Santi's bank accounts have been drained. She split the funds between Dessa, the club, and donated the rest to a few worthy causes."

My brow furrowed. "How the fuck did she have time to do all that?"

"I didn't ask. She'd just tell me a bunch of shit I don't understand. I asked Wire how he'd been taken if Lavender was still free. He said they claimed to have her and his kids. Since they hadn't been home with him, he didn't know if they were lying or not and decided to err on the side of caution."

"Right. Because everyone knows we're a bunch of overprotective assholes who will do anything for our family," I said. Even if my efforts did end up getting my wife hurt. I tried to push down the guilt. If I hadn't busted loose, would he have shot her?

"As to how they got in, you're going to be pissed."

"That seems to be the general theme for the night," I said.

"Will was watching the gate. One of the women came up and told him she'd had a flat tire. Asked if she could wait inside the gate until the tow truck arrived. Since she was one of our club whores, he let her in. When he turned his back to the gate, one of the others bashed him over the head. The doc stitched up his head. He has a concussion and will be out of commission for a day or three."

"Anything else?" I asked.

"I think that covers it for now. Saint isn't leaving Sofia's side. You're at the hospital, and so is Tempest. He's in the waiting room until he finds out if Dessa is okay. Anyone in particular you'd like to put in charge until you're back?" Grimm asked.

"You and Royal. I think it may take the both of you, considering how fucked up tonight has been."

"How's Ares?" he asked.

"She's going to be okay. They want to keep an eye on her overnight, but she's been awake and talking. I sent Prophet to get coffee. He seemed reluctant to leave her side."

"Sorry to say this, but I have a feeling he's marked Ares as his."

"I figured as much by what he said at the house earlier. I also know he won't do anything until she's eighteen, so I'm not too worried. Although Ares didn't seem too excited about it. She may bludgeon him to death if he hovers too much."

"I don't envy you. I'll let Royal know we're riding herd on the club until you get back. Let us know when you hear something about Dessa. We'll all hoping she makes a swift recovery."

Yeah, I was too. I ended the call and went back to sitting and waiting.

Epilogue
Savior
One Month Later

I stared out across the picnic area and smiled at the children running around. It had been pure hell up until a few days ago, but the club was slowly healing. I'd called an impromptu picnic for everyone as a way to let off some steam and enjoy family time. My gaze settled on Dessa, and I swallowed down the pain.

Not only had I nearly lost her, but we'd lost our child. I still remembered the numbness I'd felt when I heard the doctor's words, followed by an all-consuming grief.

"Your wife is out of surgery. I'm sorry, but the baby didn't make it."

"What baby?" I asked.

"Your wife was about one week pregnant. I'm afraid she won't be able to have children. Between previous damage and scar tissue, plus the bullet we pulled out of her, she won't be able to get pregnant again."

I knew it would devastate Dessa. Hell, it hit me hard too. I'd looked forward to having more children with her. We still could. We'd just have to adopt them, like we had with Ares and Judd. The thought of my only biological child being with a club whore and not my wife made me want to hit something. Not that I loved Junie any less because of who her mother was.

"Your wife coded twice. We were able to bring her back, but her condition is precarious for the moment. We'll keep a close watch tonight and tomorrow. After that, you should be in the clear as long as her wound doesn't get infected."

"Thank you, Doctor."

Dessa had cried for hours when I'd told her about the baby, and that we wouldn't be able to have another one. The fact she was alive was enough for me. I scanned the area again and saw Judd and Junie in the sandbox with two other kids. Lavender and Pepper stood nearby, keeping an eye on them.

Ares sat at the table with Dessa, and I noticed Prophet sat beside her. Even though she pretended to ignore him, whenever she thought he wasn't watching, she'd look his way with a soft expression on her face. I knew I'd have my hands full with the two of them later.

I walked over to Dessa and leaned down to kiss her. "Need anything?"

"Just you," she said softly.

"You have me. Always."

"Eww." Ares scrunched her nose. "Can you two do that when I'm not within hearing range?"

"Leave them alone, Ares." Prophet placed his hand on her back. "They're allowed to be affectionate."

She huffed, but I saw her cheeks turn a bit pink. I gave Prophet a nod of thanks before sitting next to Dessa. Wire made his way over and handed me a piece of paper.

"What's this?" I asked.

"Show your wife," he said.

I held the paper where both Dessa and I could read it. What the… "Wire? What the hell?"

"One of the club whores involved in our recent troubles had a kid. She's five and has Down Syndrome." Wire handed us more papers. "Since we made sure that bitch wouldn't cause trouble for anyone ever again, it's left that little girl without a mother. Not that she was much of one, anyway. These are your official adoption records for Marnie. I know the two of you took it hard when Dessa lost the baby. This won't make up for your loss, but that little girl needs a home. I couldn't think of two better parents for her."

I noticed Dessa had tears in her eyes. She gave Wire a smile. "Thank you."

He nodded and backed away. "I will text the directions to you within the hour. You can enjoy the picnic a little while longer. As for where she'll sleep, I'll ask the old ladies to figure something out while you're gone."

"When will the new house be finished?" Ares asked.

"Not for a few months. Why?" I asked.

She shrugged a shoulder. "Take the queen bed out of my room and put in two twins. I don't mind sharing. It's only temporary, right? We'll all have our own rooms at the new place?"

"Right," I said. "You really amaze me sometimes, Ares. Thank you."

Dessa took my hand. "We have another daughter."

"They outnumber poor Judd." I kissed Dessa's cheek. "Guess he better become a tough guy to protect all his sisters."

Someone cried, and I looked over to see Judd standing above Cole, who was bawling his eyes out. What the hell happened?

"Um, Dad. I don't think he'll have any problems. Cole tossed sand onto Junie, and Judd just knocked him down." Ares snickered. "Give him a few more years and he'll be like all the other guys around here."

It had taken me forever, but I had what I always wanted. A family. I adored my wife, and our family kept expanding. It didn't matter if I'd donated the DNA for the kids or not. They were all mine, just like they were Dessa's. Sometimes family went beyond blood. "Love you, Dessa." I kissed her cheek. "I have something for you."

"It better not be a puppy. I'm not cleaning up

puddles," she said.

I shook my head. "Nope. Not a puppy. Wait here for just a minute." I went out to the truck and got the box out of the back seat. I'd had to swear the kids to secrecy so they wouldn't blab before we got here. I carried it back to the picnic area and placed it in Dessa's lap.

Before she had a chance to open it, Tempest joined us. He cleared his throat to get her attention. When Dessa looked up at him, she gave him a fond smile.

"If it isn't my hero…" Ever since she found out he was the one who took her from the clubhouse and drove her to the hospital, she'd started calling him that. I got a laugh out of it since it usually made him blush like a damn schoolgirl.

"When Savior first brought you here, I gave you a shitty apology for the way I acted the night we came to get Junie and Judd. I didn't give you a chance to prove yourself, and I'm sorry. You're a perfect match for Savior, and a welcome addition to the Dixie Reapers. I hope you'll accept my sincere apology."

"You're forgiven. However, in the future, you should try not to judge someone without knowing all the facts."

He gave her a nod, then waited while she opened her gift. He knew what was inside, since he'd helped me plan part of it.

"It's not my birthday," she said.

"It's not that sort of present. This is more of a thanks for loving me gift." She slowly opened the box and I saw her lip tremble as she lifted out her property cut. "You were supposed to get it the night Bridget caused all that trouble. Then I had to wait until you came home from the hospital. The timing always felt off. Until now."

"Help me put it on?" she asked.

I took it from her, then slipped it over her shoulders as she leaned forward. I smoothed it down and adjusted it for her. "There's something else in there."

She pulled out a car key and stared at it. When she didn't say anything, I started to think I'd fucked up.

"Dessa, are you all right?"

"You got me a car?" she asked.

"And a hand brake. I know transferring isn't the easiest thing for you, but when we discussed cars two weeks ago, you said you didn't want the kind you had to roll up into. It's a small SUV that sits low to the ground. You should be able to get into it without much trouble. You can break down your chair and still have room for the kids."

She reached for me, and I leaned down. Dessa put her arms around my neck, then kissed the hell out of me. "Thank you."

"Anything for you." They weren't just empty words. I couldn't think of a single thing I wouldn't do for her -- except let her go. She was mine. Would always be mine. After nearly losing her, I knew I'd die without her.

Our lives weren't perfect. They were messy. Dramatic. Sometimes painful. But they were also full of love and family, and I couldn't ask for more than that.

Harley Wylde

Harley Wylde is the International Bestselling Author of the Dixie Reapers MC, Devil's Boneyard MC, and Hades Abyss MC series. When Harley's writing, her motto is the hotter the better -- off-the-charts sex, commanding men, and the women who can't deny them. If you want men who talk dirty, are sexy as hell, and take what they want, then you've come to the right place. She doesn't shy away from the dangers and nastiness in the world, bringing those realities to the pages of her books, but always gives her characters a happily-ever-after and makes sure the bad guys get what they deserve.

The times Harley isn't writing, she's thinking up naughty things to do to her husband, drinking copious amounts of Starbucks, and reading. She loves to read and devours a book a day, sometimes more. She's also fond of TV shows and movies from the 1980s, as well as paranormal shows from the 1990s to today, even though she'd much rather be reading or writing. You can find out more about Harley or enter her monthly giveaway on her website. Be sure to join her newsletter while you're there to learn more about discounts, signing events, and other goodies!

Harley at Changeling: changelingpress.com/harley-wylde-a-196

ChangelingPress.com